# burned
## **deep**

# burned
## deep

## CALISTA FOX

st. martin's griffin ≈ new york

BURNED DEEP. Copyright © 2015 by Calista Fox. All rights reserved. Printed in the United States of America. For information, address St. Martin's Press, 175 Fifth Avenue, New York, N.Y. 10010.

www.stmartins.com

Designed by Anna Gorovoy

The Library of Congress Cataloging-in-Publication Data is available upon request.

ISBN 978-1-250-07251-1 (trade paperback)
ISBN 978-1-4668-8419-9 (e-book)

Our books may be purchased in bulk for promotional, educational, or business use. Please contact your local bookseller or the Macmillan Corporate and Premium Sales Department at (800) 221-7945, extension 5442, or by e-mail at MacmillanSpecialMarkets@macmillan.com.

First Edition: October 2015

10 9 8 7 6 5 4 3 2 1

This one is for the people in my life who have to suffer through the "writer's existence," right along with me. There is not enough praise or gratitude in the world for your endless support.

# acknowledgments

I am forever indebted to my wonderful editor, Monique Patterson, for the way this trilogy came about. It was a golden opportunity to present the initial proposal, and I'm so thrilled it hit all the right notes. The entire process was fantastic, and I'm so happy we connected through this story.

I am also grateful to my agent, Sarah E. Younger, for seizing the opportunity to hook me up with Monique. It came about unexpectedly, but offered me the chance to stretch my writing wings and delve into a meaty series. Thanks, Sarah!

I've met some of the St. Martin's team, and have thoroughly enjoyed those interactions and appreciate all that you do. For those I haven't met who are working behind the scenes, thank you so much for your support and enthusiasm.

To my family and friends, I love you.

To my readers, old and new, I am always in awe of your dedication, and I thank you greatly for your support and your wonderful e-mails! Please keep sending them!

To Stephenie Meyer, who wrote a gripping series that made me fall in love with dark, gothic heroes, you created memorable characters that live on.

# burned
## deep

# chapter 1

"Where's my groom?" I muttered under my breath.

Tamera Fenmore tore her gaze from the dark clouds rolling in—
the same ones I kept my eye on. "Just saw him a few minutes
ago." The tension in her voice mirrored mine.

She was the officiant I'd subcontracted for this extravagant
creekside wedding at a renowned resort in the intimate upscale
community of Sedona, Arizona. Unfortunately, our unpredictable
monsoons made late summer a sketchy time of year for outdoor
events. A torrential downpour could obliterate this ceremony with
very little warning.

That was only one of my worries. We were surrounded by lush
green grass, full sycamore trees, and breathtaking red-rock canyons,
yet all was not right with this scene—and it wasn't just the crackle
of electricity and the scent of rain hanging in the air that set
me on edge.

Keeping my voice low, between us, I said, "My groomsmen are
missing, too."

I'd only turned my back briefly to mend the strap that had pulled too tight and snapped on the maid of honor's dress. Suddenly I was missing half of my bridal party.

Tamera frowned. "Now would be a good time to panic." Even her lovely British accent couldn't mask her dread.

"This can't be happening." My stomach knotted.

Sure, I'd dealt with MIA grooms before. Ones who'd had their bachelor parties on the eve of the big day—*never* a good idea—and ended up in the emergency room after a barroom brawl, passed out in a back alley or on a great escape to Sin City.

I hadn't considered Sean Aldridge a flight risk. My bad, because he and his buds were nowhere in sight. While two hundred guests waited for the nuptials to begin, nervously stealing glances at the increasingly ominous sky.

Tamera was all set to head to the front of the event lawn just before the sun started its gradual descent, hopefully breaking through the cloud cover to splash radiant color across the white caps of the flowing rapids. The sound of water rushing over smooth rocks filtered through the trees, mingling with the rustle of leaves as a breeze picked up. Another bad sign. If a storm hit, microbursts and downdrafts could rip through the partially covered east patio where the cocktail reception was to be held, effectively destroying that portion of the evening as well.

Inclement weather had posed a threat for me before, but this was my biggest event thus far and the last thing I needed was drenched and disgruntled guests glaring at the wedding planner—even if it was the bride who'd waved a dismissive hand when I'd repeatedly warned her of the dangers of monsoon season. For fear tents would mar the scenery she'd insisted none be erected.

Meghan Delfino currently paced the polished wooden floor of the elegantly rustic cottage the resort had comped her, so no one caught a glimpse of her stunning one-of-a-kind Carolina Herrera gown. Not until that precious moment when Meghan stepped out of the thicket and paused at the top of the short set of stone steps built into the grassy knoll above the lawn.

Even the steel-nerved father of the bride was ready to walk his pride and joy down the aisle that was lit by ornate lanterns and accented with dozens of elaborate sterling silver and white rose bouquets. Though his patience crept toward agitation, if the darting of his alert hazel eyes was any indication. And they kept landing on me.

Tamera consulted her platinum boyfriend watch. "We're straight-up seven o'clock, Ari. Sun'll be on the move in eleven minutes."

"Damn it. They must be in the bar." I whirled around and marched off. My low heels crunched the underbrush of the nature trail woven through the heavily wooded property and I dodged wayward branches that jutted out onto the path. The wind whispered through the trees, taunting me with its potential to become a menacing howl. Deep-vibrato, rust-colored chimes hanging from limbs added a ghostly effect to the overcast evening, bringing on a razor-sharp vibe. Or maybe that was just my nerves getting the best of me.

I reached the outdoor dining area along the water's edge, the servers already cranking down the tall umbrellas to keep them from toppling over if a violent gust whipped along the creek.

I required less than forty-five minutes of tame weather—the ceremony was to be a quick one. I could move the predinner reception inside if need be, but I desperately wanted the vows to be as Meghan had envisioned.

Not to mention, I needed referrals from this wedding. Bridal consulting wasn't exactly a lucrative business in such a small town, especially when you were an independent planner. And rent didn't come cheap in Sedona.

I blew into the bar with a stiff draft that sent cocktail napkins flying from tables. Gazes snapped to me, but I ignored them, due to my current tunnel vision.

As I'd suspected, I found the rest of my wedding party congregated around two high tops they'd pushed together in the middle of the bar, slamming shots of tequila.

My pulse racing, I simply said, "Gentlemen, tick-tock."

"Hold up. I've got one more round coming," the groom told me before sucking a wedge of lime between his teeth. As though time were not of the essence here.

"You've got a bride ready to say *I do*," I pointed out, trying to keep the anxiety from my voice. "And a storm brewing."

Sean seemed like a good kid. At twenty-two, he was four years younger than me. Fresh out of college. A bit too early in his adult life to tie the knot, in my opinion, but with his twenty-year-old girlfriend of eight months in her first trimester, it was no surprise a shotgun wedding had been in his immediate future. Especially when said girlfriend was the former Valedictorian of a legendary all-girls Catholic school and the only child of a global communications tycoon.

"Join us, Ari," insisted Kyle Jenns, the best man. He was an easygoing sort, with sandy-brown hair, sky-blue eyes, an athletic build, and a gorgeous smile, all pearly white and vibrant. A college friend of Sean's whom I'd just met when the whirlwind planning had begun. They'd both attended Arizona State University in Phoenix, played football together, and belonged to the same fraternity.

Today was the first time I'd seen Kyle in something other than a tight T-shirt that showed off all of his muscles, the hems of the sleeves always straining against his bulging biceps. Even wearing a tuxedo now did little to conceal his solid frame. Obviously, he hadn't quit the gym after his last season as quarterback.

"You look like you could use a drink," he said in his amiable tone. "One for her, too," he told Grace Hart, the bartender setting out the shot glasses.

"Hi, Ari."

"Nice to see you, Grace." She and I had gone through senior year of high school together. Like me, Grace was one of the very few who'd stuck around after graduation, despite the sparse career opportunities a community of eleven thousand offered. Some of us just couldn't shake the allure of what *USA Today* called the most beautiful place in America.

"You sure you want one?" she asked.

"If it'll get them closer to the altar, bring it on."

Kyle's grin widened. "Now *that's* a wedding planner, people. One who'll do a shot with the groomsmen."

Sean nodded. "Give Ari three weeks and you, too, can be on your way to wedded bliss—in first-class style from start to finish." He didn't bother hiding the grimace—not at all directed at me. I couldn't fathom the pressure he was under with his new Forbes list in-laws and a baby on the way. I empathized with Sean, having high hopes for this marriage.

I had high hopes for *every* marriage. An inherent dream following the horrific parental breakup and subsequent financial fallout I'd lived through years ago. The exact reason why *I* wouldn't be escorted down an aisle anytime soon. As in *never.*

"How many has he had?" I asked Kyle.

"Going on his second one. Sean won't slur his vows, I promise. Just needed a little fortification so he doesn't sphincter up when the *I now pronounce you husband and wife* part comes." He winked. "Couple of wedding-day jitters, that's all. Nothing to worry about."

"Hey, I love Meghan," Sean assured us. "But, come on—she's only *two* months pregnant. What's the rush?"

Kyle snickered. "You're a lucky SOB and you know it. Meg's a knockout and you're marrying into a crazy-rich family. Too bad she doesn't have a sister. But, hey, if I catch the garter, that means I'll find my own pretty little love slave, right?" His gaze swept over me.

"Use a condom," Sean lamented. "That's all I'm saying, man."

Kyle leaned in close—*too* close for comfort, making me flinch. I didn't like anyone invading my personal space unless invited.

Despite being good-natured, Kyle exuded enough self-confidence to convince me he had a way with the ladies—and wasn't the least bit hesitant to use that particular gift to his full advantage.

So my nerves jumped to attention when he gave me a suggestive look.

"I'd be *your* love slave," he said in a low tone. "You can tie me
to the bedposts, if you want."

"That's, um . . . not really my thing."

"You're not married, are you, Ari? Or otherwise spoken for?
'Cause there's a whole night of dancing ahead of us—"

"Dude." Sean fake-punched his best man in the arm. "She's
my wedding planner. Don't hit on her. At. My. *Wedding.*"

Kyle said, "Weddings are the perfect place to meet new women,
amigo. And this one's beautiful, smart, possibly single. So why
wouldn't I find out if there's something to pursue here?"

I suddenly felt another set of eyes on me. From behind. It was
an eerie yet unmistakable feeling.

As Sean and Kyle bantered like I wasn't standing next to them
in earshot, I glanced over my shoulder. And lost my breath.

The argument faded into oblivion as my pulse echoed through
me, drowning out all other sounds, thoughts, everything.

In the corner up front sat two men, paperwork sprawled across
their table. One salt-and-pepper-haired, distinguished looking, older.
The other dark-haired and dressed all in black—jeans, boots, and a
button-down shirt with sleeves rolled up to reveal impressive forearms. Late twenties, maybe thirty. He had a very mysterious air
about him, and he was staring at me.

*Right at me.*

His onyx hair was sexily tousled, as though he'd just rolled out
of bed with a woman who'd enjoyed mussing the thick, silky-looking
strands. His piercing green eyes held a hint of intrigue and a hell of
a lot of *don't mess with me.* Contradictory signals that sparked my
interest.

His face was a chiseled masterpiece. He had strong features with
a stone-set jaw, balanced brows, not too thick, not too thin, and a
nose that might have been punched a time or two, given the slight
bump close to the eyes, but which still managed to look specially

crafted to keep harmony with all the sculpted angles. A mouth that easily drew my attention, my gaze lingering on it until I caught myself.

All in all, he was devilishly handsome. Darkly beautiful.

It struck me that I would never consider a man beautiful, thinking it would undermine his masculinity. Not so with this one. He was beautiful and virile. Downright heart-stopping.

I felt a peculiar stirring deep within me. An innate reaction to his edgy perfection.

It seemed as though the blood moved a bit slower through my veins. Thicker, warmer. Molten.

My gaze lifted, our eyes locked, and I was riveted. I still couldn't breathe.

Something flickered in those hypnotic emerald pools of his. Something curious, like a warning to be heeded. Not menacing, but . . . definitely intimidating.

Unnerved and surprisingly, intensely aroused, I tore my gaze from the sexy stranger just as Grace brought my shot.

"So, bottoms up," I said as I reached for the tequila, my voice a bit shaky from the unexpected encounter. I finally pulled in a long breath, then gave a quick toast, brevity being the order of the moment. "May the new Aldridge family be blessed with a lifetime of health and happiness." We all touched rims and threw back the booze. Even the burn of alcohol couldn't compete with the simmering inside me created by that heated gaze. But I had business to focus on and resisted the temptation to look over my shoulder again. "Okay, guys. Showtime."

"Damn, you love to crack the whip," Kyle said. "Maybe you ought to rethink your stance on bondage." He raised a hand as though to rest it at the small of my back and escort me out. I instinctively leapt a bit too far out of his reach—and stumbled into a trio of men just coming through the door.

One of them caught me around the waist and held on tight. "Hey, hey there, pretty lady."

Behind us, I heard the scrape on the stone floor as a chair shoved back. A powerful sense of awareness jolted me. I knew *exactly* who was about to intervene if anyone got too touchy-feely.

But why?

Mumbling an apology, I wrenched free from the semi-embrace of a twenty something with spiky blond hair and an intricately designed diamondback snake tattoo slithering up his neck. A lascivious glint lit his brown eyes, pricking my nerves. He spared a glimpse at Kyle and the others, then asked me, "Looking for real men to party with, sweetheart?"

The entire atmosphere turned tense and everything that followed happened quickly.

Kyle came immediately to my defense, saying in a suddenly sharp tone, "Back off, pal." His chin lifted, his chest puffed out.

Snake-tat guy grabbed me again, more forcefully than I thought he'd intended. I winced as he tugged me to him. "Doesn't look like she was interested in leaving with you, *pal*."

Three groomsmen instantly threw off their jackets, fueled by tequila.

"No fighting!" I cried out, panic shooting through me. I'd never get another planning gig in this town if I delivered a bloodied bridal party to the event lawn—the Delfinos would make sure of it.

The darkly handsome stranger swooped in, pushing Kyle to the side with a solid palm to the pecs—clearly agitating Kyle further, because his fists balled at his sides. A breath later, the stranger had the spiky-haired blond by the forearm.

"Hands off," he all but growled.

Alarm flashed in the blond's eyes at the sudden and vehement reaction from the intruder—and likely his commanding presence. Snake-tat guy released me instantly. Even his friends backed off.

The stranger twisted the blond's arm and jerked it behind his back before slamming his shoulder to the table, as if freeing me wasn't justice enough.

"Jesus, Bax," the salt-and-pepper-haired companion grumbled, a hint of admiration mixing with his shock as he scrambled to collect the papers getting crinkled.

In a deep, rough voice, the man called Bax said, "Doesn't look like she's interested in leaving with *you*, either."

Air rushed from my lungs. I stood so close to him, I felt his heat, inhaled his expensive-smelling cologne, absorbed his raw intensity. He glanced my way, his green eyes entrancing, though something foreboding edged the rims of those brilliant irises.

A scowl darkened his visage even more, turning him dangerous in a recklessly thrilling way. I wasn't the reckless sort, yet a scintillating sensation flared within me.

His gaze remained connected with mine as he spoke to the spiky-haired guy. "I think you owe the lady an apology."

"I didn't know she came with a bodyguard," the blond ground out. Craning his neck to look around the broad-shouldered man caging him, he acridly added, "Sorry, sweetheart." The stranger released him and stepped away. The blond skulked off with his friends, muttering "Asshole" under his breath.

"Come on, Ari," Sean said as he gently took my hand—the first wholly innocent gesture in this incident.

Yet I recoiled again, breaking the trancelike gaze with emerald eyes I would never forget, and hissed out, "Everybody stop touching me." My heart thundered as anxiety mounted.

I sidestepped the group. A concerned Grace asked, "Are you okay? I called Security."

"We're good—I'm good," I told her. "Sorry for the trouble. That was all my fault."

"No, it wasn't. I called Security on Tattoo Guy," she said. "He shouldn't have grabbed you. Looked like it hurt."

"It's fine," I lied. My arm smarted.

She whispered, "Who's Dark and Dangerous?"

Clearly, she meant the gorgeous green-eyed stranger. "I don't know."

"Interesting," she murmured. "He's been watching you since

you made your grand entrance. He is smokin' hot. The best man is damn good-looking, too. Lucky you, all the way around."

Heat burst on my cheeks. "Not interested," I said, trying to compose myself as the groomsmen paid up and I herded them toward the door.

My pulse still jumped. Not just from the sexy stranger—and the way he'd put an immediate stop to what could have been a disastrous altercation. Competing with the excitement he elicited was a bit of apprehension, because I didn't like anyone moving in too close. These guys bumped against my boundaries. Only *one* of them hadn't touched me, or tried to.

"Relax, Ari," a groomsman scoffed as he shrugged into his jacket, not knowing the true source of my consternation. "Weddings never start on time."

"Mine do." Feeling that smoldering gaze again, I turned around. The stranger stood facing me—an impressive six-foot-two or-three inches tall. Muscular. Strong. Powerful. Formidable.

His eyes narrowed. My stomach fluttered. I couldn't explain why.

"Thanks," I said tentatively.

His emerald gaze flicked to Kyle before the now-disgruntled best man disappeared out the door, then returned to me. "Try to be a little more careful."

"Right." I bristled slightly at the admonishment but brushed it off. I needed to leave, yet my feet remained rooted where they were. His mesmerizing gaze held me captive. I couldn't breathe again. It took several seconds to return to myself and head to the door.

"Ari."

His tone was low this time. Rich. Sensual. The warm timbre worked its way through my body and slid slowly, tantalizingly down my spine. Chasing away the apprehension. Making me shiver and inciting a tickle along my clit that had my inner walls clenching as my thighs pressed together.

I glanced back. "Yes?" My voice was suddenly much too soft and breathy. I was deeply aroused by the way he so intimately said my name—the fact that he'd paid close enough attention to pick up on it.

His jaw clenched briefly. Then he asked, "Are you all right?"

I stared at him for several suspended seconds. Why did it matter to him?

Given his size and agility, he probably felt duty bound to rescue girls like me, who never went looking for trouble but somehow inadvertently found it from time to time.

"Sure," I finally said, then dragged my gaze away and forced myself to walk out.

I left the bar and directed the men to their places by Tamera, an electric current moving under my skin even though I'd broken the intense eye contact and was no longer in the riveting presence of the devilish stranger.

The changing of color overhead began. The cumulous clouds had miraculously thinned into wispier ones and they captured the light as the sun burned through them, dispersing it in all directions so that fiery blood-orange, gold, and vermillion painted the sky and cast dazzling hues over the sparkling water.

From a parquet platform set off to the side, a pianist and harpist took their cue and eased into a gorgeously haunting version of Aaliyah's "One in a Million." The last of the guests settled in and I signaled the bridesmaids. The adorable six-year-olds serving as ring bearer and flower girl followed.

I slipped off to get the bride, my gaze flitting toward the restaurant, my interest thoroughly piqued.

*Bax.* What kind of a name was that? First? Last? Short for Baxley or Baxter? I shook my head. No, he definitely did not seem like a Baxter.

Who was he and what had made him come so swiftly to my defense? Even when it had just been Kyle flirting with me, Bax had seemed disturbed by it.

Curiosity clawed at me. I was dying to figure out what the hell had happened in less than fifteen minutes that had compelled him to save me from the claim two men had instantly staked.

A rumble of thunder in the distance caught my attention, pulling me from my errant thoughts. I entered the cottage and prepped Meghan for her breath-stealing appearance. As her father escorted her down the aisle, my eyes flashed from the sky to the bridal party to the guests and back. I silently prayed the weather would hold out. I wanted everything to be perfect, but I couldn't control the climate—nor could I keep my mind from wandering. I swore I felt his gaze again. But that was impossible. He wasn't one of the guests.

Clearly, I *wanted* to feel his gaze.

Heat blazed through me at the mere thought of him, making me uncomfortable, what with the addition of the thick humidity. I wiped a bead of perspiration from my brow. I was more than intrigued, though I doubted that was wise. He wasn't the kind of man one trifled with, and he was quite obviously out of my league. *Way* too potent, likely the reason for all of that forewarning in his eyes.

Unfortunately, he lingered in my thoughts.

The ceremony turned out flawless—to the casual observer. No wedding ever went off without a hitch, but it was how you smoothed the wrinkles with no one noticing there was a hiccup that made an event a true success.

During the vows, I checked in with the staff responsible for the cocktail reception and the band that would entertain the guests while the bridal party and parents posed for pictures. They were all on standby to move everything indoors at a moment's notice.

Then I headed into the lodge to confirm the dinner preparations were all seen to. I took in the formal setting with a critical eye, ensuring the floral arrangements and intricate decorations were in their appropriate place, all of which created a no-expense-spared ambience—yet another reason I meticulously surveyed the surroundings.

Inspecting the rounds of ten filling the enormous ballroom, and the extended head table at the far end where floor-to-ceiling win-

dows showcased the strategically lit grounds and red-rock forma-
tions, I spied a few fixables.

Lifting a tulip champagne flute, I said to the Banquet Manager
following me around, "This glass has spots." I handed it over, noting the tremble in my fingers. That was odd. I was usually a very
steady person when in my element. But everything about the potentially dangerous encounter in the bar had left me a bit off-kilter.

I examined the plates and flatware to make sure they were all
polished. Found two more glasses with smudges. A few napkins
with slightly tattered edges. Votives that needed to be replaced. The
staff rushed about, adjusting everything to my specifications.

I wasn't obnoxiously OCD. People paid me good money to en-
sure every little detail was taken care of and that their event was
extraordinary and memorable. I owed it to them to have the food
and wine served on time. To make sure no one waited for plates to
be cleared from in front of them. To keep servers on their toes so
they delivered another fork to a guest before the first one even hit
the floor.

My painstaking attention to all facets of the process from start
to finish was also born of the incessant need to occupy every waking second of my day and keep my mind on all things fresh and
new and awe-inspiring—like the symbolism that weddings and
other events evoked. I put substantial effort into stepping away from
the pain wrapped around my parents' hostile, failed marriage and
the inevitable suffering that came from being an only child caught
in the cross fire.

Around the last ten or so minutes of the cocktail hour, the sky
conspired against me and opened up. The deluge began. A few fat
drops served as a prelude before the heavy shower hit. Everyone
scrambled to get into the lodge as I urged them off the patio. Three-
pronged lightning flashed wildly and the crack of thunder eclipsed
the crashing of cymbals as the band's equipment was hastily moved
to the foyer.

A harsh wind roared through the terrace while I rushed about with the staff, collecting vases of flowers and hurricane lamps containing pillar candles—now blown out by the gust, the smoky scent wafting on the night air. A couple tipped over. The one I reached for flew off the table.

The shattering of glass on the Saltillo tile lent to the suddenly eerie atmosphere and the sense of urgency to gather everything up. Kyle jumped into the mayhem, snatching decorations quicker than I could and adding them to a service cart. Strands of hair slashed across my face as the undercurrent gained strength.

"Get inside, Ari!" he shouted.

"This is my job!" I insisted as more jagged bolts lit the night. "You're a guest. *You* get inside!"

"Yeah, right. And leave you out here?" He rounded up the last of the arrangements and all but dragged me into the lodge. We set everything off to the side with the gift table.

My breath labored from the scurrying around—and how close the lightning had struck.

The guests remained dry, thankfully, and incredulous conversations over how fast and furious the tempest had hit were in full swing.

Meghan hurried over, delicately holding up the hem of her gown. "Ari, you're drenched!"

She dropped one side of her fluffy skirt and snatched a clean linen napkin from a high-top table set up specifically in the event the rain didn't hold off until dinnertime. She handed the napkin over and I dabbed at my cheeks and throat while my pulse raced.

"You were so right about the monsoons," she said, contrite. "But at least we got through the ceremony and almost all of the reception. Everything's just gorgeous, Ari!"

"I'm glad it worked out—for the most part."

She waved her manicured hand in the air as she was prone to do. "It's all fabulous. Exactly what I wanted. Well, with the exception of you getting soaked."

"It was worth it. We salvaged just about all of the arrangements."

Meghan had asked me previously to make sure the florist returned for the bouquets at the end of the evening and distributed them to hospices and funeral homes to brighten someone else's day. I thought that was a beautiful gesture.

She leaned forward as though to hug me. My hand jerked up to ward her off.

"Don't you dare," I hastily said, "or you'll ruin your dress." I wouldn't have minded the friendly bit of affection coming from her but I feared spoiling her gown. "You need to get upstairs so dinner can start. And I need to find some towels."

Sean came for her and I turned to Kyle, who was shaking off the rain from his jacket. He gave up and slipped out of it. He raked a hand through his hair and managed to appear dashing despite his slightly unkempt appearance. The wet look totally worked for him.

"Thanks for the save," I said.

"Had to redeem myself, right? I didn't exactly get to be the hero in the bar."

"You really weren't given a chance." It was unfortunate that I couldn't release the image from my mind of the man who *had* been the hero. Albeit a reluctant one. His scowl had spoken volumes.

Kyle told me, "I'd offer you my jacket but it's no drier than your own clothes."

"I'll be fine."

"What else can I do to help?"

I laughed softly. "I think you've earned your wings, by a lot. You'd better get going, anyway. Formal introductions are about to be made." According to my careful planning.

"You'll save me a dance, right? Or a few?"

His sudden mega-watt grin was contagious, despite my mind being elsewhere. "I'm the wedding planner, remember? Here to work. But you . . . Go. Have fun. Enjoy. Eat too much cake."

I tried to shoo him off with a wave of my hand. He lingered a moment or two, as though he had something else to say. He really was very sweet. Valiant. I liked him, no doubt. But didn't want to lead him on. So I was relieved when he spun around and sauntered off, heading to the second floor.

I ducked into the bathroom and used a few plush hand towels to dry my skin and the ends of my hair. I ran one over my blouse and skirt to sop up the drops of water. I couldn't wring out the garments or the material would rumple miserably. I was stuck with moist, clinging clothes because the gift shop was already closed and I hadn't brought a spare outfit. Lesson learned there.

Thus, I kept to the periphery as I made sure the dinner service went off without a hitch. Finally, I consulted with the DJ, who'd take over from this point.

Sometimes I hung around to watch the dancing, because brides and their families typically asked me to celebrate with them, and tonight was no exception. But I was exhausted, having pulled off this particular wedding in such a short, frenzied period—an emotional time, what with the tension gripping everyone over the impending Mrs. Aldridge's delicate condition and concern that the news would ignite a scandal for the high-society Delfinos.

Not to mention all the drama created by the inclement weather and the men I'd encountered this evening. I'd be out like a light when I got home. Looked forward to a sound night's sleep, instead of waking up ten times to run through my mental checklists.

I'd also caught Kyle stealing glances my way, and I really hated the idea of turning him down again. Clearly, he was a good guy. Much more on par with where my interests *should* lie—rather than with the magnetic stranger, so intriguing and darkly gorgeous. Primed to come to my rescue—

I shook my head. I definitely shouldn't think about him.

After delivering congratulations and good-byes, I went downstairs to the lobby of the main lodge, a log structure that belonged in the mountains of Aspen, but which stunned visitors as it sat nestled in this artistic canyon. The two-story windows highlighted an inspirational landscape that left one speechless the first, tenth, and one-hundredth time they admired the view. Even more so tonight, as they showcased a spectacular display of purple-and-gold lightning veins rippling across the clouds.

I passed through the tall double doors and was greeted by a valet. "Another happily ever after, Miss DeMille?"

"What a lovely way to put it, Alex. And yes, I think the newly-weds have a very pleasant future ahead of them."

Envy seeped through my veins, but I ignored the sensation. It happened on occasion. Was to be expected, I surmised. I was twenty-six years old, with very few friends—really just a handful of people who knew me from the weddings I worked with them. I dated every now and then, but trying to build my rep as the "It" event planner in the Southwest kept me busy.

I had a very specific goal in mind, a career I was devoted to, one I was completely immersed in and was already plotting to take to the next level. That hadn't exactly panned out for me yet, but I remained diligent. So much so, I'd developed an eagle eye for de-tails, could anticipate needs before expressed, was thoroughly aware of my surroundings so that very few wayward scenarios took me by surprise.

But *he* did.

# chapter 2

I sensed his presence a breath too late, so that he was standing next to me before I had the chance to sidestep him. Put a few feet between us. My body tensed.

"Did I startle you?" he asked.

"Yes," I admitted. It was both unnerving and enticing that he noticed so much about me. It wasn't something I was accustomed to.

"My apologies." His voice was that warm timbre that ribboned through me.

I turned to face him, the devilish stranger. The dark, mesmerizing man who had the potential to haunt my mind and plague my fantasies from this day forward. I used the word *plague* because I didn't need anyone specific hovering in the back of my brain when I conjured erotic images to enhance a quick go-round with my very straightforward, get-the-job-done vibrator.

I kept my fantasy men nameless and faceless—though that defense mechanism was probably shot to hell now that I'd gotten a glimpse of the *ultimate* fantasy man.

I didn't even delve into identities when I had the rare one-night stand—a term I used *very* loosely. Typically, it was someone I met at a hotel where I held an event, someone I'd never see again, would never run into at the grocery store. Men who were more than happy to indulge in spontaneous, impersonal sex. Mostly me bent over a desk or pressed up against a wall in their room. Always over within a concise amount of time. Then I shoved my thong and skirt into place and reached for the doorknob before they lobbed a "Maybe the next time I'm in town . . . ?" my way.

Not appealing to everyone, but it worked fine for me. When you'd slipped into the role of loner because you'd spent so much time avoiding screaming parents, true intimacy was a foreign concept. I'd discovered it was best to limit physical contact. The less you knew of it, the less you craved it.

"Looks like you got caught in the rain," the sexy stranger said, a hint of amusement in his tone.

"Occupational hazard."

"That and getting hit on by groomsmen?"

I sighed. "That was all a bit bizarre."

"I hope the jerk who grabbed you didn't leave a bruise."

"It stung a little, but I'm okay."

His jaw clenched, as though hearing I'd been hurt angered him. His irises actually darkened. "I should have taught that guy a lesson about keeping his hands to himself."

The sharp intonation to his voice, the slightly gritty inflection, made the hairs on the nape of my neck stand on end.

"Think you made your point loud and clear," I said. "He got the picture."

"It's not something he should have gotten away with, that's all I'm saying."

"Sooo . . . what? You wish you'd punched him in the face for good measure?"

"I was thinking the gut, but breaking his nose probably would have given me equal satisfaction."

I couldn't tell if he was kidding . . . or deathly serious. That raw intensity I'd noted in the bar still exuded from him. He had a very dangerous edge to him, one that made my nerves jump but which excited me all the same. A surreal combination. Definitely not a sane elixir to be tempted by, and yet . . . I *was* tempted by this man.

For reasons I couldn't fully fathom. Reasons that went well beyond a simple attraction. I was drawn to him in a compelling, unshakable way.

Eventually finding my voice, though it sounded a bit breathy—as it had in the bar—I said, "Thanks again. Especially for keeping my wedding party from a scuffle. We had enough to contend with because of the storm."

"You handled it all well—until someone decided to manhandle you." He shook his head. Ground his teeth. He wasn't letting the slight go.

I wanted to ask him why it bothered him so much. Kyle and the others had clearly been ready to come to my aid. Why had this man felt it necessary to do so, particularly with the whole *don't mess with me* vibe he had going on?

I eyed him closely, taking in his sculpted features and mysterious air, and found myself wondering if perhaps he had a different agenda . . . though I couldn't for the life of me imagine what it might be.

"Would you like me to bring your car around, Mr. Bax?" Alex asked courteously, interrupting the broken silence. I'd forgotten all about the valet. Nothing else had existed for several minutes—except the two of us.

"I'd appreciate that," he said, his gaze still on me, though he spoke to Alex the way he had with Tat Guy. When we were alone, he introduced himself with an efficient, "Dane Bax." His eyes glowed, and his voice was low and seductive. Making me nearly lose all coherent thought.

Luckily, I remembered my own name. "Ari DeMille."

He extended his hand. I stared at it for a second or two, hedging against that anchoring temptation.

Then I employed my common trick of reaching for a business card in my oversized tote bag, filled with all manner of wedding-emergency necessities—soon to be home to a backup outfit. I placed the card in his palm to avoid an actual handshake. I didn't need to feel his skin on mine. His voice would no doubt spring to mind when I was between the sheets. I didn't need anything else fanning the flames.

Several moments passed before he dragged his gaze from me and glanced down at the white linen cardstock bearing my logo and *Simply Elegant* printed with a flourish in rich, glossy obsidian. The back was a reverse color scheme, black with my Web and social media addresses in white script.

"Stylish. Representative of the woman herself."

"Right," I scoffed as my cheeks flushed. "I'm a drowned rat."

He didn't seem to think so. His beautiful eyes slid over me. Taking in my sensible shoes with a modest, chunky heel for extensive time on my feet, up my bare legs to the black pencil skirt I wore, paired with a silver satin buttoned blouse and Tahitian pearl necklace. My clothes were still damp, as was my dark-brown hair. It hung loose about my shoulders, the strands originally curled in fluffy beach waves. Now they were straight and combed away from my face with my fingers.

I applied more makeup during events than my normal business day and had turned my blue eyes smoky and added an extra coat of mascara for the occasion. Thank God it was waterproof.

His attention lingered for endless seconds on my glossy lips. Then his gaze slowly lifted to meet mine again.

My breath caught. Heat fringed the emerald pools and one corner of his mouth lifted.

"Your name is rather unique," I said by way of idle chitchat as I willed my pulse to ease up a bit. Seriously, it was a wonder I got the words out. Desire flowed through every inch of me. My inner thighs quivered. My nipples tingled. All with just a blazing look from the sexiest man I'd ever laid eyes on.

"'Bax' is from the German *bagan*—to fight." Ah. Didn't that explain oh so much? Even the way he said his last name held a discernible *I don't let people fuck with me* connotation. He added, "I thought perhaps we'd met before, but I was mistaken." A flicker of something contemplative and beyond my comprehension replaced the heat in his eyes. But then he grinned again, chasing away the moment or two of disquiet.

No, we definitely had not met before. I would remember this man.

I will *remember this man.*

It was an inescapable reality.

Maybe it was the fact that we seemed to be so aware of each other that had given him the impression I was familiar. Maybe that was why he'd stepped in at the bar. I'd probably never know for sure.

With a fluid movement he whisked out his own business card and handed it over. I studied the thick pewter-gray matte stock with his contact information in a satiny accent a hue lighter than the card. Very avant-garde. On the back was a rendering of an astonishing hotel facade.

"*Oh.*" I glanced up, realization dawning. I'd seen this particular schematic for the ultra-lavish resort that was being touted as the West's Plaza Hotel. Though larger. More extravagant. More exclusive. Members only, along with elite guests upon special invitation. Rumor had it, the Bellagio rolled into Caesars Palace couldn't compete with the glitz and glamour of this destination hotel. "You own 10,000 Lux?"

"Yes." His smile was more engaging this time, showing me straight, snow-white teeth against his tanned skin.

I fought the gravitational pull that coaxed me to take a step toward him. Not at all a common urge. If anything, I typically took steps backward when I felt crowded.

But this man—Dane Bax—was a magnetic force difficult to ignore. Difficult to break free of, even though I didn't know him. Couldn't afford to know him, or get tangled up in the mystery of him. I was smart enough to quickly deduce he wasn't anyone with whom I should get involved.

With a mental shake of my head, I reminded myself that I didn't get involved period.

Yet I found myself saying, "I applied online for the Event Manager position a couple months ago." I gave a small shrug and added, "Never heard back."

"We've had some complications that have slowed our hiring process. In fact, I've pushed the grand opening to December."

I let out what sounded too much like a dreamy sigh—planner's curse. "That'll be sensational with a light dusting of fresh powder on the sandstone buttes, and all the holiday lights and decorations." I had no doubt they'd be gold and glittery and completely over-the-top.

"As long as nothing goes awry." The tinge of angst in his tone made me wonder what sort of *complications* he'd encountered. They sounded serious, given that he'd had to move the launch.

"Well, I hope everything works out for you." That seemed the polite thing to say to someone who'd rescued me. Not to mention, he might still be a potential employer.

"Thank you." His gaze turned intently scrutinizing as he asked, "Why would you give up independent wedding planning for events at the Lux? You appear to be quite good at what you do. I snuck a peek at the festivities. Very impressive."

So I had felt his gaze again. A little thrill zapped all of my erogenous zones so that I had to tamp down a moan. The man lit me up like nothing I'd ever known before.

Forcing an even tone, though fiery sensations raged through me, I told him, "It was *this close* to perfect." I held up my hand, pinching my forefinger and thumb almost together.

He brooded some more. "Nothing you can do about the monsoons, Ari."

My stomach flipped at how my name fell so smoothly and easily from his lips. His extremely kissable lips.

It took a few seconds for me to catch up with the conversation. "I enjoy the weddings, absolutely." But a grand opening, PR functions, and galas at a resort such as 10,000 Lux—a venue that would nab five stars right out of the chute, maybe even the elusive six— was an exhilarating prospect. It'd also keep me beyond busy. And I could use the steady paycheck. Plus . . . "It gets a little lonely working mostly by myself. Being part of a team would be nice. I don't have justification for staff at the moment. I don't bring in that sort of income."

"Money's an issue for you?"

"Um . . ." That was a hugely personal question. Though hadn't I just divulged personal things about myself? "I didn't really mean it like that. Just, you know . . . Planners can spend weeks or months—even years—on a wedding and we generally only make ten to fifteen percent on the overall cost, so without a large company capable of handling numerous events at once, I have to schedule accordingly and—"

Christ, I was rambling. Thank God I didn't go off on a tangent about the cryptic e-mails I'd recently received from my estranged mother. I had a very good idea what they were all about, even if dollar signs hadn't flashed on the screen. Like my father, I literally could not afford to get caught up in whatever scheme brewed in the back of her devious mind.

It was difficult, though, to open my mouth and *not* spew when it came to Dane. The way he stared so fixedly at me, the way his eyes bore into mine . . . I found it challenging not to bare some of my soul. Completely out of character for me, but still. He was captivating in the most alluring way. Scary-captivating, which made anxiety skip through me. And yet he was so damn electrifying,

I wanted to stay stuck in this moment with him, no matter what I gabbed about arbitrarily.

Having a conversation with a man who sparked my interest and left me ridiculously breathless was all very new and stimulating.

I found his brooding nature gripping in itself. His powerful presence thoroughly entranced me. But his hypnotic eyes . . . They were impossible to look away from, impossible to deny in that peculiar *I'm desperate to know him* sort of way.

So very dangerous.

Clearly, I wasn't inclined to play it safe. Otherwise, I would have made an excuse and hid out in the resort until he drove off.

He studied me closely as he said, "Money can be the root of all evil. Haven't you heard?"

"Says the man building the most luxurious hotel on the continent," I half joked.

He didn't smile. Mine faded. He wasn't being cliché. Or glib. His entire visage turned stony with hard angles, which only made him more intensely provocative, more fascinating.

"I'll be sure to have my Vice President of Human Resources take another look at your résumé," he said, effectively dismissing the previous topic.

A few tense moments passed between us. Then the soft, elegant purring of an engine drew my attention. A heartbeat later, Alex joined us. I wanted to send him away. Steal more time with Dane Bax.

"You're all set, Mr. Bax. And the rain has stopped. We kept your car covered."

Dane appeared to reluctantly pull his gaze from mine. He fished a tip from the front pocket of his jeans and handed over the cash.

Alex beamed brightly, then said, "I'll get yours next, Miss DeMille."

"Thank you." Not surprisingly, Mr. Bax ranked much higher in priority than Miss DeMille.

Dane's head tilted and his eyes slid over me again. Unabash-
edly. Unapologetically. "It was a pleasure to meet you, Ari. I look
forward to seeing you again. Soon."

He stalked off, all stealthy and pantherlike, as I fought the urge to
gape—and wondered why I couldn't breathe normally around him.

As I stood there awestruck and shell-shocked—*so* embarrassing—
Alex said, "Seriously cool sports car, huh?"

My gaze followed the shiny silver vehicle until it disappeared
into the inky night. I'd never seen anything like it, with aggressive
lines and a low profile.

"What is it?" I asked, trying to get my mind churning once
again, instead of leaving me in a mental standstill while my insides
burned.

"Hennessey Venom F5. Only thirty are being made. Base model
is like one-point-five mil or something, but Mr. Bax optioned his
to the hilt. It's a blast to drive. I'd kill to take it up the switchbacks."

My gaze shifted to the young valet. "I can see you're in a hurry
to trade that thrill seeker's experience for my sensible Kia Sorento."

He laughed. "I'll just be a couple minutes."

"Thanks."

My thoughts returned to Dane Bax.

*I look forward to seeing you again. Soon.*

What had he meant, exactly?

And did I really want to know?


"Time for the hand wedge, Ari." My dad gave me that disappointed
look any golf professional would throw his daughter's way when
she'd just hacked the hell out of a bunker.

I scooped up the ball and tossed it haphazardly onto the green.
Then I raked the sand trap and climbed out of it. Joining my dad—
former PGA golfer Bryce DeMille—I said, "It's always this last
hole that kills me."

I'd just added five unnecessary strokes to my scorecard, devastating my respectable showing.

"You've got to let the sand work for you, sweets. Get underneath the ball and blast it out. I tell you this every time."

Maybe it was my OCD that made it so difficult to create my own sandstorm just to get my ball onto the green. I was the same on the fairway, hating to leave divots, even though I always replaced the patches I took out when trying to avoid a worm burner.

"Easier said than done," I muttered.

He chuckled. My father was the type who struggled to appear good-natured in order to cover a sullen disposition. The result of his doomed marriage and career. He and my mother had started going at it with venomous words not long after I'd turned five. The terrible twos had nothing on their tantrums. Apparently, when your heart had been ripped from your chest—as was my dad's case when he'd discovered my mother had cheated on him, *repeatedly*—you checked your civility at the door. And there was residual bitterness, no matter how hard you pretended to be "over it."

They'd stayed together until I was thirteen. All those years, I'd spent an exorbitant amount of time wearing headphones blaring music to tune them out. And picking up the broken pieces of glass or porcelain when one of them got particularly miffed and hurled something at a wall or slammed a door too hard, making windowpanes rattle and picture frames fall to the floor.

It'd been a toxic state of affairs for all parties concerned. My maternal grandparents had suffered the same nasty fate, rivaling *The War of the Roses*. Leaving me full-on convinced it was genetic and I should therefore avoid romantic relationships and marriage at all costs.

Kind of a painful bane of existence, given that I loved weddings. Obviously. And I'd be lying if I said I didn't make believe that all of my brides and grooms were as deliriously happy the day after they'd exchanged vows as they were during those few magical moments. I was pretty good at creating my own little Emerald City so that *I* wasn't bitter.

Reaching for my putter, I lined up my shot and employed a nice, clean sweep toward the ball. It rolled tried-and-true to its target, made one pass around the rim of the cup, then popped up and out, rolling downhill. Even farther away from the pin than where I'd started.

"Son of a bitch," I grumbled.

My dad laughed a bit heartier this time. His cerulean eyes crinkled around the edges. He was of medium height with brown hair several shades lighter than mine. Perpetually tan from his hours spent on the course. A handsome man in excellent physical shape for his forty-seven years, with the exception of the crushed rotator cuff that had been operated on twice, along with a semi-detached bicep muscle. The very reason he'd gotten so close to a championship but hadn't been able to pull it off. Something we never talked about, though I knew it was a lost dream never far from his mind.

"Circle of love?" I asked of my wayward ball, calling on the sympathy factor that would put me out of my misery without adding more strokes.

I'd tried all morning to keep my focus on my game—mostly for my dad's sake. But in the back of my mind were thoughts of Dane Bax and 10,000 Lux. I tried to play it off, to myself, that all I was really interested in was a call from the HR department about my application. Another internal lie, of course. I wanted to see him again. I wanted to know if that magnetic force had been a fluke. Though that sort of curiosity wasn't exactly sane.

"Let's move along," my dad said. He glanced toward the fairway and the foursome who had been breathing down our necks— my fault—since we'd started earlier in the morning. "They didn't want to play through, but let's not needlessly hold them up. Especially when there's a storm moving in."

He was so golf-PC. I grabbed my ball and clubs and we headed to the cart. He drove us up to the clubhouse and we found a table on the patio overlooking the eighteenth hole—the one that had just slaughtered my confidence. Making the gloomy weather quite suitable.

While the server brought our usual round of drinks without us even placing the order, since my dad was well known on just about every course in the Southwest, he finished tallying his score, three under par. His shoulder must be hurting him. He'd left the limelight years ago and was now the GM and occasional instructor for a private golf club.

Tossing aside his pencil, he asked, "How was yesterday's big soiree?"

I gave him a knowing smile before taking a sip of iced tea. "You don't really want to talk about that. You hate weddings."

And I didn't like torturing him with details of starry-eyed couples. Nor was I inclined to mention my chance meeting with Dane Bax. It already felt too obsessive that, as exhausted as I'd been the previous evening, when I'd closed my eyes it was the gorgeous man with the hypnotic green gaze that flashed in my mind.

"Everything else okay?" my dad asked.

"Sure." I didn't worry him with the mini–rescue scene that had played out at Grace's bar. Though that wasn't far from my thoughts, either. Particularly Dane's role in the whole thing.

Changing the subject to a safer one, I chatted my dad up on news of The Open Championship while we ate lunch. Then we parted ways outside and I loaded my clubs into the SUV and drove to my townhome.

I spent the first part of the week reorganizing myself following the rushed preparations for the Delfino-Aldridge affair. I had papers strewn all over my kitchen counters and table. Meghan's mishmash of ideas for flowers and decorations were plastered across the corkboard that hung above my desk in the spare bedroom, mostly pages from magazines that we'd torn out or images from the Web she'd given me so that I could get a full visualization and come up with more definitive suggestions for her.

I was long overdue for actual office space, but since I always met clients at their venue of choice or in their home I chose not to waste the money. Not that I could really afford the extra expense at the moment without making serious sacrifices to my budget.

I wanted an office, though. Dreamed of someday having a large, elegant one that would bedazzle my brides and their parents. A little more hustle and bustle would be nice, too, as I'd mentioned to Dane.

Not surprisingly, I checked my smartphone about a dozen times more frequently than normal, hoping for a call or an e-mail from 10,000 Lux. Though there was no sense in denying that I wished *he* would call. He had my number, after all.

I found myself fantasizing about him asking me to bring a résumé to his office, personally, saying mine had apparently gotten lost in cyberspace. I was actually tempted to do just that without the open invitation. In fact, the more I thought about it, the more appealing the idea became.

When I had everything in order, I wrapped up a few details for a Halloween wedding still a couple of months away and prepped for a new client I'd be meeting with the following week. I also had a bridal show in Phoenix that required paperwork and a vendor booth selection to consider.

All of that taken care of, I printed my résumé with the Delfino-Aldridge wedding added as a highlight. I willed myself to find the nerve to drive to 10,000 Lux and deliver it to Dane. But then I thought back to the last visual he'd had of me—soaked to the bone—and decided he'd likely forgotten all about me the moment the door had closed on his Venom F5.

Too bad I couldn't dismiss him quite so easily.

Too bad I was preoccupied with him every moment I wasn't engrossed in something that required my full brain capacity. The very reason I kept myself immersed in details, details, details.

I even stopped in at Grace's bar over the weekend. She complained about her latest date not being able to tear his gaze from the TV when they'd stopped into a pub for a drink before dinner the night before. It'd gone downhill from there. I commiserated with her over a glass of wine.

The following Wednesday, I parked in the partially paved, partially dusty lot of Tlaquepaque, a rustic yet high-end complex of restaurants, art galleries, and boutiques in a lovely traditional Mexican village setting, complete with cobblestone walkways and vine-covered stucco walls. The full sycamores created a canopy overhead and the sound of Oak Creek running strong and steady echoed through the archways along with a trilling breeze laced with sultry humidity.

El Rincon was one of my favorite restaurants, with a patio on the bank of the creek. I'd reserved a table for the consultation with my new client and her extremely excitable mother. The future mother-in-law was also present, looking anxious and trepid, as though she really didn't want to be there. I was used to this sort of dynamic and knew to work the group to make sure everyone felt included and involved. It also helped to order margaritas.

We debated the pros and cons of three local resorts they were contemplating for the reception that would follow the ceremony in a friend's backyard, which had an astounding view of the Mystic Hills and the glass-veneered Chapel of the Holy Cross that sat amid red-rock buttes, looking like a giant cross wedged between the rocks. A stunning sight to see, but the sacred Native American land was also believed to emit an energetic spiritual force, its vortex drawing the New Agers and worshipers to it in droves. Not something I'd wholly subscribed to, but I still found it all very interesting.

I was in the middle of my spiel on the difference between popular resorts L'Auberge and Los Abrigados when I saw him.

Every fiber of my being went on high alert. I faltered mid-sentence, my gaze following him across the patio as a flurry of dried leaves nipped at his heels. Dane Bax joined three others at a large, round table, one of them being the same salt-and-pepper-haired man he'd met with in Grace's bar.

Dane wore black pants with a robin's-egg-blue dress shirt, the sleeves rolled up his sinewy forearms, displaying an expensive-looking watch. Titanium, I guessed. He took a chair, set his laptop bag at his feet, and dug out a slim black leather portfolio that he placed before him.

When he glanced up, his eyes landed on me. A flicker of surprise crossed his face. Then his look turned intense. Smoldering. Heat flashed through me.

I had no idea how many seconds—minutes?—passed. Eventually, he released me from his captivating gaze and launched into reviewing paperwork with his associates.

I vaguely heard my name in the background, along with the distinct sound of a knife tapping gently against a water glass.

"Ari? Something you'd like to share with us?" Shelby Hughes, the bride-to-be, teased in her singsong voice.

It took all the willpower I possessed to divert my attention from the sexy stranger who so mesmerized me.

Shelby gave a coy smile, her tawny eyes sparkling. "Someone you know?"

"I, uh . . ." I shook my head. Swept a few wayward strands of my blowout style from my face. I'd lost all train of thought the moment I'd caught a glimpse of Dane. My pulse spiked and adrenaline flooded my veins. "Sorry," I added. "What was I saying?"

She laughed. "I know that look all too well. Every time Matthew walks into a room, I'm utterly speechless."

Mrs. Hughes smiled and patted her daughter's hand. "You're such a sweet couple."

I'd met Matthew Barnes and was inclined to agree.

"Sooo . . . ?" Shelby prodded with wagging brows.

I tried to fight the blush, to no avail. Even the mother-in-law seemed to take great interest in this turn of events, perking up considerably. I shook my head again, mostly to dislodge the vision of Dane Bax that burned a hole in my brain. I said, "I actually don't know him." That was pretty close to the truth.

I spared a peek at my notes and then picked up where I'd left off, clearly disappointing my audience. But what, exactly, was I going to say about the man? That I had no idea who he really was and yet I was absurdly fixated on him? Desperate to speak with him again, even though it'd be a pointless endeavor?

When I'd finished my dissertation on the various resort offerings, I reached for my margarita and nearly downed the entire thing in one long gulp. My insides were on fire, just knowing Dane sat tables away, with me in his direct line of vision. Did he steal glances my way? I was dying to find out but didn't dare look over my shoulder. Not this time.

I wrapped up my meeting in a breathy tone and with slightly shaky fingers that made it difficult to write as I added details to my planning book. With nothing more to discuss at the moment, I said, "I'll type all of this up and send it in an e-mail so you can peruse it again, make some decisions or come up with more questions. Ping me anytime, for anything. I'll share with you everything I possibly can about the venues and vendors we've talked about."

"This is really great, Ari," Shelby said. "I'm a little brain fried from all the information you've given us."

"Take your time looking through it all." I handed over the packet I assembled for bridal parties, with the pertinent ins and outs and protocols neatly, concisely described so no one was too overwhelmed. It was a futile attempt to keep everyone calm, because there were just so many decisions to make and so much to do to pull off fairy-tale weddings. And Shelby's had Cinderella Moment written all over it.

The threesome left me and I jotted down more ideas as I polished off the rest of my marg and grew a bit antsy over the rumble of thunder through the clouds.

Suddenly I felt that emerald gaze. Tried to ignore the tickle against my clit it evoked. I needed to focus on immediate action items. Though the Hughes-Barnes wedding wasn't scheduled until the following summer, there were always things to accomplish and put on the radar right off the bat.

I tapped the end of my pen against my notebook as it started to dry up. I had a few more things to scribble down, but the ink ran out.

"Damn it," I mumbled as I scrawled against the paper in a vain attempt to get a little more out of the ballpoint. No such luck.

Seconds later, a fancy Montblanc fountain pen rested on my planner, with the initials *DBB* inscribed in gold script.

My heart nearly jumped from my chest and I swear there was a sparkage factor between my legs that had to be illegal. I pressed my thighs together as the thrumming started deep inside.

Lifting my gaze, I found Dane staring down at me, an arrogant smile on his too-handsome face. As though he knew he so easily set my body on fire.

"You can return it whenever you're done."

His laptop bag was slung over one impossibly broad shoulder, so I guessed he'd concluded his own business.

I handed the pen back. "I'm good. Thanks." Every thought, save for one, had just fled my mind, so I had nothing left to write. Except the fantasy of him pushing my skirt up and taking me right then and there.

*Oh, wait.* We were in the middle of a busy restaurant.

I shook the mental image from my head. Tried to breathe like a normal person, not a lust-crazed one.

He tucked away the pen and then gestured toward the chair Shelby had vacated. "May I?"

"Of course."

*Crap.* I'd had two margaritas, which took way too much of the edge off. I felt all warm and fuzzy and that just would not do at the moment. Why couldn't he have caught me after I'd taken a tour through the art galleries, as I had planned for the afternoon?

I reached for my water as Dane said, "You clearly don't lack for clients."

I sipped, then set aside the glass. Even ice water couldn't cool my blazing insides. "I get a decent amount of referrals now. Word of mouth, or people who were guests at one of my weddings."

He retrieved a magazine from the side pocket of his bag and dropped it on the table. My face smiled back at me.

"Congratulations," he said.

It was the latest issue of *Southwest Weddings* magazine, in which I was featured in as an up-and-coming wedding planner, following an event I'd orchestrated at the private Forest Highlands country club outside of Flagstaff, just north of us. The son of an eighties rock musician had married a Malibu Barbie type and the wedding had been sensational, with the gorgeous San Francisco Peaks as the backdrop.

"Are you in the habit of reading bridal magazines?" I asked, my tone low and provocative. I couldn't seem to find my real voice when I was around this man.

"The cover caught my attention," he said, a hint of mischief in his words. "Turns out you're exactly what I was looking for." Excitement flared in his eyes—warning signals went off in my head.

Still, I said playfully, "I'm not the marrying kind."

He smirked. And oh, what that sexy look did to my insides was nothing short of volcanic!

Even light flirting with him was dangerous. My gaze dropped as I tried to regroup. Then I forced myself to make eye contact again. Not exactly a good thing. I was way too entranced, way too hooked on how he looked at me, the way his eyes glowed seductively, the way the corner of his mouth lifted slightly, revealing the shadow of a grin.

"What *were* you looking for?" I managed to ask.

His gaze dipped to my rapidly rising and falling chest. Which made it all worse for me. My nipples puckered behind the tight bodice of my lavender summer dress as desire flitted across his chiseled features. I fought the insane urge to have his hands and mouth all over my body.

Another blush crept up my neck. *Damn it.*

*This* was what I carefully avoided in order to stay focused on my dream, and to keep from falling into the trap of mediocre dating that always left me lonelier than I was before I'd met someone new and had given him a chance.

Though, without doubt, there was nothing mediocre about Dane Bax.

His gaze shifted to my face and he continued our original conversation, as if he hadn't just stolen more than a quick glance at my breasts and responded as heatedly as I had. The intense humidity in the air didn't cling to my skin the way his bold gazes did. I felt tingles along my bare flesh and had to reach for my water again.

He said, "We located your application at the hotel—a glitch with the new system." A troubled expression flitted across his face but quickly disappeared. I surmised there were plenty of *glitches* when it came to bringing a resort online. One of this magnitude was likely rife with challenges and setbacks. I suspected that was the reason for his vacillating consternation—when he wasn't scowling over me being in the clutches of another man.

Continuing, Dane said, "You started your company when you were twenty, while getting your business degree."

"I took online courses. Ended up with a good deal of time on my hands for weddings. No commuting to class."

"Right." He gave a half snort at my easy explanation.

No, school had not been a breeze for me, especially while actively farming for clients. But I'd wanted my own LLC initially and needed to know how to run it. Plus, I'd always considered eventually becoming a corporate planner, so I'd committed to professional training and industry certifications.

"According to this article," he said, indicating the magazine, "you're on a distinguished list of preferred planners."

"A celebrity wedding helps to put one on the map."

"That and the Delfino event."

"Yes." I'd already had media inquiries to talk about some of the arrangements I'd made. Mr. Delfino had me sign a nondisclosure statement but it only applied to family information—most specifically, his daughter's pregnancy—not anything related to flowers, decorations, et cetera.

"What's the largest number of guests you've worked with?"

I eyed him speculatively, my stomach fluttering. "Is this a job interview, Mr. Bax?"

His dazzling grin took my breath away. "Perhaps the start of one." He leaned in, pinning me with an engaging look. "And call me Dane."

I opened my mouth to speak. No words came out.

His grin widened. "Have dinner with me Saturday night at the hotel and I'll explain." His voice alone did the most insane things to my inner thighs, making them burn.

Everything within me went haywire. Yet a hint of panic crept around the fringes.

"Dinner?" Not a daytime meeting in his office? Or with Human Resources?

"Are you available?" A mischievous glint edged his beautiful irises.

*For dinner, or . . . ?* I had no idea where this might be going.

"I promise it'll be worth your while," he assured me. The panic must have flashed in my eyes, because his tone changed to one that resonated *no is not an option, Ari.* "I'll send a car for you. Seven o'clock. I'll meet you in the lobby."

"I—"

"No point in driving yourself. The gate's heavily guarded at present, while we're still in construction phase."

"I—"

"Don't stay out here too long," he said as his gaze darted to the clouds overhead. "You'll end up soaked again."

He stood, hefted his bag, and sauntered off.

Leaving me reeling. Once more.

And wondering if Dane Bax always got what he wanted.

I waited for a water refill and then promptly drained the glass. I stole a few glances toward the small walkway just outside the patio that led from the shops to the parking lot. Dane was texting on his phone. Moments later, a woman joined him.

Statuesque, slim, honey-blond hair. Perfectly sleek and highlighted shiny honey-blond hair, to be exact. She wore skinny jeans, six-inch heels, and a blouse that hung open to reveal the scalloped lace of her bra. Aviator sunglasses covered her eyes and she carried a Louis Vuitton bag on her forearm, said arm crooked, palm up in that society way with which I was all too familiar, because my mother possessed the same air of Scottsdale haughtiness and chic entitlement.

Dane's companion held her phone in the other hand, as though missing a call would result in dire consequences, and she waved her arm emphatically as she spoke with him. I watched with morbid curiosity as she gave him a sudden grave look, listened to something he said, smiled vibrantly, and then leaned in to give him double-cheek air kisses. Her breasts brushed his chest. I tore my gaze away. Paid the bill. Gathered my belongings and ducked into the ladies' room.

When I emerged, Dane and the Heidi Klum lookalike were nowhere in sight. I sighed in relief, not wanting to have to skirt past them. Oddly, a tinge of envy over how cool and aloof the blonde had appeared crept in on me. I was a tangled mess of nervous energy and tingling body parts around him. She'd been collected, affectionate, alluring.

I forced myself to wave off the feeling of jealousy over their obviously close relationship. Accepted the reality that Dane Bax likely dated a half dozen women at any given time, all living in sophisticated places such as New York City, San Francisco, Milan, Paris . . .

With a shake of my head, I left the restaurant and went about my day.

# chapter 3

That night, I started sifting through my closet for the perfect outfit. By Thursday afternoon, I'd torn through every article of clothing I owned, trying on each ensemble and discarding it into a wrinkled heap on the chair sitting next to the full-length mirror in my bedroom. Nothing I owned seemed worthy of 10,000 Lux. Or Dane Bax.

Friday morning, I made my apologies to my dad and bailed on a nine-hole round on the executive course in Flagstaff, in lieu of another trip to Tlaquepaque. There was a boutique that specialized in cocktail dresses I'd always admired; they were just typically way out of my price range. I wasn't one to splurge, but desperate times and all that . . .

I scoured the racks, handing over possibilities to the salesclerk for her to add to the changing room she'd designated for me. I was three quarters of the way through the store, with only a few dresses selected, when I hit the back wall and stared up at the strapless mini on display.

A smile spread over my lips.

"That's the one," I said to the clerk.

"You're in luck. It's a one-off we received by mistake. I believe it's your size."

I'd never been into the whole cosmic-kismet-destiny stuff like some of the New Agers in town, but I knew a sign when I saw it.

The garment was a deep emerald, as close to Dane's eyes as one could get, because nothing quite matched their dynamic magnetism. The dress was amazingly beautiful and I couldn't resist it. I'd made my mind up before I'd even seen the price tag, which did make my heart stutter.

Luckily, the Delfinos had already paid me in full for my services, sending the last installment with a gorgeous *thank you* bouquet last week. Along with an invitation to the second reception they'd planned for the newlyweds in Scottsdale, upon their return from a honeymoon cruise and two weeks in Aruba.

I also needed a new pair of black shoes, since mine were more functional and less complementary of my purchase. So I added four-inch heels to my shopping spree and hoped like hell I wouldn't hurt myself when I wore them.

Returning to my townhome, I left the dress in its sealed bag, hanging it in my now-empty closet. I'd have to deal with that disaster later, because I still had work to do. I went into the spare bedroom and sifted through e-mails and then magazines, looking for visuals that would inspire me when it came to some of Shelby Hughes's scrambled thoughts on decorations and themes. I liked the creative process, understanding that not every bride had a full idea of what she wanted, just bits and pieces that needed to be puzzled together.

As the sun dipped over the golf course on which I lived, my stomach grumbled. I made pasta and considered watching a movie, but my mind wandered too much. I grabbed my tablet, flipped the switch on the gas fireplace—since tonight's storm brought the temperature down as the rain fell heartily—and settled on the sofa with a glass of chardonnay.

I needed to do a little research.

Dane had studied up on me; it was time I did the same.

I Googled him and found all kinds of links that led to articles, interviews, and, of course, a Wikipedia page. The latter was a little disconcerting. Actually, every item I devoured was disconcerting. Not just because the word *billionaire* jumped out repeatedly— completely unsettling me. It was the lack of any substantial details that alarmed me most.

I learned he was six-foot-three, though I'd already suspected that. Thirty years old, born to a Philadelphia society family—also lacking details aside from their extreme philanthropic efforts decades ago and the very simple *d.* that denoted they were both deceased. No explanation given. No dates.

That was definitely odd. Causing a chill to run along my spine.

I further learned Dane had graduated from Harvard summa cum laude, having completed the Thesis Track in Economics. He'd built his first boutique resort in Lake Tahoe. Then revived a hotel/casino in Las Vegas. And now he had the Lux.

Just like that.

I frowned. Literally, those were the most revealing details of the man that I could find. Nothing at all personal.

Had he played sports in school? Did he date supermodels? (The blond-haired woman from El Rincon flashed in my head.) How the hell had he made all of his money—was it strictly from an inheritance?

And who was capable of containing so much information so that only the essentials were provided? How much did *that* cost?

My stomach twisted as I recalled his comment regarding money being the root of all evil . . . and the ensuing hard set of his features. This intrigued me the most. It was a strange thing for a billionaire to say.

Then again, I imagined there had to be a dark side to amassing such wealth. My parents were a prime example on a much, *much* smaller scale. Finances had always been an issue for them. My mother had been obsessed with being one of the pampered "ladies who lunch" in Scottsdale, where I'd been born. She'd spent just about every penny my dad brought in from his PGA tours. She'd put substantial pressure on him to win a championship, a Masters, *anything and everything* that would garner the massive bucks. And when he'd failed because of his injuries . . . things had taken a serious dive.

He'd been devastated all the way around. Afterward, when the electricity or water was sometimes shut off, he'd shrug and say he'd forgotten to pay the bill. Around the time I was sixteen or so, I'd discovered the truth. He was flat broke. She'd taken him to the cleaners, big-time—financially and emotionally. And it hadn't been until he'd scored the GM position at the club in Sedona that he'd dug himself out of the hole.

There were so many things about my childhood that made me shudder when I checked my own balance online. Though I had a safety net with a savings account, I still lived in fear of not being able to make ends meet. Especially since we'd moved to a sketchy part of downtown Phoenix after the fallout. I honestly couldn't take scorpions crawling up the walls again or crouching in corners if I had to leave Sedona and find something more affordable in the Valley.

I'd been so relieved when my dad had moved us here with his new job. So relieved, I'd cried for a week. He'd never really known why, because we kept stuff like that to ourselves.

Setting aside the tablet, I reached for my wine and sipped while I pushed aside my dismal and sometimes horrifying childhood and instead contemplated the ambiguity around Dane Bax.

Why so secretive? And what drove him to build, according to all news reports, what was projected to be the most lavish resort in North America? What was his next goal—a hotel to rival the only seven-star resort in the world, the Burj Al Arab in Dubai?

That extraordinarily ambitious aspiration made my palms sweat. Because the determined set of Dane's jaw and his steely gaze made me believe it was a distinct possibility. And he was only thirty, after all.

Anxiety roiled through me.

Maybe it was best not to know so much about him.

As I tried to alter my mind-set from the gorgeous billionaire, while streaming *Breaking Bad*, my phone buzzed with an incoming text. I paused the show and read, my spirits plummeting.

*Saw your feature in* SW Weddings, my mother wrote. *You must be doing well for yourself.*

I stared at those words, fighting the dread that came with the sinking feeling of *what is she up to now?*

Late Saturday afternoon, I tried to relax with a bubble bath— *impossible*—then carefully did my makeup and hair before slipping into my new dress.

The driver arrived promptly at seven. We left the townhome and drove through Sedona, heading west, then north to a striated red-rock canyon. The scenery was spectacular as the sun began to set over the mesas. I loved this time of night, because of the way the rays illuminated the various hues of orange and red on the pinnacles, which ranged in size and shape from mountainous to tall, artistic sculptures and spires.

Set amongst it all was 10,000 Lux, also situated near several ponds and streams with placid mirrored surfaces. The grounds were lush and stunning, the foliage all meticulously trimmed and vibrant. I caught glimpses through the decorative black wrought-iron and gold-leaf fencing that stretched between cream-colored columns topped with enormous gaslit lanterns, winking seductively against the encroaching twilight.

A sense of exclusivity enveloped the property, the kind that created in people of lesser good fortune the mysterious yearning to be a part of something beyond their reach.

We passed through the guards' booth at the gate and took the winding stone driveway lined with trees and beautifully crafted fountains to the enormous circular entrance, surrounded by more manicured lawns, topiary hedges, and waterfalls. Being one of those people of lesser good fortune, I stared out the window in complete awe.

The resort itself was sensational, even in its reported state of late construction, of which there was no evidence in the front. The lobby was four stories of large, symmetrically shaped windows, all illuminated with a golden glimmer that came from chandeliers so huge I could see them from the drive.

Full vines climbed the stone walls, strategically placed, impeccably arranged. I'd expected a fancy porte cochere out front but then realized a ramada would detract the eye from all the grandeur. Clearly, I wasn't the only one who'd deduced that.

All in all, I was thoroughly mind blown. And I hadn't even gotten out of the gleaming Jag yet.

A valet swooped in, already in uniform despite the hotel not being open. He wore stylish black tails with white gloves. I instantly felt underdressed, though I loved the mini and had spent enough money on it to give myself heart palpitations.

*Damn—shown up by a valet.* I should have pulled out my prom dress from the closet in the spare bedroom.

But no, that would have been complete overkill.

Unless, of course, Dane sported a tux, too.

Panic slithered down my spine. I really had no idea what I was getting myself into with him. This was supposed to be a job interview, right? Except that it was also dinner, and I'd dressed *that* part, hadn't I? I should have played it safe and simple and worn a business suit.

As I waded through my confused thoughts, the spiffed-to-the-hilt gentleman opened my door and greeted me with a friendly smile. "Welcome, Miss DeMille."

I slipped from the leather seat, staring up at the gorgeous facade of 10,000 Lux.

"Mr. Bax is waiting for you just inside the entrance. I'll escort you."

My breathing turned shallow. I hoped like hell I didn't botch this. I was already nervous over the fact that I'd applied for a position here and, of course, seeing Dane.

Or, more accurately, having dinner with Dane. Being alone with Dane. Being within fifty feet of Dane.

I had no delusions; I knew I was in over my head. Did that stop me from proceeding with caution? No. I was too sexually charged, too intrigued, to give in to my wary side.

The valet pulled open one of the tall wood-trimmed glass doors and gestured for me to lead the way. I stepped into the lobby, doing everything in my power to appear calm and collected. No-go, really.

*Holy shit.*

There he stood.

Dane Bax.

I couldn't breathe again.

Only he could outshine and outclass his surroundings.

I could probably come up with some clever and evocative words to describe the inside of 10,000 Lux. At the moment, all I saw was the veined creamy marble floor that led straight to Dane. It took several seconds for anything else to register.

He stood alongside a gorgeous round mahogany table that served as the focal point of the lobby and that likely would fill my living and dining room combo. A gold, silver, and copper-painted vase about as tall as I was in heels stood sentinel in the middle of the table, filled with ecru blooms and dripping verdant leaves. Above it hung the mammoth chandelier. Others decorated the ornately designed ceiling, defying gravity throughout the cavernous reception area. All impressive, but the main fixture was a showstopper.

My wide-eyed gaze dropped to Dane. He glanced up from his iPhone and our gazes locked. He grinned. The ultra-sexy one that was really just the hint of a smile.

My heart skipped a few necessary beats.

"Good evening," he said in a somewhat formal tone.

I lost my voice again.

The grin deepened—he must have known he left me speechless.

He took several long strides toward me, since I'd barely made it through the doors when I'd gone into shock. Everything was just so . . . perfect.

Especially him.

Dressed in a black suit with a pewter shirt opened at the neck, he was devilishly handsome. His hair was a tousled mess, wildly stylish. His emerald eyes glowed warmly, invitingly.

"That will be all, Brandon," he said to the valet, dismissing him.

"Of course. If you need anything, Mr. Bax, I'll be right out front."

Not that he had guests to assist. Must be a quick slip outside for discretionary purposes.

"Are you all right?" Dane asked as he regarded me closely.

"Sure," I managed to say. Then, hoping to break the ice, I added, "Should I be wearing a hard hat?"

He chuckled, low and deep. The sound resonated within me, heightening my arousal. How was that even possible? I was absurdly turned on from just the sight of him.

"You're safe, I assure you. The construction's complete in the main building. We're just finishing decorating of the suites upstairs and the penthouse. The casitas on the back portion of the property and the indoor aquatic center and its two restaurants are still being built."

"I was thinking more along the lines of the chandelier." I spared another glance at the one we stood under. "Looks like it'd wipe out an entire village if it fell."

"I promise it's not going anywhere."

"Right. Okay." Butterflies got the best of me. I was nothing but a bundle of nerves—not all of them emotionally jumping. Most of them were sizzling and snapping at the hint of his cologne wafting under my nose and the fact that Dane Bax had the most spellbinding presence I'd ever encountered.

He stepped aside and said, "Shall we?"

I finally noted that he'd kept a respectable distance when he'd joined me. Not crowding me at all. And he didn't take my hand or offer his arm.

He'd seen my reaction to Kyle Jenns when he'd reached for me—not to mention everyone else who'd laid a hand on me the day of the Delfino-Aldridge wedding. He'd come to my rescue because of it all.

Clearly, he'd picked up on my minimal-touching stance. A thought that really should have pleased me. So why didn't it?

*Because you want* him *to touch* you.

All. Over.

*Good point.*

Regardless, I maintained a few feet between us and started walking.

"Up the stairs to the mezzanine," he instructed, following along with a slow, measured gait.

I eyed the elegant sweeping staircases on either side of the main portion of the lobby and asked, "Does it matter which one?"

"No. We're heading straight out to the veranda."

I ascended the marble steps, holding on to the fancy black wrought-iron banister because my legs shook a little from nervous anxiety—or were my knees weak from Dane?

"Did you design this place yourself?" I asked.

"Yes. Over the course of several years and with help from engineers and architects, naturally."

I wanted to ask him how someone so young could afford to finance such extravagance but that seemed rude. And I wasn't sure I wanted to know the answer. I was already sufficiently overwhelmed and intimidated by everything about him.

Except that his disconcertion over the money comment he'd made while we'd waited for our cars at the resort still ate at me. There was something there, something to latch on to. I just didn't know what it was and that perplexed me greatly.

I tried to stay on safe ground. "What about the name?" I inquired. "I suspect it's not Lux as in *luxury*, though this is certainly the very definition of posh. The pinnacle of it, really."

He kept a span of two steps between us. Not that I could breathe any easier because of it, but at least I could speak now.

His eyes held a roguish shimmer. "What do you think it means, then?"

I smiled. "*Lux* is an industry term. Well, in audio-visual, that is. It's the luminance of light boxes or projectors. Ten-thousand lux is the equivalent of full daylight on a surface. Brilliant light."

He grinned again. An appreciative one. "You catch on quick. Very few others get it—just my A-V guys."

"Hmm." I figured that was one more exclusionary element to this breathtaking venue. "Clever."

He winked. My pulse shot through the roof.

We reached the mezzanine and he directed me through more intricately trimmed doors to a long terrace with the same railing as the stairway and outer fencing, rounded where a portion of the veranda jutted out in a semicircle over the magnificent courtyard.

This particular spot was just the one to show off the vast grounds and striking outbuildings. I couldn't even fathom how many acres the resort sat on. It was like we'd entered another world. A glittery, astounding one that boggled the mind. Disneyland wasn't this magical. And, wouldn't you know it? The clouds had thinned out for the remainder of the sunset and it was as awe inspiring as everything else surrounding us.

"What do you think?" Dane asked in a quiet voice.

"I think you're a genius."

He chuckled. I stared at him over my shoulder.

"I was hoping you'd like it."

"What's not to like?" I asked.

"Indeed." His gaze turned smoldering and I knew he wasn't talking about the resort. "You fit in here."

Flames danced along my skin at his sensual look. My internal temperature soared, even though it was a balmy seventy degrees outside. He moved next to me and rested a forearm on the railing, casual and yet . . . so engaging. My eyes followed his graceful movements.

"I'm trying to be cool and not trip on these shoes as I take it all in," I admitted.

"You're doing just fine."

"I'm used to thicker heels, mostly because they don't get stuck in the grass like tent spikes during outdoor weddings and garden receptions."

And there I went again . . . rambling.

"Doesn't matter what you're wearing. Though that dress is sensational. Interesting color choice." He gave me a knowing look.

I flushed. "I happen to like green."

"Hmm," he said, using my own vague response. Apparently, he'd deduced why I'd chosen this particular garment. He stared awhile longer, an all-consuming gaze that sparked a peculiar yearning deep within me. Then he pushed away from the ledge and moved past me, pausing to lean in—close enough that his very essence surrounded me despite him not being *too* close—and said, "You're stunning." He strolled off.

I stood where I was, the yearning becoming a dull ache that pulsed erratically in my pussy, a radiant longing for something elusive. It was almost painful—because I liked how my body responded to Dane. Even though I knew I shouldn't.

I turned and joined him at one of the pretty glass-top tables set for two. Candles were lit all around us. I heard for the first time the sultry sound of muted trumpets and the soul-stirring wail of a saxophone drifting on the night air. I couldn't seem to notice anything beyond him when he stood next to me.

Dane held out a chair for me, then sat at the opposite side of the table. Another tuxedo-clad man appeared and gently placed a linen napkin in my lap and offered me champagne.

"That would be nice. Thank you." He disappeared. I asked Dane, "Isn't this a bit much, a bit unorthodox? I mean, for a job interview . . . ?"

Though I supposed it wasn't totally unconventional. I'd had plenty of dinners and lunches with prospective clients. We usually sealed the deal over dessert and espresso.

With his sigh-worthy grin, he said, "I like it when you're all breathless and wide-eyed. I thought this place might do that to you."

"You think it's the hotel?"

His grin turned devilish. Something sexy and evocative flickered in his eyes. A shiver ran down my spine. I was perfectly aware I was playing with fire—and could easily get burned. But I couldn't seem to help myself.

The server returned a few minutes later with a freestanding chiller.

"Watch this," Dane said, a hint of intrigue in his voice. "Miyanaga is an expert at serving champagne."

The other man stood back from the table and made a production out of removing the foil and wire cage with precise movements. Then he whipped out a short sword from the sheath I hadn't even realized was strapped to his waist. He pointed the bottle toward the grounds, away from us, and placed the blade flat against the seam, sliding it slowly up to the flange. Then he swiftly and efficiently sabered the neck.

The cork went flying, Miyanaga bowed, and I clapped enthusiastically. I was certain someone had been hired specifically to retrieve the corks from the courtyard—and probably had a haughty French title to go with the position.

To Dane, I said, "How'd I know this wouldn't be a normal evening?"

# chapter 4

Mischief made Dane's eyes sparkle. "Life's too short to settle for normal."

I cringed. *I* was normal. There was absolutely nothing extraordinary about me. Except that I could take ten hodgepodge ideas and turn them into one glamorous or intimate spot-on wedding.

Yet the way Dane looked at me, the way he *watched* me, made me feel as though he actually did find something fascinating here. I wished he'd tell me what it was.

Miyanaga wrapped a linen napkin around the bottle and splashed a sample of champagne into a delicate flute for me to sip.

"Cristal," I ventured, having a fairly defined palate, given my profession.

He revealed the label and I nodded my approval. He poured for both of us.

Dane tipped the rim of his glass to mine and said, "To your health—*à votre santé.*"

Miyanaga returned the bottle to the bucket and asked, "May I serve?"

My very sexy host gave me a keen look. I nodded again.

We started with Blue Point oysters, which happened to be my favorite variety; perhaps I'd mentioned that in the bridal magazine feature?

As I sprinkled the shallot-and-red-wine vinaigrette on one, I asked, "Why'd you choose Sedona for the Lux?"

"The seclusion of the canyons. I like the temperate, sometimes moody weather as well, and the fact that we're far removed from a bright-lights-big-city atmosphere, where guests can lose themselves in the beauty of their surroundings without too much hindrance from the outside world."

I knew from experience that cell reception in this general area was sketchy. And calls dropped farther along the outskirts of town where the signals were nil, particularly in the box canyons. Every time I worked a wedding at the Enchantment Resort, not far from here, I had to use resort-issued walkie-talkies to communicate with staff and critical bridal-party points of contact, because our cells were useless. Even in the age of smartphones and satellite service. Some claimed it was a result of our infamous vortices. I just figured we lacked for towers.

Oysters were followed by the richest, creamiest lobster bisque in small, artsy bowls. Next came an exquisite salad of heirloom beets, goat cheese, figs, and pecans.

Our entreé arrived and my stomach did a little happy dance over bone-in rib eye with the most aromatic crab béarnaise sauce drizzled over the prime cut, and accompanied by grilled asparagus spears.

"*Oooh*." I all but salivated when the plate was set before me.

As if Dane didn't serve as the most exciting stimulant known to womankind, he sent me over the edge with decadent aphrodisiacs. Between him and the food, I practically melted off my chair. I knew he was trying to impress me with the chef's talents, but

Dane's selections were all at the top of my list. Prompting me to
ask, "How did you know . . . ?"

He gave a wicked smirk that did me in. I had to tamp down the
moan bubbling in my throat. And what continued to happen between my legs was altogether scandalous.

Dane said, "I do my homework. I never enter negotiations without knowing exactly what I'm getting into and *exactly* what I want
to get out of it."

I stared at him, completely caught off guard. Why was he so
good at that when I'd devoted so much time to being cognizant of
any potential surprise coming my way?

"I didn't realize we were in the midst of negotiations," I said,
my tone tentative. "We haven't really talked about the position."

He sliced smoothly into his steak, chewed a bit, washed it down
with champagne. Meanwhile, my stomach begged for the same,
but apprehension whirled within me and I set aside my flatware.

Dane frowned. "I had that specially prepared for you."

"I'm aware of that and I appreciate the gesture," I said, trying to
sound nonchalant, though my pulse was totally off the charts.
Clearly, he'd learned enough about me to know my preferences.
Though flattering, it was a bit unsettling.

I took a sip of champagne, then asked, "Why am I here?" I gazed
expectantly at him.

As casual as could be, he said, "I want you to work for me, of
course." He gave a half shrug of his broad shoulders and added,
"We'll have to figure out the rest, naturally."

*The rest* aroused my interest even more than the job offer and
sent a wave of heat rushing through me. But I focused on the first
issue at hand.

"Doing what, specifically?"

"Events Director. In charge of everything. Reporting straight to
me."

My palms turned clammy. I wrung them in the napkin in my
lap.

"I think there's been a mistake in HR. I applied for the manager position."

"And I see you as the director."

I swallowed hard. My mouth turned as dry as dust. I reached for my champagne and sipped. Then I started small. "Events Director with no VP above me?"

"No. Just me."

And damn if that little sentiment didn't hold all kinds of innuendo. Didn't help that lust, raw and intense, flashed in his eyes. I swear he fought a suggestive crooking of his brow.

I returned my glass to the table because my fingers trembled. I brimmed with a burning desire unlike anything I'd ever known. And he hadn't even touched me.

"So, um . . ." I tried to concentrate on the topic on deck. It was next to impossible to get my mind moving in the right direction, but thankfully, I spoke coherently. "I don't think I have the qualifications for something of that magnitude."

Sure, I'd pulled off some amazing weddings, but I still needed to cut my teeth on other functions. And the Delfino-Aldridge soiree was the largest one I'd handled so far. 10,000 Lux would host *thousands* of celebrity and other VIP guests. I wasn't on par with that. In fact, the mere thought scared the shit out of me as much as it excited me.

"Ari," he said as he leaned forward with a serious look on his face. I got lost in his deep-green eyes for a few moments. He continued, despite my mental stammering that matched the crazed beating of my heart. "Anthony Delfino is a very, *very* important man. One of the wealthiest in the country. You skillfully executed an event under the intense scrutiny of someone significant. A man who wouldn't want a hint of a flaw to mar his only daughter's big day."

"He has two other receptions planned," I informed Dane. "One at his home in Scottsdale and another at the Plaza. He didn't ask me to coordinate either. And, the truth is, the Aldridges had heard of me from friends. Of course they'd hire me."

With a sharp shake of his head, Dane said, "Don't for a second think that Anthony Delfino would go along with anyone's suggestion without investigating all possibilities and coming to his own conclusions. He was the one footing the bill, after all. He could have easily flown in a premier planner from New York. Delfino chose *you*. The additional receptions are basically for networking purposes, a great way to appease and connect with business associates. Also," he continued rather forcefully, "his little girl's happiness on her wedding day would be *nothing* to discount. He wouldn't risk it."

Dane's intensity was enthralling. My breathing slowed to a paltry crawl.

He added, "Once again, I've done my research." His tone became more insistent, ever more entrancing. "This is the position I want you in, Ari."

*Events Director?* Beneath *him? Both?*

Needing a moment to collect myself, I pulled a classic avoidance move by digging into my steak. When I felt his gaze boring into me, I said, "I'm not really sure about this."

As much as his job offer, and everything else about him, enticed me, I had to admit I wasn't ready for something on this scale. Something so . . . grandiose.

Dane sat back, obviously knowing he'd pushed boundaries. He reached into the inside pocket of his suit jacket and extracted a dark-gray envelope that matched his business card, though larger and rectangular in shape. He set it on the table.

My full name—Aria Lynne DeMille—was neatly, artistically centered in the middle.

"I've set the date for the grand opening. New Year's Eve. We'll start off the new year—the first year for 10,000 Lux—with a huge bash the night before. I want you in charge of it, and all the associated functions leading up to it, including the soft launch and the press events. And think of the weddings and galas we'll host here." With two fingers, he pushed the envelope toward me. "Take a peek." The flicker of excitement in his eyes had curiosity clawing at me.

I wasn't sure this was a sane path to travel. But I couldn't stop myself from reaching for the envelope. I untucked the flap and withdrew the matching card inside.

There was nothing on it, save for two numbers, centered as my name had been and stacked on top of each other. Figures that made my heart nearly leap from my chest.

I tore my gaze from the cardstock and asked, "Are there typos here?"

He smirked again. "No typos."

"You're serious?"

He nodded. "First one's an annual salary. I also provide a rich benefits package, including free golf for my senior executive team, of which you'd be a part."

My brow dipped. Did he know who my dad was?

Not missing a beat, Dane added, "The second figure is your yearly budget."

"Oh." *Wow.* My fingers trembled again as I held the note card.

"Consider your environment, Ari." He spread his arms wide, indicating all that was 10,000 Lux.

"Sure, but—" All these heart palpitations couldn't be good for me. "Dane." I glared at him, incredulous.

He glared back. "Not enough?"

I was just about to launch into an all-out *this offer is obscene and I can't do this!* when he stood abruptly.

"Why don't I show you to your office?"

"My—" *Oh, crap.* My office?

He really was the devil. He knew all the threads to pull in order to unravel me.

Rib eye and crab béarnaise be damned, I was on my feet in a heartbeat. He grinned knowingly. I ignored his arrogance. Despite

the daunting flash in my mind of *this could be an episode of* 666
Park Avenue *unfolding*, I followed him.

He ushered me inside and down the hallway to a discreet bank
of elevators. Exhilaration chased through me. I'd devoted so much
of my time and energy to fulfilling others' wishes, it was surreal to
be thrust into my own fairy tale. Even when I wondered if giving
in to my dreams might bend more toward nightmarish than fantasy when it came to a man who seemed determined to win at *all*
costs. A man who seemed resolute about possessing . . . *me*.

We left the elevator on the top floor and traveled the wide, marbled corridor. Dane stopped halfway down and retrieved a card
key from his inner jacket pocket, swiping it over the electronic
reader. He opened the door and we moved inside.

My gaze swept through the room, my jaw falling slack. It was
huge, with floor-to-ceiling windows showcasing the gardens and
fountains, the majestic canyons in the distance. A plush white sofa
and two stylish armless chairs were situated on one side with a glass
coffee table in the center, along with matching end tables and tall
exotic bamboo trees and birds of paradise to accent the living room
setting.

The floor was a dark, polished hardwood that set off all the pristine white. In the far corner was a large desk situated on the diagonal, also with a glass top. There was a conference table that
accommodated eight, and a marble-countered wet bar. I had no
doubt it was fully stocked with FIJI water, champagne, and scotch
for the Lux's upper-echelon clientele.

"You don't have to keep this furniture," he said from behind me.
"We can replace all of this and decorate it however you want. I
thought it'd give you a better point of reference than an empty
room."

"No," I said as myriad emotions pressed in on me, all too overwhelming to dissect or process. "This is stunning. I wouldn't change
a thing."

He'd captured my attention. *Big-time.*

It was way over the top, of course—that seemed to be his style. Best of all, I had my own showstopping chandelier.

"So . . . what do you think?" he asked as he guided me to the sofa against the wall and I sank onto the plump cushion. Oversize pillows filled the corners, one set piled atop a luxurious satin pale-gold quilt that was arranged artfully at an angle.

"I think I'm afraid to see what *your* office looks like."

He chuckled.

Yes, I was back to being awestruck. There was no escaping it when it came to Dane. "This is all so incredible."

He stood alongside me, his hands in his pockets. "I haven't even given you the grand tour of the resort yet."

I must have stared up at him invitingly, because he eased onto the seat next to me.

"I think I can trust you, Ari. That's what I need. Everything built around the grand opening is extremely important and confidential. And *that* event—every facet, the absolute smallest details—has to be *perfect*."

Yeah, no pressure *there*.

I swallowed hard. He draped an arm along the back of the sofa and leaned in as his gaze captured mine. He was so close, the moment turned intimate. I could feel him all around me. Smell him. A hint of sandalwood mixed with his heat. An erotic scent.

My breathing was sparse, because all I had to do was inch the tiniest bit forward and our lips would touch.

My gaze dropped to his mouth. I absently nibbled my lower lip. Then raised my eyes to meet his again.

I wanted him more than I'd ever wanted anything—including an enormous office, the title to match, and a paycheck and budget with too many zeros.

My pulse continued to race. But my mind was absurdly clear. "We're mixing business and . . . pleasure?"

His jaw clenched. "You haven't said yes yet."

To his offer? To whatever was causing my heart to beat wildly?

"You'd be my boss," I pointed out.

"And what we do behind closed doors is strictly between us."

A little red flag waved in front of my face. "What if something goes wrong?"

I didn't have to be specific—he was astute enough to know I was talking about sex, not the job. Though that was of concern as well. If I took him up on his offer, I wouldn't be able to afford losing the paycheck, since I'd have to give up independent weddings and bridal shows. I'd no longer have that source of income. I'd have to start fresh, mining for brides. He had to know this was all a huge risk.

Did he care? Or was his need to draw me into this world of his too great? And . . . *why me?*

He swept a wayward curl from my cheek. His skin was warm. Soft. I sucked in a breath. And involuntarily shrank back.

Tension instantly radiated from him. "Sorry," he murmured. He stood in a swift move. "That's going to be a problem."

"It just happens," I said in sort of a floundering way. I stared up at him, my stomach twisting. "There's nothing for you to apologize about. It's just—" I gave a small shrug. "I get a little uncomfortable. Sometimes."

He eyed me closely for endless seconds, obviously trying to interpret everything about me. Maybe I wasn't normal after all. Wouldn't most women want this sort of attention, especially from *him*? Particularly when they lusted after him in turn?

Yet somehow, the reality of him touching me—someone so anti-intimacy, while he clearly fought his aggressive nature—was a difficult wall to scale.

Finally tearing his gaze away, he spun around and crossed the room to the wet bar. I felt a peculiar void as he broke eye contact and gave me his back. A strange chill slithered through me. Not eerie, but . . . empty.

*Okay, Ari, be honest. At least with yourself.*

I'd liked sitting next to him, our thighs pressed together. I'd liked his fingers brushing over my cheek. I'd like the way he'd stared so intently into my eyes.

I even liked how he filled my mind just about every second of the day. There was something about him, something about *us*, that made me wonder if that crazy day in the bar had been fated. Had he been there to rescue me in more ways than just keeping me out of the clutches of a spiky-haired blond with a creepy tattoo, or even the good-looking, flirtatious Kyle Jenns?

Or was he someone offering things a woman such as myself shouldn't get wrapped around the axle over? Was he a savior? Or was he detrimental to the perfectly constructed life I'd built following all the troubles I'd encountered as a kid?

I had no answers, and that scared me all the more. But eclipsing the fear was the arousal that seeped through my veins when he turned back to me and I took him in from head to toe—breathing him in, getting lost in every magnificent fiber of his being.

He returned with a glass and handed it over.

I took a long sip of scotch, then set the cocktail on the end table and said, "It'd be okay if you sat next to me."

Joining me once more, he gave me another of his scrutinizing looks and asked, "Are you afraid of me?"

"Not in the way you might think. You're intimidating, yes. But, it's more like . . ." I didn't really know how to explain, exactly what to say. No one had asked me that sort of question before. No one had really wanted to know why I kept my distance. And I truly wasn't sure anyone would understand.

It'd taken me a long time to notice how I always lingered on the fringes, even when wholly present in a conversation or with my wedding planning. I had a simple theory, really. Not touching, and not being touched, led to not missing physical contact when instances of it were so few and far between.

I'd never put stock in affection. My parents weren't of the sentimental, demonstrative variety—except when they were hurling things at a wall. Nor had the half-dozen guys I'd spent brief time with employed any sort of finesse beyond the few thrusts it took to get off.

Something else occurred to me. I had never felt the electric currents I did when Dane was close, when he looked at me, when his fingers grazed my skin.

He waited patiently for me to elaborate, but I couldn't quite summarize for him how keeping the bottom from falling out of my life—the way it had for my dad—was imperative.

Dane didn't seem inclined to let me off the hook, though. Continued to gaze at me expectantly.

Finally, I said, "It's sort of a self-imposed thing. Don't take it personally."

"Impossible," he murmured.

Heat erupted in my belly. Spread outward. A tempting, tantalizing sensation.

I got to my feet, albeit shakily. I crossed to the patio doors and stepped onto the terrace, needing the respite of cool air. The scenery really was too fabulous for words. The most stunning scenario to find myself in.

And the most amazing, breathtaking man I'd ever known— would *ever* know—offered me my own slice of the gorgeous pie.

When I felt him standing behind me, I dared to ask, "What, exactly, do you want from me—aside from accepting the director position?"

"You already know what I want." He stepped closer, so that I inhaled his rich scent, more intoxicating and decadent than the most expensive champagne.

"Be specific," I implored. Because I knew I dug a deeper hole every second I stayed here. I was entranced, hopelessly drawn into his beautiful, magnificent world. Entangled in a mysterious web I knew was dangerous to get caught in, but it was one I couldn't seem to find the good sense to escape. Even when I had the chance.

His fingers gently swept my hair over one shoulder, purposely not grazing my skin. His head dipped and I felt his warm breath on my nape. A delicious shiver rippled down my spine.

His lips were so close to my neck, I could almost feel them. Though I knew I imagined that—because I *craved* the feeling. The one thing I avoided most in life. The ultimate threat.

"Dane," I urged him to lay it all on the line. Because this was hazardous.

He whispered against my throat, "I want to touch you." His breath rustled the wispy strands of hair, teasing me further. But he wasn't done. "Ari," he said in his sexy, enticing voice. "I want to *taste* you."

# chapter 5

I didn't breathe for several seconds. *Couldn't* breathe.

I'd never felt so surrounded—so permeated—by male heat, strength, aggression. It swept over my skin, burned through my body. The overwhelming desire to have Dane's hand at the small of my back, a gesture I'd always deemed too intimate, took hold of me and wouldn't let go. I willed it to happen, wanting the physical connection to coalesce with the visceral.

But that was impossible.

Just as I felt him make the move, I stepped away. Though liquid fire still rushed through my veins. I returned to the office. Dane closed the terrace doors behind us and followed me into the wide corridor.

We walked to the elevators in silence. When we reached them, I asked, "Is this the normal interviewing process for all your female executives?"

I instantly thought of the statuesque honey-blonde and wondered if she worked here. Had he enticed her with a fabulous office, breath-stealing words, and a salary to keep her closet stocked with Louis Vuitton?

I grimaced inwardly. That thought didn't exactly gel in my mind. Dane didn't seem like the type to burn both ends of the fuse when they could meet explosively in the middle.

And his sharp look said he wouldn't dignify my question with a response.

I was afraid that would be the case. My instincts were a little too fine-tuned when it came to this man.

We entered the elevator and it took us down to the second floor. Miyanaga had covered our food with metal domes to keep the steaks warm. Not necessary for me. I'd lost my appetite. Nothing could compete with the inferno, raging out of control. I snatched my clutch and the note card and held on tight—so I wouldn't touch Dane.

I wanted him in ways I couldn't fully comprehend. It went beyond just having his hand at the small of my back. Far beyond my simple fantasy of him shoving my skirt up and thrusting into me. This wasn't something I could get out of my system by asking him to take me to one of the hotel rooms for a quick fuck.

This wasn't *anything* like my past hookups. For God's sake, it wasn't even a hookup and still I felt deeply entangled in something I could neither dissect nor wrap my arms around. I was so ensnared that the only word tripping through my mind was *inevitable*.

An alarming fate from which I couldn't break free. Worse, I wasn't sure I *wanted* to break free. Perhaps that was why I found it so alarming.

Rallying a bit of resistance, I told him, "I need to go."

His hands were in his pockets and, once again, he didn't crowd me. He shifted slightly and I walked past him, onto the mezzanine. He was by my side as we descended the stairs and crossed the vast lobby to the front doors. It started to rain. The valet, Brandon, opened a large black umbrella with the resort name in gold script across it.

Dane finally spoke. "I want an answer by five o'clock on Monday."

I glanced at him, taking in the hard set of his jaw and the steel determination in his eyes, rimmed with lust. My stomach fluttered.

"For which?" I asked, a bit breathless.

"For both."

"Dane." Nervous exhilaration shimmied through me. "You can't put a time line on—" I shook my head. This was all happening so fast. He was certainly determined—and obviously willing to press my hand.

A scowl canted his mouth, as it had in the bar when he'd rescued me. The same expression that darkened his features and made him even more mesmeric. I wanted to be alone with him even though that had already proved dangerous. I wanted Brandon to disappear so I could stand there and breathe in Dane along with the rain-scented air.

Desire was such a tricky beast, such a double-edged sword. I wanted him, but I didn't *want* to want him. It was cruel, really. Painful.

I tore my gaze from his and headed to the Jag, Brandon falling into step with me. I slipped into the vehicle and tried to still my frenzied insides. A worthless effort. The car pulled away, circled the mammoth waterfalls, and started down the long drive. I turned in the seat and stole a look out of the back window.

Dane stood just outside the main doors, beneath the slight overhang of 10,000 Lux, as the downpour turned violent and lightning streaked the sky. He remained there as we turned the bend.

Watching me go.


"You should be practicing your chipping and pitching," my dad said as I joined him on the driving range of the private club where he worked.

I dropped my bucket of balls on the ground, whipped out a tee, and stabbed it into the damp earth. I grabbed a driver and whacked the hell out of three balls before I said, over my shoulder, "Chipping and pitching take thought and concentration." Teeing off helped to relieve sexual tension. Granted, I could spend a week at this and I'd be just as wound up as I had been from the moment I'd laid eyes on Dane Bax, but still. It felt good to assert myself.

"Something wrong?" my dad asked, concern lacing his tone.

"Not really. Just a lot on my mind."

"Humph." He went back to working on an already perfect swing, stopping about ten minutes later to say, "You've really improved over the past few years. We should get out more frequently."

"We golf twice a week, Dad. And then spend Sunday morning here."

"I was just saying."

With a laugh, I asked, "Is that guy-speak for 'I'd like to see you more often'?"

"Something like that."

If it were anyone else I was talking to, I'd suggest he find himself a girlfriend. But that was a volatile subject, so I avoided the land mine. "Chances are, I'm about to be busier than before," I warned.

"Oh?"

I stepped away from the tee and faced him. "Have you heard anything about 10,000 Lux?"

"Sure. It's created quite the buzz around here. Five golf courses by the best designers, including Nicklaus and Engh. Member fees are through the roof—too rich for my blood."

I smiled, about to make his day. "You might get to golf there for free."

His head snapped up from his shot and he speared me with a look. "You win the lottery?"

My dad never messed around when it came to playing world-class courses.

With a noncommittal shrug, I said, "Not exactly. Well, sort of, but not in the traditional sense. I met the owner of the resort. He offered me a job."

My dad whistled under his breath. "At 10,000 Lux? You realize it's featured in all the national golf magazines?"

"Yes, and in newspapers. The position is Events Director. Totally in charge of all festivities." Anxiety tripped down my spine. I ignored it.

"Wow, Sweets." His brows knitted. "That's . . . Uh. Wow."

I grimaced. "Translation: 'way the hell over my head'?"

"I didn't say that," he was quick to assure me. "It's just that . . . I've heard enough about the hotel to know they'll host events several levels above small weddings in Sedona."

"Numerous levels," I corrected. And the anxiety mounted. "He seems pretty convinced I can handle it."

"He?" My dad's voice hitched to that *uh-oh* octave.

I was *so* there with him.

"Dane Bax." That was all I planned to say about the man I couldn't get off my mind. The one I'd lain in bed last night obsessing over, fantasizing about. I'd never been fixated on a man's hands, on his lips, on his entire being, so that no sensible thoughts formed in my head the way they should when I entered risky territory.

Then again . . . I'd never met anyone like Dane Bax.

To diffuse whatever might next come out of my father's mouth, I added, "The grand opening is New Year's Eve. I'd get to plan it. Since there are pre-launch events, I'll be decking the halls with boughs of holly."

"You're not really the holiday type," he reminded me. We hadn't been particularly festive around the DeMille household when I was growing up.

"It could actually be fun. Something different. *Fa la la la la, la la la la.*"

"Cute," my dad said. "The owner has already made you an offer?"

I nodded, knowing it'd be best not to mention the astounding salary that came with the outrageous yearly budget. I really didn't want to get into a discussion over that. I was still reeling from those figures.

"Anyway, I'm seriously considering it." How could I not? It was a castle in the sky job with the sort of office I'd longed for and knew I'd never be able to afford on my own.

Plus, there was a certain thrill that came with being a part of Dane's world. Being a part of something that meant so much to him. My dream meshing with his dream.

The only thing keeping me from accepting was Dane himself. I was tempted, *too* tempted, by him. How involved would I be in something that didn't just bump my boundaries but barreled right through them?

And then there was that not so tiny insecurity that I might fall flat on my face and ruin his launch. Lots of responsibility to shoulder there.

I went back to hitting balls and my father let me maintain the silence until our buckets were empty. No more discussion of 10,000 Lux or Dane Bax. I certainly didn't mention my other source of consternation—my mother's sudden communications. No need to stress my father out more, especially where she was concerned.

When we were done, we returned the drivers we'd demoed to the golf shop.

"So, let me know how this pans out," he said as we stood in the entryway, removing our gloves. His office was upstairs and he was on duty in half an hour.

"I will. I think it'd be pretty incredible. It's just extremely overwhelming at the moment."

"I'd sure enjoy the links out there." He winked.

I laughed and said, "Had a feeling that would get your attention. We'll see." I kissed him on the cheek and then left to run errands.

That night, I prowled my townhome, restless and torn. I knew what I wanted. It was the price to be paid that worried me. Given what was truly on the line for someone like me, it honestly did feel as though I'd be handing over my soul for a gorgeous office—and to an even more gorgeous man.

The latter was of great concern because, honestly, I couldn't begin to fathom what Dane saw in me. Why he wanted me. My fear was that his attraction was wrapped around the challenge I presented—my obvious need for physical distance and my low tolerance for romance. Though I wasn't even sure he wanted to romance me. Or if he'd just gotten into the thrill of the chase and was now ready for the kill.

What would happen if he broke through and I became one more notch on his bedpost?

Another huge red flag. I had no doubt sex with Dane would be like nothing I'd ever experienced, read, or fantasized about. And I wasn't exactly worldly in the bedroom, so how fast would it be before I bored him to tears? What sort of work environment would *that* create?

I shook my head as I paced the living room. As long as I didn't fall in love, I could accept when he was done with me and let it lie. Right?

*Right.*

I wasn't wired to fall in love, anyway. I'd never even been in deep like.

As always, this would just be sex. Well, okay, with Dane it'd likely be amazingly hot, singe me to the core of my being sex, but again . . .

Just sex.

*Maybe.*

I frowned.

The rain fell steady and straight, flooding my small patio. The flashes of light illuminated my dim living room. If I were a superstitious person, I'd add another element to my freak-out over

Dane. I'd call all of this dark and ominous weather an omen. The fact that I didn't subscribe to signs didn't mean I dismissed them entirely—especially with this particular scenario. I still had warnings to heed. The most prevalent one being the foreboding that flickered in Dane's eyes when he looked at me.

I had a very strong sense of what that was all about. The man was a take-no-prisoners type.

He wanted me, and he'd already let me know it wouldn't be a casual fling.

My *right* that had morphed into a more tenuous *maybe* was now a solid *oh, shit*.

I spared a glance at the clock. Twenty after ten, and my mind was much too preoccupied for sleep. I went into the room that housed my desk and opened the Web browser on my computer. I pulled up the 10,000 Lux site that I'd viewed when I'd submitted my application. I sifted through the hyperlinks again, noting they'd added more photos and information.

I clicked on the "Careers" section, curious to know what positions were being advertised in the Events department that still needed to be filled. Those employees would be my staff, after all. Another concern to mull over. I'd never really managed anyone, other than subcontractors who already knew the business, knew exactly what they were doing.

I ran through the list anyway, happy to see there'd be a robust team of planners and support staff. I was about to move on when my gut twisted. It suddenly dawned on me that the Events Director position was no longer posted.

Had Dane pulled it? Was he *that* sure he'd snagged me?

I let out a hollow laugh. "Of course," I mumbled.

*I never enter negotiations without knowing exactly what I'm getting into and* exactly *what I want to get out of it.*

Given his aggressive nature, I'd say the more appropriate sentiment was that he never entered negotiations without knowing exactly what he would—*for certain*—get out of it.

This wasn't even a negotiation. What was there to reconcile? He'd laid the world's most tempting cards on the table—and had thrown in the possibility of sizzling sex for good measure.

As I considered how easily I'd stood under his net and let it fall on me, the Web site turned a sinister onyx, with the words *Under Construction* suddenly flashing in the center in red, along with a sequence of numbers in the bottom right-hand corner. Moments later, the text and numbers turned to crimson splatters against the background, then dripped away. Leaving nothing but pitch-black.

*Huh.*

I reached for my phone and tried to pull the site up on that device. No dazzling Lux lights, just eerie darkness. That was strange and deeply disturbing. Dane was actively hiring now that he'd set the date for the opening. Why would he take the site offline now?

Finding that curious, I grabbed his business card, which I'd pinned to my corkboard. I tapped the cardstock against my palm for a second or two, debating whether I should alert him to what could be his latest glitch.

I hardly thought I'd wake him. A man of his caliber and grand success probably didn't sleep much.

*What if he's with another woman?*

Okay, that one stung. When I knew it shouldn't. We had no claim whatsoever on each other. Yet the mere idea of him tangled in the sheets with someone else made me absurdly and vehemently jealous. Ridiculously tormented.

*Now* I knew I was in over my head.

I dialed before I could stop myself or think this through. He picked up on the second ring.

"You came around a bit faster than I'd expected."

I cringed at how my call screamed *eager beaver* when it came at nearly eleven o'clock at night. On a Sunday.

Pushing that aside, I asked, "How'd you know it was me?"

"I've seen your number on your business card and application, remember?"

And what, had *memorized* it?

That sent a much too wicked thrill down my spine.

"Still with me, Ari?" His tone was low and sensual. The most seductive bedroom voice imaginable. My inner thighs flamed. My stomach quivered. And we were just on the phone!

*Potent* was a mammoth understatement for this man.

"I'm still here," I said, my own voice the soft, sultry one that seemed to be reserved specifically for him. Which was just one more intimate thing between us when intimacy was what I wanted to evade.

"So, you've made up your mind about the director position?"

I sucked in a sharp breath, let it out slowly. "Actually, that's not why I'm calling." I still needed more time to wade through all the exciting yet conversely troubling nuances presented. "Are you alone?"

*Whoa.* I winced inwardly. Where the hell had *that* come from?

Unfortunately, I knew precisely from where. I couldn't let go of the image of the Heidi Klum lookalike grazing her breasts against his chest, smiling beguilingly at him.

He was quiet for several seconds that felt more like an eternity, leaving me to grind over how possessive I'd sounded. That was his department, not mine.

Eventually, he asked, "What would make you think I was with someone?"

"I just—I—" *Oh, Jesus.* "I saw you with a woman at Tlaquepaque. I just assumed—"

*Ugh!* I bounced the heel of my hand off my forehead a few times. I was a colossal idiot.

"So that's what that bizarre question about interviewing female executives was all about. You should have said something sooner."

"I shouldn't be saying anything at all," I lamented.

"Ari, she's a friend," he explained. "Her name is Mikaela Madsen. She and her boyfriend, Fabrizio Catalano, are trying to open a shop in Old Town Scottsdale. They import gourmet olive oils, wines, meats, cheeses, and the like. All from Brizio's family village in Italy. They've run into a few snags with zoning and City Council and Mikaela asked for my help."

I sighed despondently. What was worse than a colossal idiot? A monumental one?

"So . . . you're jealous?" he asked with interest in his tone, while I backpedaled in my mind. "Because, Ari," he added, "that's sexy. But not warranted. I wouldn't have said what I did last night if I weren't serious about being with you."

*Being with you . . .*

Those words caused apprehension and excitement to crash over me. I struggled for a way out of this conversation that *I'd* started. But my thoughts were all twisted and nonsensical.

I hastily said, "That's not at all what I meant. Not the reason I'm calling." My heart thumped ridiculously fast. *Geez, just shoot me now.* "Do you know your Web site is down?"

*"That's* why you're calling?" He made a *tsking* sound, so cool and nonchalant. While I could barely breathe. "Now I'm disappointed. I was hoping you were tossing and turning in bed, thinking about me and wondering what I might be able to do about your restlessness."

"I—" I shook my head. I *was* restless. How had he known? Was I really this transparent with him?

"If you're interested in a bedtime story, I'd be happy to make one up for you," he taunted in his sexy voice. "But be forewarned: It's no sweet, innocent fairy tale."

*Of course not. Because you are the devil.*

A hotter than hell one at that.

"I'll pass on the story," I said. *Coward.* "Is your site scheduled for maintenance tonight?"

"Not that I'm aware of," he told me, the discontent over my avoidance thick in his tone. I heard his fingers click on the keyboard, so he must be in his office. Or he could be working on a laptop at home. I almost asked but pressed my lips together to keep from sounding as though I were stalking him. "That's weird," he muttered. "It's solid black."

A crack of thunder made me jump. Rain pelted the windows. All I needed now was a terrifying flock of ravens perched on the tree limbs outside and I could call it a day.

I said, "There was an *Under Construction* tag with some digits at the bottom, but they only flashed a few times before trickling away."

"Digits? Do you remember what they were?"

"Not really. Started with a five . . ."

He fell silent again. Tension arced between us. I could *feel* him brooding. Could picture the furrowed brow and the clenched jaw. Something definitely was not right with the problems at 10,000 Lux.

"One more complication?" I ventured.

"I'll get it fixed in the morning." His tone was still low and sexy but decisive. "Now, about the job. Say, *Yes, it's everything I've ever wanted,* and then we can wrap up the business portion of this call."

That spark only he could ignite made my clit tingle. The ache inside me sprang to life—an incessant need that consumed me. A demanding, erratic pulsing in my core that would only intensify if I stayed on the phone with him.

"Ari," he said, his tone coaxing. "What's the point in stalling? What more can I offer to make you agree?"

"Nothing," I told him. "Everything you've put on the table is . . . perfect. Yes, everything I've ever wanted. *The rest,*" as he'd termed it during dinner the night before, "is something entirely different."

"I've explained about Mikaela. And I've been patient with you. You can't expect me to wait forever."

"Dane, we've known each other for, like, two weeks."

"Yes," he said, the sound of his laptop snapping closed and him settling into a chair or sofa echoed his frustration. "And I haven't laid a hand on you. That's killing me, Ari."

Exhilaration shot through me. The throbbing in my pussy had me squeezing my legs together.

"Dane," I grumbled. God, he lit me up so easily. *Too easily.*

"Tell me what you sleep in."

My eyelids closed tightly as magma started to flow in place of blood.

"Ari," he prompted, a hint of need edging his voice, tearing at me. "Give me something to work with here."

My cheeks warmed. "Nothing provocative, sorry. I've got on a faded Edmonton Oilers T-shirt, ripped at the neck."

"Mm." He sounded a bit more satisfied. "Number?"

"Ninety-nine, of course."

"The Great One. Wayne Gretzky. I wouldn't take you for a hockey fan."

Shoving thoughts of how much more thrilling a response someone like Mikaela Madsen would give to his question, I stood and flipped off the light switch, then returned to the living room. The storm was a bad one, and it made me a little nervous as I thought again of its warning, the potential for it to truly be an omen. Though I fought that odd notion tugging at me. Monsoons were unpredictable and they could be mild and last two weeks or torrential and last two months. Total crapshoot.

*Not an omen, Ari.*

Curling up on the sofa that faced the patio doors and the golf course beyond, I dragged the throw from the back of the couch and draped it over my bare legs.

"My dad got me into hockey," I said, "when Gretzky coached the Phoenix Coyotes. He never missed a game on TV. He and Gretzky played a pro-am tourney together. That's when I met him."

"Bryce DeMille is your dad—I read that in the bridal magazine feature. I've seen him on ESPN. He had a very promising career."

"And a bad shoulder."

"He'll like the courses at the Lux."

"I haven't said yes yet."

"But you will."

I couldn't help the smile. "Okay. You win."

"I had every intention of winning." The dark tinge around those words made me fear them even more than before. "Now, tell me what kind of panties you're wearing."

I gasped. Not so much at his demand, but at the way he so deeply aroused me.

Still, I hedged, fighting for at least a tiny patch of safe ground. "You're not seriously asking a new employee about her underwear."

"No. I'm asking *you*."

"Why?"

"Because I want the visual, damn it."

I sighed. He had lust flashing through my body with such little effort on his part. I was so out of my league with him, but I felt the tether. I felt the tug as he pulled me slowly to his side. Even my convictions couldn't anchor me to that safe patch I'd sought.

"I meant, why me?"

He was quiet again. I wondered if I exasperated him, but then he said, "I can't really explain it. You came through the door of the bar at the resort and my papers flew off the table. It was like . . . a silent call, grabbing my attention when it was so set on business. I watched you cross to your wedding party, every single thing about you instantly registering in my mind. *Burning deep* into my mind."

He let out a sexy, irritable sound—like he couldn't quite figure out his own reaction to me. It sent heat waves along my skin.

Continuing, he said, "Your hair, the sway of your hips, the way you carried yourself, those seriously gorgeous legs . . . I didn't even get a good look at your face until you glanced over your shoulder, and yet I was hooked. And when you finally turned toward me . . . Christ. You stole my breath."

The air rushed from my own lungs. "I felt you staring at me. When Kyle was flirting."

"I didn't like him moving in so close to you," he admitted, his tone dark again. "I could see you were uncomfortable. You flinched—I didn't like that he'd done that to you. The tat guy, either."

My eyes closed as fire flared. "Why did you step in?" More silence. His tension seeped into my soul. "Dane?"

"I don't want anyone else touching you, Ari. I thought I made that clear from the beginning."

"*Oh.*" His words were jolting. He'd marked his territory from the onset?

And how long did that branding last?

I gnawed my lower lip as I considered how strong this undertow was, and whether I'd surface when it released me. Or—

"Tell me about your panties."

"You can't shift gears so fast, Dane. I'm not a Venom F5."

"No shifting. I told you I wanted you the second I saw you. Tell me what *I* want to hear."

He was slightly infuriating but mostly irresistible. Impossible to deny. "Boy shorts. Pink lace."

A low growl filled the line. "Now I'm hard. I want to peel your shirt off."

My breasts felt instantly heavier, fuller. My pulse beat deep in my core. "Dane."

"I want to rub my fingers over the lace between your legs. Stroking slowly."

I fought a gasp.

"No, I want you naked," he amended, his voice rough with desire. "Beneath me as I sink into you."

I could easily picture him stretched above me, naked, all of his muscles hard and flexed. Then pumping slowly into me, my hips lifting to meet his full thrusts.

A soft moan escaped my parted lips.

"That's a start." He added, "I want to know all the little sounds you make when you're hot for me. I want to hear you moan as I'm exploring all of you, staring into your eyes. I want you wet and calling my name when I make you come."

I was so, so close. It was surreal, crazy even, the way my body responded strongly to the sexy things he said. I couldn't for the life of me imagine how I'd ever survive the real deal.

If we ever made it to the real deal.

I should put a stop to this. *I should.*

"Dane."

He whispered, "I need to be inside you, Ari."

That was all it took. I pressed two fingers to my clit and came, grinding out an, "Oh, God," as the fiery sensations tore through me.

# chapter 6

"What are you doing?" I demanded in a quiet tone, my breath still coming in heavy pulls as orgasmic aftershocks ricocheted through my body.

"The same thing you're doing."

"No." My chest heaved. "You didn't just come."

"Because I'm waiting to be in your mouth or in your pussy when I do."

*Christ.* I'd never win this game—he kept me hot and restless just with his words.

"Exactly how long do you think you can hold out?" I dared to ask.

"I've waited a long time for you, Ari. And I'll wait more if you need me to. You're worth it."

"You don't know that." A hint of insecurity crept in on me. I didn't consider myself inhibited by any means. But this was different from anything else I'd experienced. *He* was different. I tried to get a firmer hold on all of this, asking, "What do you mean you've waited a long time for me? We just met."

"I meant in the ethereal sense. That innate knowledge that someone is out there, and she's going to be everything I didn't even know I wanted."

"Oh, God." My spirits sank. "You really are going to be disappointed."

Ignoring my dismal comment, he said, "At first, I wasn't inclined to accept how powerfully I reacted to seeing you. Then you got tangled up with the two other men, and I knew it was inevitable."

I sucked in a breath. He'd just described the exact way I'd felt the previous evening. That *same* word had popped into my head.

"So far," he said while I tried to catch my breath, "you're exceeding expectations."

"I haven't done anything yet," I muttered.

That delicious growl of his met my ears. "You're insanely beautiful. You know that, don't you?"

My heart fluttered. "I've been told something along those lines a time or two." Not that it mattered, since I wasn't looking for anyone to get hooked on me. For some reason, though, hearing the sentiment from him did all kinds of frenzied things to my insides.

"It's not just your body that attracts me. It's everything, Ari. Everything about you captivates me—your face, those big blue eyes, how breathless you are around me."

His lusty tone compelled me to say, "You seem to like my breasts, too."

"Mm, yes. You have a nice ass as well."

The aftershocks kept coming.

He added, "I liked how seriously you took your job as wedding planner and yet you were flexible and personal enough to do a shot with those guys. You seemed to grasp how nervous the groom was and helped to calm him. Plus, you were meticulous about the entire wedding. I admire that sort of dedication and talent."

"As you mentioned, the smallest of details are crucial. It's the special touches that make events sparkle."

"You'll do a great job at the Lux. Don't think you're going to let me down there. Not a chance."

"I was thinking more in terms of—"

"I know what you were thinking. And you're wrong," he said with conviction.

Exhilaration hitched a ride on my racing pulse. But then a loud clap of thunder reverberated within me and the rain fell even heavier. My heart thumped harder.

"I have to go," I said suddenly. Omens weren't anything to mess with, even if you didn't believe in them.

"You only get so many hasty retreats, Ari," he warned.

"Good night, Dane."

I disconnected the call. Closed my eyes. Wondered what the hell I was doing.

I'd just consented to work at 10,000 Lux. I'd just let my new boss talk dirty to me—and I'd liked it. I'd had an orgasm while *on the phone* with him.

And then he'd told me I was everything he'd never even known he wanted.

I pulled in several deep breaths. They didn't steady me, because a very disconcerting thought haunted my mind: How long could I avoid *the inevitable*?

One would think a seriously powerful orgasm inspired by a seriously hot man would take the edge off a seriously sexually deprived woman. In my case, one would be wrong.

All it did was make me want Dane more.

He called around nine the next morning. I wished he'd have asked me again what I was wearing. This time I could have give him a sexier answer, since I'd just stepped out of the shower.

But he was all business.

"Can you come to the hotel around eleven?" he asked without preamble. Tension tinged his voice.

"Sure."

"I'm on my way to the airport. I have to go to Paris for some meetings. I'll be gone all week."

Why did that make my stomach knot? Was it the thought of not seeing him?

"Everything okay?" I asked.

"It will be when I'm done." His determination echoed in his voice, a dangerous edge I didn't miss, couldn't deny. It evoked a razor-sharp vibe that made warning signals go off in my head once more. The hairs on my arms stood on end. What was I *really* getting myself into?

He said, "I need you to see my VPs of Human Resources and Legal Affairs. One of them will meet you in the lobby. There's paperwork to fill out, contracts to sign. I've also arranged for Amano, my head of Security, to give you the tour of the property, since I won't be able to do it myself." This time, it was regret I heard. As though it meant a lot to him to be the one to show me the resort. I supposed it would, since the Lux was his pride and joy.

Continuing, he said, "The rest of the week will be filled with meetings between the heads of the departments you'll be working most closely with—Sales, Banquets, Security, Marketing, and Public Relations. Also reps from the salon and spa, for your clients' personal needs. My assistant has set everything up. She's left a schedule on your desk. Her name is Molly Albright. Whatever you need, ask her."

Apprehension skipped through me. "So, how does this work? I just dive in and clear things with you along the way?"

"Initially. So we're on the same page to start. Then I'm sure you can run with it. I have other things to keep an eye on."

That sounded ominous. "Dane, is there something serious happening—"

"I trust you, Ari. Implicitly," was all he said.

He couldn't put me off so easily, though. The whole mystery of him and the resort prompted me to ask, "Why didn't I see you around town until recently? At the very least, I would remember seeing that car of yours in a parking lot or on the street."

"I've spent most of my time on-property or in New York with my investment group. And the car was just delivered a couple of weeks ago."

"Hmm." A convenient answer, but one I couldn't dispute.

"Anyway," he said, "I have to go."

"Oh, wait!" I suddenly recalled my previous engagements. "I'll need some time off in October and a few days next summer for weddings I have on the books. And I'll need to be out of the office around five this Friday for the reception Anthony Delfino is hosting at his home in Scottsdale."

"I've been invited as well. It's more of a networking thing—we're professional acquaintances."

"I didn't know." Dane would be at the party, too? That meant Friday couldn't come fast enough. *Great.* How the hell would I concentrate all week?

He said, "Have one of the hotel limo drivers take you to Scottsdale. I'm flying in that night. We can ride back from the reception together."

My stomach fluttered. I clumsily pulled the towel more firmly around my body, juggling the phone. "An hour in the back of your limo will likely land me in a compromising position, won't it?"

The wicked dripped from his voice as he said, "There's a good chance of that."

A flicker of heat between my legs told me I wouldn't mind. The staccato beat of my heart told me I just might.

*Here we go again with the tug-of-war.*

"Wear the green dress," he insisted in a low tone.

Excitement rippled through me. "It's new."

"You bought it specifically for our dinner?"

"The color reminds me of your eyes."

"And I couldn't take them off you."

Mine squeezed shut for a moment.

*Breathe, Ari.*

"I'll call midweek to make sure you have everything you need," he said.

"Including Valium when the size of my salary and budget finally *fully* hits me?" Not to mention the fact that I'd had a stellar orgasm from his voice alone.

"You'll do just fine, baby. I have complete faith."

*Baby.*

I swallowed hard. Had I heard that right?

*Baby. Ari.* Yeah, there was no mistaking one for the other. Unless my mind was playing tricks on me and I'd wanted to hear the term of endearment.

But, no. That wouldn't be like me at all.

I said, "Travel safe." And ended the call before I dropped the phone as panic seized me.

I hurried about, dressing in my favorite black suit and the new heels. All the while, I kept wondering, *Are we . . . dating?*

I tried to focus on anything other than the staggering situation I was suddenly embroiled in as I drove to the resort. Dane had been right about Lux security. The gate was heavily guarded and I had to show two forms of ID and let them jot down my license plate number. Then I traveled to the entrance and Brandon was there to valet-park my SUV. 10,000 Lux was no less intimidating the second time around.

Inside, a fortysomething blonde whom I easily dwarfed greeted me.

"Patricia Lansing," she said in a clipped manner. "Vice President of HR. Mr. Bax said you'd be expecting me."

"Yes, of course. Paperwork and whatnot."

"There's a lot of the 'whatnot,'" she told me with a tight smile. "Mr. Bax is very thorough, and security is of utmost importance here. I'll take you straight to the clearance office so they can issue your personalized electronic badge. You'll need it to access the floors of the west wing, where all of the offices are located. The east wing is strictly suites and the penthouses. The conference center is located on the south lawns, but Amano will be the one to give you the tour of the resort, per Mr. Bax's request."

"Okay." I was already overwhelmed and I'd been here less than ten minutes.

"Also, you need the badge to access the top floor from inside the stairwell, and for your office door. You can leave it open when you're in there, but Mr. Bax insists the doors are all closed when you leave, even if it's just to visit the ladies' room. And your card will only get you into the reception areas of each department, not individual offices."

Super-duper tight security. Interesting. But then again, he'd told me everything related to the grand opening was confidential, so I was sure he didn't want anyone unauthorized rifling through files.

Once I'd signed for the photo ID card and various security forms, we went to the fourth floor and swiped our badges to pass through a door that opened to an inner sanctum for HR and Legal. All overly opulent and pristine.

In a conference room, there were dozens of papers spread out on the oval mahogany table.

Patricia introduced me to Margo Tomlin, General Counsel, and she explained about the contracts, no-compete clauses, nondisclosure statements, conflict of interest documents . . . the list went on and on. Patricia covered all the benefits information, payroll, and tax forms. My head spun. Then they collected up the tall stack and handed it over.

Margo said, "You'll want to read everything carefully before you sign."

"In blood?" I quipped. Seriously . . . this was *a lot.*

The two VPs exchanged a look. Neither smiled at my joke.

"Mr. Bax told me you've already seen your office, so you know where it's located." This from Patricia.

"Right across the hall."

"And your staff will be one floor down, once hired. See Margo or myself if you have questions or need anything."

"Thank you."

I left them and balanced the paperwork as I flashed my electronic card against the reader to gain access to my office. I dumped my armful on the desk and surveyed my surroundings. Everything was exactly as it'd been the first time I'd walked in with Dane.

That memory came rushing back. My cheeks burned and my insides ignited as I thought of the racy words he'd whispered against my neck. The man was scandalous. And I was already addicted to his devilish side.

My gaze roved the room, landing on the huge all-white bouquet in the middle of the coffee table. Okay, that was new. Spying the small envelope alongside the elegant vase, I snatched it up and pulled out the card.

*Next time, I want to hear you say my name when
I make you come. . . . Dane*

I fanned my face with the card. *Next time.* Oh, boy.

I tucked the missive into my purse and returned to the desk. As I eased into the gorgeous white leather chair, a roaring sense of *Oh, my God, I'm really doing this!* washed over me.

My stomach churned at the same time adrenaline pumped through my veins. My palms were a little clammy as I reached for the decorative gift box on the leather blotter. I pulled the satin ribbon and opened the long, narrow box. Inside was the same type of Montblanc fountain pen Dane had tried to lend me at El Rincon. Only, instead of initials, the inscription read: *10,000 Lux.*

Must be a signing bonus—apropos, given the endless amount of paperwork to which I'd have to add my John Hancock.

I read the accompanying card, this one appropriate for our *professional* association.

*Welcome to the Lux, Miss DeMille. Thank you for*
*helping us to make the resort a success.*
*Dane B. Bax, Owner*

I stared at that last word.

This dual predicament sent a tickle down my spine. Turned out, I found having a little something covert on the side exciting. Except that it was my boss I played this wicked game with—detrimental to both me and my career.

I didn't have time to dwell on that perilous thought, though. I had forms and policies to read, and then the resort tour, taken mostly by golf cart. I was exhausted by the time I got home. As I fell into bed later, my phone jingled from its perch on the nightstand, signaling an incoming text.

It was Dane. I smiled.

*How was your first day?*

I typed: *Busy. And my hand is cramped from signing my name so many times. Seriously?*

*I don't like anything falling through the cracks.*

Not a surprise when it came to him. I texted: *Thanks for the flowers. They're spectacular.*

*So are you. Now go to sleep. You have an even busier week ahead of you.*

With a nod he obviously couldn't see, I wrote: *I suspected as much.*

*Sweet dreams.*

Clearly, I found it impossible not to nibble on the lure.

*You, too. Whenever it is that you sleep.*

I returned the phone to the nightstand, drifting off with thoughts of Dane and 10,000 Lux racing through my head.

The week was a blur of activity. There were so many people to meet, so many different offices to try to find, so many things to learn about hotel life and how everything worked. Then there were the multitude of discussions on all of the opening events, guest lists, and planning to be handled. I was utterly brain fried—now understanding why my brides always stared at me with deer-in-the-headlights, glassed-over eyes during their initial consultation. The tables had been turned.

Dane called on Wednesday night, but I missed his call, because I was dead asleep. He texted, concerned. I immediately replied when I woke in the morning, telling him I was basically a zombie at this point but really, really excited. I didn't hear back, likely because it was the middle of the night for him.

On Thursday afternoon, I inspected the conference space and grand ballroom—and by *grand* I meant absolutely breathtaking. I stood in the center of the enormous room, envisioning black-and-white galas held under the glittery rays of chandeliers that sparkled like diamonds.

I'd been told by someone in Engineering that the artistically painted panes covering the domed ceiling could be diffused with the touch of a button to reveal a crystal-clear night sky. Or a stellar blue afternoon. Whatever. It was totally over-the-top. No surprise there.

I left with that overwhelming feeling I couldn't seem to shake when I was on-property. Down the wide Italian marble corridor, also lined with gorgeous chandeliers, I located the media room, beautifully laid out, all the equpiment and controls marked with their corresponding conference rooms. Nothing was on, and I was tempted to power up, because that panel was clearly labeled as well.

Eyeing the switches for the ballroom, I wanted to test the sound system. I liked to know well in advance how the acoustics were and the level of clarity of the speakers. My fingers itched to give it all a whirl.

But my good sense won out—what if I fucked something up? Dane had enough on his hands. No need to add media operational issues to the list.

I'd wait and ask the A-V guys to walk me through it all. They'd handle events, but it'd be helpful to have the knowledge in case of emergencies.

Tearing my gaze from the even more tempting remote panels nestled in their wall-mounted docking stations, which *were* powered on, I reached for the lever on the door, ready to head back to my office. I gave it a tug, but the door stuck. That happened sometimes at my townhome, when there was a lot of humidity in the air. The wood would swell and fill the door frame.

I pulled a little harder. Behind me, I heard a *thump*. Moments later, there was a strange crackle in the air.

I moved away from the door and surveyed the equipment again.

Another buzzing, hissing noise and my brow furrowed. I got down on my hands and knees, following the sound. Under a narrow table stacked high with opened boxes filled to the brim with packing slips and materials—and more were tucked under a portion of the table—I spied a panel of multiple outlets.

And, above it, I fixated on the stream of water flowing from a small hole down the wall that led to the plugs.

A spark made me gasp. A heartbeat later, a sharp sizzle had me jumping to my feet. The lights in the room flickered, then shorted out, making me panic. The remote units remained aglow, obviously holding a charge, though their docking station indicators dimmed. I had enough illumination to find the door. I yanked on the lever with force. The door flew open—just as the sparks ignited the twisted brown paper overflowing from the boxes.

*Shit!*

I barreled into the hallway and yelled, "Fire!"

One of the Electrical staff was close at hand—and instantly on his radio. A flurry of activity ensued with more staff rushing toward us, fire extinguishers at the ready. Before I knew it, Amano was at my side, ushering me out of the conference center.

My pulse raged. My chest heaved. Within seconds he had me in a golf cart speeding toward the main building.

"There was water leaking down the wall," I told him.

He got on his own radio and relayed the information. By the time we reached the lobby, it was reported to him that the flames were out and they'd never gotten high enough to cause much damage or—thankfully—set off the sprinklers. I thought of all that media equipment and the extreme expense of replacing it and breathed a sigh of relief.

"So, what happened?" I asked, still reeling.

"Just a leak from one of the pipes."

His normally stoic features appeared uncharacteristically tense. I studied him a few moments before he directed me to the bank of elevators.

He said, "I'll escort you upstairs. Why don't you stick close to your office this afternoon? You look a little pale."

I pulled in a few deep breaths, then told him, "The door was stuck. I think the humidity made the wood swell."

"I'll look into it."

Why did that sound so . . . cryptic? Like he didn't believe that had been the cause of the jammed door?

He walked with me to my office. I swiped my badge and entered. He asked, "Are you okay?"

"Sure. That was just a little . . ." *Terrifying.* "Unexpected."

"There are bound to be some mishaps here and there, while we work out all the kinks and get everything running smoothly. Lots of trial and error before the grand opening."

"I get it. This is a huge project. Lots of bumps in the road."

Though I found it hard to shrug off the fact that I'd almost been trapped in a room about to go up in flames.

"Why don't you sit for a while, have some cold water?" he suggested. "Get your color back."

"Good idea." I gave him a weak smile. I was still jittery, still breathing heavily.

"If you decide to check out the sights again, let me know. I'll take you around."

"Amano. You have plenty to do. No need to babysit me. It was a fluke and I'm okay. In fact, it'd be all right with me if you didn't mention this to Mr. Bax."

His brow crooked—a total *as if* look crossed his face.

"Right," I grumbled. "Wishful thinking on my part."

"Let me know if you plan to leave the building." He disappeared.

I would have spent the rest of the afternoon dreading the big deal Dane would make of this except that he called less than ten minutes later.

"Why didn't you tell me what happened?" he asked—demanded? I couldn't tell. He sounded worried, angry, and irritated all at once.

"I had a feeling you'd hear about it from Amano within two seconds of him leaving my office."

"I did."

"So, you have the full scoop. What else was I going to disturb your day to say?"

"Naturally, I want to know about any issues with the hotel," he informed me in a tight voice. "Especially when they involve an employee."

I ventured to ask, "And when that employee is me . . . ?"

"Then I want to know immediately—from you. Amano can only tell me what happened. And that it appeared to shake you up. Are you okay?"

I thought back to the bar, after Dane had rescued me from the blond with the diamondback tattoo. He'd wanted to know if I was all right—like it meant something to him. I had a feeling it did. A bit more now that we knew each other better.

"It all happened pretty quick," I told him. "Yes, it freaked me out a little. But I escaped easily enough. After that, I was mostly concerned about all of those expensive media components."

"Baby, I have insurance to cover that stuff."

He caught me off guard again with the term of endearment.

So I hadn't imagined it the first time. That was surreal.

We were both quiet a few moments. The curiosity of what had him suddenly tongue-tied ate at me. Did he regret the slip?

"You still there?" I finally asked, my stomach now resembling a pretzel.

"I'm not happy about what happened to you." His tone held that distinct edge that made me wary. I could picture him twisting Snake-Tat guy's arm around to his back and slamming his shoulder to the table. I'd already learned that Dane didn't let slights go.

But there was nothing he could do about an accident. Maybe that was what had him so aggravated?

I surmised it was best that he didn't have anyone to blame. I'd gotten a glimpse of his wrath at the bar. I didn't want to know how he might take care of this situation if there'd been someone specific at fault.

"Look," I said, hoping to bring the intensity down a notch or ten. "I'm fine. It was a leak, and like Amano told me, this is all a trial-and-error process as the hotel comes online. I understand."

He still didn't say anything.

"Dane." I tried to coerce him into chilling out, because the broody vibes reached me despite his being a continent away. "Everything's all right. And I absolutely love all of the work I have at the Lux."

"Ari—"

"Just do what you have to do in Paris. All's well here. I promise."

"I'll be back tomorrow night," he reminded me.

"The party." Even the hustle and bustle at the resort—and today's scare—couldn't make me forget the upcoming opportunity to be with Dane.

His voice turned low and sensual as he said, "I'm looking forward to seeing you."

A little thrill ribboned through me. "I want to see you again, too."

"Get a good night's sleep."

I didn't miss the hint of mischief in his tone.

"And what are you doing?"

"Heading into a meeting. Otherwise . . ."

He didn't need to elaborate. I had a very good idea of what he'd do if he were alone and not wrapped up in business—had a very good idea that I'd be coming again while simply listening to him tell me the things he wanted to do to me.

"Go," I said. "I still have work."

# chapter 7

Friday arrived in the blink of an eye. I changed into the emerald dress at the hotel and let a driver take me down the hill to the Valley and to Anthony Delfino's mansion in the exclusive Mirabel Country Club community. These were my mother's dream residential estates, so I was well versed in its prestige. Thank God she didn't know I was attending a party here, or she would have invited herself along, now that she was suddenly pinging me. Totally out of the blue, which still made me uneasy.

"Ari!" Meghan greeted me with a bright smile and the flash from three lightning-quick photos she took. "We're so glad you came!" She was such a perky thing, all blond and beautiful and bouncing on the soles of her designer shoes.

"Thanks for asking me. This is a real treat. How was the honeymoon?"

As she regaled me with details of the trip in her dreamy voice and showed me pictures, Kyle joined us and handed me a glass of champagne. I smiled my gratitude. He wore his dark-gray suit as well as he had the tux at the wedding, the deep blue in his silk tie bringing out the color of his eyes, which glowed warmly.

He had an easy grin, still infectious, reminding me that if I was going to date someone it should probably be him—someone a bit closer to my level who wasn't shrouded in mystery and oozing an edgy vibe and raw sensuality.

Speaking of Dane . . . I couldn't help but steal glances around the room, wondering if he'd arrived yet.

At the end of Meghan's recap, Sean collected her to entertain more people, leaving me with Kyle. I wondered if that had been planned.

"You look great," he said as his gaze slid over me.

"Thank you. I've recently developed an appreciation for green." I fought to keep my tone even, not provocative, because I was thinking of Dane. I added, "You certainly do that suit justice."

"College graduation duds," he said with a dismissive wave of his hand. "My keeping up with the Joneses is basically keeping up with Sean now that he runs with the Forbes crowd, and Meghan is snap happy with the camera. I look like a slug in my T-shirts and jeans when that girl's around."

"Hardly." I'd seen him in casual attire—and I'd caught the collective, not so subtle adoration of the bridesmaids during the wedding planning. In fact, as I scanned the crowd once more—anxiously seeking out Dane—I noted the women from the bridal party hovering close by as though keeping tabs on Kyle. Perhaps waiting for that perfect moment when I stepped aside so they could swoop in?

He didn't lack for admirers, that was for sure.

Which prompted me to ask, "Did you bring a date? If not, I think there's a line about to form."

He chuckled. "I can't afford Meg's friends. Their fathers have private jets and islands, and they're all obsessed over the perfect mani-pedi. What the—?"

I laughed. "Never underestimate the value of a good manicure and pedicure."

With a roll of his eyes, he lamented, "See? Was that really so difficult? They can't even throw in a little guy-speak to help a dude along?"

I sipped my champagne, then said, "You'd do just fine with them. Meghan mentioned that you took the summer off to travel Europe. That makes you worldly, you know?"

His grin could light the entire room, without a doubt. "Right. Me and my backpack stuffed with just three changes of clothes, a translator because I only know a little Spanish and was on the wrong continent for that, and a list of hostels where I could crash—and share a bathroom with a half dozen other students. That'd impress the ladies who prefer the Ritz-Carlton and spa days."

"I don't know," I said with a shrug. "Sounds adventurous. Totally off the beaten path. If I were at the Ritz, I'd spend all my time poolside and never actually see the sights."

"You would have liked my itinerary then. I skipped all the major cities and stuck to the villages and wine country. Although, I had to make a stop in Monte Carlo for the casinos. Just 'cause, you know?"

"That does sound intriguing. I suppose I'd have to hit Casablanca, since it's my favorite movie."

He looked taken aback. "You seem more like the *Princess Bride* type. You know, weddings and romance and happily ever afters. All that stuff."

"Every fiber of my being swears my brides and grooms are the happiest people on the planet. But something about torn endings calls to me—like an untold story awaits a rainbow. Rhett walking out on Scarlett, or Nick Nolte going back to his wife even though he was totally hooked on Barbra Streisand in *Prince of Tides*. Rick Blaine sacrificing everything for Ilsa Lund, so she could leave Casablanca with Victor Laszlo. It's tragic, sure. But we only see *that* part of the love story. Maybe a silver lining is right around the corner. . . ."

I likely felt this way because I privately wanted my dad to bounce back from his disastrous marriage and find someone new—someone worthy of him.

Kyle's brow lifted in a speculative way. "So," he mused with interest in his voice. "Ari has a dark side mixed with eternal optimism. Very deep."

Since I hadn't weirded him out, I said, "It's all about the potential, you know?" I conspiratorially added, "And yes, I ate up the whole *Princess Bride* 'true love' theory."

It wasn't anything I subscribed to in my own life, obviously. But that Emerald City of mine would always exist, keeping up my high hopes for wedding couples.

"Your secret's safe with me." He seemed to give more thought to my contradictory view of love and romance—embracing the bad because I knew it existed but still hoping for good to win over, no matter what the situation. I liked that he put so much thought into my personal views. Though my stomach plummeted when he grimaced.

"What?" I asked, trepid. "You think I'm a nut job, right?"

"No. I'm just wondering . . . what is *he* doing here?"

I was about to ask, *He who?* but somehow already knew to whom Kyle referred. I felt Dane's burning gaze on me.

*Uh-oh.*

Tossing a cautious look over my shoulder, I found him staring at us, his brow crooked.

Anxiety rippled through me—along with unadulterated lust.

Glancing back at Kyle, I said in what I hoped was an even tone, "He knows Anthony Delfino. They're business associates or something."

"Why is he always scowling?"

I didn't bother to look back to see the dark expression on Dane's face. It was pretty much engrained in my brain. And it made my toes curl and exhilaration shimmy down my spine.

"He's just that way. Don't make anything out of it. Brooding type." My willpower lasted only so long, and I spared another glance his way. Dane had that *you're poaching on my territory* expression on his chiseled face—directed at Kyle. Things went a little haywire inside me. "His name is Dane Bax. He owns a new resort in Sedona. Where I now work."

Kyle's gaze snapped to mine. "What? Why?"

"Why, what?" I countered, confused.

"Why did you go to work at a hotel?"

"Oh, well, I've always wanted to do corporate planning in addition to weddings, and he sort of . . ." *Made me an offer I couldn't refuse.* Yeah, that definitely sounded way too *666 Park Avenue.* With a nonchalant shrug, I said, "The timing just worked out and it was an amazing deal all the way around."

Including the boss now being in hot pursuit of me.

"Are you talking about 10,000 Lux?" Kyle asked.

I had a little trouble concentrating on the conversation. I knew Dane was watching us. I knew he'd be annoyed that Kyle and I were still chatting. I also knew that Dane was steel and I was a magnet and I felt the intrinsic pull that made me desperate to extract myself from Kyle and make a beeline for Dane. Though I shouldn't—we weren't a couple. Were we?

Besides, he was in the middle of his own discussion.

So I said to Kyle, "That's the one. The grand opening is scheduled at the end of the year."

"I searched for marketing positions online before I went to Europe. Several jobs at the Lux came up."

"They're actively hiring. Do you have a portfolio?"

He reached for his phone and accessed the Web browser. Then he handed the device over. I scrolled through the photos, whistling under my breath at his projects. "Nice work."

"I did those during an internship. I have more to post, but it's a start."

"Hey," I said, not catching myself before I blurted, "you should apply at the resort. With the launch coming up, incredible things are happening. It'd be a great opportunity to pump up your portfolio."

"Yeah, I'll bet. Except . . ." He looked around me and frowned again. "Something tells me Surly over there wouldn't go for it. What *is* his problem?"

*You're talking to me.*

"He's just sort of that way," I said arbitrarily. "E-mail me your résumé. I'll pass it on to HR."

"I could definitely use the job, now that the fun's over."

I drained the remainder of my champagne and set the glass on a silver tray as a server wandered by. "You can get my e-mail address from Meghan or the Internet." I didn't dare whip out a Lux business card that had already been personalized for me—including a picture from a photo shoot we'd had earlier in the week for a press release. With Dane watching us so closely, I knew better than to add fuel to the fire. "I think I'll grab another drink."

Kyle opened his mouth—likely to offer to get me one—but I whirled around and headed toward the bar.

I lost sight of Dane in the throng of people milling about. I accepted a glass of champagne from a tuxedo-clad server and took several sips to cool my blazing insides. Really, that intensity of Dane's was its own highly intoxicating sexual stimulant.

Eventually I made my way toward the terrace. He fell into my line of vision once more while he talked with a different group.

One that included Mikaela Madsen and a twentysomething attractive Italian man who must have been Fabrizio Catalano.

The discussion looked heated, with Mikaela gripping Dane's arm from time to time and leaning in close. *Really* close. Like *we know each other intimately* close.

I was tempted to seek out Kyle, just to even the score. But that was juvenile. And Dane had been adamant when he'd expressed that he and Mikaela were only friends. That I was the one he wanted to be with. So I tamped down my insecurity.

The crowd shifted as I approached him. Rain fell in the background; the lightning was stunning as the pink-and-purple streaks flashed across the mountains in the distance.

Dane murmured something to Mikaela, disentangled himself from her, and took a few long strides toward me. He was dressed in all black again, stealing my breath. The glower on his face only ratcheted up my excitement.

Here I'd been all tormented by her nearness, but it was Dane who radiated a possessive vibe, wrapped around me.

Was *he* the jealous one? Of Kyle?

Tingles ran rampant through my body. Dane closed the gap between us and the world fell away.

He'd been gone nearly a week. It was five days too long.

"Hello," he said, all secretive and sexy. Though with the slight edge I'd anticipated.

"Hi."

"I see you still have someone waiting in the wings."

I fought the smile over his possessiveness. It'd only irritate him, I surmised. "Kyle's a friend. That's all. Like Mikaela."

"Definitely not like Mikaela." He gave a sharp shake of his head. "That's not how I see it at all. He looks at you as though he's about to ask you on a date. Or kiss you."

I could say the same for *his* friend but refrained. "I doubt he'll do either. I certainly haven't encouraged him. And you keep getting in his way."

"Good."

The corners of my mouth quivered. I couldn't hold back the smile this time. "Could you be any more alpha . . . territorial?"

"No one knows we're together, and that's fine for now. But he doesn't need to be sniffing around."

Similar to when we'd been on the phone, I mentally tripped over the *we're together* part. And the fact that he'd likely go through the roof if he knew I'd told Kyle to apply at the Lux. I figured it was best to keep that to myself for now.

The salt-and-pepper-haired associate or friend of Dane's from the bar suddenly appeared at his elbow. "Dane. We have a chance to speak with Delfino about Mikaela's Old Town market."

"Of course." As usual, Dane spoke to someone else while staring at me. It took him several seconds to tear his gaze away. He said, "Ethan Evans, Ari DeMille. She works at the hotel now. Events Director. Ari, this is Ethan. A former Harvard professor and one of my investors."

"It's a pleasure to meet you, Miss DeMille."

"Call me Ari, please."

"I'll be back in a few minutes," Dane told me—warned me? "Try to stay out of trouble."

They left me on the terrace. I strolled over to the railing where there was an overhang that protected me from the torrent. I believed we were about to set a record for most rainfall in decades.

Thankfully, the wind remained calm. The Phoenix area could be exceptionally dangerous during monsoon season because of the dust storms, or haboobs, as the local weather people called them. They could be up to sixty or so feet wide and several kilometers tall, completely blanketing parts of the city as the wall of dust rolled through. We didn't have that threat in Sedona, but we still experienced the violent thunderstorms.

"He is so not good at hiding his bad mood." Kyle joined me again.

I innocently asked, "Who?" Though, of course, I already knew the answer.

"Your boyfriend."

"He's not my boyfriend. He's my boss."

"He acts likes he's your boyfriend."

"Boss," I simply contended. No need to stir the pot. And I still wasn't totally sure *what* Dane and I were. Another reason not to stress over Heidi Klum.

*Easier said than done.*

"So, that makes you available?" Kyle asked with his engaging grin.

Okay, Dane had been right.

I said, "I'm basically committed to my career, so—"

"Getting together for a beer wouldn't be out of the question, though?"

I had to give Kyle credit for even making the suggestion when Dane had been so visibly agitated at seeing us together.

"I'm not one to date," I said, clearing the air. "But I'd meet up with you, Meghan, and Sean for a couple of drinks. As friends," I added with a placating look.

"Well," he said, appearing mildly disappointed, "I suppose that's a start. It could always lead to dinner."

I laughed at his persistence. Then launched into less-risky conversation as Meghan and Sean came over. Fifteen or twenty minutes later, I caught sight of Dane out of the corner of my eye. I decided *irritated* was much too mild a word for him, despite the fact that I wasn't alone with Kyle. He wasn't monopolizing me. Though I supposed just standing in close proximity to me was bad enough in Dane's eyes.

"I have some business to take care of," I said before leaving the group. I met Dane halfway across the terrace. "It's not what you think." That wasn't entirely true, but why make a scene?

He said, "I've accomplished what I needed to, so let's get out of here before I have to convince him to stay away from you."

"Just friends," I repeated. "I made the distinction *very* clear."

"And I can see he's totally on board with that. Especially when you're so nice to him."

"Am I supposed to be a jerk?"

"No, that's my job if he keeps hitting on you."

How had he known?

"Let's go," Dane insisted. He didn't take me by the hand or arm, for which I was grateful, but his tone certainly left no room for opposition. My God, he really was annoyed that I'd spent time with Kyle. And coming from Dane, it was the sexiest damn thing. A little alarming, too, in a thrilling way. This level of intensity wasn't something I was used to, nothing I'd ever encountered. That it was all because of me was deeply arousing.

I said my good-byes—with Kyle eyeing me suspiciously—and Dane and I left the party. The limo pulled around and the valet held the door open for us. They must have loaded Dane's bags in the trunk when the driver had picked him up at the airport.

I slid in first and felt a modicum of nervous energy with Dane sitting so close to me. I crossed my legs and gripped my clutch in my lap.

He'd removed his jacket before getting in and tossed it onto the seat across from us. Then he loosened his tie. His hand rested on my leg, at the hem of my short skirt.

"I'm not having sex in a limo," I diligently informed him, my gaze flitting to the raised partition. I didn't have a specific aversion to the prospect. I was stalling, especially after his power play inside and how his dominance turned me on. I needed to get a grip on the situation before it spiraled out of control.

Unfortunately, I suspected it was too late for that.

He gave me his half-assed grin. "I had a foot massage in mind. These shoes must be killing your feet when you're not used to wearing them."

I'd told him they weren't my style before. It was kind of sweet that he'd remembered.

His fingers trailed over my skin, making me tremble. They swept around to the underside of my knee. Slowly, they grazed downward, over my calf to my ankle. Such a simple touch, as though he were acclimating me to it, and yet so electric.

He slipped off the high heel, then started rubbing, with just the right amount of pressure, not tickling my sensitive soles. Caressing perfectly. A sigh fell from my parted lips. He grinned again.

Only Dane Bax could make a foot massage so amazingly sensual. It felt heavenly but also highly arousing. The thrumming inside me was a demanding cry for another release. A demanding cry for *him*.

My hands remained curled around my purse when they wanted to be buried in Dane's lush-looking hair. His cologne and heat teased my senses. His nearness taunted me. His head dipped and his warm lips brushed over my bare thigh. Tempting me.

Nerve endings sizzled. My nipples puckered against the shelf bra in my dress.

He uncrossed my legs and parted them slightly. Then he eased off the other shoe and rubbed that foot. I came alive under his touch, the thrumming turning into a sharp throb.

"Dane," I whispered. That word was the most I could get out, because a lust-induced haze clouded my thoughts. And I was breathless once more.

He glanced up at me and the need I felt must have been reflected in my eyes. His jaw clenched briefly. He stopped what he was doing and pulled apart the ends of his tie and unbuttoned his shirt, yanking the tails from his pants.

I took in his sculpted chest, so beautifully defined with hard pecs that rose above ripped abs. All that tanned skin. Jesus, he was stunning.

Without a word and without breaking our eye contact, he reached for the clutch I'd pretty much mutilated with my death grip. He pried it from my hands and set it aside. Then his palms splayed over the tops of my thighs and he pushed my skirt up. I lifted off the seat and he bunched the material at my hips.

He spread my legs wider and wedged himself into the vee they created. One arm snaked around my waist and he tugged me closer to him, so that my satin-covered sex pressed firmly against the corrugated grooves of his stomach. The aggressive move and erotic touch jolted me.

I grasped the edge of the seat with both hands on either side of us. His hands moved over me, up to my breasts. He squeezed them roughly, enough to convey his desire and spark a frenzy of excitement.

He leaned close and his mouth swept over the rounded tops cresting the tight bodice of my dress.

"You smell like rain and sex," he rumbled against my skin.

My hips jerked at his words.

"That's it," he murmured, softly kissing his way up to my neck. "Rub your pussy against my stomach."

His hands slid around to my back and then lower to clasp my hips. He guided me into a slow, sultry rhythm that had me grinding against his muscles, the satin swath of my thong slipping and sliding along my swollen folds and clit.

"Dane . . . Oh, Christ." Heat flared between my legs. My inner thighs quivered. My belly tensed and released as the feel of solid, rippled sinew caressed the heart of me, pushing me up, up, *up* . . .

He found a particularly tender spot just below my ear and pressed his tongue against it, then nipped gently.

"*Oh*. Oh, God." My head fell back on my shoulders and he continued the delicious torment.

"You're wet for me," he said against my throat. One of his hands relinquished my hip and he reached between us to whisk aside the triangle. Then his flesh was against mine and I let out a small cry at the velvety feel of skin that covered his steel abs. I writhed on the seat, rubbing against him as heat and sensation swelled in my core.

"That feels so good," I said on a sharp breath.

"Wrap your legs around me."

I did as instructed. Leading me, he picked up the pace.

I panted in harsh rasps of air. "I'm going to come."

A low growl escaped him. "You make me so damn hard."

His teeth grazed my earlobe, biting lightly.

"Fuck. Oh . . . yes . . . oh . . . oh, God . . ." The swelling expanded and exploded. I called out, "Dane!" as fire blazed through me, consumed me. My fingertips pressed into the leather. My inner walls clenched as I held on to the orgasm, prolonging it, savoring it. Vibrating from it.

"I like hearing my name on your lips," he said as he kissed my neck. "Now I want to hear you beg. For me."

# chapter 8

He released my hips, shifted away. Dane sank into the seat across from me and our gazes locked. I could barely breathe and my pulse jumped in wild beats. But I hadn't missed a single word he'd said.

Reaching for a packet of Wet-Naps on the bar, he wiped his hands. Not his stomach. That sent more zings through my body than I could process all at once.

"Are you a virgin, Ari?"

"Of course not." My chest rose and fell sharply with my rash breathing.

He dragged his gaze from mine and it flashed to my fingers, still grasping the edge of the seat. His eyes lifted to my face. "Did someone hurt you?"

"No. Nothing like that. It's not—it's not that."

He tried a different tactic. "How do you like to be fucked?"

I pulled in a slice of air. "Hard and fast. My clothes still on."

His brow knitted. "Every time?"

I nodded.

"Tell me about the last time. No, don't." He raked a hand through his hair, as though knowing the details would torment him. "Give me an idea, so I know what we're talking about here."

I wasn't sure this was the right path to travel, but I offered the highlights. "I'll see a man in a hotel bar, sit next to him, let him buy me a drink or two. I'll suggest we go to his room—or he will. I don't need to know his name. I don't need to know anything about him. We go at it. No foreplay. Not much touching. No kissing. Five, ten minutes later, I leave."

His jaw tightened as he took this all in. Then he asked, "Why so impersonal?"

"I don't want to get involved. Intimacy gets too complicated. It leads to emotions you can't control. Ones that can be . . . devastating."

The furrowed brow jerked up. "And you don't consider what we just did intimate?"

I nodded slowly, steeling myself. "Yes. And that's dangerous."

"Why?"

"Because I know what happens when things like this go wrong. My grandparents, my parents . . . really volatile splits. Also"—I gave a small shrug, though this was no minuscule matter—"My dad was totally blindsided by my mother's cheating. It destroyed him. For quite some time. He was a mess. And that wreaked havoc on his career. His life. My life."

Dane rested his forearms on his thighs and leaned forward. "You think history will repeat itself?"

"I do believe it's genetic."

"Cheating?"

"No," I was quick to say. "I would never do that to anyone. Especially since I know the kind of pain it causes. I just don't think I'm wired to get deeply involved."

"So . . . no kidding when you told me you weren't the marrying kind."

"No kidding."

"Hmm." His dark eyes clouded as he sat back in his seat.

"We're just talking about sex, right?" I dared to ask. "Between us. Anything more—" I shook my head.

I suspected the socialites in his circle fell hard and fast for him, that he was used to it. How could he not be? He was rich, gorgeous, intelligent, and powerful. And I'd seen the extraordinarily beautiful Mikaela Madsen fawn over him. Which probably drove Fabrizio nuts.

Not to mention, Dane knew how to make a woman come hard enough to see stars. I'd learned that firsthand, and he hadn't even touched me, not really. So it was an easy assumption to make that he left plenty of wet thongs and broken hearts in his wake.

He asked, "You're kind of young to be this jaded, don't you think?"

"I'm twenty-six."

"I know."

Of course he did.

"I don't really consider it being jaded," I told him. "I consider it being smart."

He ground his teeth. Then he said, "Come here."

I stared at him.

He grabbed his jacket and dropped it on the floor between his parted legs. Then he crooked his finger at me. "Come. Here."

Apprehension moved through me. I took a few deep breaths. Then I did as he'd asked. Demanded. Whatever.

I knelt before him. He dragged one end of his tie down his shirt, slipping it off. "Hands behind your back."

My stomach flipped with excitement. Yet tumbling from my lips were the words, "Not a chance in hell."

His gaze didn't falter. "Do it."

Against my better judgment, I did. He reached around and deftly secured my wrists. I gasped.

"What are you doing?"

"Teaching you a lesson about control."

"Dane," I said, my panic bouncing off the walls of the car.

"Don't worry," he told me, a hint of edginess in his tone. "I won't do anything you don't want me to do."

"Then why tie me up?"

"You'll see."

The challenge in his eyes was enough to make my heart skip several beats.

One of his beautifully sculpted hands slid along my cheek and cupped the side of my face, his fingers burrowing in my hair. His thumb swept over my bare lips. I'd not applied more lip gloss after drinking champagne.

His other hand rested at the dip of my waist, where my skirt was still gathered. It didn't faze me to be half dressed the way it unnerved me to have found myself in the compromising position I'd been concerned about when he'd said we'd ride back together in the limo.

The thumb stopped sweeping. His head dipped and his soft lips grazed my temple, then my cheekbone. The throbbing in my pussy returned full force. He tugged gently at the corner of my mouth with his lips. I started. He was going to kiss me.

"Dane," I said in protest. A measly one. It was only vaguely audible.

"That's not the word I wanted to hear," he murmured. "I want you to beg, remember?"

*Oh, God.* My eyes squeezed shut. My insides rioted.

He nipped at the other side of my mouth as his hand at my waist held me steady, although the road to Sedona was fairly smooth. It was Dane who made me vibrate from head to toe.

He smelled sinfully delicious. So masculine. So enticing. And being this close to him . . . it did the craziest things to me. My palms itched to splay over his bare chest. My heart pounded. My core tightened and my inner walls contracted, once again in search of something elusive.

Need burned through me. Not just the need to touch him but the need for him to possess me. To take what he wanted from me.

"Please," I whispered before I could stop myself.

"Better." Then he kissed me. Sexy, tongueless kisses that did exactly what I knew he intended—tease me. Seduce me. Bring me over to his dark side.

I leaned into him, melding to him as best as I could. He let out a low, strangled sound that sparked more carnal cravings. I wanted him desperately. It was terrifying yet too thrilling to stop.

My eyelids fluttered closed as his lips twisted and tangled with mine, our breaths becoming one.

The hand in my hair shifted and slid down my body to my slightly parted legs. He yanked the strand of my thong down one side, then the other, so the panties rested mid-thigh, further restraining me. His fingers glanced lightly over my slick folds. A small cry escaped me as his touch sent lightning bolts through my body.

He continued to engage me in his sensuous kisses as he stroked leisurely, tauntingly.

"You're so wet," he said against my lips. "I want you wetter."

He massaged my clit, picking up the pace.

I gasped and he used that opportunity to slip his tongue inside, toying with mine at first. Then he deepened the kiss. And moved his other hand to my backside, his fingers gliding along the cleft of my ass. He eased one into my pussy, penetrating from behind. My hips bucked.

Dragging his mouth from mine, he said, "You're tight. My cock will be a snug fit."

Fiery sensations sprang to life.

He wedged a second finger inside and pumped vigorously as he continued to rub the sensitive bud between my legs, with a bit more pressure and speed.

A moan leapt from my throat. My heavy panting filled the cabin of the limo.

"You're close," he said. As usual, cataloging everything about me.

"Yes."

He worked me a bit faster and I felt the threads unravel.

"Dane." I had no other thoughts in my head. Sensation consumed me. The blaze brightened and then, when his teeth pulled on my lower lip, I lost it completely. "Oh, God!" I cried out as I shattered at his mercy. "Dane!"

I came even harder this time. Every fiber of my being lit, every feeling to the depths of my soul centered wholly on him and the intense pleasure he gave me.

His fingers continued to massage and stroke as the orgasm went on and on. My inner thighs quivered again. My stomach tightened.

A strong, erratic pulse echoed in my ears. Irrational, raw urges clawed at me. I *had* to touch him. I had to press my body to his. I had to have him. *Now.*

"Dane," I said, my voice a mere wisp of air. "Untie me. Please."

He didn't. Rather, he lifted the hand at the apex of my legs and swiped the tip of his finger over my lips. Then his tongue smoothed over it, tasting me, before he kissed me. Deeply. Passionately. As though he couldn't get enough.

His fingers were still buried in my pussy and I came again, a powerful ripple that echoed through every inch of me.

He captured my whimper with his kiss, not breaking the contact.

*Oh, fuck.* I was so out of my element, so lost in him.

So very, very screwed. Because I needed him more than I needed my next breath.

When he pulled away, disappointment flashed through me— likely across my face, too.

"See?" he said in a darkly triumphant tone. Not exactly a gloat, but more of a silent *I just proved an invaluable point.* "You can't have it both ways, baby. Either you want me to kiss you . . . or you don't. Either you want me to touch you—and you want to touch me in turn—or you don't."

"You win again. Untie my hands."

The desire raging within was like nothing I'd ever imagined, nothing I'd ever believed I could feel.

Dane pulled the knot loose, freeing my wrists. This time, I kissed him. And shoved him back toward the seat. He clasped me by the waist and hauled me up and against him, shredding one side of my thong so that I could more easily straddle his lap. I pressed my chest to his.

It wasn't enough.

Breaking the kiss, I sat back and ran my hands over his cut abs, up to his well-defined pectoral ledge, to his wide shoulders. Then back down. Over and over, I absorbed the feeling of him beneath my fingertips, my palms.

His muscles flexed. His breathing turned ragged. His eyes smoldered with lust and longing.

He wanted me. Bad.

I felt his erection along my sex. I writhed against the hard length of him.

"Glad to see you couldn't resist for long," he said in a strained voice.

"I know better than to do this," I confessed. I knew better than to let myself get caught up in him. Yet here I was, completely entranced, enthralled.

His. All his.

Anxiety lingered on the periphery, but I chose to ignore it. I knew what I wanted. What I couldn't go a second more without.

I slipped between his legs again, kneeling on the floor of the limo. I worked the fastening of his belt. Too slowly, apparently. Dane joined in, undoing it quickly along with the top button while I worked the zipper. He shoved his pants and briefs down just enough to free his cock. I gaped.

Not that I hadn't expected everything about him to be magnificent—perfection personified, really. But . . . Good Lord. He was wide and thick. Beautifully hard. Amazingly tempting.

I wrapped my fingers around his base. His body jerked at my intimate touch. One of those primal growls that elicited my extreme excitement met my ears. He definitely wasn't immune to me.

I bent my head to him and licked my way up his shaft, teasing the underside of the head with my tongue, then licking some more.

"Fuck," he ground out. His hands plowed through my hair, lifting strands away from my face and off my shoulders. "I've thought about you doing this since we met. Jesus, you make me hot."

Spurred by his enthusiasm, I whisked my tongue over the indentation at the tip of his cock and then closed my lips around his head.

His hips rose and he said, "Take all of me." He let out a frustrated sound. "As much as you can."

I sheathed his erection with my mouth, down to where I still held him.

"Yes," he said in his strained voice. "Suck me hard."

I did. His hips bucked. "Damn, Ari . . ." He held my head in place as he pistoned into me, fucking my mouth. "Shit." His breath came in heavier pulls.

I took him deep once more.

"Oh, yeah. Just like that. Do it again."

My head bobbed as my lips slid up and down his shaft, pulling him in, sucking him harder.

"God, Ari . . ." A coarse sound slipped from low in his throat. His hips lifted again. I kept at it. "Swallow me down, baby." He came hard, his heat and salty taste flooding my mouth, sliding easily.

His release set me on fire again. I looked up at him, watching me. Desire and yearning raced through me.

"Dane."

He must have heard the need in my voice. His large hands gripped my biceps and he brought me up and onto him once more, my legs spreading to straddle his lap. Then his hand skimmed my ass and suddenly two fingers pressed into me from behind. He stroked quickly, confidently. I'd never needed this so much. I'd never greedily sought these powerful releases.

His mouth sealed to mine, adding to the pleasure, pushing me closer and closer to the edge. He kissed me as though he knew the frenzy raging inside, like he had every intention of making me burn brighter.

He worked a third finger in and pumped steadily. The sensations were too sinful not to give in to them. I cried his name as I came.

Wave after sizzling wave crashed over me. My fingers curled into his shoulders and I collapsed against him, sprawled across his chest.

"Oh, my God," was all I could say. *Finally,* some of the sexual tension had eased.

While I tried to calm my rapid breathing, Dane smoothed a hand over my hair. He withdrew his fingers and wrapped his arm around my waist. I pressed my ear to his heart and listened to the strong, steady beats. They were a bit faster than I thought was normal and I smiled.

"Well, this is fortunate," he murmured.

"Hmm?" I was too spent to really speak.

"No way for you to make one of your hasty retreats when we're in a moving vehicle."

I supposed it wouldn't kill me to admit, "I kind of like this spot."

His low chuckle rumbled in his chest. "I'm sorry about your thong."

"No, you're not."

Another soft laugh. "No. I'm not."

We fell silent for several minutes. I stared out the window as we turned off I-17 and headed toward Sedona. I hadn't even realized it'd started to rain.

I gave a half snort. *Figures.*

"What's so funny?"

"Nothing. It's not really funny at all. It's just . . . We're driving through another shower and I didn't even notice until now." Even though the rain *ping*ed against the roof.

A hint of anxiety encroached on my tingly afterglow. I slipped from Dane's loose embrace and returned to my seat, pulling down my skirt and whipping off my semi-shredded thong. I stuffed it into my small purse as he zipped up, though his shirt still hung open. The sight of all that smooth skin over rigid muscles was too tempting by far. My hands burned to touch him again.

He scowled, apparently not liking the distance I'd just put between us. "We're still twenty minutes away from your townhome."

"You know where I live?"

"Résumé," he simply said.

"Right."

"So, what's the problem?"

In other words, why couldn't I handle more than a few minutes of cuddling? I sighed. "Everything ceases to exist sometimes when I'm with you. It's like people, the rain, it all melts away and there's just . . . you."

His brow crooked. "And that's a bad thing?"

"It's dangerous," I reminded him.

The brow dropped and the disconcertion deepened.

"If you're worried about what sort of impact this has on your job, believe me when I say I can separate the two."

"Of course I don't want to lose my job. But it's more than that. I don't want to get all tangled up in . . ." *You.*

Yet . . .

Even as he sat there brooding, I wanted him. Even though his features were darkened and there was a hard glint in his emerald eyes, I wanted him. Even though I knew this had the potential to end horrifically for me, I wanted him.

"Maybe we should set the record straight," he said. "I'm not interested in just one night in the back of a limo with you. I'm not interested in your type of fast fuck in a hotel room before you bolt for the door."

My breathing turned shallow. His eyes locked with mine and I felt his intensity to the depths of my soul.

"This isn't something casual, Ari. It isn't something fleeting. I already know it. However long it takes for you to realize it, fine." He tried to cut me slack, but I could see the impatience rimming his eyes. A certain restlessness to his entire demeanor that was now quite familiar. I felt it, too.

The question that had invaded my mind the morning after he'd made me come with his sexy tone and dirty talk crawled to the forefront. I asked, "What exactly are we doing, Dane? Are we dating?"

"Call it whatever you want," he said without hesitation. He clearly had this worked out in his head, while I still bumbled along. "We're involved."

*Oh, God. That* word.

He continued, since I couldn't find my voice. "I want exclusivity. No more picking up men in hotel bars."

"That's not anything you have to worry about. It's been a while."

"How long?"

I shrugged. "Over a year."

"Good." He seemed pleased I wasn't sleeping around, but I also felt the undercurrent of tension radiating from him and I wondered if it had something to do with thoughts of other men touching me. He'd already proven himself territorial about that.

In turn, I probably should have asked about his sexual history but didn't really want to hear that he'd dated Mikaela, Kate Upton,

Jennifer Aniston, or some heiress to a gold mine. I had enough to contend with at the moment.

However, I did tell him, "I highly doubt you'll be entertained by me for long. In fact, I'm sure you'll lose interest quickly."

Sort of a painful confession but certainly an honest one.

He leaned forward. "Don't be so sure. You have hands-on experience of how hard you make me. Even when we're just on the phone, you get me going in a heartbeat. That won't go away overnight."

Flames flickered over my skin.

"I don't want you to have any inhibitions," he said. "Nothing's off-limits, Ari. *Nothing*."

I swallowed down a lump of panic. "What do you mean?"

"The things I want to do to you—they're going to push all these boundaries. And you're going to let me do them to you. You're going to *beg* me to do them to you."

I *had* begged him. Within seconds, it'd seemed.

"Or say no." His voice was clipped. Jaw set, eyes fixed on me. "Right now."

I'd just come multiple times . . . and now he was giving me an ultimatum?

"Ari," he prompted.

"That's a lot to ask." From *me*. The woman with endless boundaries.

"I told you," he said, his expression a dark, compelling one. "I want you."

The standoff ensued. I had no idea how to react. What to say. Ask for some actual definitions or . . . trust him?

My head spun. And despite the fact that we'd arrived at the row of townhomes along the seventh hole, I knew he wouldn't let me off the hook.

He did give me a reprieve from the mouthwatering sight of him as he buttoned his shirt. He collected his jacket, shook it out, and handed it to me. "Put this on."

I draped it around my shoulders, still a bit stunned at how everything had unfolded this evening. And because of his latest demand.

He reached for my shoes. "You'll ruin these if you wear them."

The door opened and he climbed out while I dug around for my keys. Then he scooped me into his arms, so I didn't have to wade through an inch of rain flooding the parking lot. The driver held a large umbrella over our heads, having to extend his arm to accommodate Dane's stature.

I directed him to the end unit and miraculously managed to shove the key in the hole while my fingers trembled. I pushed the door open and he set me on my feet just inside the foyer.

Turning to his driver, Dane said, "Thanks. You can return to the car."

"Very good, sir."

He tried to pass over the umbrella, but Dane shook his head. "I'm fine." The driver left us.

Butterflies took flight in my stomach. *Now what?*

Dane gave another one of those steely gazes and asked, "Have you made up your mind?"

The butterflies became more like screeching crows. I didn't know this man. Not really. He was secretive. Mysterious. There were things happening in his world that I knew nothing about, but I could see they troubled him when I caught glimpses of his clenched jaw or flashes of consternation in his eyes.

I understood what he was trying to do with me—break down my walls. But I was entitled to something in return.

So I bucked up and said, "I can't deny the physical attraction between us."

"Well, you did just come four times in an hour."

*Ah.* So he had a sense of humor. See? These were things I didn't know about him.

"I'd be lying if I said that was enough. It's not."

He closed the scant gap between us and bent his head to mine.

In my ear, he whispered, "I will give you many, *many* more orgasms. All delivered my way."

I lost my breath.

"I'll give you anything you want, Ari. But that means that you give me *you*—no holding back."

# chapter 9

He rendered me speechless for some time. His gaze didn't falter.

Finally, I told him, "I won't regret letting you do to my body whatever you want, but—" I delivered my own ultimatum. "I want to know who you are, Dane. Who you *really* are."

A sexy grin pulled at the corners of his mouth. "Clever tactic. And you think I'm going to lose interest quickly?"

"This is all new to me." Hell, I might as well be a virgin. Except I doubted virgins had such explicit thoughts running through their minds. I knew exactly what I wanted him to do to me. But I still had doubts. "I'm not really sure how—"

"Stop second-guessing yourself, Ari." Heat flared in his eyes. "I'm one-hundred percent sure about this. Which room is yours?"

"Not my bedroom," I blurted. "I can't—not in there."

His gaze locked with mine. "I told you this wouldn't be like your hotel escapades."

"It could never be like that with us," I assured him. "This is different. So different."

I reached out and fingered the first button he'd fastened below his collarbone. I felt the warmth he emitted through the material of his shirt. Smelled the intoxicating scent of him. My breath quickened as an intense longing seeped through my veins.

Freeing the small disk from its hole, then continuing down the line of buttons, I said, "I don't think about those other times. But they did happen." Staring up at him, I implored, "Erase the memories from my mind. Completely obliterate them."

His beautiful irises darkened. "When I'm done, I'll be the only one who has ever had you."

I nodded. "Just you."

He yanked the tails from his pants, undid his cuff links, and tossed off his shirt. "You have no idea what you do to me."

"Show me. Right here. Right now."

I needed this replay of past encounters because I knew he'd take it to all-new levels. I knew he'd prove those other men meant nothing and that what I'd done with them was simplistic. Nongratifying for one very specific reason—none of those men had been Dane.

My palms flattened against his chest as he slipped the jacket from my shoulders. He extracted a small foil package from the inside pocket before haphazardly draping the garment over a chair at my kitchen table, which we stood alongside.

Dipping my head, I left feathery kisses on his hot, smooth skin. My palms slid lower, to his abdomen.

I loved the feel of him, the taste of him.

His fingers twisted in my hair. "No holding back," he murmured. "This is our deal."

"I won't." I shook my head slightly. "I'll try." My tongue flicked over his small, hard nipple and his fingers tightened around my long curls.

"This is already out of control." He released the strands he held and cupped the side of my face, tipping it up to meet his searing kiss. My lips parted and his tongue delved deep.

He backed me up against the wall and pressed his powerful body to mine. There was no better feeling than being pinned to him, crushed against him. All of his rigid muscles, his unyielding strength, were their own aphrodisiacs. I was instantly high on his forceful claiming of me.

My hands glided up his bulging biceps to his broad shoulders. The sinew flexing under my touch drove me wild. One of my hands slipped around to his nape and I held his head to mine, letting him kiss me senseless as I went up in flames.

He was so right about this already being out of control. My body ached for him and, deep in my soul, I knew I had to have all of him—and give him all of me—no matter the consequences.

My mind was a hyperactive mess. I wasn't sure where to start with this man. All I could fully process was that I needed him. This instant. Buried inside me. Thrusting hard.

Tearing my mouth from his, I said, "Do something. *Now*. I can't wait a—"

His lips sealed to mine again. As he kissed me passionately, he worked his belt and zipper, ripped open the condom packet. He shoved my skirt up. Then his hands gripped my ass and he lifted me. I wrapped my legs around him. A heartbeat later, he plunged deep, mercilessly, fantastically.

I broke our kiss and cried out, "Oh, God!" A vehement reaction I'd never experienced. "Oh, Jesus, Dane!"

He filled me completely, stretching me and pressing so far into me, I immediately came.

"Oh, fuck, Ari," he groaned as I erupted around him, clenching him as my orgasm roared through me. "Ah, damn," he whispered, his voice rough yet intimate. "That's so hot, baby."

I trembled and panted from the quick, unexpected release. "You feel unbelievable." I held him tightly as the current of ecstasy raged on.

Dane slowly moved inside me, giving me a little time to adjust to him, though that was moot, not the least bit viable. He was huge. Thick and hard. Rubbing a particularly sensitive spot that kept me charged, kept me clutching at his cock as he stroked skillfully.

"Dane," I murmured, a quiet plea.

He kissed me once more, a demanding, hungry one that set me right back on course for another electrifying orgasm. He pumped into me in a masterful, commanding way. My fingers gripped his shoulder as my other hand twined in his hair, curling around the soft strands.

Dane dragged his mouth from mine and kissed his way over my jaw, down my throat. Against my skin, he said, "Come for me."

"So close . . ." I could barely keep up with the frenetic sensations.

He swiftly shifted us from the wall and, holding me to him with one hand, he jerked a chair away from the table so he could set me on the ledge. Hooking his arm in the crook of my knee, he lifted that leg up, spreading me wide as he thrust deeper into me.

I lay back against the smooth wood of the tabletop and raised my hips, greedily meeting his long, full strokes.

"Oh, God," I mumbled. He made me so restless, so hungry for more. It was near impossible to cling to all the emotions he incited, to sort them all out and find coherent thoughts. I wanted more. So much more. That was all that registered in my head. "Fuck me harder." The words rushed from my mouth on sharp breaths. "Dane."

My fingers wrapped around as much of his biceps as I could manage and I held fast to him. He drove deeper, harder. I moaned and whimpered, completely lost in the strongest vortex of all time.

Everything inside me collided and I screamed his name as the orgasm ignited.

"Shit, Ari." He plunged farther and then I felt his cock swell and throb as he let out a hoarse, "Fuck, yes. Squeeze me tight."

My inner walls clenched and released, prolonging my climax and drawing his out, too.

"Oh, goddamn," he muttered as he buried his face in my hair, partially covering my neck, though mostly fanned across the table.

I couldn't get a single word out. Dane had set me on fire in the limo. That had all been fevered and crazed, but this . . . *This* was pure magic.

How could I have even said I'd had sex before?

"Ari." His sensual voice cut into my thoughts. He stared down at me.

I tried to focus on him but my eyes seemed to dance in their sockets. I was literally rocked to the core of my being.

"Are you okay, baby?"

I grinned. A loopy one, I was sure. "Never, ever, *ever* better."

He gave me his sexy smirk. "You're definitely something else. I can't believe how quickly you made me come. Christ."

He kissed me in his electrifying way, keeping the juices flowing, keeping me boneless and excited. It was all I could do not to claw at him, to beg him to fuck me again.

Eventually, Dane straightened and hauled me up. I was ridiculously limp, needing to plant my palms alongside my hips to steady myself for a few seconds. He eyed me curiously and grinned.

"Don't look so pleased with yourself," I teased. "You could pretend you put a little effort into leaving me dazed and spineless."

*Thoroughly ravaged* was probably the more appropriate term. My mussed hair fell over my bare shoulders. My skirt was still bunched around my waist. I had no idea what my makeup looked like. No doubt I wore a *very* satisfied smile on my face.

He reached for my hem. "Lift up."

I did as instructed and he moved my skirt into place. Then he discarded the condom and cleaned up at the sink. I was still nowhere near in touch with myself as I finally slipped to the floor and padded my way into the bathroom. I took a quick shower, did a light blow-dry of my hair, and pulled on my Edmonton Oilers T-shirt. Then I dragged on a pair of red lace panties.

Dane stood in my living room when I returned, his hip propped

against the back of the sofa. He'd put his shirt on. He'd left it unbuttoned, the tails out. I wasn't quite sure what the next move was
supposed to be—or who was supposed to make it.

I wrung my hands, unnerved. "That was . . ." I didn't have words
for *what that was.* Even a cool shower couldn't alleviate the fiery
sensations that still flickered within me.

"I didn't hurt you, did I?" His look was a grave one.

"Of course not. I'll be sore in the morning, but in a really good
way." I already felt it coming on. The throbbing within me didn't
abate and my inner thighs burned. My stomach ached, too, as
though I'd just done a million crunches. It all felt exhilarating. Like
a nonstop reminder of how much we'd wanted each other. A constant memory that he'd been so very deep inside me. That he'd
fucked me hard—as I'd wanted him to do.

Yet he didn't seem pleased with my answer. "You're incredibly
tight. Small. And—"

"Dane." I crossed to where he stood and gazed up at him. "Try
to understand. This is the first time I've actually had earth-shattering
sex. I mean, I always thought that term was such bullshit, such an
exaggeration. Now, I get it. And the fact that I can *still feel* everything
you did to me . . ." I might have worn a silly expression. "Like, my
body is just—"

My fists balled at my sides. I couldn't explain how unbelievable
it felt to have every inch of me singed by his touch, his thrusts, his
kisses.

"Trust me when I say, you gave me exactly what I needed." I
stretched on tiptoe and pressed my lips to his.

He quickly took over the kiss—apparently I was too tentative.
And Dane knew exactly how to turn something sweet and spicy
into something scorching hot. I loved it.

When he eventually pulled away, he whispered, "Touch me,
Ari." His breath blew against a few strands of hair on my temple.
"Anywhere. Everywhere. However you want."

My fingertips grazed the corrugrated grooves of his stomach, up to his stonewall of a chest.

"I've never actually seen anyone this cut in person," I told him. "How do you find time for the gym?"

"I started working out with a trainer when I was a kid. I've always kept with it."

"You're unbelievable," I simply said. There really wasn't a better description.

Slipping out of his shirt, he laid it across the back of the sofa. Then he gathered me in a tight embrace and delivered yet another passionate kiss. Leaving me breathless.

His hands slid under my shirt and caressed my sides, before one slid to my butt. He palmed my ass cheek and gave it a titillating squeeze.

"It's too bad I only had the one condom."

I frowned. "That is too bad. I don't have any, either."

"I should have considered that before I sent the driver back to the hotel. He could have made a drugstore run for us."

I started. First at the thought of the chauffeur picking up condoms and bringing them back here. And second . . . "You're staying?"

His eyes bore into me. "I told you very specifically this wouldn't be a fast fuck in a hotel room before you bolt for the door. I believe those were my exact words."

"Actually, I think I'm mostly surprised you'd want to sleep over, knowing we won't be having sex again."

"This isn't just about sex, Ari."

*Wow.* Not only was he a literal man, he also clearly wasn't one to look for the easy way out of a tricky situation. Because his staying *did* make things infinitely more serious between us.

"Just so you know," I felt compelled to say, "this is something else I've never done before."

"I suspected that. Which is why I provided the simple solution of sending my driver away."

"Now who's the clever one?"

With a smug look on his devilishly handsome face, he said, "You still haven't told me which bedroom is yours."

I pointed to the one closest to the patio.

He scooped me into his arms and carried me to my bed, where he set me gently. I watched with bated breath as he stripped down to his black briefs. He was just so fantastically built, I feared there might be drool forming at the corner of my mouth.

That wasn't the only thing I feared. He climbed in beside me and pulled me to him. His arm draped over my shoulder and he coaxed me into resting my head on his chest. My hand splayed over his stomach.

"Relax, baby," he whispered in the dark. "You're much too tense."

It'd hit me suddenly, invading my post-sex serenity. "How long can I lay here before your arm falls asleep?"

"That's what you're worried about?"

"I told you. I've never done this before."

One hand stroked my hair. He also twined his fingers with mine as they lay against his abs. "You're very endearing."

"Is that a polite way of calling me naive?"

"I don't think that at all." He kissed my forehead. "You gave me valid reasons for why you've avoided intimacy. The truth is, it makes me happy that you haven't shared yourself like this with anyone else."

It would never be like this with anyone else; I was sure of it. There was something so mesmeric about Dane that had me easily caught up in the connection we'd made. Not just the physical one, but the emotional side of it as well.

"It's late," he said. "Try to sleep."

"You did wear me out tonight."

"I did everything you asked."

"And then some. It was pretty damn sensational."

"So take a few deep breaths," he told me in a low voice, "and know that I'm perfectly content right here, whether my arm falls asleep or not."

"You're really very sweet when you're not looking as though you want to rip Kyle's head off. Or you're scowling at me."

"Hmm." Apparently, that was all he intended to say on the subject.

So I did as he'd recommended, slowly inhaling, slowly exhaling. I tried not to think of insane things like how heavy my head might be on his chest. How erratic my pulse was—could he feel it? How noisy my breathing could possibly be.

*Damn it.* I should have turned on music. For that matter, why the hell wasn't it raining, when I needed the camouflage sound now more than ever?

"Ari," he whispered against the top of my head. "Baby. You're squirming like crazy."

"I am?" I forced myself to still.

"Nothing to be antsy over."

I swallowed hard. "You'd feel differently if you were in my shoes."

He chuckled, a sexy rumble that reverberated throughout my body. "Fine. I have a better thought."

Gripping me around the waist, he hauled me onto him, so I lay against his hunky torso, propped on my forearms at his pecs, my legs between his.

"Dane."

"Shh." He swept my tumbling curls off my shoulders. Then his hands skimmed down my back to my ass. "I like you on top of me."

"You can't sleep like this."

"Obviously, neither one of us is interested in sleeping just yet."

My stomach fluttered. "You do make me restless."

His hands shifted and he clasped the hem of my shirt, pulling it up and over my head, then working it off one arm at a time.

"Mm, that's nice," he mused. "Your nipples pressed to my chest.

And they're hard." His fingers skated along my skin, on either side of my spine, down to my tailbone, making me shiver with delight.

He let out a primal groan. His erection pressed to my belly. "So am I. So quick."

"You're insatiable," I said playfully.

"It's you." His tone was serious, sincere.

I stared at him, his beautiful emerald irises shimmering with heat in the soft, silvery moonlight that filtered through the vertical blinds covering the sliding glass doors.

He gently kneaded my ass cheeks as his thick cock throbbed against my stomach.

"You're not at all what I expected when I met you," I confided.

"What did you expect?"

"I don't know. You were so intense. Still are. Still electrifying. But also . . . tender."

He gripped my ass more firmly. I let out a soft laugh.

"And so wicked."

He kissed me, then said against my lips, "Be wicked with me."

Lust shot to my core. But I reminded him, "We don't have a condom."

"We don't need one. You've been celibate for a year. You must have a vi—"

"Dane." I cut him off, instantly knowing where his devilish thoughts were headed.

He teased my lips again with his and then glided his tongue over the bottom one before nipping at it with his teeth. "Let me watch."

"What?" I stared down at him, excitement and shock warring within me.

"You heard me," he said. One hand remained splayed across my ass. The other smoothed up to my shoulder and then around to my front to slip between us. He palmed my breast, massaging and whisking his thumb over my puckered nipple.

He was seducing me again, and he was so damn good at it.

The hand on my breast slid to the lace covering me and he

pushed my panties down my legs as he rolled us so I was on my back. He tossed aside my lingerie. Kissed me senseless.

His hands were all over my body, as though he couldn't get enough of me. I was on fire, his fingers and palms blazing a trail along every inch of me. Teasing, caressing, tempting me to do whatever he asked of me.

His head dipped and his tongue fluttered thrillingly over my nipple, making it unbelievably hard. Making my breasts ache for more.

"Dane," I whispered in complete surrender. I reached above my head, to the nightstand, and jerked the drawer open. I fumbled through paperbacks, tissue packets, and throat spray for when the air got too dry.

Stretching beyond me, with a longer arm span, Dane grabbed my vibrator.

He eyed the battery-operated device. "Not one for bells and whistles?"

"Totally utilitarian," I said.

He let out a *humph*, then handed it over. He went back to expertly massaging my breasts, rolling and lightly pinching my nipples, until I writhed beneath him and flames danced through my veins.

I turned the knob on the base. The low buzzing that suddenly filled the quiet room made me nearly heave the thing back into the drawer and slam it shut. Heat burst on my cheeks.

This was crazy. What the hell was I doing?

Dane kissed the tops of my breasts, then along my collarbone and up my neck. His teeth grazed, then nipped at my sensitive skin, just below my ear. That drove me wild. Spurred me on. Made it impossible for me to stop what he'd started.

I pressed the length of the shaft along my slick folds and a moan escaped my parted lips. I absorbed the tingles along my clit. Dane's mouth wreaked havoc on my throat, finding the most delectable places to lightly bite and tease, heightening my arousal.

My eyelids drifted closed. Heat burned through me. I slid the vibrator back and forth, over my swollen, dewy flesh. Dane's hand covered mine, adding a bit more pressure.

He murmured, "I want you to come again."

I was amazed I could be so sexually charged. Fascinated by it as well.

Dane kissed me while coaxing my hand beneath his. The shaft penetrated my opening and he pushed it in deep. Pumped slowly.

The toy was narrow and not nearly as filling or gratifying as Dane's cock inside me. But he worked me with faster strokes now, hitching my breath. He must have known some creative way to maneuver it between the V of his fingers and his palm, because his thumb was free to rub my clit.

He drew one of my nipples into his mouth and suckled deep. My fingers plowed through his hair.

I'd honestly thought I was too much of an intimacy-phobe to get into this, but Dane had me frantic for another release. My hips rolled and my hand at the back of his head kept him locked to me as his tongue and mouth did the most amazing things to my breasts and the taut peaks that begged for more and more of his attention.

I was a bit crazed.

"Fuck," I mumured. "This really shouldn't feel as good as it does."

My vibrator couldn't hold a candle to Dane, of course—and I felt his erection against my side, taunting me. But good Lord, he knew how to send me straight to the edge.

"Slips and slides nicely because you're so wet."

"You make me this wet."

I didn't bother giving credence to the blush crawling up my neck to my cheeks. I'd never been a prude, but with Dane, I was downright shameless. An addictive sensation. *He* was addictive.

More throaty moans fell from my lips as he worked me skillfully. My inner walls clutched tight and though I knew precisely what my body sought—Dane—I couldn't deny the tension mounting within. He did the most incredible things to me.

"I thought you wanted to watch," I mumbled as the breaking point neared.

"I am watching. But I need to be the one who makes you come."

That did more insane things to my body.

"You're so good at everything you do," I said.

"Come for me. Now."

"Yes. Oh, God . . . Yes!"

My hips raised and I let go under his talented command, whimpering his name as tremors rolled through me and exhilaration consumed me.

"Oh, God!" There were plenty of aftershocks to keep me charged.

Several suspended moments ticked by, with me not quite catching my breath. Dane withdrew the vibrator and managed to jerk a tissue from its packet and set the toy on the nightstand, all with one hand. His other arm remained wrapped around my waist.

"Oh, Christ." I could barely breathe. "Now *that* was nice."

I saw his smirk in the pale moonlight. "Just *nice*?"

"Downright deviant?"

He laughed quietly. "Hardly."

"Well, I will admit you're much better at that than I am." Yet I still ached for him. How was that possible? And what did it mean?

I'd crossed a number of personal lines this evening. Since I'd met Dane, really. I couldn't seem to help myself. He was good at guiding me and I was hooked on following.

But similar to him needing more when he was touching me, when he was inside me, I couldn't find a satiable medium. I literally craved more of him. So much so, my private companion for years had been reduced to an impersonal substitution for the real thing—for the only thing, I feared, would ever fulfill me. *Dane.*

Since I couldn't have his cock buried deep, I clasped his hand

and dragged it to the apex of my legs. I couldn't explain the urgency of the moment, other than to say, "I need to feel *you*."

His sexy growl sparked my nerve endings, instantly lighting me up like the Vegas Strip.

"You make me so damn hot," he whispered into my hair. Two fingers plunged deep. I let out a gratified cry.

His skin, his heat, his very essence . . . I needed it all.

As Dane massaged my inner walls with just the right rhythm, I carefully lowered his briefs so I could curl my hand around his cock.

"Ari," he said on a gruff sigh. "You'll make me come."

"That's what I want," I told him. "I want to feel you come in my hand, on my stomach—"

His mouth crashed over mine and he claimed it with passion and aggression. I was suddenly lost, drowning in a sea of erotic thoughts, sensations, desires.

I pumped his thick erection in my fist, moisture from the indentation in the tip of his head helping my hand to glide smoothly, with just a hint of friction. His hips bucked in time with my ministrations. All the while, his fingers inside me caressed masterfully.

When my breath caught in my throat, I had to tear my mouth from his. I was so close to falling apart again.

"You know the perfect spot," I said, thinking of what he'd done to me in the limo, when my hands were tied behind my back.

The pads of his fingers rubbed my g-spot as though the man had the ultimate road map to my erogenous zones. He knew my body—had learned those intricate nuances so quickly.

"Dane." I moaned, pleasure rippling through me. My foot flattened on the mattress, my hips lifted. "That's it." I panted. "Oh, God. Right there."

His mouth was on my neck again. His fingers stroked expertly. I felt myself unravel.

My hand pumped faster, closing over his head and then sliding down to his base before gliding back up. His breathing was as erratic as mine. His cock pulsed against my palm. The rush of getting him so worked up mingled with the sizzling between my legs and deep in my core.

"Squeeze me tight," he whispered. I did. He grunted. "Yeah, just like that."

His eyes locked with mine in the shimmery slivers of light. I was so dazed, so hypnotized by the sensual feelings, the burning in his eyes, the intensity of the intimate moments we shared. I wasn't at all myself. I seemed to float in a different realm, collecting all the flashes of excitement, disassociating myself from everything around me except for Dane. Vibrating from head to toe as the anticipation built between us, a near palpable sensation that enveloped us.

"Ari," he murmured.

I knew he was as close as I was. I could feel it, home in on it. I wanted him to explode at the exact moment I did.

"Come with me," I urged.

His fingers moved quickly within me. My pulse kicked up. I pulled in ragged slices of air. My lids grew heavy.

"Keep your eyes open," he demanded.

The tension escalated. A tremor ran through me and then spread in all directions. My entire being stretched much too thin as Dane's gaze remained unwavering while he played me just right and I used his own pre-cum to pump him faster, more firmly.

"Jesus," he ground out. "Fuck."

I couldn't hold on a heartbeat longer. Everything inside of me erupted in a firestorm that singed me to the core. "Oh, God!"

"Ah, yeah, Ari. Baby. Just like that!" His hot seed coated my skin, his orgasm fanning the flames.

"Dane!" I screamed as excitement rocked me and I soared higher. My body shook violently, the trembling not just a physical response. He'd touched me so deep inside, so much deeper than the part of my body I'd considered to be the most intimate. He'd gone far beyond that.

And that left me stunned, blissed out . . . and terrified.

———

It took a short eternity for me to come down from my high. For me to break free of my lust-induced haze.

Dane carried me to the shower and I remained in my euphoric state as his soapy hands skimmed over my body. I returned the favor, exploring every inch of him, completely mesmerized, mystified. He was too incredible for words.

My hands trailed over his lean hips as I circled him in the over-sized tub, the only thing about my modest townhome that could be considered large. My fingertips grazed the base of his spine and then my hand slid over his ass. He shot a heated look at me over his broad shoulder. I felt a blush coming on, but ignored it.

I stepped around Dane and faced him. I took in his powerful, virile body and it made my heart skitter.

When my gaze finally lifted to his devastatingly handsome vis-age, I still saw every inch of him in my mind's eye.

"You're beautiful," I told him.

"Ari."

"Really," I said, breathless. "So beautiful."

My palms splayed over his pecs as I went up on tiptoe to kiss him. His arms wound around me and he crushed me against him, holding me tight as he took over the kiss and turned it searing and sensational.

The spray of hot water against my back couldn't compete with the scorching feeling of his hard body against mine.

My fingers tangled in his wet hair. I held on for dear life as he kept me energized with his perfect kiss.

I was clearly beyond my passion threshold, by a lot. But Dane was in my house, I was in his arms, and since I really didn't know what tomorrow would bring—whether he'd still want me or not—I took advantage of the opportunity presented.

More than that, I just plain needed him. Desperately.

I broke our kiss and merely whispered, "Dane." I nuzzled his neck, kissing the crook at his shoulder.

His hands swept over me. "Again?"

"Yes."

He carefully turned me around. His hands cupped my breasts and his fingers toyed with my nipples as his mouth skated over my throat, tenderly biting.

"I don't want to make you too sore."

"I'm fine." Then I gave a slight shake of my head. "No. Not fine. I'm burning up."

One of his hands slipped between my legs, his fingers sinking deep. The other arm spread over my chest, palming my breast, still teasing my nipple. He held me firmly. Stroked confidently.

I leaned forward, flattening a hand to the wall to stabilize myself. My legs quaked, my stomach quivered. I was trapped once more in his vortex, that disconnection of my past, who I used to be, as everything about him poignantly pressed in on me so that all that registered were the moments with Dane.

His strokes quickened along that spot inside that set me ablaze and made me ridiculously aroused. Seconds later, all the intensely erotic sensations he evoked burst wide open and I came again, calling his name.

"God, Ari," he said against my temple as I rode the waves of ecstasy. "You have no idea how much I want you."

"Can't be more than I want you," I insisted as my body continued to tremble.

He held me awhile longer, until the shaking was a little more under control. Then he released me and shut off the water. He stepped out of the tub for towels and wrapped one around me before securing the other at his waist. He helped me out of the shower and I used the hair dryer while he disappeared into my room. Moments later, he strutted back into the bathroom, vibrator in hand. He dumped it in the trash.

"You won't be needing that again," he said simply, smugly.

I watched him strut out. A tickle of delight ran along my skin.

When I lost sight of him, I spared a glance toward the wicker garbage bin. To the budget-minded, that was thirty bucks wasted. I didn't care. It'd never provide the same purpose following this evening.

I stripped off the towel, turned off the light, and went into the bedroom, pulling my Gretzky tee and panties on. I settled on the mattress next to Dane, who was propped against a pile of pillows. The rumpled covers were strewn haphazardly across his hips, just barely concealing what was an impressive bulge.

"So . . . ," I ventured as my fingers skimmed over his abs, which bunched beneath my touch. "This has been an interesting evening."

He grinned. So lazy, cocky, sexy. "How many times did you come?"

"I lost count."

"I didn't."

Tiny microbursts exploded between my legs. *Amazing.*

"I think you've finally exhausted me," I confessed.

"Then curl up with me and sleep."

I did as told. "You'll still be here in the morning when I wake up?"

He kissed the top of my head. "Don't doubt it for a second."

There was definitely something to be said for the adage *be careful what you wish for.*

In the morning, while we were still snuggled under the covers and his hands were roaming my body, Dane coyly suggested we have lunch together.

As in . . . a date. A real one. Not an interview that felt like a date. Not a meet-up at a party. An actual, honest-to-God date.

Panic slithered through me. But I had a legitimate excuse to evade him.

"That'd be great," I said, "except that I'll be in Phoenix. Peoria, more specifically. My dad and I have a ten o'clock tee time at Trilogy at Vistancia while there's a break in the weather."

"Excellent course." He palmed my breast and lazily swept his thumb over my hard nipple, making it nearly impossible to focus on anything else. I barely heard him ask, "Have you played Blackstone?"

I all but purred under his touch but managed to say, "The private country club in Vistancia? No. My dad hasn't, either."

"Would you like to?"

My stomach fluttered—not just from Dane's light teasing of my nipple. The devil knew all the right buttons to push.

"It'd be a highlight," I dared to admit.

"Then cancel Trilogy and go to Blackstone instead. I'm a member. I'll leave your name with the guard at the gate."

"You can't seriously get a tee time there at the last minute."

"It won't be a problem." Of course not. I'd forgotten who I was talking to—whatever Dane Bax wanted . . .

He pushed my shirt up and flicked his tongue over the taut peak, igniting my insides. Then he drew my nipple into his mouth and suckled deep. I moaned.

"Ten o'clock," he said in a low voice, his warm breath on my skin keeping me highly aroused. "Ethan and I will meet you there."

My body stiffened. "You're going to golf with us?" The panic hit full-on. I pushed him away, yanked down my shirt. This was serious business. I wouldn't let him distract me. Difficult as it was to have him stop. "With my *dad*?"

"Yes. I have to meet him sometime, right?"

I sat up. Dane didn't bump boundaries—he bulldozed right through them.

I couldn't even challenge him and demand to meet his parents. They were deceased.

Shaking my head, I said, "That would be a huge mistake of epic proportions."

"I promise not to mention how many times I made his one and only daughter come last night."

I laughed, despite the anxiety rushing through me. "It's nice to know you can tell a joke from time to time."

He gave me a seductive grin. "Did you doubt it?"

"Please. Even you can't dispute that you're incredibly intense." Edgy. Sexy. Dangerous. Too, *too* desirable.

I bit back a lusty sigh.

"I have a lot on my mind," he said by way of a vague excuse.

Honestly, I was dying of curiosity to hear all about it. Was it just the hotel that made him so conflicted? Did it have anything to do with his massive wealth? His parents' deaths?

I considered the hint of guilt that had flitted in his eyes at one point, when we'd been waiting for Alex to bring our cars after the Delfino-Aldridge wedding. What would a man like Dane Bax have to feel guilty over? Had he decided to lie, cheat, and steal his way to the top? Or did he suffer survivor's guilt because he was alive and his parents weren't?

*Questions, questions.* I needed some answers.

"So if I let you meet my father," I ventured into risky territory, "will you tell me why there's almost next to nothing about you on the Internet?"

"You Googled me?"

"Naturally." I wouldn't apologize for it. He'd researched me before offering me a job.

"We'll talk later," he said as he threw off the covers and got to his feet. "I have to call Amano for a ride and make the reservation at Blackstone."

His tone was clipped. He didn't like having the tables turned on him—clearly didn't appreciate that I intended to push back.

*Too bad.* Even Satan had pesky archangels with whom to deal.

Dane dressed, kissed me, then said mischievously, "I also have to make a drugstore run." He winked.

"Don't you dare flirt with me on the course. In front of my father . . . Ethan . . ."

*Oh, crap.* I was in way too deep here.

Dane gave me another kiss—a slow, sexy one—before adding, "Get ready, or you'll miss our tee time."

Then he sauntered off. Leaving me to wonder how he managed to talk me into everything he wanted.

# chapter 10

I didn't bother informing my father of the venue change. I figured I'd surprise him, since we had to drive in the same direction as if we were playing Trilogy. I picked him up and we headed out of Sedona, then south on I-17. I tried to ignore the reminder of being on this highway just last night, with Dane doing orgasmic things to me—and having his cock in my mouth.

Making a man like him come was equivalent to locating the Holy Grail. I still couldn't believe I'd gotten him so hot and bothered. Had then gotten him off.

And what he'd done to me afterward, in my townhome . . .

My stomach flipped. Though now was hardly the time to think about all that. Instead, I engaged my dad in idle chitchat. When we reached the exit for Loop 303, I peeled off the highway and headed west. The temperature in the Valley had dipped with the nearly endless rainfall and it was a virtually unheard-of seventy-five degrees, according to the digital readout on my rearview mirror.

A half dozen hot-air balloons rose above the desert landscape, with low mountains in the background.

The sun was cloaked by a gray sky but the chance of precipitation was low. It looked like the breeze was minimal, since none of the brush or wildflowers blew in the wind. All in all, a great early-autumn day to hit the links. A nice change of pace from golfing when it was a hundred and fifteen out and my dad itched to play one of the Valley courses.

I took the exit for Lone Mountain and we entered the back portion of the master-planned community of Vistancia. But rather than take the parkway to Sunset Drive, I slowed at the cobblestone entrance of the country club and turned in.

My dad spared a glance my way.

"Wishful thinking?"

I laughed. "Change in plans."

"This is a private development, Ari."

"Yeah, I know." I pulled under the porte cochere and waited for the security guard to approach the driver's side. Sliding down the window, I said, "Hi. Ari DeMille. We're guests of Dane Bax."

"Of course. Welcome to Blackstone, Ms. DeMille. Mr. Bax and Mr. Evans are already here, at the country club. Do you know where you're going?"

"Not exactly."

"Follow this road until you reach a stone bridge. There's a sign and the club is on the left."

"Thanks." I waited for the double wooden gates to open. Then we passed through.

Every minute that ticked by was filled with both excitement over seeing Dane and dread that I'd have to introduce him to my father.

I eyed my father a moment. He looked a bit perplexed and befuddled. He'd go through the roof if he found out about me and Dane. I was sure of it. My dad had always been protective. So much so that he'd gone toe-to-toe with my mother and the high-priced lawyer she'd secured—at my dad's expense, since Kathryn De-Mille had never worked a day in her life. My mother had wanted full custody. Not because she adored me so much that she didn't want us separated. That had never been the case.

What she'd wanted was a bargaining chip. I'd been it. She'd told him she'd give up all parental rights . . . for a price. That price had drained his savings account and wiped out every single one of his investments. He'd had to give her the house, too. On top of that was alimony, since she was pretty much unemployable with zero experience and no career aspirations above being a professional bitch.

Yes, I could say that about my mother. I'd lived with her long enough to formulate the educated opinion. The very reason I'd been ignoring the sudden texting she'd tried to engage me in.

"So, what are we doing here?" my dad asked.

I pulled into the drive and slowed, taking in all of the self-parking and the valet ahead of us.

"Seriously?" I said, skirting his question. "The parking lot is like feet away from the entrance and people actually valet park?"

"Comes with the membership at places like this."

"Jesus." Sure, I grasped the concept of *privileged*. My dad had been a mover and a shaker in his heyday. We'd had country club memberships when I was a kid. Still . . . We could manage to walk a short distance from the car to the club.

I bypassed the valet and easily found a spot. I shut off the engine and we collected our bags from the back.

Now I had some explaining to do. "Mr. Bax booked our game," I said, hoping like hell to keep the *I am completely enthralled and desperately hot for my boss—and oh, yeah, I'm sleeping with him!* from my tone. "He and one of his associates will be joining us."

My dad gave me a *you're shitting me* look. "Why are we golfing with your boss?"

"He wanted to meet you, of course." I shrugged. "You are sort of famous, Dad. A consistent contender for the championship. Any-

one who golfs knows who you are and Dane—Mr. Bax—is probably curious to get your take on his courses. It's only logical that he'd
want to meet you here so that you can gauge the tracks of a Jim
Engh–designed course."

There. That sounded reasonable. *Right?*

Unfortunately, my dad didn't look wholly convinced. But I could
tell the prospect of a morning on Blackstone fairways was too tempting to pass up. The devil likely would have known that. He seemed
to be one step ahead of me.

I gave my name again at the check-in stand under the tall archways. The valet suddenly hopped to and I snickered, knowing it had
nothing to do with me.

"Mr. DeMille," he said, as though I didn't exist. "It's an honor
to meet you. John Halston. If you need anything at all, let me know."
He grabbed my dad's clubs.

I resisted the urge to clear my throat and remind John I was
standing there with my own bag slung over my shoulder.

My dad took my clubs and handed them over.

John, whom I pegged for mid-forties, recapped a few of my
father's most prestigious on-camera shots and I let him bask in the
glory. I'd always been proud of him. Even when my mother trashed
him. Her tirades had been completely unnecessary, unwarranted,
horrendous. I'd always wondered what her deal was. My dad was
well respected within the golf community and amongst media and
fans. He was also a very generous man, who volunteered his time
to teach kids the basics of the game, especially those in low-income
environments.

But he'd married a Scottsdale prima donna addicted to plastic
surgery and double martinis. Big, big mistake.

When John's hero worship began to make my dad visibly uncomfortable, I asked him to direct us to the golf shop. The country
club was quite beautiful, with a hacienda feel, and was a straight shot
from the courtyard that boasted numerous fireplaces and plush
patio furniture to the event lawn beyond. Excellent for weddings.

I followed my dad to the shop and browsed while John set up our cart. I snuck a peek at a few price tags and cringed. I wouldn't be picking up any cute skirts and tops here. Not that I really needed them. I practically lived in golf clothes when not working, so I already had a closetful. Came with the territory.

As I scanned the racks, I caught a glimpse of Dane out a side window. He wore black pants and a black polo shirt with thin white horizontal stripes and the Blackstone logo on the left chest. He literally was too captivating for words and I was inexplicably drawn to him.

I left my dad—discussing with the golf shop pro a putter he wanted to demo—and joined Dane on the patio.

"This is incredible," I said, luckily finding my voice. It was difficult to latch on to coherent thoughts, other than those wrapped around everything he'd done to me last night. How I'd responded. How I'd begged for him. Begged for more.

"I'm glad you like it." He gave me a sigh-worthy grin. "You look damn pretty this morning."

"I look like a watermelon," I quipped as I slid a glance over my fuchsia-and-lime-green-blocked sleeveless collared shirt, paired with a fuchsia skirt. "It was cute on the mannequin at my dad's golf club, but now that I'm wearing it . . . Hmm . . ."

Dane's head dipped and he said quietly, "You're gorgeous."

"No flirting, remember?" Though my toes curled in my spikes. I knew to stick to safer territory, so I kept to small talk. "The valet gushed over my dad. Definite ego stroke. You didn't pay for that, did you? Grease the wheels?"

"Absolutely not. I only gave your name."

His cell rang and his shoulders instantly bunched.

"Something wrong?" I asked.

He hedged. I stared fiercely. I wouldn't back down from my demand to know more about him. A few suspended seconds ensued. He ignored the call and said, "Yes. The furniture for the penthouse and third-floor suites was delivered to a five-story apartment in a new Monaco skyscraper."

"Monaco?" *Holy shit.* How could anyone make *that* sort of mistake?

"Apparently, the front desk staff there signed for it and the deliverymen unloaded, unboxed, and set everything up. So I can't exactly have it reshipped here."

"Well, if no one's really touched any of it—"

He shot me a dour look. "Ari."

"Right. Damaged goods even if in mint condition."

"Everything for the grand opening has to be *new*—never-before-slept-in beds, never-before-eaten-off-of plates. . . . You know what I'm saying. Even if they're just taken out of the packaging somewhere other than the Lux, they're used."

"Of course." I felt horrifically bad for him. Found myself asking, "Are these normal setbacks?"

As he stared at me for more endless moments, I wondered if *he'd* be the one to retreat. Close off this part of himself. But he didn't. And I admired him for it.

He said, "I've dealt with plenty of obstacles with my other two properties. These are just more . . . tedious."

"Versus?"

His jaw set. Amazingly, I *knew* that look. Within a month of meeting him, I could identify the dark expression that screamed his desire to sidestep my question.

"Dane." I refused to be sidestepped.

He regarded me awhile longer, then said, "Legitimate."

I didn't exactly follow. He caught on.

"The troubles I've seen in the past with bringing up a hotel were all predictable. Textbook, really, so I'd anticipated them and could easily combat them. What's happening at the Lux . . ." He shook his head. Angst rolled off his tongue as he said, "This is more targeted."

His eyes deepened in color, his forehead crinkled with dismay. I reeled from just one word.

*Targeted.*

As in, specific issues, an expensive prank of sorts, or . . . sabotage?

I didn't get the chance to ask and was stuck with my off-the-charts inquisitiveness where Dane was concerned. My father and Ethan joined us. I made the introductions.

"Thanks for inviting us," my dad said as he shook Dane's hand. My dad wore a guarded expression and his tone was a bit strained. He totally knew something was up. Did Dane and I exude our attraction to each other? Granted, he did stand a bit too close. Couldn't seem to take his eyes off me.

"It's nice to meet you," Dane said. "I'm a fan."

"You're not old enough to remember me."

"Sure I am," Dane insisted with a smile. "I started golfing when I was in high school. You were in The Open that year."

He'd retired not long after that.

"Well, it wasn't a win, unfortunately."

"But an incredible showing."

"Thank you."

Dane didn't overdo it. He said, "Shall we?"

We each grabbed a club from our cart and warmed up, me putting and the guys pitching and chipping. At ten o'clock, we hit the first tee. Dane and Ethan demonstrated impressive drives, though my dad edged them both out by several yards on the fairway. I smiled inwardly. Dane would naturally draw out my father's competitive side and it'd be fun to see him so into his game again.

I teed up last, from the women's ledge, and my ball landed not too far from Ethan's.

Dane grinned. "Excellent swing, Miss DeMille."

I smirked, since no one could see it as I sauntered past him. "Smart-ass," I whispered. "Call me Ari."

"That's not exactly what I want to call you, either."

*Baby* popped into my head. A thrill ran down my spine. "Don't you dare!" My cheeks flamed.

He chuckled. "Just keeping the ball in my court."

So he was on a power trip . . . because I'd been poking and prodding?

I joined my dad in our cart and we were off.

The tracks ran fast and I had to adjust my game a bit to accommodate the challenging fairways. It was a fabulous course. Although I was a bit disgruntled over the strokes I racked up, I said at one point, "This is almost on par with the Robert Trent Jones Golf Club on Lake Manassas."

"You've played his Virginia course?" Dane asked, looking duly impressed.

"Sure. My dad was always getting invitations to exclusive clubs. He took me most of the time."

"No wonder you're so good," Dane said as we walked toward the green.

"I should be better," I admitted. "I need to get out more."

"That shouldn't be a problem now. I do have five new courses for you to explore." He winked.

I couldn't help but think, once again, that perhaps meeting him really had been fated. I wasn't sure a supermodel would be excited by the prospect of playing award-winning links.

Dane chatted up my dad on the next several holes. Though I could tell my father was a bit suspicious, he couldn't seem to help but like Dane—that magnetic personality again—laughing heartily at some of his jokes and giving him pointers on his swing.

My good time, however, came to a screeching halt when I dropped in a bunker.

"Fuck me," I grumbled under my breath.

"I will again," Dane muttered from behind. "*Soon.*"

Heat rushed through my veins. "Don't you have a ball in the rough to go find?"

He gave me his sexy smile. Yeah, my game was shot to hell now. I nearly tripped over my own two feet at the way he looked at me, all possessive and brimming with lust.

While he went in search of his ball from his only slice, I caught up with my father and grabbed my sand wedge and putter. He'd overshot the green and left the cart to trudge over the hill. Ethan was the only one who'd neatly landed close to the pin.

Softly swearing a blue streak, I took three swings at my ball. It hit the wall of the trap each time.

Suddenly there were strong arms around me, large hands covering mine on the club. Dane's deliciously hunky body pressed against my backside.

"From this angle," he said as he put my arms in motion, "come down right behind the ball. Really slam into the sand." He guided me confidently through the practice swing.

Seriously? He expected me to concentrate on golfing when he was wrapped around me, fully surrounding me, his commanding presence seeping through my body?

*Not a chance.*

"This is the bane of my game," I told him. "I hate making a mess."

"Sometimes it's necessary in order to get what you want."

"Are we still talking about my swing?"

"No time to waste. Your dad is almost at his ball." Currently his back was to us.

"It's not exactly easy to focus on anything other than you when you've got your arms around me." And with all of those rigid muscles melding to my curves . . . Lord have mercy.

Dane's lips grazed my temple as he murmured, "Glad I get you all worked up."

"You don't know the half of it," I confessed.

A dark sound fell from his lips, arousing me further. "Probably a good thing, or I'm going to have trouble walking. Your father will slug me and I'll have to let him, because it's well deserved while I'm thinking about how tight you are and how wet you get for me."

I smiled through the lusty sigh swelling in my throat. "We'd better get out of the bunker or he'll catch us like this and slug you anyway."

"Do what I said," he instructed.

"So bossy."

With a snicker, he said, "You don't know the half of it."

"Funny."

"Do it." He continued to guide me, though he mostly allowed me to pull back, then sweep forward with the club, hammering the bowl of the trap with so much force, sand went flying—so, too, did my ball. Right up and out of the bunker and onto the green, rolling sweetly to the hole and plopping in.

"Holy shit!" I shrieked.

Dane's arms instantly dropped and he took a step back. My dad's head whipped around and he gave us a curious look.

My pulse raced from Dane and my great shot. "It's in the hole!" I yelled at my father. "No hand wedge this time!"

His gaze narrowed on me. Then shifted to Dane. I felt like a teenager busted for breaking curfew. And with a man four years older than me—one my father did not appear to approve of me hanging out with.

*More tension ensues.*

"Grab your ball," Dane said. "I'll rake."

While he tidied up, I retrieved my ball. Ethan and my dad putted theirs in. Dane chipped onto the green. His ball also rolled straight into the hole.

"Show-off," I teased quietly.

"I like to win, remember?"

Sure enough, he trumped my score and Ethan's. Came in several strokes away from my dad but that was to be expected when you played with someone of PGA caliber.

We left the clubs for the staff to clean and I hit the ladies' room inside the lobby of the gorgeous restaurant that featured a patio almost wrapped all the way around it and overlooked the lush lawns. Across the courtyard from the dining room was an outdoor cantina, where I met up with the men.

A Bloody Mary bar was set up and I loaded a small plate with bleu cheese–stuffed olives and shrimp-and-bacon skewers. I dropped a cilantro sprig into my cocktail.

A cool breeze swept through the covered patio. The huge double-sided fireplace was lit and tall heaters with glass pyramid-shaped tops had roaring flames inside them. Not exactly necessary but they added to the ambience.

We settled at a round stone table for four and talked about the course and the club. Although it was quite striking, it didn't compare to 10,000 Lux by any stretch. Even the Robert Trent Jones property couldn't compare to the Lux. It was in a class unto itself. As was its owner.

I tried not to hang on his every word, but that was near impossible. I tried not to stare too long at him. That, too, was near impossible.

He sat next to me and I could feel his heat, sense his presence, drown in all the tingly sensations he so easily evoked, without even touching me.

And that was another ragged-edge feeling, because I wanted his hands and mouth all over my body. Desperately. Like nothing I'd ever imagined.

I pressed my thighs together as desire hummed between my legs, taunting me. My napkin slipped from my lap and Dane and I reached for it at the same time, my shoulder bumping his rock-hard biceps.

"Sorry," I mumbled.

He collected the napkin and lightly placed it in my lap. My pulse spiked. I was sure my father caught the hitch in my breath. Ethan, too. *Damn it.* I willed some composure. But I was just so intensely aware of Dane. And my body was so responsive to him that his nearness sent me into sensory overload.

Lust quickly vanished, however, when I caught sight of Mikaela Madsen strolling casually across the courtyard. Heading in our direction. My spirits plummeted with every step she took toward the busy cantina. Naturally, she'd be a member at this exclusive club.

She reached our table and the men stood as Dane made introductions. I reluctantly followed suit.

She was gracious, dripping saccharine as she greeted Ethan and Dane—her hand on his arm, as seemed to be her custom. As though she had some sort of claim over him.

*Did she?*

Eventually, she turned fluttering eyelashes on my father and damn it all to hell, she knew exactly who he was. And he didn't mind in the least the way she fawned over him.

When her attention finally fell on me, she said, "I've seen you with Dane—at Tlaquepaque and then at the Delfino's last night."

"Yes. Meghan is a former client. And a friend."

"She's very sweet. We play tennis together on occasion."

"Are you joining us for a drink?" Ethan asked.

"I'd love to, but Brizio is already warming up. We tee off in a few minutes. I just stopped by to say hello. And Mr. DeMille, I must say, it's quite an honor to meet you in person."

I resisted the urge to roll my eyes.

To me, she said, "And a pleasure to meet you as well, Airy."

"Ari," I corrected.

"Right. Sorry. Have a great day, everyone!" She gave Ethan and Dane air kisses and then swept off toward the course.

I fought the urge to grind my teeth. Luckily, my father and I had finished our Bloody Marys. I was ready to be on our way, needing a chance to regroup. The intertwining of my dad and Dane—and Mikaela Madsen?—in my life was a complicated predicament. One I needed to untangle as quickly as possible.

A server came by and my dad asked for the check, pulling out his credit card.

"I'd like everything on my account, please," Dane said to the pretty brunette who had as much trouble tearing her gaze from him as I did.

"Of course, Mr. Bax."

To my father, he added, "Please, allow me. It's not every day I get to golf with someone of your skill."

"Thanks, Bax," Ethan lamented, albeit factiously.

My dad graciously shook hands with the two men, thanking them for the outing. He invited them for a complimentary round at his club and they both agreed they'd take him up on his offer.

My dad said, "I'll bring the SUV around and get our bags."

I handed over the keys. Ethan told Dane he'd have the valet fetch his Mercedes and their clubs. He left with my father.

"You two valet-park here?" I asked Dane.

"Of course." He leaned in close and said, "See, that didn't go so badly."

"My father is onto us. He'll grill me the entire drive home."

"Why? Because I couldn't help watching you walk the fairways?" Desire tinged his emerald eyes. "You have the perfect sway to your hips. Feminine. Sexy. Tempting."

"You just love keeping that ball in your court, don't you?"

The corner of his mouth lifted. Devilishly. "Are you wet for me right now?"

I fought the blush. To no avail. "Yes."

"Good." He took my hand. I gave a slight tug but he didn't let go.

Hemming and hawing was a hard habit to break. He tilted his head to the side and scowled.

I heaved an exasperated sigh. "You don't seem to get that *this*"—I motioned to our linked hands—"is a big deal for me. You're moving too fast."

"What are you so worried about?"

"Everything."

"I'm not going to hurt you," he insisted.

"You can't make that promise. Shit happens." I shrugged, though this was no nonchalant matter. "There's nothing you can do about it. When it's over, it's over. And someone always gets hurt when the end comes."

His expression darkened. "I asked you last night if you'd been hurt. I'd meant physically, but now I'm asking about emotionally."

"I told you no—that applies to both. Emotionally, I've never allowed myself to be in a vulnerable position."

Until now.

Because I clearly couldn't control what transpired between us. He'd proven that when he'd tied my hands and kissed me until I'd begged him for more. Until I'd absolutely had to touch him or die.

He led me out of the cantina and across the courtyard. He stalked, I tried to keep up. When we were almost at the archways of the entrance, I pulled my hand from his. He drew up short and glared at me.

"I don't care if he knows," he said of my father.

"I do."

His jaw clenched.

"Dane," I said, hearing the compelling plea in my voice. "I don't know what I'm doing. I don't know what's really going on with us, except that I can't seem to stop it or slow it down. I'm constantly thinking about you."

I winced at that particular confession.

His jaw loosened and his bunched shoulders relaxed. "I don't have a problem with that."

"What *do* you have a problem with?"

"This isn't exactly familiar territory for me, either, Ari. But I don't know how to hold back when there's something I want. I go after it."

"Regardless of consequences?" Not that I really thought he'd suffer repercussions from pursuing me. Men like Dane Bax could contain their degree of *involvement*; not fall in love; fuck without turning it into anything too personal. He was powerful and very much in control of his environment. I'd witnessed this, experienced it enough with him to state it as fact.

I faced the firing squad alone. Not exactly a comforting thought.

He said, "I evaluate the risks. But this is something I'm committing to despite whatever dangers you think it poses to you. This is inescapable, Ari. Even you have to admit that."

I took a deep breath. Let it out slowly. Why did I have the feeling that if I'd not sought out Sean, Kyle, and the others in the bar that day I'd still have found myself in this predicament with Dane? Fate was a crazy thing, after all.

"My father's waiting," I said as an excuse to step away from the flame and try to get a better handle on the situation.

"You can't pretend this isn't happening," Dane warned.

"I know. It's just—"

"I'm staying in Scottsdale tonight. At the Four Seasons. I bought a table at a fund-raising gala and I'm in a charity golf tournament tomorrow. So you get the weekend. Rest up." He stared solidly for a few moments, then gestured for me to precede him to the archways.

I mentally stammered over the *rest up* portion of his little speech.

We parted ways in the drive and I endured my father stealing glances at me until we reached I-17 and he blurted, "Something going on that I should know about?"

My pulse still raced from Dane and his words. Now I had apprehension to contend with because I didn't lie to my dad. Sure, I bent the truth on occasion when it was for his own good. Just like every other person on the planet. But this . . . Wow. What to say?

"I suppose we have a little flirtation going on." I grimaced. That was much more than a bit of bending. I'd had a searing orgasm last night just from his large body wedged between my parted legs and his mouth on my neck.

"He's your boss, Ari," my dad said in a stern, fatherly tone. "And older than you."

"By only four years, Dad. Not a big deal at my age."

"He's just not—"

"In my tax bracket? I'm well aware of that. But it's not the class difference that's the pro—"

My mouth snapped shut.

My dad gave me the full-on parental disapproval now. "I don't like where this is headed, Ari."

"Dad, you had a good time today. You enjoyed his company. Ethan's, too. Dane respects your talent and your opinion; that has nothing to do with me. He likely would have sought you out about his courses whether we'd met or not. You're a resident expert in Sedona. And for the record, we sort of got to know each other before he even learned I'd applied at 10,000 Lux and way before he offered me the job."

*Okay, TMI?*

My dad grunted despondently. "I don't want to know about this, do I?"

"Don't get so worked up. I have conflicting feelings. And he's perfectly aware of my . . . issues."

My father settled back in his seat and pondered this for a while. We were nearly to the turnoff to Sedona when he said, "It always has bothered me that you don't date."

That almost broke my heart. "Dad."

"I know it's because of your mother and me. Your grandparents. All the screaming. I never wanted you to witness any of it, Ari."

I'd suffered a peculiar side effect to all the volatile arguments. To this day I couldn't be in the same room with people screaming at each other or around sharp disagreements. Even on TV, when voices escalated I changed the channel.

Having been my own shrink for my instabilities, I'd realized that surrounding myself with gushing brides and grooms, vibrant flowers, gorgeous decorations, new beginnings, and all that had been the perfect escape. Nothing dark and haunting about weddings.

Which made it incredibly disconcerting to be hooked on a dark, foreboding man.

Didn't that go against every conviction I had?

My silence prompted my dad to ask, "Something wrong over there?"

"Just concentrating on driving," I said.

A much safer topic than Dane.

Though I had another shocker waiting for me right around the corner . . .

# chapter 11

Sunday morning at the driving range was followed by brunch at the golf club. My dad did that fatherly speculative-gazing thing from time to time but didn't bring up what he suspected might or might not be going on between me and Dane.

Relieved to have endured a few hours unscathed, I returned to my townhome to shower and change into jeans. I texted Grace to ask whether or not she was working. Since she was, I told her I'd stop in at the bar later in the evening.

In the meantime, I had résumés to look at for the staff I needed to hire. While in the midst of that, there was a knock on my door.

I didn't get many vistors, so I made a very quick guess as to who it might be—and leapt up from the kitchen table, rushing to the small foyer.

Yanking open the door, I said, "I thought you were at the Four Sea—"

My mouth snapped shut.

On the other side of the threshold stood Kathryn DeMille. My

mother. As though I'd summoned her evil presence just by thinking of her yesterday. Though she'd been texting me of late, so
maybe this face-off was destined to be. I hadn't texted her back,
after all.

"Darling," she said as she swept into the entryway, all but brushing me aside with the witchy wave of her manicured and bejeweled hand. "You've had me worried sick."

"Oh?" I found that *very* hard to believe.

"Well, I haven't heard from you in so long, darling," she said in
her cultured tone that, at the moment, held the hint of a pout. "I
was just so certain something horrible had happened to you that I
had to drive *all* the way up here to see for myself that you're still
alive."

My gaze narrowed. "How'd you find me? You've never been to
my house before." Which left me with a sinking feeling in my gut.
This would not be a pleasant visit.

"I had your address from the last birthday card you sent, along
with the Dillard's gift certificate. I still have it in my wallet if you'd
like to use it."

"I bought that for you, Mother." I resisted the urge to grind my
teeth. "Something wrong with Dillard's?"

"Well, it's not Nordstrom, darling."

I seethed inwardly. Showing any sort of outward emotion in my
mother's presence was futile. She only saw what she wanted to see.

So I skipped over it and asked, "To what do I owe the honor?"
My tone held a biting edge that I couldn't disguise. Perhaps it was
her air of superiority that grated on my nerves, in addition to the
way she'd treated both my dad and me.

My mother was a petite brunette with the right hair, the perfect pallor, the tiny frame suitable for all upscale fashions, and the
richest fragrance to make one think she dipped herself in gold every
morning. Her crocodile leather handbag—Prada would be my
guess—dangled from her dainty forearm as she pointed a finger at

me and said, "It's been much too long, Aria Lynne. You never come visit me."

She always used my full name. As though that made us royalty or something. She'd truly missed her calling as a Southern belle or privileged debutante. I could see her delivering the most polished curtsey imaginable and then setting an entire room aglow with her UV-ray smile. Serious overkill on the bleach, but it was all part of the Kathryn DeMille Big Top circus.

"I've been a bit busy, Mother. Sorry."

She surveyed my small space—the foyer that opened into a kitchen and the living room beyond. The corner of her mouth twitched, but of course she wouldn't give in to a frown for fear she'd wrinkle.

Setting her large tote on my table, she extracted two items. The first was today's *Arizona Republic*, the Phoenix paper. It was already opened and folded over to reveal pictures from Friday night's extravaganza at the Delfino estate.

"I had no idea you kept such prestigious company these days," she cooed.

In the center of the page was a photo of me with a grinning Kyle, Meghan, and Sean. I bit back a grunt of *oh, shit, please don't let Dane see this*. But he would. Seeing me with Kyle would create a bit of friction. No need to delude myself.

"I planned Meghan Delfino's wedding," I told my mother.

"And you're now BFFs? Darling, that's *fab-ulous!*" She drew out the last word as though I'd miraculously procured the Hope Diamond.

"Just friends," I mumbled as I moved past her. "Do you want some water? There's no Evian, just tap, but—"

"You really should be more prepared for guests, Aria Lynne."

"I don't get many, Mother. Why are you here?" And why did I feel as though a million tiny spiders had suddenly crawled under my skin?

She set out the other item she'd brought with her—another bridal magazine. "There's an article in here about all the preparations you made for the Delfinos. So impressive." Her sculpted brows would have arched for emphasis if they weren't already at the perfectly elevated degree.

The creepy sensation grew. My mother was up to something. No doubt about it. I decided to cut to the chase.

"Again, is there a specific reason you're here?" I asked.

"Naturally, I've wanted to come see you. I've had so much on my plate, though." She launched into the luncheons with the Junior League and Soroptimist and so on and so forth. There were fund-raising galas she simply *had* to attend—not volunteer for, mind you, but purchase an expensive seat in order to be "seen."

I halfheartedly listened, still trying to pinpoint what it was she truly wanted from me. A good five minutes later, I started to piece it all together.

"Well, you of all people know how important it is to be appropriately attired for all of these functions, and to wear the same dress is absolutely *not* an option. Darling," she said, "I'm sure that my attendance does so much good for the community but it's drained my finances completely."

"You have alimony from Dad. And it's never been paltry," I reminded her. I'd suffered the consequences of the payments he made. She had a lovely condo in Scottsdale. We'd lived in a run-down duplex in a not-so-great part of Phoenix.

"Times change, Aria Lynne," she said in a dismissive tone. "Inflation and all that. I literally cannot be expected to—"

"Whoa, wait." I raised a hand to cut her off. "Are you here for money?"

She didn't even bother looking taken aback. Rather, she appeared indignant as she said, "I can't be expected to live in squalor."

"Squalor?" I nearly spat out the word. "Seriously, Mother?"

She moved past me and took the five-second tour of my living room. Staring out at the golf course, she said with disdain, "You just can't resist the fairways. Like your father."

"You didn't come here to talk about golf. What's going on? Tell me straight, because you don't make house calls out of the kindness of your heart."

Flashing me a stern expression I figured was meant to be maternal, though it came out more snide because I was onto her, she told me, "It's extremely expensive to maintain my lifestyle."

"So find a different lifestyle," I snapped as thoughts of walking through seedy neighborhoods to get to school and having no lights from time to time—sometimes no water—came rushing back to me. All the while, my mother had enjoyed her posh existence because of my father's money.

"Do not be disrespectable, Aria Lynne."

"Okay, so find a new husband. One who can afford you."

She crossed her arms over her surgically enhanced chest, as she was prone to do when she wanted to tell me to watch my mouth. Maybe it was because I was older and disassociated from her that she didn't press this time.

"Men don't want women in their forties," she informed me. "They want girls your age. A little tidbit you should tuck away."

"Then I don't know what to tell you."

She gave me a contemplative look, studying me closely, which set me on edge. Finally, she said, "I just need a little supplement, Aria Lynne. Considering that wedding you recently pulled off, I wouldn't think it'd be asking too much to help out your own mother. The woman who gave birth to you. If you understood the expense of Botox, chemical peels, eye lifts . . ." Her sudden disgruntlement actually brought out a few creases. I'd never seen her go that far.

A part of me wanted to assure her she had nothing to worry about—my mother was a very beautiful woman. But I'd witnessed this ploy before. It started out all *woe is me* and morphed into Bitchville in the blink of an eye.

I knew to tread lightly. "I really can't help you, Mother. Money's been tight for me as well."

She had the audacity to scoff. "Please, you don't attract the sort of media attention you've been receiving without the money to back it up."

I didn't feed into her theory. That didn't stop her from expounding on it.

Dropping her arms, she gave me the real-deal Kathryn De-Mille. "Do you know that I never once mentioned the names of the men I had affairs with while your father was on his tours?"

Unease flitted through me. "Meaning what, exactly?"

"Of course, I didn't want to implicate anyone. They'd all been contenders in their time. Some more successful than others . . ." She slowly circled my living room, taking in the minuscule space as though to silently point out what a disappointment my town-home was—thereby emphasizing the opinion that I wasn't on par with the men she'd slept with or the women she associated with. Like I fell short in her eyes the way my dad did.

My blood boiled. I didn't mind that she judged me. But to be cruel toward my father when he'd been so in love with her, so supportive. And so devastated when he'd learned the truth about her . . . That irked the hell out of me.

"What does your past have to do with your present?" I asked, not sure I wanted to hear what she had to say.

"Simply that I never took the opportunity to share with the world some very burning questions about breakups in the pro golf community right around the time—"

"Oh, you have got to be kidding." I glared at her, incredulous. "You feel it's some sort of civic duty to set the tawdry record straight twenty-one or -two years after the fact?" The cheating had started before I was in kindergarten.

Not the least bit contrite, she said, "You don't seem to understand the value of mainstream media, Aria Lynne. It's all the rage to divulge secrets after the fact, as you put it. Look at Bobbi Brown's book on all the rock stars and A-list actors she had sex with—I'm sure she made a lot of money with her tell-all."

My stomach roiled. "Are you saying . . . You'd go public for cash? Knowing you'd crush Dad all over again?"

*How on earth was I even related to this woman?*

"I have a synopsis written. And I've already picked several agents to send the proposal to." She gave me a reflective look I knew was feigned. "I just need a working title."

"Oh, my God." I felt sick. "You can't do that to Dad. To me. Moth—"

"I just need a little money, darling," she said. "It'll be nothing to you, with all your grand success of late."

I hated every word she said. Hated that I asked, "How much?" My insides twisted in knots, but all I wanted was to get rid of her. If only I could afford it.

Her expression turning shrewd, she said, "Five thousand isn't too much for your own mother."

I pulled in a deep breath. *Shit.* Five grand would drain half of my savings account. I had rent and a car payment. But I quickly deduced that I'd get my first paycheck from 10,000 Lux before they were due.

So I stalked into my pseudo-office and opened the drawer of my desk. I collected my checkbook, scribbled out the amount she wanted. Tore the paper loose. Then I marched into the living room and handed it over.

"Don't come back," I said, my heart breaking yet again. Because for just the briefest of moments, when she'd first arrived, I'd held the tiniest bit of hope that she'd been here to celebrate my business ventures. To say she was proud to see me in magazines and newspapers. And to actually *be* a mom.

I should have known better the second I'd seen her perfectly made-up face.

Sure enough, the *pity me* facade she'd flaunted faded and I saw nothing but triumph. Which not only worried me but also made the tears trickle as she whirled around and disappeared out the door without so much as a thank-you or a good-bye.

Dread mixed with my dismay. The way she'd breezed out of here. I couldn't help but wonder if this was just the beginning of her torment.

I survived the weekend. That was the best summation I could provide.

Unfortunately, I'd spent two nights restlessly missing Dane and once again wondering if he was spending *his* nights alone.

He didn't call or text, and I had a very good sense of what that was all about. He was forcing my hand. It was a *commit along with me or walk away* kind of thing, I suspected. Which made me put serious thought into what I might actually be committing to and how fucked up I could be in the end.

The reality of the situation, however, was that every torturous minute that passed without him proved I'd be screwed either way. I couldn't stand not being with him. Especially knowing what he was willing to give in return by way of the hottest sex I'd ever known.

Thankfully, I had a ton of work on Monday that required my full attention. I met with Patricia to discuss all of the event staff applications Dane had approved for the posted positions.

We were in the middle of discussing interviewing schedules when I caught sight of him. He strutted toward us as we sat at one of the round glass-topped and black wrought-iron tables in the courtyard. His purposeful stride gave me pause.

Patricia noticed she'd lost me and stopped mid-sentence. Dane reached us and he politely asked if she'd mind giving us a few minutes alone.

I gnawed my lower lip in consternation.

"Certainly, Mr. Bax. I'm due for a refill, anyway." She lifted her cappuccino mug from the table and gestured toward mine. "Ready for another?"

"No, thanks," I said. "I'm good." I didn't need anything else making me jittery. Dane's stern expression did that all on its own. Not to mention, he looked hotter than hell in a dark-gray suit with a crisp white shirt, unbuttoned at the neck to reveal that pulsating spot at the base of his throat I wanted to press my lips to—and the strong angles of his collarbone that I wanted to run my tongue along.

My fingers twitched. If I could just unbutton the rest of the shirt flap and splay my hands over his hard pecs, the way I'd done Friday night . . .

Sliding into the chair across from me, he set a slim black leather folio on the glass and pushed it my way. "Did you really think you were going to slip this by me?"

The challenge in his voice was tinged with displeasure.

"I'm not sure what you're talking about."

His brow jerked.

Had he somehow found out my mother's devious plot—and that I'd attempted to pay her off with a measly five grand? Measly by her and Dane's standards, because it was a hell of a lot of money to me.

I tried to breathe. How could he possibly have learned of that? And why would he care, anyway?

I flipped open the folder and stared at the piece of paper inside. Kyle's résumé.

*Oh, boy.* This might be worse.

"He's really very talented," I said in Kyle's—and my—defense. "I've seen his portfolio. When we were at the Delfinos' house. He showed me the Web version on his phone."

"He's not working here, Ari." Dane's tone was flat and decisive. "You think I don't know his intentions?"

"Dane. I told him to apply. It wasn't even his idea. It was mine."

Dane stared at me as though I'd grown a third eye. "Are you kidding me?"

"No." I braced myself for his angst. "It's not a big deal. He and I are not . . . anything. Just friends, like I keep saying. So it'd be okay. And, let's face it, you need people who are gifted and trust-worthy."

Sitting back in his chair and crossing his arms over his massive chest, he speared me with a firm look. "How am I supposed to consider him trustworthy when every time I turn my back he's coming on to you? What makes you think I'll tolerate that after the arrangement *we* made?"

That jealousy bit again. It did the craziest things to me. I fought the smile, because it would only piss him off, I was sure. "You don't have to trust him. You have to trust *me*."

His expression turned ever more somber.

I sighed. "Personally, I think he's a good guy. And he wants the job. As it relates to me . . ." I rested my forearms on the table and leaned toward Dane. In a soft voice, I said, "You can't honestly think, for one single second, that Kyle poses any sort of threat."

He didn't appear convinced. "Maybe you don't realize that heads snap in your direction when you walk into a room. I see it."

"You really notice stuff like that?"

"When it comes to you," he said, his gaze deep and intent, "yes."

I pulled in a steadying breath.

"Sharing you isn't a possibility."

"You don't have to share me," I assured him. "You wanted exclusivity. I'm not my mother. I'm not a cheater. But . . ."

Dare I ask the question practically burning a hole in my head?

He eyed me speculatively. "But what?"

I swallowed hard. I risked pissing him off further, but I just had to know. "You didn't call me all weekend. If you had a table at the fund-raiser that likely means you had a . . . a date. I want the same terms from you that you demand of me—mutual exclusivity."

God, that sounded so small and petty. Yet, it wasn't. Not when it came to Dane. The mere thought of another woman on his arm, even just for social appearances, shredded me. I didn't even want him to notice other women, let alone be with one.

Which meant it took all the willpower I possessed not to bring up Mikaela—and ask if she'd been at the fund-raiser as well.

In a tight voice, he said, "I've made my intentions *very* clear. I gave you some space this weekend. Under no circumstances should that ever be misconstrued as me being with another woman. Ever."

His green gaze bored into me and my pulse jumped.

"It was strictly business," Dane added, "with associates. No date."

"Oh." I inhaled deeply. "Okay." I was extremely unnerved to discover *I* had a jealous streak. There'd never been any cause for it before. Yet with Dane I was filled with anxiety just thinking of the number of batting eyelashes that came his way.

"Ari," he said, snagging my attention. "That is absolutely the last thing you have to worry about."

Thank God, because I already had a lengthy list of worries.

"Fine. But that goes for you, too. Especially where Kyle is concerned."

"About that—"

"Hey," I said with a somewhat imploring look. "What happened to giving me anything I wanted?"

His eyes smoldered. "You're going to owe me for this one." Then he got to his feet and sauntered off.

Leaving me dying of curiosity to know what *that* meant.


"More catalogs for you, Miss DeMille."

"Ari is fine, Jason. And thank you."

The mail clerk hefted a stack of high-end catalogs I'd ordered off the Internet that contained holiday and other decorations. I'd decided that in addition to jumping on hiring staff, I needed to quickly formulate a plan for all the Christmas and event accessories. Since the pre-launch activities occurred prior to New Year's Eve, around Christmastime, and we'd no doubt leave up the decorations into the first week of January at least—it was an easy theme with which to work. But I'd need lots of decorations and, knowing it'd take some time to wade through all of the offerings, *sooner rather than later* was my current motto.

Jason left me and I started scouring the pages, ripping them out whenever something caught my eye. Several hours passed and my conference table was covered with images. I hadn't even made it all the way through my stack.

I glanced at the wall behind me, eyeing the space.

"Assessing pictures to hang?"

My head whipped around. Dane stood just inside my office, closing the door behind him. Since it had an automatic lock, excitement gripped me. It was after seven and I suspected most everyone on the floor had gone home.

Trying not to sound all breathy and awestruck at the sight of him, I said, "I was just thinking that I need corkboard on the wall so I can hang some of these decoration ideas. I need them staring me in the face to help spark my creativity."

"I'll take care of it," he said.

"I'm sure you have more important things to do."

"At the moment, yes." He crossed to the tall windows and pulled the drapes. The room immediately dimmed, since the chandelier was the only light I had on and it was at a low setting.

I didn't have time to process all the electric undercurrents running rampant at his suggestive gaze. He popped the buttons on his suit jacket and I just about incinerated at his feet.

Moving closer, he reached for my hand and pulled me to him.

"We really shouldn't at the office," I weakly protested.

"You don't leave me many options when you work late."

"I have a lot to do."

"Mm, so do I." His eyes dropped to my mouth. "Starting here." His warm lips brushed over mine.

Our lips tangled. Slowly. Seductively. Had it been anyone else guiding me in this direction, I would have said it was pointless to try to engage me in this manner.

But I wasn't dealing with just *anyone*.

Dane knew how to draw me in, completely and provocatively. So that I eased toward him, wanting more. So that I responded by curling my fingers around his biceps, hating that his suit jacket kept me from getting a better grip on him.

His tongue swept over my bottom lip and a moan lodged in my throat. He took that as encouragement and his tongue slipped inside, twisting and teasing. His arms slid around my waist and he hauled me up against his solid chest and abs.

The kiss went on and on. Becoming more seductive. More searing. More powerful.

In the hazy part of my mind, I finally understood why I'd never gotten seriously involved with anyone. No one had ever affected me like this. No one had *ever* kissed me like this. So that my hold on him tightened and I met the changing inclination of his head, testing all the different angles, not breaking the intimate contact. So that I tasted him, breathed him in, experienced all the passionate nuances of a scorching kiss that pushed everything from my mind except the excitement coursing through my veins and the feel of Dane responding so vehemently, so skillfully, that I could think of nothing but him.

I didn't even hesitate, didn't balk, when he led me to the sofa, still kissing me deeply. The backs of my legs bumped the couch and we eased down onto the plump cushion. I rested against the pile of pillows in the corner, the satin quilt beneath me. His fingers grazed my bare thigh, at the hem of my skirt.

The incessant throbbing within me began again. I instinctively clenched my legs together in hopes of staving it off, to somehow quell or slow the need building much too quickly.

He broke our kiss and against my lips simply muttered, "Ari."

My eyelids fluttered open. His gaze was fixed on me. Fiery and demanding.

"Don't stop me."

My chest rose and fell in sharp, staccato beats that matched my heart. My pulse jumped at pressure points that made me insanely aware of how much I wanted him, how much I *didn't* want to stop him.

But my legs remained pressed together.

He kissed me again and it sizzled. We sizzled. I got ridiculously caught up in the heat of the moment, swept away by the sort of sexual chemistry that made sensible women do irrational things. Like shove a man's suit jacket over his shoulders and down his arms as he continued to do sinful things with his tongue. Like fumble hopelessly with the buttons on his shirt, fingers trembling because I wanted him so much that he had to help.

As the material hung open, I ran my hands all over his hard chest, his cut abs, even reaching around to his back and splaying my palms over muscles that flexed beneath my touch.

He was so hot, so beautifully chiseled. I wanted to strip him bare and crawl all over him, rubbing myself against him, feeling his skin on mine.

He kept kissing me as though he couldn't get enough of me. The thought sent a thrill down my spine.

With deft fingers he undid my blouse and then palmed my breasts through the white lace of my bra. His thumbs swept over my pebbled nipples, puckering them even more, making them tingle.

Another moan welled in my throat. He dragged his mouth from mine and his lips skimmed over my jaw and down my neck, nipping along the way.

I was instantly restless and in desperate need of him. "Dane," I pleaded.

His head dipped farther and his tongue flicked over my nipple, the lace creating extra friction.

"Oh, God." My head fell back, my eyes closed as he lavished my breasts with fluttering licks, then deep suckling. I writhed beneath him, drowning in the smell of him, the feel of him. Losing myself in the erotic sensations burning through me.

He squeezed my breasts roughly, conveying urgency, impatience. A sharp moan fell from my lips. My fingers plowed through his messy hair. I felt his erection against my leg and I knew this wasn't going to be slow and leisurely. It would be fevered and intense, like Friday night.

"You have a sensational body. I want to see all of it. All of you."

He whisked off my blouse and bra. Shoved my skirt down my hips as I raised them. He tossed my clothes aside. I was sprawled on the gold satin quilt in nothing more than a white lace thong and high heels. Cool air blew over the newly exposed flesh and it was a welcome relief, because I was on fire. His fingers trailed along my skin, over my quivering belly, to the apex of my legs. Enticing me, exciting me.

His gaze held mine. His fingers skimmed over the lace.

"Dane." I couldn't seem to think beyond him. Beyond my need for him.

He stared at me in his smoldering way as I tried to catch my breath. His jaw clenched. I was held prisoner by his intensity, by the lust that rolled off him in waves.

And then he started stroking. A featherlight touch.

Our eyes remained locked as his fingertips gently massaged my folds, heightening the dull ache inside me. He pressed a little firmer, stroked a little faster. His lips tangled with mine again. Sexy little kisses that taunted the senses.

My other hand shifted from his back and pressed to the side of his neck, keeping his head bent, keeping him kissing me.

His fingers slipped behind my panties and he caressed masterfully. The skin-on-skin contact made my hips jerk. I was hypersensitive to his touch, so charged it was a wonder I didn't vibrate from head to toe.

He rubbed my clit with just the right amount of pressure, gradually picking up the pace to match my choppy breaths.

My nipples tightened, begging for his attention again. My hips rolled of their own accord, silently demanding more. Lusty whimpers fell from my lips.

His mouth glided over my chin and down my throat, kissing, biting.

"You're so wet for me," he murmured.

"Yes."

He eased a finger inside my pussy.

Lightning seemed to zap my core.

"So tight," he said in a strained voice that was sexy as hell. He worked in a second finger and pumped quickly, deeply.

My heavy lids fluttered closed once more. The heel of his hand massaged my clit as his fingers stroked almost forcefully. As though he *needed* to get me off. I felt his gaze on me as ecstasy crept around the periphery, enveloping me in its sultry embrace. I knew he watched me as my throaty moans turned erratic while he increased the sensual rhythm, pushing me right to the edge.

"Come for me," he said, his tone low and husky.

"Yes. Oh, God, yes." The tension mounted. A vibrant, blazing sensation swelled to a boiling point. Then erupted. "Dane!" I cried out as the orgasm flashed through me, powerful and pulsating. "Oh, Christ!" Everything ignited within me. He kept stroking as my inner walls contracted around his fingers, clenching and releasing while I rode out the climax.

"Oh, shit. Dane." I really didn't have a clever thought in my brain—it was filled with him. "Fuck me. *Please*. Now." I couldn't stand another second of not having him inside me. I had to feel him filling and stretching me. Needed him to pump into me and make me come again.

He slipped away and knelt on the floor. His fingers hooked in the thin strands of my thong and he tugged. I lifted my hips so he could drag the material down to my ankles. He freed me of the panties and they went the way of the rest of my outfit.

A flicker of wicked intent in his emerald eyes made my clit tingle. His head lowered and he nipped at my inner thigh. The tingle deepened, becoming a dark, greedy sensation.

Anticipation built as Dane's mouth moved closer to the apex of my legs. He was about to do to me something no other man had ever done—and I wanted it. Badly.

Yet apprehension slid through my veins. "Dane—"

He cut me off with a look full of sexual promise.

But I managed to tell him, "Another something I've never done before."

His gaze narrowed. "Too personal? Too intimate?"

I nodded. Okay, so maybe I didn't really need to explain anything to him. Maybe he just knew.

He went back to his expert seduction, his tongue swirling over my flesh, inching closer to the spot that ached for him. It was perverse of him to toy with me like this . . . but I loved every tortuous second of it.

He glanced up, spearing me with a heated expression as he issued a reminder. "*Nothing* off-limits, Ari."

I was naked on the sofa in my office, my legs spread wide. One foot was on the floor, the other on the cushion, my fingers wrapped around the heel so that I didn't poke or rip the seat.

As I internally searched for acceptance of this risky endeavor, this personal compromise, his cell buzzed. I started. Yet again, the outside world had ceased to exist.

Dane glanced over his shoulder at his jacket, strewn across the coffee table. Listened a moment. Then returned his attention to me.

"Don't you need to get that?"

"Not when I'm between your legs," he said.

I sighed. The man was all kinds of sexy.

The phone quieted.

"Now," he said, "do you want me to make you come several more times, or not?"

I sucked in a breath. He was so demanding. And so impossible to deny.

I opened my mouth to speak. His cell started up again. Only this time, it was an actual ring. A frantic tempo that practically screamed, *Don't ignore me!*

"Fuck," Dane hissed. "This one I have to take."

He didn't move away, though. Instead, he took my hand not holding onto the shoe and kissed the inside of my wrist. My pulse soared.

Against the sensitive flesh, he whispered, "I want you to touch yourself. I want to watch."

"What?" I choked out.

"You heard me." He placed my hand on my glistening mound and added, "Do it." His eyes lifted to my face. "But don't come. I'll get you off when I'm ready."

"Dane—" Christ, I could barely breathe.

"Do it. Keep me hard."

# chapter 12

He stood in a fluid motion and snatched his jacket from the table, extracting the iPhone.

I wasn't sure what to do. Here was my chance for a neat, clean escape. I could make one of my hasty retreats, gain a little space to process this latest request. Both of them, actually, because I still reeled when it came to the *nothing off-limits* demand.

I could collect my panties and slip out. Except that he snatched those, too, and rubbed the damp crotch between his finger and thumb, giving me a devilish look.

With his other thumb, he connected the angry-ring call.

I couldn't quite get my body moving—to leave even without my thong. I was so tightly wound with anticipation over what he intended to do. And the fact that I wanted him, despite the intensity factor that alarmed me.

In an abrupt tone, he said into the phone, "What is it?" He listened. While his gaze was riveted on me. A dark brow jerked upward in silent challenge.

I had no idea what possessed me—perhaps the fact that he was so magnificently gorgeous, his shirt hanging open to reveal all those sculpted muscles, and the fact that I wanted him.

I started to rub my clit with the pads of two fingers. A slow, circular motion.

His eyes blazed as he stared. And continued listening to his caller. Even when he spoke again, his attention remained focused on what I was doing.

"No, that's not what I think. This is a problem. No, I don't want you to do anything just yet. I need to assess it further."

He was quiet a few moments. Still watching. I dipped a finger into my pussy and stroked slowly. The fact that I was doing something like this, which went against convictions I'd clung to for so long and threatened every wall I'd built, was a bit terrifying. But I didn't want to stop. Couldn't stop. Because he was enthralled by it—by *me*—and was so hard his cock strained against the fly of his dress pants, spiking my arousal and my boldness.

He held my panties to his nose and inhaled deeply. Liquid fire roared through my veins.

I released the heel of my shoe and cupped my breast, squeezing as roughly as he had. Dane let out a low, sexy grunt. I rolled my nipple between my finger and thumb as I worked a second finger into my pussy and pumped a bit faster. Throaty pants escaped my lips. I swear I could come just from him staring, his jaw working rigorously, his eyes deepening in color.

To his caller, he said in a curt voice, "Don't do anything right now. Wait for me to contact you." He hit the disconnect button and dropped the iPhone and my thong onto the mound his jacket created. Then he knelt between my parted thighs, his gaze on my hand as I pleasured myself. He eased in two fingers, along with mine, filling the tight canal.

"Dane." My hips bucked as I accepted the added pressure, the additional width that felt so amazing.

I continued tugging on my nipple, the prickly sensation mingling with the sizzle between my legs and deep in my core.

Dane's free hand slid behind mine as I kept time with his quick stroking. His thumb rubbed my clit with lightning speed. He leaned forward and his mouth captured my other nipple. He suckled hard, then flicked his tongue over the aching tip. I couldn't quite keep up with all the high-voltage zings that pushed me so, so close to another powerful orgasm.

"Dane," I repeated. My hips gyrated; my head fell back on the pillows. "Christ. That is unbelievably good. I'm—oh, God—I'm—"

Cogent thought fled. Heat and vibrancy collided and exploded. I screamed his name as I reached a phenomenal peak.

"Holy shit!" I cried out. It was so good. *Too* good. The pulsing reverberated deep, prolonging the release.

"Oh, fuck," he groaned. "You're driving me crazy." He withdrew his fingers and brushed away my hand. While I still reeled from the scorching climax, his mouth covered me. His lips swept along my pussy lips, and then his tongue fluttered over that highly sensitive knot of nerves.

I let out a breathy moan. I'd never felt anything so exquisite. He went at it with gusto, teasing my clit with the tip of his tongue before tugging gently on my slick folds with his mouth, then returning to the flicking and suckling that made me want to cry from the pleasure he evoked. I was still in the throes of one orgasm and felt another one coming on.

My body trembled and my sharp whimpers filled the cavernous room.

"That's it," he whispered against my clit. "You're dripping wet. And you taste so damn good."

I flushed.

His tongue swirled around my opening, pressing in.

"Oh, God, Dane." My hands fisted around the satin material of the quilt. "Christ. I'm going to come again."

"Yes," he all but growled. "Come for me, baby."

He slid two fingers in and pumped vigorously. His tongue worked skillfully, fluttering over my clit. He added a third finger and thrust deep.

I lost it completely, calling out as I shattered once more. Every fiber of my being, every nerve ending, igniting.

"Dane!" It was all so overwhelming. All-consuming. So incredibly delicious, I was obsessed by how intensely he made me come, how wildly passionate he made me when I'd never once considered myself the type.

He let me ride this release out, but his labored breath on my pussy kept my insides blazing.

I had no idea how much time passed before I felt his gaze on my face. My heavy lids reluctantly opened. He wore a serious expression, though it held desire and white-hot need.

In his seductive voice, he asked, "Are you ready to give me everything I want from you?"

I stared at him for endless seconds, my breathing coming in sharp pulls.

I had not expected the gauntlet he'd thrown down.

"Ari."

He clearly was not a man to let any opportunity slip through his fingers.

Though I was still breathy and lost in a lust-induced haze, I said, "We're even with Kyle." Since I'd let Dane go down on me—something that was hugely personal in my book. And I'd followed his *other* request, so we were more than even. "Yes, I am ready. I refuse to be circumvented, though. You have to give in return. I want to know what's going on at the Lux. With you."

I didn't let him off the hook, somehow feeling I had enough power at the moment. He was still hard, still had lust and need raging in his eyes.

"I'm not accustomed to bargaining," he said, not at all pleased.

"I can believe that. But there's too much at stake for me to be lax about this. The things you've already done to me . . . the way you make me feel . . . this is all too much to not ask for something in exchange. To not know *exactly* who I'm involved with—what I'm involved in."

He glared unyieldingly. "You might not like all the answers."

"Maybe not. But I still need them."

"There's something I have to deal with right now. It's urgent."

"I gathered that."

Neither of us moved, just stared at each other. Deeply disturbed by the torment suddenly eating at him, I reached out a hand and smoothed the crinkle between his brows. Didn't seem to help much. I could see his mind churned with what appeared to be ominous thoughts, if the hooded look in his eyes was any indication.

It was a bit insane how easily he shifted gears. But when you had so much riding on a multibillion-dollar venture and whatever the hell was transpiring between us, I supposed that was natural.

Finally, he stood and handed over my clothing. I dressed quickly, which was no easy feat because I felt liquefied from the explosive climaxes.

"So, what's happened?" I asked, thinking of the call he'd taken.

"Beavers chewed through the security wire on the north end, by the streams."

My brow crooked. "Beavers?"

"We've lost camera monitoring capability throughout the property. We have to rewire."

"That sounds painful. At least it's not an infestation of rattlesnakes and scorpions." I shuddered.

"Not a fan, I see."

"I'm terrified of both. Like, nightmare terrified."

"We don't really have that problem this far north."

"I know. That's one of the reasons I like it here."

"Anyway, this will be an extensive undertaking. But a necessary one." He shook his head and looked a little lost in thought . . . that dark place in his mind where he sometimes went.

"Dane?" I had no idea what else to say, but—

A quick rap on the door startled me. I jumped.

Dane broke free of his trance. He put the phone in his pocket and buttoned his shirt. Then he stuffed the hem into the waist of his pants and held out his hand. "Come on."

I gazed at the hand that had brought me so much pleasure just minutes before. At this point, it made no sense to deliberate over the intimate gesture. But I did. Because there was something ominous in his eyes, similar to when we'd been in the bar and I'd turned to find him staring at me after Kyle had flirted.

I couldn't decipher the look. Obviously, I had no idea what sparked it. But I felt a peculiar warning that caused my hesitation.

Dane said, "I'll have Amano escort you to your car."

The corners of my mouth dipped. "I can find my way out of the hotel. I've been doing it for a week now."

"Please cooperate." He kissed me again, the taste of my arousal on his lips and tongue.

When he pulled away, I let him guide me to the door with a hand on the small of my back. As with every other touch from him, I found I perilously liked how it felt. Protective and possessive, coming from a man such as Dane Bax.

We stepped into the hallway and I was surprised to discover the mammoth dark-haired, stoic Chief of Security standing outside my door.

"Take Miss DeMille downstairs."

"Of course."

Dane had gone from seductive to troubled to in charge in less than two minutes. He was wildly sexy in all iterations.

"Please," Amano said as he gestured for me to precede him down the wide marbled corridor to the elevators. I wrenched my gaze from Dane.

"I prefer the stairwell, if you don't mind." With all the sampling of decadent food I partook of every day at the Lux, I needed all the exercise I could squeeze in.

Halfway to the door at the end of the hall, outside of Dane's office suite, I glanced back. He remained standing in the middle of the corridor, focused on me. Ethan stepped out of the elevator at the opposite end of the floor. He wore a grim expression.

Dane's intensity was one thing. The fact that they were both agitated was something altogether different.

What the hell was going on?

The next morning, I was alternately sifting through catalogs and surfing the Web for more ideas when Dane's executive administrative assistant, Molly, stopped in. She let me know he'd be off-property for the next couple of days.

I found it interesting that he hadn't called or texted with the news himself. Then I realized he was the one who needed space this time. He had to concede that I was right—that I deserved to know more about him and his troubles at the resort. Why he and Ethan were always so locked in deep discussion.

And, for that matter, I wondered if it had been Ethan on the phone—the angry-ring call. Did he have some sort of vested interest in 10,000 Lux?

Most important, would Dane give me the answers I required?

The following days I spent mostly in interviews—and praying like hell I wouldn't hear from my mother again, because I was seriously stressing over the money I'd given her. Thank God I had a job to cover forthcoming bills.

I did my best to focus solely on my hiring objectives. There were plenty of viable candidates from whom to choose, the vast majority of them coming from prestigious Phoenix and Scottsdale resorts, others from California, Florida, and even New York. I was hugely relieved to be on the cover of *Southwest Weddings* magazine this quarter, because it gave me instant credibility. I could see from many of the applicants that they hadn't expected me to be so young.

That I came from a strictly-wedding background didn't help

matters, either, when my applicants boasted of the budgets and events they worked with or managed. But a large percent of them followed industry news and were not only impressed by my professional designations but also that I was on a list of preferred planners and had orchestrated two illustrious weddings, in addition to my other upper-echelon ones.

I actually found it a relief in one respect that Dane was absent from the Lux. I wasn't looking for him around every corner, nor did I have to worry if anyone saw us together and speculated whether something was going on between us. I suspected it was more and more difficult for us to hide our attraction because it was so all-consuming. Even my dad had caught on. That was saying something.

Conversely, I missed Dane like crazy. A part of me also considered if he'd done it on purpose—disappeared for a spell with no connection just to make me grind over him and transition from a *demanding to know things before we proceed* stance to a *fuck not knowing anything, just let me have at him* one.

I took him for the strategic type, and it was a good possibility I was correct with my take on the current situation.

Another thing I found interesting was the way Amano loitered about. Sitting outside my office in one of the plush chairs that accompanied the long glass-topped decorative tables, usually on his iPad or phone. Taking his coffee break at the same time I did. Appearing in the courtyard when I met other executives there instead of on the fourth floor. He greeted me out front in the morning and walked me out to the valet in the evenings. No matter how late I stayed.

Did I have a bodyguard now?

And . . . why would I need one?

Just a comfort level for Dane? Part of protecting his territory?

Granted, that seemed just like him. So I didn't balk or tell Amano—an extremely professional and nice man, despite the scare factor that came with his six-foot-six-inch stature and the *I could kill King Kong with my bare hands* disposition—that I didn't need a shadow.

Though I had a feeling Kyle would take one look at him and head for the hills, never to contact me again.

That could be another Dane tactic. He operated in varying degrees I simply couldn't keep up with.

On Wednesday afternoon, I received a call I wasn't the least bit interested in taking.

Since I hadn't yet hired my own assistant, Molly announced over the speakerphone, "Kathryn DeMille on line three."

I stared at the handset, debating my options. But if I ignored her, she'd only show up at my townhome. She'd already proven that.

I snatched up the phone. "Hello, Mother."

"Aria Lynne, darling."

The double suck-up. I rolled my eyes.

She said, "I just saw the fabulous spread on the executive team of 10,000 Lux, and there was my little girl, front and center. My, oh, my, how you've climbed the corporate ladder. So quickly. I've told all my friends. They're so impressed I have such a successful daughter."

I reached for my pen and absently tapped the end on the blotter before me. I had a bad feeling about this call. My mother's sudden interest in me did not bode well for any part of my life.

God forbid she should ever discover I was involved with Dane. She'd latch on to that like a dog with a bone, given his social and financial status. When it came to the two of them, I was definitely of the *never the twain shall meet* mentality.

"I'm in the middle of work at the moment," I said, "so if we can talk la—"

"Well, I was just thinking," she interjected. "A trip to New York would be so wonderful this time of year. All the fall colors and festivities. And I've never been to Manhattan. . . ."

I felt the knife twist. "Why would you be going to New York?"

"To meet with agents, of course. For my book."

I had to curb my temper. "I thought we'd agreed that was over."

"For five thousand dollars?" She made a soft *tsk*ing sound. "Aria Lynne, you are a senior executive at 10,000 Lux and you're going to let your mother suffer through her last pennies?"

*Really?*

I wanted to scream. Cry. Nothing would *ever* be enough for this woman!

And now that my name was showing up in papers and magazines, she wanted to swoop in and pretend to be the doting mother she'd never *once* been?

I didn't know what to make of her. I didn't know what to do with her. After I'd turned eighteen and no longer had to legally spend any time with her, I'd stayed in Sedona with my dad, not venturing to Scottsdale to visit her. She hadn't complained, nor had she traveled up the hill to see me. Birthday gifts from her? Nonexistent. College graduation congrats? Not a peep.

She'd cut me off long ago, clearly finding no value in our association.

But now that it seemed I had some relevance in the world—a little more clout and a little more money—who was beating down my door?

I was furious that she'd do this to me. I'd moved past the drama. The trauma. Everything.

Yet here she was, suddenly threatening my dad's reputation and perhaps even his livelihood. Not to mention hinting at a scandal that could damage my image and career.

I abandoned the tapping of the pen and demanded, "What is it that you want, Mother?"

"Well, I've been watching a lot of Oprah lately—I would just love to be on her show—and it seems that a book such as mine could land me an advance somewhere in the hundred-thousand-dollar range."

My heart nearly stopped. "I don't have that kind of money."

"But you must be making six figures at 10,000 Lux. Correct? I'm sure we can come to an agreement."

Fury tore through me. "I always knew you were a piece of work, Mother, but this is downright evil. If you think for one minute—"

"I didn't tell you this before, but I've written the first three chapters already. I started off with some of the bigger names, just to make things juicy right off the bat."

My stomach roiled.

"Five thousand *a month* would be oh-so helpful, darling." Her tone was sugary sweet.

She was insane! Maybe all that Botox had contaminated her brain.

"Think about it, Aria Lynne. I'll be in touch."

The line went dead. I stared at the receiver for endless moments, my mind racing. What in the hell was I going to do with her?

# chapter 13

I didn't get much sleep that night and was monumentally relieved the next day when Mr. Mysterious texted to take my mind off my mother. I was in the middle of a meeting with PR, discussing initial guest lists for the myriad pre-launch festivities. The VIPs astounded me, and we hadn't even yet touched on those invited to the grand opening.

*Amano will pick you up at seven tonight.*

I had no idea what compelled me to be sassy—it wasn't exactly advisable with this man—but I typed: *I'm not dating Amano. Pick me up yourself.* Maybe I was just that desperate to see him.

*I have business.*

I frowned. Wished he could see it. I replied: *Is this a professional request?*

*You want answers, don't you?*

My heart picked up a few extra beats. Had I *really* gotten through to him?

*Someone will have to drive me home since I have to be in the office in the morning.*

*So do I. Bring a change of clothes.*

I sucked in a breath. All eyes at the conference table snapped in my direction.

A blush crept up my neck. Covering my faux pas, I said, "Sorry. A vendor just confirmed the garland I want is available."

"I swear you have the coolest job here," Lacy Jackson said. She was head of Food and Beverage.

"For me, yes," I concurred. "But PR hobnobs with society types at galas. Marketing is being wooed by every Southwest athletic team for joint ventures, and you get to sample food and expensive wines and liqueurs all day long."

"So true." She beamed. "It's not a position I'd trade for all the chocolate made from Venezuela cacao pods in the world."

"And companies send it to you in bricks, it seems," said Carter Moore, the VP of Marketing.

They all went off on a dark-chocolate and red-wine tangent and I stole another glance at my phone.

*I'm waiting.*

I smirked, feeling his impatience.

Then typed, *Yes.*

Thank God I'd reserved the afternoon for ordering decoration samples. Although this was a critical part of the launch—everything had to look just right and be as magnificent as the Lux itself—I wasn't making any sort of concrete decisions at the moment. Just examining and contemplating options.

Had I needed to focus on the budget or selecting employees from the first round of interviews, I would have been screwed. I couldn't keep my mind from wandering to Dane and whatever he had planned for the evening.

Well. I had a fairly good idea of the latter. He'd told me to pack clothes, after all.

I left the office at five and, once home, took a shower and changed into a red dress I thought he might like. I did my hair and makeup. Debated on what to bring by way of sleepwear, though I suspected it was a clothing-optional sort of evening. I packed yoga pants and a tank top. Added all the necessities for doing myself up in the morning. Then grabbed a black suit and a white buttoned shirt from the closet. I was ready when Amano knocked on the door.

Thankfully, he was the silent, alert type who didn't bother with small talk. He seemed to grasp that was perfectly acceptable to me and didn't even try to engage beyond the polite, "Good evening, Miss DeMille."

We wound our way up the very breathtaking Oak Creek Canyon, a dark setting because of overhanging trees and a cloudy night sky. Several back roads later—I would never actually be able to find this place on my own—we waited for the massive security gate to open and then pulled alongside a glass-and-wood-enclosed house on the creek. There wasn't a neighbor within two miles of us and the sound of rushing water mixed with the sway of leaves and their gentle scraping against one another, the windows, and the detached garage.

Dane stepped through the double doors and took my bag from Amano. "That'll be all for the evening. Thank you."

Amano turned my way. "Take care."

"You, too."

Dane ushered me into his gorgeous home, lit by streaks of lightning in the clouds and candles in tall hurricane lamps.

"That's some dress," he said as his arms slipped around my waist from behind and he left featherlight kisses along my throat that made me melt.

"I wasn't sure what to expect. You weren't very specific."

"That's because all I could think about was you naked."

I resisted the urge to turn in his arms and demand he take me to his bedroom. Though that desire wasn't easily dismissed.

I said, "You do intend to feed me, right?"

"Greek salad with chilled prawns already prepared. Chef D'Angelo says it's your favorite."

"Yes, and he toys with me by not making it a regular menu item. Total hit or miss as to when it's available. Makes me crazy."

Dane chuckled sexily. "Consider it on the menu whenever *you* want it."

"Thank you." A nice perk that came with being in the boss's bed.

He directed me to a great room, with a tall fireplace at one end and a wall of floor-to-ceiling bookcases at the other end, with a sliding ladder attached to a metal railing. Tables, chairs, sofas, and coffee tables were scattered in between. The enormous windows and glass doors showcased the forest and creek beyond a vast patio. All amazingly beautiful.

I said, "This is exactly the sort of place I've dreamed of. But creekside property for sale is rare in this village—and when it does appear on the market, the prices are astronomical."

"I bought this house last year through a private sale," he said. "I had Sotheby's contact the owners. Made them an offer they couldn't refuse."

"Why am I not surprised? I suspect you make those offers frequently."

He didn't bother to respond.

There was a low flame in the hearth and more candles lit all around the room, casting shadows in the corners and flickering illumination across the stone floor. It was every bit the darkly alluring fairy tale I'd had no idea I believed in. As I surveyed the expensive-looking vases and artwork, I noted there wasn't a single framed photo of Dane—or of anyone, for that matter.

"Not big on selfies?" I quipped.

"I'm not one to collect mementos like that. They're mostly all committed to memory."

I couldn't argue the point without being a hypocrite. I'd never been the sentimental type myself.

My fingers brushed over a lovely glass pitcher. Then I stood before an artistically crafted table that not only fit the eclectic array of furniture and knickknacks but also stole my breath.

"This is so pretty," I said of the Parisian bistro set.

"It's new. Well," he amended, "new for me. It's from Napoleon's Fontainebleau palace. The collection was recently at auction—Marie Antoinette had tea at that table."

"Incredible."

He joined me, setting a delicate-looking box on top of the marble surface. "I also picked this up in Paris. For you."

My heart fluttered. "That wasn't necessary."

"I figured you'd say that. So consider it a gift for me, if you want."

His intimate tone seeped through my veins, making me sigh. I pulled the white satin bow and swept the ribbon away. Then I lifted the dove-colored lid and brushed aside the sparkling silver tissue paper.

My fingertips grazed over sensuous deep-gray satin and exquisite crystals and Tahitian pearls.

"I like the Gretzky tee on you, but this reminded me of the first time we met—your blouse and necklace." His warm breath teased the shell of my ear as he stood partially behind me. Heat flared low in my belly.

He lifted the full-length nightgown from the box. Still buried in tissue was a matching robe.

Handing it over, Dane said, "Why don't you change? Get more comfortable? Take those shoes off. The stone is heated."

I shook my head. "You're really too much. You know that, right?"

"Tell me you like it."

"You already know I like it."

"Everything," he insisted.

"Yes. Everything."

I held the garment to my body, the silky material caressing my skin. It felt heavenly—smelled that way, too. Like lilacs in the spring.

He gestured toward a twelve-foot-tall door alongside the fireplace. I grabbed my tote from the pewter-colored chair he'd set it in and closed the door behind me.

I stared into the mirror for Lord only knew how long. I employed deep-breathing exercises. I tried not to freak out because that I was going to be wearing this incredibly gorgeous gown for, like, minutes, I was sure. And then . . .

*Calm down.*

I willed it.

*Chill out.*

I set aside the endless flow of satin and slipped out of my red dress.

The nightgown was rich and sensuous and slightly cool against my flushed skin. It skimmed over my breasts, my stomach, my hips. Fell to the floor to swirl around my ankles and bare feet. I studied myself in the mirror again, wondering whether to leave my hair loosely up or around my shoulders. I decided to pull out the pins. The fat chocolate-colored curls tumbled down my back. The nightgown dipped to my tailbone. My hair fell about midway.

I wiped off the crimson lipstick I wore with a Kleenex and used a glossy balm instead. My fingers shook slightly as I packed up. Leaving my tote on the counter, I left the bathroom. Dane was setting out salads at one of the larger tables. I crossed the cavernous room and joined him.

He swept his fingers through my hair and his thumb whisked over my jaw.

"You are the most beautiful thing I've ever seen."

My breath hitched. How could he possibly say that?

"I'm sure Jennifer Aniston proves otherwise."

"No." His head dipped and he kissed me. All slow and provocative, as was his way when he warmed me up. "I'm completely hooked on you, baby."

I stared up at him. "Then tell me what's really happening at the Lux."

His eyes narrowed for a moment. Then he stepped around me

and pulled out my chair. I sat and stressed over whether I'd pushed a bit too hard.

Dane poured a fragrant pinot grigio and sat across from me. I picked at my salad, everything about it tempting, but my stomach coiled. I set aside my fork.

With a low grunt, he took a sip of wine and then got down to it. "I had an original investment team for 10,000 Lux. Nine of us. Colleagues I trusted." He stabbed a prawn, sliced into it, and chewed. Aggressively. Then he added, "Things changed with five of them. I learned more about their business practices—their financial scheming—and I had to cut them out. I didn't want them associated with the Lux."

"Wow."

This was a mega-resort we were talking about. The sort of aspiration that meant every single thing about it had to be perfect because the investment was much too big, much too risky. A Jenga puzzle where pulling the wrong piece could make the entire empire crash to the ground."

"Corrupt?" I ventured hesitantly.

"Yes," Dane said in a terse tone. I felt his jagged edge of torment over trusting someone who betrayed him, and possibly the bitter need for revenge.

"Dane . . ."

"It's these unexpected glitches that are proof they're fucking with me, Ari."

"A beaver chomping through—"

"There were no beavers." Dry lightning flashed against the large windows, emphasizing his words. "I lied. To protect you. I don't want you to know about all of this. I don't want you in a position where you're aware of things I'm involved in that could put you in a dangerous situation."

"I'm already in one, Dane. What *we're* doing is dangerous. To me, at least."

"No," he insisted. "You think being romantically involved is hazardous and that's not true. But these men are."

"Have you ever had the rug pulled out from beneath you?" I demanded. "Have you ever even been in love?"

"No," he said, a bit contrite.

"It can tear you apart," I told him. "I've seen it happen."

"But it's never happened to you," he countered.

"I saw the destruction. The devastation. With my parents." My heart twisted. "And I was a pawn. My mother used me. I believed she loved me. I thought—"

I pushed back my chair and stood. I paced alongside the windows as a breeze rustled the trees.

"I thought the same thing every child thinks when it comes to their parents," I said. "That they both loved me. They both wanted me. That they'd fight to the death for me—proverbially speaking, of course. But no."

He stood as well. Stuffed his hands into the pockets of the loose black pants he wore with a white-linen buttoned shirt. His feet were also bare. The casual look was a sexy one on him.

I told him, "My dad was one-hundred percent into the family unit and all he cared about was keeping me out of her clutches. Because he knew what she really wanted. He refused to tell me, *for my own protection*—ironically enough—that all my mother cared about was money."

That was obviously still the case.

In a grave voice, Dane said, "Then you understand why it's important for *me* to protect you."

I debated sharing my mother's attempt to extort money—hardly a mere *attempt*, since she'd already cashed one check written by me—but decided it was best to deal with this situation on my own.

"That's not your job."

"Yes," he protested vehemently, "it *is*."

I walked away. Stood in front of tall glass doors.

His big career ambition was being sabotaged. That would have been beyond my comprehension were I not suddenly being black-mailed by my own parent.

Dane felt something so strongly for me that he wanted to shelter me from *everything*.

But that was impossible. And again . . . not his job. I'd always taken care of myself and would continue to do so.

He was persistent, though. His fingers brushed my hair over one shoulder. Then the tips grazed slowly down my bare spine. Flame after flame ignited against my vertebrae.

"You have to accept that I wanted you in my life, I pulled you in, and I'll do whatever it takes to keep you. And to keep you safe."

Everything about that delicious statement sent a tremor through me, yet I asked, "That means hiding things, whatever's happening at the Lux?"

"I consider it more . . . selective sharing."

With a shake of my head, I said, "That's not fair. Nor is it what I want."

He let out a long breath that teased my skin. Then he took my hand. "Fine." He led me back to the table.

We sat and I picked at my salad.

Dane didn't seem particularly pleased with this change in direction but told me, "I graduated high school when I was seventeen and went to Harvard. When I was nineteen, I had Ethan as a professor and he mentored me, in a way. We became business partners on a few smaller projects. Then I built a boutique hotel at Lake Tahoe."

"I read that on the Internet. And, by the way, I still want to know how you've so carefully contained information about yourself and your family. There are hardly any pictures, too. I'm literally shocked you're not a billionaire playboy whose mug graces every society page in the world."

"You really take me for the playboy type?"

I studied him for a moment. I wanted to ask, *How would I know the difference?* since he was so secretive. But I did have enough to go on, from a personal point of view, to be able to draw a few conclusions. His intensity alone negated any sort of carefree existence.

"Okay, you have me there," I admitted. "But still—"

"Donations," he offered. "That's how I do it. I have someone on my staff who monitors everything posted about me, and I can have it removed by throwing money at it. Mostly sizable contributions, but well worth the investment."

"Why?" I asked, distressingly fascinated and alarmed at the same time. "Why's it so important to only have content *you* want posted?"

The grim look returned. "My privacy is crucial, Ari. You just have to understand that it is."

More secrets. I went back to my salad, agitated. Yet trying to reconcile who he was and what he was up to.

Finally, I posed different questions. "If you think you know who's causing problems at the resort, why can't you stop them? I mean, you're capable of controlling every other facet of your life. Who are these people that they're powerful enough to pull off this mayhem that trips you up? And, for that matter, why are they concentrating on 'tedious' mishaps? Granted, the security-wiring snafu is a larger hindrance, but something like furniture being sent to the wrong continent is really a minor setback when you can just reorder the pieces."

He grimaced, almost painfully it seemed. "I appreciate your train of thought. You're very intuitive. First, with regard to the Lux, it's not exactly a simple matter of calling up a few companies and asking them to reship our goods. Those pieces were specially crafted. Second, the wires were clipped in various places, strategically so, leaving me no choice but to rewire the entire perimeter. I had originally wanted a more sophisticated Wi-Fi–type electronic monitoring system, but with the sketchy signals in these canyons, I couldn't rely on it. I had to go old-school. Well, relatively speaking. It's a hugely expensive system."

"Oh." I pushed aside my plate, losing my appetite. "So when you said 'tedious,' you really meant fairly monumental and costly."

"Yes."

I reached for my wine and sipped. "You didn't tell me why you can't put a stop to it all."

His teeth ground together in frustration. Then, "I'm not sure exactly who's behind this. I have my suspicions, but nothing concrete. And those I do believe are involved are extremely prominent people, Ari. As you've surmised. Not ones to mess with arbitrarily, without a solid plan. This all started happening just a couple of months ago and I'm . . . struggling . . . to find my course of action. Trust me when I say, these aren't people you want to poke with a stick. Unless you know you have the bigger stick."

But they *were* fucking with him—I couldn't help but think about the media room fire—and I could clearly see that tore at him. Dane Bax did not strike me as the type of man who let anyone screw with him, let alone destroy something that meant so much.

An insidious shiver made me squirm in my seat.

He was definitely mixed up in something shady. Something volatile.

I didn't do shady and volatile.

So why was I still here?

I drained my glass and tried to calm my tormented insides. Why was I so wrapped up with this man that I couldn't see the trouble for what it was and walk away?

He said, "You can understand now why I wanted to keep you out of this?"

"And yet . . . here I am."

"Yes." He also pushed aside his plate. "I want you to do me a favor."

"Anything." That was how persuasive my attraction was—it could easily be leveraged against me. Somehow, walking away was actually *not* an option.

"Let Amano stay close whenever I'm not around. Not that

I think you're in any sort of physical danger," he quickly added. "Just so that I can concentrate on what I need to do without worrying about you every second of the day. Not that I won't, but—"

"Yes," I said. "If that's what you want. If it'll make you feel better. Yes."

He nodded, looking greatly relieved. "Thank you."

I pushed back my chair again and stood, facing the windows. It was a blue-black night, with gray around the fringes as a light fog ribboned through the dense forest. The creek water ran steadily over the jutting rocks, creating whitecaps on the rapids. The shrouded moon dispersed silver hues through the clouds. It hadn't rained in days, and I figured the monsoon season had finally abated. Though a sultry climate remained.

Dane crossed the room to stand behind me.

"I didn't scare you, did I?" he murmured against my temple as his arms slid around my waist.

"No. It just seems that these complications are merely warnings. If these guys are so powerful, wouldn't they—"

"I'm not sure what they plan to do. That's why I want you to let Amano do his job. And once we have all of the security up and running, I'll figure out what's really going on and that'll be the end of it."

He sounded so certain that I couldn't lob any sort of challenging thought his way. I honestly didn't think that, now that he'd pinpointed the issues and possible culprits, he'd allow anything else to go wrong at 10,000 Lux. He was powerful, too. Anything standing in his way was but a roadblock to bulldoze through. I had complete confidence in him.

His lips brushed over the column of my neck and then he placed kisses along my shoulder. I watched him as my gaze lingered on the glass pane before me, the reflection of us a sensual one. He practically engulfed me with his large, muscular body, his strong arms encircling me.

Maybe there were menacing things happening. I knew to tread

lightly. I knew to follow Dane's instructions. Yet I couldn't imagine any sort of personal threat. No one knew about my involvement with him. Hell, *I* wasn't fully sure of my involvement with him. There was still so much to learn about the man. I didn't even know when Dane's parents had died or from what cause. And I was so new to the Lux that I didn't know much about it and couldn't be used for confidential information.

I'd definitely be the last person on anyone's radar at this point. *If* they got personal. So far, Dane was right. The program at the Lux was being jacked in ways that didn't prove bodily detrimental to Dane or anyone else. I had a very strong suspicion that was because whoever was responsible—one or all five members of the investment group he'd cut out—didn't want major setbacks because they still wanted a piece of the pie.

If the Lux failed, they wouldn't gain anything. If, however, they could convince Dane to call a truce and let them back in . . . They wouldn't want to have wreaked too much havoc that would prove counterproductive to them in the long run was my best guess.

I latched on to this reasoning, mostly because it seemed the incidents were just nuisances. Again, costly for Dane and troublesome for his launch. But certainly possible to overcome. If someone was really out for bitter revenge, they'd mess things up significantly. Wouldn't they?

"I know you're not going to give up on fixing things at the hotel," I said.

His warm breath teased my skin as he said in a low voice, "I'm not giving up on this, either."

# chapter 14

Exhilaration shimmied through me. "Thank you for confiding in me. I needed to hear more about you."

His mouth swept up to my earlobe. Just below it, he nipped softly. "I need *you*."

Those rock-hard arms tightened. I felt his erection and it completely undid me.

"Dane," I whispered in the quiet room. My heavy eyelids dipped. "Whatever you want."

It was all I could think to say. I needed him just as much. Craved him in the most overwhelming way.

He kissed my neck as his arms unlocked and his hands swept upward, palming my breasts. His touch wasn't gentle. It was insistent. Greedy.

A sharp moan fell from my lips.

"I told you I've been patient," he said. "As much as I could be when it comes to you."

"And now?"

His hands shifted to my waist and he turned me around. His mouth sealed with mine and he kissed me deeply, passionately. Thank God he held me, because my knees all but knocked together and every inch of me went boneless against his masterful commanding of my body, my senses.

My arms wrapped around his neck and I clung to him as he continued the kiss. One hand splayed across my lower back. The other swept downward and cupped my ass, squeezing the cheeks and pressing me firmly against his erection.

"Dane," I repeated breathlessly as his lips tangled with mine, "I want to feel you inside me."

He guided me to the sofa in front of the fireplace, still kissing me. His hands moved to my hips and his fingers curled around the satin at my legs, gathering it up as he sank onto the cushion and I straddled his lap. His hands slid under all the luxurious material and caressed my skin.

As he kissed me deeply again, I lost all touch with reality. Nothing existed but him. Not even trouble at the Lux.

His palms glided over my belly and ribs. Then shifted from beneath the nightgown. One cupped the side of my face, his fingers sweeping through my hair. The other massaged my breast, his thumb teasing my nipple tight. His kisses were hot and passionate, stealing my breath.

He kept my head to his, our lips seductively twisting as he threaded his fingers in the thick strand of satin at my shoulder and tugged the material down my arm. Half the bodice slipped away with it and his hand caressed my breast. A soft moan fell from my mouth at the intimate touch. His head dipped and his tongue fluttered against my taut nipple, making it even harder. He suckled deep and my moan turned into a sharp whimper.

"Oh, God, Dane." My fingers combed through his lush hair as his tongue curled around the puckered peak. Then he drew it into his mouth again. My pulse jumped. Every inch of flesh tingled. He didn't let up, and the tension built as he left kisses along the tops of my breasts, across my collarbone, up my neck, and over my jaw.

"Do you feel how hard you make me?"

I rocked slightly, his erection full and tempting between my legs. Especially given the loose material of his pants and the fact that I'd stripped off my panties when I'd changed into the night-gown. No need to complicate matters with extra clothing. I knew what I was getting myself into here.

"I think you're teasing me," I murmured. "You should be inside me already."

"Now who's the impatient one?"

"I haven't exactly been playing hard to get. Just cautious."

"I understand why now. And I'm relieved you got over your aver-sion to being touched—by me only, of course."

"Of course." I kissed him, tasting the distinct flavor that was his alone. A combination of heat and wintermint. Pinot grigio laced his breath and it was even more enticing.

His hands slid under the satin again and he lifted the garment up and over my head, gently laying it on the cushion next to us. His eyes roved my body, fire blazing in them. Flickering flames from the candles cast shadows over his devilishly handsome face as he stared at me with awe and raw need.

"Stop looking and start touching," I coaxed.

"You're breathtaking." His palms skimmed over my thighs and to my hips. "Lift up slightly."

I did and he worked around me to shove his pants down his legs and kick them off. I yanked off his shirt and tossed it aside, mar-veling over his perfection.

"God, I want you," he said in a gruff voice.

"I'm not on the Pill. Not much call for it, you know?"

I heard the hint of disappointment in his tone as he said, "Sofa table behind me."

I stretched forward and snagged a foil packet from the accent table that was covered with a gorgeous arrangement and several interesting curios.

"Do you always use condoms as decorative items?"

He plucked the little square from my fingers and set it next to us. "Smart-ass."

I laughed softly. "Guess by coming here I made myself a sure thing."

"No. But I had to be prepared this time. I couldn't let the opportunity slip away again over something like this."

I gnawed my lip a moment and then ventured, "You'd rather forego the condom?"

"Yes. That's not a good idea, though, since you're not on the Pill."

"Right." Regret swept through me. I would have preferred to forego the condom as well. Any type of barrier, really, when it came to him.

Despite the necessary conversation, Dane was still hard. I wrapped my fingers around his base and pumped slowly, eliciting a guttural sound from deep in his throat. His fingertips grazed my flushed skin, along my arms, and up to my shoulders. He brushed my hair off them, so the plump waves cascaded down my back.

In a lust-roughened tone, he asked, "Are you ready for me?"

"Yes." There was no hesitation on my part. Not even the hint of *tread lightly* that I'd experienced earlier. I knew what I wanted, without a tinge of doubt.

He ripped open the packet. I released him and he rolled the condom down his thick shaft. I positioned myself as his cock slid over my slick folds, back and forth, teasing me further.

"No fair," I complained.

"I want you to go slow."

"That might not be possible." I was dying to feel him—all of him.

My hips pressed down and he penetrated my opening, just an inch. Enough to make me gasp. And send white-hot adrenaline through my veins. Slow be damned, I had to have him.

I lowered myself while straddling his lap. He sensed what I was up to, though, and caught my hips in his large hands, keeping me from my prize.

"Dane," I hissed as I gripped his shoulders to steady my suddenly vibrating body.

"I know how tight you are. I don't want to hurt you."

I brimmed with excitement, wet and wanting him. The tension was almost unbearable.

"Now's not the time to be all gallantlike. Now's the time to fuck me."

I dropped my hips; he sank in deep. I cried out from the intense sensation of him filling and stretching me.

"Oh, Christ," I said on a long sigh. "Oh, God."

He hadn't even moved inside me yet but I felt the tremors run from head to toe. And then the pleasure erupted in my core and I called out his name as I came.

My fingertips pressed into solid muscle. My chest rose and fell with heavy pants of air. Within me, the sizzling of nerve endings and the throbbing of unadulterated need burned brighter than ever before.

"Shit," I ground out. "That keeps happening with you. I can't control it."

"Don't bother trying. I like it."

"Fuck me. *Please.*"

My hips rolled, even as he gently tried to restrain them. His jaw was set in a hard line. His emerald irises glowed brilliantly.

"Dane," I insisted.

He looked a bit dazed. A bit . . . twisted up. As though I tested *his* control.

The thought made me smile. "Hey," I said, still all breathy and lusty. "You want to make me come again, right?"

"You have no idea how this feels."

"Yes, I do. And I desperately, *desperately* need more."

His teeth clenched. Then he said, "You might be the death of me."

"Doubtful."

He guided me into a slow, sexy rhythm that set my pulse racing. He was huge inside me, and buried so deep, I was sure it'd take mere seconds for another orgasm to hit.

"This is so good," I whispered against his lips. "So amazingly good."

"Just get used to me for a minute."

"I came the moment you were inside me. There's no *getting used* to this, Dane. It's exciting, thrilling. So fantastic."

He let out a strained laugh. "I haven't even done anything yet, Ari."

"I know. That's what makes it even crazier." And anticipation over all of his experienced moves had me teeming with the need to demand more from him. But I wasn't exactly well versed when it came to sex talk. When it came to asking for what I wanted. I didn't know how to describe it other than to say I needed him to go absolutely wild on me. Unleash all his passion.

Did that scare me a little? Naturally. But I didn't want him to hold back.

"You said nothing's off-limits," I reminded him. Sort of a cheap shot, but I really was desperate. And he was being much too careful. "You're not going to hurt me or break me."

"Maybe not, but the way you're squeezing me so damn tight, chances are good I'll come before the party even gets into full swing."

I bit back a gloating smile. I was making *him* crazy out of his mind.

I let him keep up the sensual pace awhile longer, cataloging the way he felt, the heat coursing through me, the way his fingers tensed as he gripped my hips. The way his chest heaved as sharply as mine and his breath came in heavy pulls.

Without my even having to encourage him further, he picked up the tempo, thrusting into me a bit more forcefully. Exhilaration skipped down my spine.

"Yes," I mumbled. My eyes locked with his. "Dane. Just like that."

*Damn it.* If only I had the words to express how incredible he felt. If only I knew how to tell him *exactly* what he did to me. How fiercely he lit me up.

"Lean back," he quietly commanded. His hands moved to my wrists and he led me to flatten my palms on the tops of his strong thighs. I arched and my head fell back, my hair spilling over his legs. "Yeah, that's right. Perfect."

Then his hands roved my body, up my arms to my shoulders and down my front, resting in the dip of my waist as he pumped into me, a bit heartier, pushing the air from my lungs.

"Oh, God." My eyelids fluttered closed. His hands slid up my body again, cupping my breasts and massaging roughly. Sparks ignited low in my belly. I rocked in time with him, meeting his demanding thrusts.

His thumbs whisked over my hard nipples, pebbling them tighter. He tugged at them and fire roared through my veins.

"Jesus, Dane." The erotic sensations swelled within me once more. How he could make me come so damn fast was beyond me. Yet I barreled toward that wicked precipice in no time.

He clutched my waist again and drove deeper, harder, faster. His low groans mingled with my throaty moans. My fingertips pressed into his thighs, keeping me steady as he fucked me.

His tone turned dark as he simply insisted, "Come."

"Yes. Oh, God, yes." I was *so* close. Trying to hold off because it was just too sinfully delicious a sensation to let go of so quickly. I wanted it to go on and on.

But then Dane's strokes became shorter and more rapid and he hit that perfect spot. I screamed his name as everything inside me ignited and exploded.

He stilled for a few seconds as I lost myself in the massive rush of heat and fervor. I was still breathing erratically and pulsing from the inside out when he started up again. Bypassing slow and picking right back up with the frenetic tempo that sent me straight into sensory overload.

For good measure, the pads of two fingers rubbed my clit, with pressure and a determined pace.

"Dane." I shifted a little. He wrapped his arm around my lower back and I sat up partially, keeping one hand on his thigh for support. I watched him piston into me, watched him stroke my clit. Beads of perspiration popped along my hairline as I continued to burn for him. My nipples were impossibly hard and I cupped my breast, massaging in the same not-so-gentle manner he would have used.

My legs were spread wide to accommodate him as I half rested on his lap, using my knees to keep me slightly lifted so he could thrust deep.

I never knew anything could be quite so sensational and addictive as him fucking me. I never wanted it to end.

"You're making me so damn hot," he grumbled. "Shit." His jaw tightened. "Nothing feels as good as you, baby."

Excitement slammed into me and I cried out again. "Dane!"

This time, the tremors didn't dim as I rode out the orgasm. I quaked and my breathing wouldn't slow. I was ridiculously turned on, rocked to my core.

I fell forward, collapsing against his wide chest. His hand moved from between my legs and he held me to him.

"Oh, God," I gushed. "Holy Christ."

My fingers twined in his hair and I kissed his neck, his cheek, his temple. I was crazed. Completely and totally spellbound, enthralled. Drunk on Dane and riding a high from which I never wanted to come down.

His mouth captured mine and he gave me another scorching kiss. I couldn't stop myself from rocking again, my hips undulating and coaxing him back into a sexy pace.

He tore his mouth from mine and said, "You're not going to be able to walk tomorrow."

"I don't care. I just . . . Dane . . . I just want you. *So* much."

Alarm edged my euphoria, but I refused to give it credence. I was enveloped in sheer bliss, not inclined to relinquish it. Not for a second.

It was a little frightening how my body trembled and my breathing wouldn't return to normal. But I couldn't escape the intensity of our desire for each other—and how vibrant and *alive* he made me feel. Like I'd merely existed before. Gotten by.

Now I was acutely aware of my surroundings. Of myself. Of him. Of every sensation blazing inside me.

His mouth sealed with mine again as we moved together. His hand slid to my backside. The finger that had rubbed my clit, still coated with my juices, circled the rim of that forbidden spot.

I broke our kiss. "Dane."

His eyes locked with mine, glowing provocatively. "I want all of you, Ari. Every piece of you. Especially if no one has ever owned you like this."

I shook my head. "No one. Ever." *Never* was more appropriate. Because I would never let anyone but him touch me like this—so intimately.

His lips grazed my neck; his teeth nipped. He pumped into me feverishly. And I was lost once more.

With skill, he rotated us to the side so I lay against the pile of pillows in the corner and he was on top of me. He sank deeper. His finger penetrated. The searing heat collided with the breath-stealing feeling of him buried so far inside me.

He moved slower now. Long, full strokes that made my spine bow and my hips rise to accommodate him, to accept more of him. All of him. My fingers tangled in his hair as he continued to kiss and lightly bite my throat, finding sensitive spots that lit me up even more.

One of my legs twined with his, the other wrapped around his hips, keeping his body pressed to me. Keeping him surrounding me. Filling me.

"Oh, fuck, Ari." His head lifted and he stared deep into my eyes. Dark, complex emotions swirled in his gorgeous green irises. Emotions I couldn't decipher, but which on some visceral level—which I couldn't begin to fathom—likely mirrored what he saw in my eyes.

My heart pounded wildly. My body writhed and arched to keep his pace and keep the intimate contact with him. The hand I didn't have buried in his hair glanced over his biceps, up to his shoulder. He increased the sexy rhythm and I moaned. My nails dug into his flesh. He pushed harder, faster. My hand dragged downward, over his collarbone, across his chest.

All the while, the eye contact didn't falter. I wasn't even sure we blinked.

I felt him swell inside me as he moved more aggressively. My breasts nestled beneath the hard ledge of his pecs. The ridged grooves of his abs pressed into my softer stomach when he exhaled in harsh breaths.

I couldn't separate all the sensations crashing over me, coursing through me. So I clung to the overall teasing, beautifully tormenting feeling that landed me once more in that place where I was about to leap from the ragged edge.

"Dane," I whispered.

"Yeah." That was all he said. As though he knew. As though he could sense it, as though he had already memorized every single change in my breath, my body, my eyes. And knew how close I was.

"I can't stop," I warned him.

"That's okay," he told me, still gazing deep. "Come with me. Right now, baby. Come with me."

He was so thick inside me, so delectable and so commanding. "Dane," I said again. A peculiar lump of emotion lodged in my throat. He thoroughly captivated me so that the only thing I focused on was his weight on top of me and the feelings that swelled and burst. "Oh, God!" I came harder than before, still riveted by his intense gaze. "Oh, Christ!"

His cock throbbed and he thrust deeper. "Fuck. Ari!" He convulsed as I squeezed him tight, prolonging my orgasm, making me soar.

The powerful release was enhanced by how vehemently he responded to me—how hard *he* came. I clenched him fiercely, not wanting to let him go.

All of his muscles flexed as he wrapped his arms around me. He was rigid, stone. I loved how the strength not only came from his chiseled features but also emanated from his every pore.

His head finally dipped and he kissed me like I'd just made his entire year. Passionately, gratefully, sensually. Insanely perfect.

When we came up for air, he burrowed his face in the spray of my hair across the pillows. And continued to breathe heavily.

"Think I could stay here forever," he mused.

I stared up at the dark ceiling, the flickering candlelight barely registering. Something stirred and moved inside me. Something unexpected and indefinable. Something that caused my heart to constrict and turned my blood molten.

Tears pricked my eyes. I couldn't explain why, except that every second with Dane inside me was amazingly, darkly spectacular. Priceless. Impossible to break free of.

So when he made to pull away, I said, "Not yet." Unable to catch myself. "That *forever* was a bit too short."

His mouth grazed my neck, then my cheek, capturing my tears.

"Ari," he murmured. "Don't cry."

"I'm not," I insisted. "I'm—"

"Ari. Baby." He stared into my eyes again. "What is it?"

"I never came before."

"What?"

"With those other men," I rushed on, to clarify. "From the hotel bars. I never once came. Not with any of them."

His gaze narrowed on me. "Never?"

My head rolled back and forth on the pillows.

"Then, why—?"

"Because I wanted to—I mean, I'd hoped . . ." I sighed, a bit frustrated that even I couldn't truly make heads or tails over those brief encounters. "I did it to make me feel normal, I guess. I engaged when it seemed necessary, but really . . . I never got anything out of it. And it sure as hell wasn't anything like this. Nothing—*nothing*—could ever be the way it is with you."

*Maybe too revealing.* My eyes squeezed shut.

"Ari." He gave me a sweet, sexy kiss. One that melted my heart. My lids fluttered open. "I've never been this consumed, either. It's different with you. Special." He shook his head. "That sounds inconsequential and temporary. I don't know the right word."

I stared at him, at a loss for words myself.

"Anyway." His lips brushed over the remainder of my tears and then he said, "Just let it be the way it is between us. Don't try to fight it or let it scare you."

"It didn't scare me," I assured him. "It should have. But it didn't. Not really."

"Then, what?"

"It was just . . . kind of beautiful. Like . . . incredibly beautiful."

He grinned, his tension easing, his bunched muscles loosening. "Now I'm catching on."

"Dane." I grimaced.

He chuckled, low and deep. "Face it, Ari. For all your hedging, you wouldn't have come tonight if you hadn't agreed we were seriously involved with each other."

"You promised me answers," I challenged.

"And told you to pack an overnight bag," he countered.

I snickered. "You don't have to win every time. You could maybe concede once in a while."

"Not really my style." He hoisted himself up. I protested with a small whimper. He added, "Don't worry, baby. I'm nowhere near done with you." With a sexy wink, he untangled himself and stood.

Sighing dreamily over the view, I watched him saunter off to the bathroom. Jesus, he was a masterpiece. I could barely take my eyes off his ass to admire his broad, tapered back. His narrowed waist. His powerful thighs.

How the hell was I so lucky that *he* wanted *me*? It boggled my mind. And that he seemed as deeply enthralled . . . That just felt crazy and impossible. Yet there was absolutely nothing about him that would make me believe that everything he said was some sort of devious mistruth. Granted, I had no basis of comparison, but the way he'd fucked me and the things he'd said . . . And then the way he'd—

My thoughts came to a screeching halt and I bolted upright. I pulled around me the chenille throw that was tossed haphazardly into the corner and covering the cushion where I was sprawled.

He'd fucked me at first. No doubt there. But then . . . He'd made love to me. When he'd been between my legs, buried deep inside me and staring into my eyes . . . He'd made love to me.

My stomach flipped.

*Okay, Ari. Time to face facts.*

Dane was absolutely right.

*This. Is. Serious.*

# chapter 15

Not just what had happened with us this evening and how I'd responded to it—to Dane—physically. But emotionally as well—most important of all, really.

That I'd not had an orgasm with another man, only my vibrator and nameless/faceless fantasies, bore its own significance. Along with the blatant reality that I'd just been scratching nature's itch from time to time. Unsuccessfully.

*This*, however . . .

Whole new ball of wax.

As Dane returned, my gaze was fixed on him, taking in every glorious inch of his tanned and toned body. The way he stealthily, confidently moved. The way he watched me watch him.

I tossed off the lightweight blanket and stood. My hands moved over his cut abs, up to his chest.

"You did say you were nowhere done with me, right?" My voice was low and sultry. Suggestive. Because I wanted him again.

One corner of his mouth lifted. "I don't want to wear you out all in one evening."

"Pretty sure I'll bounce back."

A heartbeat later he swept me off my feet. Literally and figuratively.

Wrapping my arms around his neck, I said, "You seem to like doing that."

"Well, you did call me alpha."

"Good thing I didn't say *caveman* or I'd be over your shoulder."

He carried me down the long hallway and into a bedroom. Dozens of candles ensconced in glasses of varying shapes, sizes, and heights were lit along the mantel, on the nightstands, across the wide ledge of the headboard. A fire warmed the room. No lights illuminated the space, just the flames.

The king-size bed was covered by a rich, navy-colored satin sheet, with plump pillows that had shams to match. Dane sat me in the middle of the mattress and I curled my fingers around the lush material.

"This is gorgeous," I said as I absorbed it all in awe. My gaze landed on a nightstand and I leaned forward, fingering the velvety red and white rose petals scattered about. Warmth laced through me. I glanced back at Dane. "You did all of this for me?"

"I told you this wasn't going to be like your hotel hookups. There's nothing casual about this at all, Ari."

"You're trying to make me believe in romance—in *my* life, not just with my clients?" I shook my head. "I'm not saying that lightly, because this is really sweet and thoughtful."

He said, "It occurred to me the other night that I'm not exactly romantic myself. I've never felt the desire or need to be, honestly. But with you . . . I wanted you to know what all this might be like. Granted, I'm not incredibly original, given my own lack of experience—I even forgot the music."

I smiled. "I didn't notice. And I like the crackle of the fire instead." I touched the lavish sheet again and asked, "Did you pick the bedding up in Paris as well?"

"As a matter of fact, yes."

"Well then, you're nowhere near unoriginal. And, really, Dane . . ." My heart fluttered. A foreign feeling, but one that didn't alarm me at the moment, because of his own admission. This was all new and different for him, too. Despite how he was completely in control of what we were doing, if romance wasn't his norm, either, didn't that help to put me on par with him in one aspect of this . . . relationship?

Joining me, he said, "Lay back."

He stretched out beside me, both of us on the diagonal across the bed. He raised my arms over my head, clasping my wrists in one large hand. The other skimmed the underside of my biceps, along the outer swell of my breast, across my rib cage to the dip in my waist. The slow, tantalizing progression made me burn. His fingertips grazed, his palm splayed. He seemed to take in every inch of me, not just with his sensual touch but also with his heated gaze.

His hand moved over the curve of my hip, and I breathed a little shallower as he brushed my upper thigh, then the inside, with light strokes.

I squirmed restlessly and amended that no way in hell would I ever be on par with him in any capacity, because he was a master of seduction and I was 100 percent at his mercy.

"What are you planning to do?" I asked as excitement and anticipation mounted.

His fingers glanced over my dewy folds and then he brought his hand to his mouth, tasting me.

I sucked in a breath. Let it out on one long, "*Oh.*"

He grinned mischievously. "I liked your hands bound the other night."

They remained restrained in his loose grip.

"You're going to tie me up again?" Why did that send a shiver of delight through me?

He said, "It was hugely gratifying to know you were dying to touch me. You, of all people."

"The one who doesn't like to touch or be touched."

"Mm-hmm. But you do enjoy touching me. And being touched by me."

"Insanely so," I admitted.

With a soft chuckle, he said, "I appreciate that you don't try to hide it."

"Impossible, don't you think? I mean . . . look at me."

"I am." His eyes glowed. "Your nipples are hard. Your lips are glistening. And I'm not talking about these." He kissed me. Then added in his evocative tone, "You want me again."

"Yes."

I would have cringed at my eagerness, but what would have been the point? There was no denying it. No fighting it. So I gave in to the need I had for him.

"Make me come again," I all but begged.

The pads of his fingers skated over my stomach and up the valley of my breasts. He cupped the side of my face and kissed me deeply. I could have incinerated into the mattress from that alone.

His expression was still mischievous as he released my wrists but tugged on a long silk sash attached to the bedpost that had been concealed by the sheet. He deftly tied me up before I really had any time to process the carte blanche I'd given him. He topped it off with a pretty little bow as I craned my neck to see what he was up to.

"Polite-society bondage?" I teased.

"Oh, no," he said as he pinned me with a dark, desirous look. "There's nothing polite about what I want to do to you."

My insides ignited. "Jesus, Dane." My thighs squeezed together and my inner muscles contracted as the throbbing started.

His head dipped and his tongue flitted over my nipple. Then he said, "Actually, I want you on your stomach." He helped me, since I was bound. "That's it. On your forearms and knees."

He shifted behind me and worked my legs apart. My back arched and I tossed a look at him over my shoulder. "You're not going to do anything too kinky, are you?" I returned to the insecurity of him being way out of my league.

"You're fairly safe." He winked.

"Dane."

"I'm just going to spend a little time here. . . . I don't think you'll mind." His head lowered and his tongue whisked over my slick flesh.

My hips jerked. "Oh, God." Not mind? Hell, I'd be pleading for more within seconds.

His lips tugged gently at my folds, a scintillating touch that had me instantly forgetting my trepidation. He was an expert at the quick warm-up, then jumped straight into suckling my clit and fluttering his tongue over the responsive bud. Using his thumbs, he spread me wide and dedicated himself to getting me off.

I panted harshly, the erotic ministrations setting me on fire.

My fingers gripped the thick silken sash binding my wrists. My head dropped and my eyes closed. I concentrated solely on the pleasure he brought me, his skilled determination.

His tongue circled my opening, then dipped inside. It was a wonder I didn't come instantly. But he had more in store, and the flickering of his tongue against my clit, a bit stronger and faster, had me whimpering and squirming.

"Dane," I gasped. He was too, *too* good at this. "Fuck me."

But he wasn't inclined to deviate from his current plan. He suckled my clit and everything exploded inside me.

"Oh, God!" I cried out as the release rocked me to the core.

I would never be impervious to this man or the things he did. I could barely breathe and my body screamed for him.

"Fuck me," I repeated. *Demanded.*

"You want it just like this." It wasn't even a question. He knew.

"Yes. *Now.*"

He reached for a condom on the ledge that rose above the head of the bed. He was sheathed in an instant and thrust into me from behind. Hard.

"Oh, yes!" I cried out.

As he pumped steadily, I raised my hips and ass to give him better access. He clasped my waist and fucked me with quick, full strokes. Exactly what I wanted. Exactly what I needed.

Then he pulled out all the stops and flanked my legs with his, forcing them closed as he pistoned assertively. With my thighs pressed together, I felt every inch of him, width and length, sliding in and out. Nothing had ever felt more incredible than his rock-hard cock stroking my pussy, pushing farther in. To feel him so acutely, so forcefully . . . It was mere seconds before I lost it again and screamed his name.

He thrust once more and came on a driving beat I felt deep within.

"Jesus, Ari," he ground out. "Fuck."

I clenched him tight, my spine arched, my head thrown back. If I could give him half the pleasure in return . . .

My inner muscles squeezed and released as I milked his thick shaft and he continued to shudder.

I had no idea how much time passed as we both savored the rush of heat and the intensity of the orgasm we shared. Could've been minutes. Likely it was seconds, but it felt like a small eternity.

Our heavy breaths were one as they filled the room, in time with each other, as though his heart pounded erratically with mine.

We remained joined. I had absolutely no desire to move an inch, to break the connection.

What he did to me and the way we responded to each other was so beyond anything I'd ever fathomed, I tried to hold on to every tiny bit of it. Maybe that was a bad idea—rubbing against that *once it's gone you're going to miss it horribly* theory of mine. Yet a new theory was conveniently replacing the old one. I would have missed out on *so* much if I'd not traveled this path with Dane.

At the moment, I could convince myself it was worth the risk.

Were it to disappear tomorrow . . . I'd be shredded. No two ways about it.

But it was just too incredible to give up right now for the sake of the next day's sanity.

Dane eventually withdrew from me and pulled the ties that bound my wrists. He rubbed them affectionately and whispered, "Okay?"

"In heaven," I murmured.

He gave me one of his carnal growls. "You'll have me going again in seconds."

"And that's a bad thing?"

Lightly nipping my earlobe, he said, "I've got plenty more up my sleeve for you."

Then he slipped from the bed. As he headed to a door on the opposite side of the room, I said, "You're not wearing sleeves, but I'm still expecting something clever."

His laugh filled the quiet night. Before he ducked into the bathroom, he told me, "I promise to keep you entertained."

I didn't doubt it.

With a contented sigh, I collapsed against the ultra-sensual satin sheet.

*Entertained* was hardly the word I'd use for what he did. I wasn't even myself at this point. I was some obsessed and euphoric woman whose body trembled and hummed with the sort of exhilaration that ought to be illegal. No one should feel this fantastic without giving up the rights to her soul.

It was too good. Too sinful.

Yet if there truly were something criminal about being this intensely aroused, sated, aroused, sated, aroused . . . Then okay. Lock. Me. Up.

Dane returned. I would have moved a bit to accommodate his large frame taking up so much of the bed but I didn't have the strength. And he didn't seem to mind wedging himself between me and the low headboard, both of us at an angle.

He dropped a sweet kiss on my shoulder, then reached behind him for a small glass bottle with a crooked nozzle sticking out of it.

"What are you up to now?" I asked.

"I promised not to wear you out, remember?"

"Oh, please," I begged. "Wear me out."

He laughed. "Close your eyes and enjoy."

I frowned.

"Ari." That insistent tone of his. "Try to relax."

"Yeah, right. You're naked. I'm naked. In what world would I be able to relax and not hope you're planning to be inside me again in the next five minutes?"

His sexy chuckle didn't help matters. How was I *this* perpetually turned on?

"You might like this just as much," he assured me.

"Not a chance. Whatever it is."

"Eyes closed."

With a frustrated sigh, I did as he said.

His free hand lightly twisted my long hair and tucked it in the crook of my neck. Then I felt the titillating drizzle of warm oil along my spine.

And yes. It, too, felt heavenly.

But it wasn't just the enticing heat caressing my skin that melted me. The scent was out of this world.

Keeping my eyes closed, as commanded—and because this little excursion was much more sensual that way—I asked, "What is that?"

"Frankincense."

I gave a half laugh. "Now you're teasing me because I'm twenty-four-seven Christmas decorations for the Lux."

"I hadn't thought of that. This particular scent reminded me of you."

I inhaled deeply. There was a spicy tinge to it with a hint of orange. Definitely relaxing. Soothing. Delicious.

As Dane spread the rich oil across my back, he said, "This comes from the Oman region in the Persian Gulf. Known for their fragrances. There's a woman who collects the resin from trees on Mughsayl Beach and mixes it with oils. Even sprinkles it on ice cream. It's highly addictive for anyone with a sweet tooth—one bowl is *never* enough."

"Please tell me you didn't sleep with her."

"Ari." He didn't sound amused.

"Just saying."

"If you like this, you can keep the bottle," he offered.

His hands smoothed over my body, his fingers firm and pressing into my muscles in the most sigh-worthy way. His thumbs ran along my spine as his palms splayed toward my sides. He rubbed down to my tailbone, moved back up to my shoulders, and then slowly slid down to my ass. He massaged expertly and I bit back a throaty moan.

He kneaded my cheeks, his thumbs digging into the point on the outer sides, midway. I had no idea what caused that spot to be so sensitive, but it was clearly a pressure point that not only seemed to release oodles of tension but was also erotically stirring. At least when Dane was the one unleashing the tension.

Then he spread the oil down the backs of my thighs, slowly returning to cover my hips and waist.

"Let me guess," I ventured in my now-familiar sultry voice. "You're a certified masseur."

"Not even close. But you pick up a thing or two when you own hotels with spas."

"Or it's just natural talent." Because he was fantastic.

"Really, it's just an excuse to put my hands all over you."

His palms slid around me, underneath me, to my stomach. Then eased upward to my chest. I rose slightly off the satin sheet to let him coat and caress my breasts.

"No excuse needed. Ever. I promise."

"You have a sensational body. I told you that before, based on sight alone. Touching it, enjoying it, is something altogether different."

I glanced over my shoulder. "You really can't be this fascinated."

With one of his intense looks, he said, "You really can't doubt it."

I tore my gaze from his. Dropped my forehead to the cool satin.

Dane continued his sensuous massage. The oil soaked into my skin, feeling luxurious and instantly combating the dryness that came with our usually arid climate. He rubbed my arms and shoulders and I let out a contented sigh. Though it held the undercurrent of desire.

When he reached underneath me again to palm my breasts, he whispered in my ear, "I'm hard for you." His erection pressed to my hip.

"I noticed." I tried to sound nonchalant. No such luck. My voice was breathy, lusty.

"Are you too tired? Too Zenned out?"

"I would have to be dead to not want you." There I went. A bit too revealing.

I sighed with exasperation. He chuckled.

Shifting, he slipped from the bed. My brow furrowed.

"Um, didn't you just suggest we were about to go at it again?"

"It wasn't so much a suggestion as a statement of fact," he said. He was thick and hard.

My mouth watered.

I would never get over how fabulously built he was.

He lifted me into his arms and headed to the hallway.

"Where are we going now?" I asked in between nibbling his earlobe.

"My bedroom."

"That wasn't it?"

"No. I didn't know how messy we might get with the oil, so I set up that room."

"We could have gotten messier."

He grunted in that animalistic way that sent zings through me.

"The intention was the massage. You're lucky I could contain my-self enough to give it to you."

"Oh, you definitely gave it to me," I said in a flirty tone that was wholly uncharacteristic of me. Guess he brought out my fun side in addition to the naughty one.

"Nice to see *you* have a sense of humor."

"You're right." It wasn't as though I let it see the light of day all that often.

We entered another room—an even bigger one than the last. The mammoth rock-trimmed corner fireplace glowed. No candles or other light. Just the fire.

He set me on the edge of the bed and said, "I'll be right back."

As he vanished in the direction in which we'd just come, I sus-pected he went to blow out all the candles.

I stood and took in the more masculine room, decorated with deep-bronze silk drapes and a duvet. Large, distressed brown leather chairs and round wooden tables of varying heights. Books scattered everywhere, even stacked on the wood floor. No personal pictures, as was the case throughout the house, that I'd seen. But I did spy framed artwork on the walls. Several penciled schematics of famous vessels like the *Titanic*, the *Hindenburg*, and the Hughes H-4 Hercules—the *Spruce Goose*—which my dad had once taken me to see on display at the Evergreen Aviation & Space Museum in Oregon, after it'd been moved from its previous Long Beach home.

I stole a peek at some of the authors of the hardbacks lying about. Tolkien, Browning, Shakespeare, Hawthorne, Dickens.

So Dane liked the classics. Classic literature, classic artwork—or modes of transportation, possibly. Historic, inspirational, intel-lectual things. That told me more about him than any photo snapped at the Grand Canyon could, I surmised.

I wondered if he liked *Casablanca. Gone with the Wind. The Prince of Tides.*

What sort of music did he listen to? I scanned the room, looking for an iPod speaker or other sound system. Nothing. I was curious to know if, given that he'd admitted to not having thought about adding tunes to our seductive rendezvous in the other room—when he'd gone to the trouble of scattering rose petals—he might prefer the sounds of nature. The creek, the wind, the thunder and lightning when we had it.

I found something very stimulating about that.

I sat on the bed as he returned. I slipped between the silky ecru sheets and he joined me.

"I took you for more of an absurdly high-count Egyptian cotton bedding sort," I teased.

"That would be correct."

I rubbed the lavish sateen between my fingers and thumb. "So . . . for me, again?"

He grinned. "Thought you'd like it."

"I do." The man didn't miss a thing. Even the lack of music had been perfect, whether he'd known it or not. I might have missed all of his desire-roughened breaths with something playing too loudly in the background.

I snuggled close to him. "Flannel."

Brushing a few curls from my face, he said, "You lost me."

"I like flannel sheets. In the winter. Keeps me warm."

His head dipped and his lips grazed my temple as he murmured, "I'll keep you warm."

My heart fluttered once more.

He added, "You can even rub your feet against mine if they get cold."

"That was romantic," I told him. "You're getting good at this. Not that I'm surprised. Is there anything you don't excel at?"

His jaw instantly clenched. He immediately corrected the tense gesture.

"Let's just say you inspire me."

I saw that he meant those words. I also noted that there was something ominous around the fringes. The dangerous look that crossed his face when he went to that dark place in his mind.

"You're thinking about the Lux?"

"No." His fingers swept over my cheek. "I'm thinking about you. Only you. And how much I want you again."

"*Oh.* You're in luck, then." I straddled his lap. Reached toward the nightstand where he'd dumped condoms. I did like how pre- pared he was—in mass quantity, no less. I clearly wasn't the only one thinking once would never be enough.

My fingers shook a little with anticipation as I tore open the packet. Dane's hands covered mine to steady them as I rolled the condom down his erect cock. My hand slid up and down—he was just too tempting.

"That feels good." His eyes blazed. "But you know what I really want."

Adrenaline pumped through me. "Yes."

I shifted slightly and his tip slid along my slick folds to my open- ing. His hands clasped my hips and I eased down, this time per- fectly fine with drawing him in slowly, relishing every inch as he filled and stretched me.

Our gazes connected. My fingers curved around his shoulders. He thrust deep. The air rushed from my lungs.

"Dane." He felt incredible.

He moved languidly. Heat flared in his emerald irises, but emo- tion edged in. His jaw worked. His grip on my hips tightened. I did things to this man. For the life of me, I didn't know what, but it was stamped over his hard features.

Warmth flooded me, not just from the way we made love. It was everything—the way he made me feel, the way he responded to me, the way he watched me so closely, so astutely.

He sat up, thick and hard, deep in my pussy. One of his hands swept hair from my shoulder and cheek. Then his fingers trailed along the column of my neck, over my collarbone. Downward to palm my breast. His head dipped and his tongue fluttered against my puckered nipple, eliciting a tingly sensation that spread through- out my body. He suckled deep and I gasped.

My head fell back on my shoulders, my eyelids closing. He squeezed my breast firmly and his tongue flickered over the taut peak. His other arm slipped around my waist, possessively holding me to him. I rocked slightly, losing myself in the feel of him and all the pleasure he sparked.

"The frankincense on your skin is even more addictive than the ice cream," he murmured against my breast. His warm breath teased my nipple tighter. "This scent is perfect for you."

I had to admit, it captivated me as well, one more element to make this the most sensual experience of my life.

"I'm tempted to lick it off every inch of you," he said.

A soft moan fell from my lips. "I officially concede that whatever you want to do to me will be spectacular."

"Nice to see I've finally won you over."

"Something tells me you never doubted you would."

"You do know how I feel about winning."

I briefly worried if I really was the kill he'd been searching for—and whether he'd want me now that he'd had me.

But then he leaned back against the mountain of pillows, bringing me with him. His hands returned to my hips and his leisurely pace kicked into high gear. All concern fled my mind. I didn't think about or concentrate on anything other than Dane and the excitement racing through me.

I was sprawled across his expansive chest, my fingers clutching his shoulders again as he guided me to lift a bit off him. He palmed my ass with both hands, spreading me wider, and pumped into me. Swiftly, skillfully. I let out a small cry as he thrust deep and fast, hitting all the right notes.

"Oh, God," I moaned. My breasts pressed to his pecs and I clung to him as his hips bucked wildly, pushing us both to the edge. "Yes, Dane. God—oh, God—yes!" I called his name as I came, fiery sensations ripping through me.

"That's it," he said on a low rumble. His hands on my ass forced my pelvis down and I ground against him as I clenched him. "Fuck, yeah. Just like that, baby. Just . . . like—oh, Jesus." His grip on me tensed and he thrust harder. I felt him explode deep within me. His satisfied growl filled the quiet room.

His arms circled me, crushing me to him. My head dropped to the crook of his shoulder and I breathed heavily against his neck.

"God, Dane," I muttered. "You are so unbelievably good." I'd lost count of the night's orgasms. But each one had been astounding.

My heart thundered in time with his. I felt giddy, light-headed. My entire body tingled; my skin burned.

And still, I wanted more.

He stroked my hair, my spine. I wasn't sure I'd ever catch my breath. Wasn't sure I wanted to, really.

"I'm definitely okay with nothing being off-limits," I told him.

"Good. I've only just started. . . ."

I snuggled a little closer, though I was pretty much already glued to him. Inhaling his heat and cologne, I held the scent of him in my lungs before letting out a long sigh. "You're delicious. So masculine. So . . ." I laughed self-deprecatingly at my scrambled brain. "So sexy."

His fingertips continued to graze my spine. A tantalizing touch. One that kept me aroused.

He remained quiet for a minute or two. My eyes closed. I breathed him in, wondering how I'd existed pre-Dane.

I was lost in some lustful fog when he finally broke the silence.

"It'd be all right, you know," he said in his rich, intimate voice. The one that made my insides quiver.

I lifted my head, stared into his eyes. "What would be all right?"

The corner of his mouth twitched. He held my gaze and said, "If you fell in love with me."

I gaped.

He added, "Even if it's just a little."

"*Oh.*" Emotion seeped through my veins, welling so that a hard lump rose in my throat.

He gazed unwaveringly, smoothing away hair from my forehead and temple.

I couldn't speak. Had no idea what to say.

"Ari." His lips brushed mine, tangling softly, sweetly. "I won't hurt you."

That promise again.

I had nothing to say. I could have told him I didn't think I was wired that way, that it wouldn't happen.

But the fluttering of my heart this evening and the scarcity of my breath told me I might be wrong.

I might have already fallen . . . hard.

# chapter 16

I woke surrounded by heat and hard muscles. Completely enveloped in Dane's strength, his territorial embrace. His erection pressed against my side.

I smiled.

Despite the tender spots, my body responded instantly.

I'd slept more soundly than I could ever remember. Multiple orgasms and a world-class massage left me boneless and dreamless. Relaxed from head to toe. With the exception of the electric current Dane elicited.

"Are you awake?" I whispered.

"Mm-hmm."

"Oh, good." I dragged his hand down to the apex of my legs. "Do you want to be inside me again?"

"You know I do."

Seconds later he was sheathed and sliding into me from behind. His fingers stroked my clit as he moved slowly.

"Not too sore?" he asked.

"The only thing I feel is you. And that's perfect."

He let out a soft *humph*, then increased the tempo. The quick, sexy rhythm set my pulse racing.

"God, you make me hot," he said. His arm was wrapped around me, one hand caressing my breast. Between my legs, his fingers slid along my folds, then one flitted quickly against the knot of nerves. All the while, he thrust deep.

My fist curled around the sheet and little whimpers of desire and need fell from my lips. How I'd gone from containing my physical involvement with anyone to instantly craving Dane's touch was beyond me, but I had an insatiable need for him.

"Fuck me," I whispered between torn breaths. "Harder."

He plunged into me. Pumped stronger.

"Yes. Just like that." My grip tightened on the bedding.

He kissed my shoulder, my neck. Bit lightly, making me writhe beneath him. "You like my hard cock inside you."

"Yes."

"Thrusting deep."

"Yes."

"Until you come."

"Oh, God!" I did . . . and Dane fell apart with me.

Our harsh breaths mingled in the quiet morning. The throbbing of his cock beat in time with the pulsating vibe in my core. It became another few precious moments I could have reveled in for all eternity.

He seemed to have similar thoughts. "If I didn't have a hotel to open, I'd stay buried in your sweet pussy all damn day."

I grinned. "And I'd let you."

With a low grunt, he finally disentangled himself. Then he tossed off the bedcovers and climbed out of bed. "Feel free to use my bathroom. I've got one in the dressing room."

My brow crooked. "You have a dressing room?"

"I converted a bedroom to accommodate a larger bathroom in here."

"Yes, I noticed it deserves its own zip code."

He smirked. "I'll fix breakfast before we head to the Lux. Meet me on the patio when you're ready."

"And he cooks," I quipped, admiring everything about the man. "Let me guess—you studied the fine art of crêpes suzette at Le Cordon Bleu Paris?" I said it a bit haughtily.

He chuckled and kissed my forehead. "Betty Crocker."

I watched him strut out of the room, naked and gorgeous.

This was all so surreal. Yet a shiver of excitement ran along my spine at the thought of him—and the way he touched me. The things he said. The way he made me feel.

I slipped from the bed with a smile on my face. I collected my tote and the stunning nightgown and robe and then returned to his bathroom. I showered and pulled the robe on, loving the rich satin against my skin. I did my hair, but the smell of strong coffee lured me away from the mirror.

Down the hall, I crossed the vast great room, pausing to pick up Dane's shirt from the floor, where we'd left it last night. Apparently, he'd put the drawstring pants back on, because they were missing. I held the linen shirt to my nose and inhaled deeply, savoring the scent of him. So much so, I loosened the sash on the robe and eased out of it. I put his shirt on instead and drew in another deep breath.

I turned toward the wall of windows and doors and found Dane at one of the smaller glass-topped tables. Watching me.

I passed through the opened doors to the terrace on the bank of the creek. Heaters kept the early-morning chill at bay.

Dane had the newspaper in one hand, a mug of cappuccino in the other, as I joined him.

"That was sexy," he said, lust tingeing his voice.

My cheeks warmed. "Too bad we can't bottle your scent. I like it even more than the frankincense."

He set aside the coffee and paper and reached for me, pulling me into his lap. He wrapped one arm around my waist. The other hand cupped the side of my face and he kissed me. Slowly, deeply. As it went on and on, his palm slid over my throat and down to my chest. He deftly worked the first few buttons and slipped his hand inside to caress my breast and then brushed his thumb over my tight nipple. As he paid the same attention to my other breast, magma flowed in my veins.

When he finally dragged his mouth from mine, I was burning up. No heaters necessary.

"It'll definitely be a toasty winter if you keep doing that."

He grinned. Funny how he didn't even balk at my second mention of us being together in winter when it was still only September.

My fingers skimmed over the scratches on his bare chest, running from his collarbone to his pecs. Four nail marks that clawed at him.

"I'm sorry," I said with a cringe.

"Don't be. I like you all worked up and crazed for me." His voice was sensual and arousing.

He kissed me again. Then, breathless, I got to my feet and took the chair across from him. Or we'd never make it to work.

"Keep the buttons undone," he said, his tone a bit darker.

I did as instructed.

He asked, "Which section of the paper do you want?"

"Sports."

The corner of his mouth lifted. "Why'd I even ask?" He handed it over.

I scanned scores as I dug into the omelet on my plate. Fully loaded and absolutely fantastic. I moaned. "My compliments to Ms. Crocker."

He chuckled. "Don't get too excited. I have a very limited kitchen repertoire."

"Good thing you have five-star chefs at your disposal."

"It's certainly a perk."

I went back to devouring my breakfast, including the southwestern potatoes with red and green bell peppers and onions, a hint of cayenne and paprika to add just the right amount of spice. Ravenous, I barely said another word until I reached for my orange juice to wash it all down. Then I started in on the cappuccino.

When we were finished, I stood to collect the dishes.

"Don't worry about them," Dane said. "I have someone who cleans. Rosa. She comes in at nine."

"Then I'll do my makeup and get dressed."

As much as I wanted to kiss him before I left the patio, I hesitated. All of this was out of my realm of normalcy. I didn't want to make assumptions. Though after last night . . . all the intimacy and the things we'd said in the heat of passion—

Dane caught my wrist, taking the guesswork out of how this was all supposed to go. He got to his feet, drew me into his arms, and kissed me. It sizzled as he held me tightly and his tongue delved deep, sliding over mine.

When he eventually pulled away, I was breathless. Yet somehow I managed to say, "We're going to be late. I wouldn't want the boss to think I'm a slacker."

His mischievous grin made my stomach flip. "I think you're safe." He kissed me again, another scorcher. Then said, "Take however much time you need."

"Thanks." I returned to his bathroom and wrapped up quickly.

We met in the foyer and I all but melted in my high heels. Dane wore black, too. A sharp tailored suit I had no doubt was by Armani or some other prestigious designer. A dark-gray silk tie complemented his crisp white shirt.

"I forgot how incredible you look with clothes on," I told him, admiring the view. "Though naked really is preferable."

"You're amusing."

"I'm being totally serious." And had to bite back the sigh of longing swelling in my throat.

He took my tote from me and gathered up both our laptop bags. I preceded him outside. We left in his black Escalade instead of the F5. I surmised the latter lacked trunk space. Or a backseat. There'd be no place to put our bags, except piled high on my lap.

We left the gated property and I tried to shift my attention from Dane to work as we drove into Sedona and then west toward the Lux. It was difficult to concentrate, though, when flashes of him between my legs, behind me, beneath me, on top of me, riddled my mind. It was completely insane, but now I ached for him *all* the time.

We slowed at the security booth but breezed through the gates, the guards clearly recognizing Dane's vehicle and license plate, not daring to detain the owner of 10,000 Lux. We pulled alongside the entrance of the hotel and Brandon, dressed in black pants and a black polo shirt with the Lux's crest in gold on the left chest, swooped in to open the passenger door for me. It suddenly hit me how my arrival with Dane must appear.

I quickly explained to the valet, "I had car trouble this morning. Mr. Bax was kind enough to give me a ride."

"If your Sorento needs to go to the dealer, Miss DeMille, I can arrange that for you. Pickup and delivery. You don't have to do a thing."

"Wow, you really are all about first-class service."

He smiled. "Well, it's not exactly your standard hotel."

"No, it's definitely not."

Brandon retrieved our bags from the back of the SUV and handed them over. Then he walked ahead of us to the tall doors and pulled one open. I caught sight of Kyle in the lobby and quickened my pace.

"Hey," I said. "Don't you look professional?"

He wore a navy-colored suit and what I suspected were new shoes.

"Interview," he explained. "I'm meeting someone from HR."

"Probably Patricia." I glanced at Dane, who kept up with me, given his wide strides. "You two haven't officially been introduced. Dane Bax, Kyle Jenns."

They shook, though it was that sharp, tense kind that belied the whole territory-encroachment issue.

Maybe this wasn't such a good idea after all.

But I'd already pleaded my case with Dane, and he'd agreed to let the chips fall where they may when it came to Kyle possibly working at the Lux.

"And there's Patricia now," I said as she stepped around a white marble and gold-accented pillar. She headed our way. "So, good luck," I told Kyle as Dane latched on to my elbow and started to maneuver me away. "Let me know how it goes."

We started off toward the glass-enclosed elevators. Over my shoulder, I mouthed, *Call me.* I held my hand up to my ear, mimicking the pinkie and thumb gesture for Kyle to phone.

Dane's grip tightened on my elbow and I turned back to him. "After last night, do you honestly think he's any sort of competition?"

"Haven't we already established that I protect what's mine?"

A wicked thrill shot through me. "He's no threat, Dane," was all I could say.

The truth was, it excited the hell out of me that he had this claim over me. It was completely foreign yet exhilarating.

We flashed our badges against the electronic reader he'd just had installed at the west wing bank of elevators, so that only authorized personnel could access this portion of the hotel. On the fourth floor, we parted ways at my office door.

There was no one in the hallway, so he leaned in close and whispered, "We'll have dinner tomorrow night. Pack another bag."

My pulse jumped. "Feel free to punish me if Kyle gets the job."

He scowled—though somewhat playfully. "You already know he's getting the job."

"Dane." I smiled at him.

"It's what you wanted."

"Yes, so . . . Thank you." I kissed him on the cheek, then entered my office, a bit on the giddy side. Too bad I couldn't tell my new friend, so he wouldn't stress over the interview. But I couldn't call him now that he was with Patricia.

I set my tote alongside my desk and unloaded my laptop bag. I had another huge stack of catalogs to wade through and samples to order. I also needed to take photos of the lobby to fully assess where all the decorations would go and somehow gauge how many miles of garland, crates of ornaments, truckloads of wreaths, et cetera, I'd need.

*And twinkle lights.*

Lots and lots of clear twinkle lights.

Amano waited for me outside my office when I headed to the stairwell. He fell into step behind me, not crowding me, but close enough that he could intervene in any given situation. It was a bit disconcerting to have someone follow my every move. However, if it made Dane feel better until he'd fixed all of his problems at the resort I'd do as asked and let Amano perform his duties. He wasn't a nuisance, didn't try to chat me up. Just provided a protective presence.

I snapped photos of the outer entrance of the Lux. Then the lobby and reception area. The key to the holiday decorations was to create a beautifully festive ambience but not overdo it so that anything detracted from the natural, decadent opulence of the place.

Though I was extremely good at striking a balance with my weddings, I couldn't help but fear I'd go overboard here. So much opportunity and an astronomical budget were demonic temptations to a party planner. But, again, the goal was not to have every inch of 10,000 Lux dripping Christmas decorations. I had to be strategic. What I did needed to accentuate, enhance, complement what currently existed. Not overrun the stunning fixtures and features of the hotel.

My stomach churned as I considered how seriously I could fuck this all up. And let Dane down.

I didn't even know how to calculate the amount of everything I'd have to order. I decorated a sad-sack Charlie Brown Christmas tree every year, because my dad and I didn't really do holidays. So my effort was hardly on par with what I dealt with now.

And that brought up another consideration—trees. Did I want a single tall one standing between the curving staircases? Accompanied by two skinny ones up front at the entrance? Or maybe just the skinny trees so I didn't block the view out to the grounds beyond the lobby?

*Shit.* For that matter, where the hell would I get a real tree that spanned three or four stories? Where would I get an artificial one of that magnitude if I had to go that route?

I stalked back to the stairwell, forgetting all about Amano as I stewed over my lack of experience with something as simple as holiday decorations.

I spent the majority of the day on the Internet, deciding I had to start with the tree options before I could even think of selecting ornaments. Something told me I'd need everything custom made. But did we have enough time for that?

Mid-afternoon, Molly came into my office with three gentlemen wearing jeans and T-shirts, tool belts around their waists.

She said, "Your corkboard has arrived. Is now a good time to install it?"

"Install?" My brow jerked up. What had Dane done?

I stepped around my desk and into the hallway, finding a long metal cart with a mammoth wood cabinet resting on it, protected by a drop cloth on the floor of the cart.

One of the men told me, "There's corkboard inside and also on the inner panels of the doors, so that you have more space to pin stuff. You can also close and lock the cabinet when necessary, for security."

"Wow. This is much more than I expected." So Dane-like.

"It'll take us about a half hour to install it. Just confirm where you want it hung."

We returned to my office and I indicated the wall by the conference table.

"I have a meeting," I said, "so now works well."

I gathered up my papers and placed them in a black leather folio. Then I left the workers to it. Molly and I walked toward the stairwell, since that was where Dane's office suite was located. He was just outside the door to his inner sanctum, engaged in discussion with Amano.

As we approached, Molly peeled off to enter the suite.

Dane asked me, "Where are you off to?"

"I have a meeting on the third floor with PR." To Amano, I said, "I won't be long. There are some guys in my office putting up my corkboard." I shot Dane a look and added, "Thanks, by the way. It's gorgeous. And huge."

"You have a lot of planning to do."

Hadn't I just learned the full extent of it this morning? "I do. This will be a big help."

Amano said, "Maybe I should be in there with them."

"Probably a good idea," Dane agreed.

I didn't have anything top secret going on at the moment, but given the anxiety over security that Dane had, I wouldn't add to his grief by protesting.

Instead, I assured them, "I'll just be one floor down with Traci Carpenter, VP of Public Relations."

Dane nodded his approval. I moved past them as they wrapped up their conversation. I opened the heavy door and stepped into the stairwell, trying to get my breathing under control before I met with Traci. I didn't need her seeing me all flushed and excited. She wouldn't know it was because of Dane, granted. But still. A five-second conversation with him had me all hot and bothered, so that I was—

I drew up short on the fifth step down and let out a bloodcurdling scream. My heart leapt into my throat and my portfolio went flying, all the papers scattering in the air.

On the landing not more than six or seven steps from me was a rattlesnake. Coiled and hissing.

"Oh, shit," I choked out. "Oh, God!"

Terror besieged me. The snake started to uncoil and move. Toward me. I took very small, slow steps backward, up to the fourth-floor landing. It slithered to the first step. I turned and raced the rest of the way up and grabbed the handle on the door. It didn't budge.

*Fuck!*

I swiped my badge, forgetting that I had to in order to unlock the door. The light remained red. I swiped again, yanked on the handle. Nothing happened.

I stole a glance down the stairway. The rattler inched toward me, its pronged tongue darting in and out of its mouth, its tail sounding like a sprinkler going off in the middle of summer.

I screamed again. Pounded on the door. "Dane! Amano! *Someone!*"

I pulled harder on the lever. Then my fists banged against the door again.

Suddenly the electronic reader chimed and the door flew open. I jumped back.

Dane took one look at me—likely with horror stamped across my face—and grabbed me, jerking me to him.

"Jesus Christ," he said.

"Snake." I pointed. "Don't let the door close!"

"What the *fuck*?" He ushered me out of the stairwell, his arms tight around me.

My heart had never thundered so fiercely. I couldn't catch my breath.

"What happened?" Amano demanded.

"Rattler," was all Dane said.

Amano flung the door open and saw it for himself. "Son of a bitch." He slammed the door closed. "I'll get rid of it."

"Have the grounds crew do a thorough sweep to see if there are more. Tell them to check for eggs." Dane guided me to his office.

Molly sprang to her feet when we entered. "My God, Ari! You're white as a ghost." To Dane, she repeated Amano's question. "What happened?"

I shook uncontrollably, so she likely assumed I couldn't get a coherent word out. She was probably right.

Dane said to her, "Send an e-mail to all employees to stay out of the west wing stairwell and tape signs to the outside of the doors telling them to keep out."

"I don't under—"

"Please, just do it," he insisted. "No one's to be in the stairwell."

"Of course, Mr. Bax. Whatever you say." She scurried off.

Dane led me to the sofa and I sank onto the cushion, still vibrating violently. He poured a scotch and brought it to me, sitting on the sturdy coffee table in front of me and holding the crystal tumbler so I could sip.

"It's okay," he said in a soothing voice. "It'll be okay." Tension radiated from him, undermining his effort to calm me.

After a much longer gulp of scotch, I asked, "How the hell would a rattlesnake get into the stairwell?"

"I don't know, Ari." His jaw clenched. He didn't say more. Didn't want to speculate. Just brooded in a tormented sort of way.

Several minutes passed as I polished off the drink. My breathing slowed but my pulse was still erratic. That damn snake could have given me a massive coronary before it'd even bitten me.

Amano returned. With a concerned look I appreciated, he asked, "Are you okay?"

"Getting there," I lied.

To Dane, he said, "We've got it under control in the stairwell. Couple of guys on the crew worked at a golf club in Scottsdale previously. They're used to dealing with the snakes. Keep special lassos on hand, just in case."

"They're not all that common this far north," Dane commented. "Especially not this time of year."

He shook his head and stood. Anguish rolled off him in waves, mixed with the very obvious tension over it having been me in the dangerous situation.

"Goddamn it!" he suddenly roared as his fist slammed against his desk.

I jumped.

He glanced my way and asked, "Why couldn't you get back in?"

I lifted the badge hanging on a thin, bejeweled lanyard around my neck. "Didn't work."

Amano was instantly on his cell. "Bring up Miss DeMille's account," he said without preamble. His strained tone spoke volumes, and a second later he was shaking his head, too, and pacing the floor. "Deactivated? When? . . . Twenty minutes ago. Shit . . . Not just hers? Three others." He shot a look toward Dane. "More goddamn IT issues." He listened further, then said, "Reactivate her account and monitor it regularly."

As soon as he disconnected the call, Dane told him, "I want all of the security wiring replaced before Monday morning. I don't care if your contractors have to work around the clock. Get it done. Every single camera has to be functioning before I come in."

"Agreed. The cameras in the stairwell aren't even hooked up at the moment. But they will be."

So there was no concrete way to discern how a snake had made its way into the area. A propped-open door during some routine maintenance work, or . . . Had someone on the inside known about the cameras not currently providing surveillance in the stairwell?

I was at a loss, though one thing was clear. This did not bode well for anyone. Dane in particular. And I could see the toll it took on him. But he was obviously more worried about me.

Taking my hand, he said, "Come on. We'll get some stuff from your house and then you'll stay at mine until we've figured this all out."

Panic seized me. "You don't think—"

"I don't know what to think, Ari. Except that you take that route when no one else does. So what the hell am I supposed to—"

"Dane, no one knows about us. Why would . . . ?" Okay, Amano knew. But other than that . . . "No one outside this room knows about us. And I'm not involved in anything confidential at the moment. I'm just getting started with the launch preparation."

"I'm not taking chances, okay? The media-room fire and now a snake in the stairwell?" His piercing emerald eyes left no potential for argument. "Just let me handle this, Ari. Let me take care of it."

"How?" I asked, though my voice wasn't very steady—like I wasn't quite sure I wanted to know his answer.

"I have my ways."

# chapter 17

Snake-tat guy flashed in my mind again.

"I've seen you 'handle' things," I told Dane. I got to my feet and stepped closer to him. "You're talking about violence here, right?"

His gaze narrowed on me. "I'm talking about doing whatever I have to in order to protect the Lux—and you. *Especially* you, Ari."

My heart pounded heavily. "Dane . . . I can't . . . I mean, that's—" I shook my head. Turned away. My eyes squeezed shut.

He was willing to go to any extreme to stop the attacks. To even the score. However he looked at it. And that disturbed me as much as it provided a hint of relief that he wasn't going to let anything happen to the hotel or me. That whatever the threat, he could contain it.

At the same time, I worried over that *extreme.* How far he'd actually go. I'd caught enough glimpses of his angst to know a storm brewed within him. If anything went more haywire at the Lux—and involved me—what would be his breaking point? And how volatile would the tempest be?

I wasn't a fan of rage. I'd grown up in a house full of fury and explosive tempers. There'd been a few too many instances in my life when I'd encountered someone *on the verge of massive destruction.*

"Ari," Dane said as he laid a hand on my arm. "Just take a few breaths. Trust me."

I opened my eyes and faced him. "I'm a little afraid of what you might be capable of."

A bit of an understatement, but the truth nonetheless.

He nodded. "Try to understand why it's so important to me to—"

"I don't know why anything's important to you, Dane!" I erupted. "Because you're still not telling me everything!"

Amano moved in and said to Dane, "I'll manage everything here."

"I know you will." Dane clasped the man on the shoulder, though Amano was a good three inches taller and maybe twenty or so years Dane's senior. "I trust you. Thank you."

I had no idea what their relationship was, how long they'd known each other, or what had bonded them together, but I couldn't dispute that the expression in Amano's eyes, the intensity exuding from him, confirmed he was a solid for Dane. On his side all the way. Mine, too, given my association with Dane. Amano had been worried about me. Maybe even before the snake incident, if his diligent shadowing was any indication.

Dane gathered up his laptop and some files and packed them in his bag. Then he put an arm around my waist and we left his office. In mine, the workers had finished and the new, slim corkboard cabinet was striking on my pristine white wall. But I didn't have time to get all jazzed over it. Urgency radiated from Dane. He wanted me out of here. Fast.

I wasn't inclined to dillydally. I still trembled from head to toe. He helped me get all the things I needed in order to continue working over the weekend, including carrying an enormous stack of catalogs as I slung the strap of the laptop bag over my shoulder. He grabbed my tote and we headed out.

The elevator arrived and he peered inside before letting me in. That freaked me out even more—was I going to have to watch my every step, peek around every corner, from now on?

"Dane." I swallowed hard. "What else haven't you told me?" Because I had a disturbing suspicion there was a deeper plot to this nightmare.

"Not now, Ari."

I simmered. His angst set me on edge. There was more to what was happening at the Lux. I could feel it in my bones. The investment group mishap was not anything to be discounted; I knew that. But I could sense there were things he hadn't told me last night.

We left the property and I fought to keep the questions flying from my mouth. He drove us to my townhome and I packed another bag and grabbed a couple more suits still on their hangers. Anxiety tore through me as we wound our way up Oak Creek Canyon.

It was a gloomy afternoon with a light drizzle. Not our typical autumn weather. I started to feel as though the universe conspired against Dane and 10,000 Lux.

I spared a glance at him and noted his white-knuckled grip on the steering wheel. I wondered if he pondered the same thing I did. Or if there was something a bit darker on his mind.

A chill ran down my spine. Here was the problem with being so wrapped up in this man and his world. I really didn't know him. Not as well as I should when I'd just been locked in a stairwell with a deadly snake.

I shuddered.

*Best not to think of that right now, Ari.*

I needed to calm down. I tried to force my shoulders to loosen. They remained bunched much too close to my ears. My hands still shook.

Dane reached over and covered them as I wrung them in my lap. "Calm down. You're making me even more inclined to throttle someone."

I shot him a look. "But you're not sure which someone, are you?"

"Let's just say, it's time to get this under control."

"How do you plan to do that?"

"Trust me to handle it, Ari."

I inhaled deeply, hoping it would steady me a bit. No such luck. I asked, "Don't you have other partners who are concerned?"

"Yes. Three others from the initial investment group. I'll probably spend the majority of tomorrow with them at the house."

I nodded. "I'll stay out of your way. I have a lot to do."

"You don't have to work twenty-four-seven, baby. We still have almost three months till the grand opening."

"That's really not as much time as you think in the land of event planning. And I don't mind being so busy."

It'd always been the way I'd managed my life and my emotions. Part of the avoidance theory I'd adopted at a young age. In this case, it'd help to have something to focus on other than what had happened today. And how I'd literally spiraled out of control with Dane.

I was alarmed by the inescapable acknowledgment of how deep I was in with this man and that there was no longer the retreat I was accustomed to making when the flame burned a bit too close to the skin. With Dane, I couldn't seem to keep the walls up. More than that, I didn't want to keep them up.

That meant I had to coax more out of him. Really find out what he was involved with and how it truly impacted the Lux. And me.

We arrived at his creekside, nestled-in-the-woods house and he unlocked the door for me, then grabbed our things from the SUV. He left our work bags in the foyer and I followed him down the wide hallway to a room opposite his. The dressing room.

I pulled up short and gasped at the size of it. "Good Lord, Dane."

He set my totes on the rectangular marble-topped bureau with drawers and cabinets that was situated in the center of the room. He hung my clothes on the only empty rack against the far wall, with a ledge above and below for accessories or shoes. The wood was a rich mahogany and there was a three-way mirror in the corner, along with several chairs and end tables scattered about. The room was filled with his neatly arranged suits, shirts, ties, shoes, sweaters, pants. I took it all in, awestruck again.

"I thought rooms like this only existed in movies," I said, unable to process how much the setup alone cost, not to mention every article of clothing filling it.

He opened two top drawers and relocated the T-shirts inside. Then he asked, "Will this do?"

I stared at him, now befuddled. "You're giving me drawers?"

"You don't want your clothes to wrinkle, right?"

"Right," I numbly agreed.

*Drawers.* Wasn't that a really big deal?

*Don't think about it, Ari. Just unpack.*

I retrieved the yoga suits and other items I'd brought along and tucked them away. Dane stripped down, changing into another pair of loose black pants and a black tank top that fit him sinfully well, displaying his bulging biceps and conforming to his chiseled chest and abs.

He held me spellbound as I removed my jacket and he gave me an extra hanger for it.

"Thanks," I murmured, completely captivated by him.

I fumbled with the small pearl buttons on my French cuffs. He grinned when it became all too apparent that my now-trembling fingers weren't because a snake had terrified me but because of how Dane excited me. So easily. He stepped forward and helped out, our gazes locked.

He slipped the little orbs through the holes on the flap of my blouse and slid the material down my arms. He hung up the garment, then moved behind me to unzip the back of my skirt, easing it to my ankles so I could step out of it. My shoes followed.

I opened a drawer again and skimmed my fingers over my clothes, none of them holding much appeal.

"You want something of mine?"

I glanced up. "Yes."

Rounding the bureau to his side, he pulled out an oatmeal-colored long-sleeved Henley.

"This one's comfortable," he said.

I unhooked my bra and put it in the drawer before shutting it.

"Or maybe forego the shirt altogether."

I smiled softly. "Something tells me you still have work to focus on. It's not even five o'clock yet."

He grimaced. A sexy expression like every other one coming from him. "I do have a Board of Directors conference call for a nonprofit that I need to prep for."

"Then prep." I stretched on tiptoe and gave him a kiss. "What's the organization?"

"Children's group homes."

My brows knitted. "Orphanages?"

"They don't really call them that anymore. They're privately held and funded group homes."

"And you donate your time and money to them."

"Yes."

"Huh." Warmth oozed through me. "That's pretty amazing."

He lifted the shirt above my head. "You'd better cover up or neither of us will get anything done tonight."

I slipped into the Henley and he whisked my hair from inside the collar, fanning it out over my shoulders. The buttoned neckline dipped between my breasts and he didn't bother to fasten me up, just left the material open so the rounded swells filled the gap.

He seemed to admire me for several seconds. Then his head dipped and he kissed me.

I clung to him, loving the nearness of him, the way he engulfed me with his entire sexy presence.

When he broke the kiss, he kept me in his strong embrace and whispered, "What happened to you today scared the hell out of me."

"Dane—"

"Just listen." His voice was strained, tattered. "I'd be worried and fuming over any employee or guest finding themselves in that situation. Possibly getting hurt. But the fact that it was you . . ."

His arms tightened.

"I'm okay," I tried to assure him.

"No. You've been shaking since I pulled you out of the stairwell."

My face was buried in the crook of his neck as I said, "I have a serious aversion to all reptiles. I told you that."

"Ari, if Amano or I hadn't been right outside the door—"

"Don't make me think about that. Please." I had no delusions of the trouble I'd been in. Even if my badge hadn't been deactivated, I could have been thoroughly engrossed in paperwork and bounded down those steps, right to that snake, giving it the perfect opportunity to strike.

I shivered. Dane held me firmer against his hard body.

"I wouldn't forgive myself if you'd been bitten. You know that. I'm not sure I can for—"

"Dane." I wrenched free from his embrace. "It wasn't your fault. None of this is your fault."

"Ari," he said in a compelling tone as he stared deep into my eyes, "you don't seem to get it. I'd be upset if anyone encountered what you did on my property. But again, the fact that it was *you* makes it infinitely worse."

"I'm not saying I'm not appreciative. I'm saying . . . I need to know what lies beyond all this darkness, all this anger. All this need for revenge."

He was quiet for several seconds, still gazing unwaveringly at me. Finally, he said, "You're not the only one who grew up in an environment beyond your control. I had no clear idea of what happened to my parents. I just grew up without them. And for a while, I didn't understand why Amano was always shadowing me, why I couldn't go anywhere without him."

"How do you know him? How did you know you could trust him?"

For that matter, the stunning and mysterious Mikaela Madsen flashed in my mind. What was her role in Dane's life?

He brushed strands of hair from my temple, distracting me from my wayward thoughts. "Like my lawyer, we go way back. Amano was head of security at my family's estate. He stayed on after my parents died, to keep an eye on my aunt and me. He's invaluable. I trust him explicitly."

"Was it necessary for him to stick so close to you?"

"Yes. There were threats that I eventually found out about. Against me. Against my aunt, who raised me. I didn't grasp what they were all about, until later on, when I was old enough to comprehend the amount of money I was heir to, the properties and businesses I owned."

He shook his head. My heart wrenched.

"Dane, I can't even begin to imagine how difficult that all was to process."

"It was the threats I focused on the most," he said, that tense, lethal look that I had become all too familiar with crossing his face. "My aunt made sacrifices, did whatever she had to do to take care of me. I couldn't stand anyone trying to take away what I felt she was also entitled to. The house, which I deeded to her as soon as I was able to, and a bank account that was supposed to guarantee—"

He moved away from me.

"Supposed to guarantee what?" I asked.

With another shake of his head, he told me, "We could afford the best doctors, the best care for her. She shouldn't have died."

"Oh, God," I said on a heavy breath. "Dane." I closed the gap between us and gripped his arm. "You can't save someone just because you have money. But how—?"

"Breast cancer."

I started to see things in a different light. He thought it was his duty, his responsibility, to take care of those around him, those who worked for him or had raised him. And because he'd always had a financial safety net, he'd likely considered himself invincible.

"I'm so sorry," I said. "But you can't blame yourself for the position you found yourself in, or for what happened to your aunt. You can't save the world, Dane."

This seemed to aggravate him further, if the flexing of his muscles was any indication. "You still don't understand that my obligations are—"

"I'm not an obligation," I insisted. "Dane." I searched his eyes, looking for exactly what he was trying to say to me.

"Ari. You're not seeing the biggest picture of all." Leaning in close, he kissed me slowly yet intensely. Then, against my lips, he murmured, "I'm in love with you."

# chapter 18

I didn't know what to say.

Apparently, Dane didn't have a problem with my lack of words. His mouth sealed with mine and he kissed me possessively. My body melded to his and I slipped my arms around his neck, holding on tight.

I experienced a different kind of bliss. Exhilaration over the way he fervently ignited my insides mixed with warmth from his admission until I burned with need.

Breaking the kiss, I simply said, "Dane."

And he knew what I wanted.

With one arm still around my waist, he reached for his suit jacket on top of the bureau with his free hand and dug out his wallet and a condom. He clenched the packet between his teeth as he whisked my panties down my thighs and I worked them off at my ankles.

He led us to the armless chair next to the full-length mirrors and yanked his pants and briefs to his hips, rolled on the condom, and pulled me into his lap. I straddled him and he sank in deep.

"*Yes*," I whispered along his temple. "God, you feel so good."

I rocked slightly as his hands roved my body, slipping under the shirt I wore. He clasped my waist and pressed me against him, tighter, as he thrust into me. I gasped. He was thick and full and pumping deeper, faster.

He palmed my breasts and massaged them, teasing my nipples into hard points. My head fell back and I let out a throaty moan as the sizzling sensations built. I curled my fingers into his biceps as he commanded my passion and pushed me higher.

Dane swept the material covering me up to my chest and then his tongue flicked over my nipple, puckering the bud further. He drew the taut peak into his mouth and my insides ignited.

I shamelessly, wholly sparked with this man. Everything he did sent me straight to the edge.

And he knew it.

His breath caressed my sensitive skin as he murmured, "Come for me."

My fingers tangled in his lush hair and I rocked more firmly, my hips undulating. He gripped my waist again and guided me into a quicker rhythm that made soft pants fall from my lips.

He captured them with a hungry kiss and I lost it completely. Ripping my mouth from his, I cried out his name as the searing orgasm consumed me. I squeezed him tight.

"Yes," he ground out. "Ari. Baby."

I felt him surge and pulse within me. Then his cock throbbed in wild beats as he came, his hands still holding me steady.

My head fell forward and my lips grazed his cheek, his jaw, his neck. I quietly, breathlessly, said in his ear, "Just because I can't say the words yet doesn't mean I don't feel it, too."

His arms slid around me and our bodies pressed together. "I've been patient so far, haven't I?"

I laughed. "You move fast and push hard."

"I don't see the point in wasting time when I want something.

This has been a bit different, but it's meant to be, so I'm not going to hide the fact that I'm crazy about you."

I swept a wayward lock of hair from his forehead. He'd given me something to work with here—something in my comfort zone. "I'm crazy about you, too."

"See?" He grinned devilishly. "You come around quick."

Then he gave me a sweet but hot kiss.

It was impossible to deny that I was totally wrapped up in Dane. I'd realized long ago that my feelings ran deep. A somewhat unsettling and tenuous situation to find myself in, given that I still didn't know all that much about him. Just that he wanted me and fiercely pursued this budding relationship.

When I partially came to my senses, I said, "Don't you have a conference call?"

He grunted. "I'm enjoying this much more."

"Duty calls and you're too responsible to shirk it." Okay, so I did know some things about the man.

I climbed off his lap and snatched my thong. He ducked into what I presumed was the bathroom. I hauled my totes off the top of the dresser and set them and my shoes on the bottom shelf under my hanging clothes.

It was a bit thrilling to have my own little space in his world. At the Lux. At his house.

Thoughts of the hotel brought back my own responsibilities. I had a lot of work to do.

We traveled the hall together and collected our laptop bags.

Dane kissed my forehead and said, "I'll be in my office until about eight. Make yourself comfortable."

"I like your great room."

"Switch for the fireplace is under the mantel. Password for the Wi-Fi is *bagan*." He spelled it.

I recalled he'd said it meant *to fight*. "Are you German?"

"On my dad's side."

"How did your parents die?"

His irises darkened. "Not now, Ari." He kissed me again, then turned to head into his office.

I said, "I'm sorry about them."

He glanced over his shoulder. "Thanks." As he disappeared into the other room, I wondered if I'd ever get all the facts.

I set my things out on the coffee table, lit the hearth and a few candles before firing up my computer. I accessed the Internet and went into full-on research mode, looking for the perfect Christmas tree. Or trees. I still hadn't decided on quantity. Size. Shape. *Shit.*

Shopping around, however, led me in a different direction—budget planning. A thirty-foot Rockefeller Pine would cost us fifteen grand alone. I had a sneaking suspicion Dane would not reuse decorations from year to year but would donate them and have a different theme every Christmas.

I didn't know this for sure, of course, but from what I'd gleaned thus far—and the fact that packing up all of the unused furniture erroneously delivered to Monaco and having it shipped to the Lux was an unsatisfactory solution—I had a feeling I was pretty close to right with my speculation.

I had an astronomical budget for events. Still . . . Fifteen thousand dollars for a fake tree. Holy fuck.

Around seven o'clock, my head throbbed from breaking down my allotted funds into an Excel spreadsheet and trying to disperse them adequately across twelve months, taking into account the other holidays and potential functions we'd host. Not to mention all the pre-launch and grand-opening festivities.

I was also starving. I wandered through the house until I located the enormous kitchen, filled with shiny stainless-steel state-of-the-art appliances. There was a large rectangular island in the center, intricately designed with decorative accents. A matching table that sat eight was tucked into the artistic breakfast nook in the far corner, just off the patio, where glass doors revealed another big table and an outdoor grill and cooking station.

My entire townhome could have fit into this one room.

A slow churning started low in my belly. I wasn't a stranger to the rich and affluent—not when my dad's career had been red-hot and he'd garnered invitations to lavish parties. But I'd never been intimately involved with someone who owned . . . *all this*. And 10,000 Lux.

Curiosity ate at me once more. From where had all of Dane's money come? Sure, he'd inherited his parents' fortune. But how vast was it? And what had he done to put himself in the position to build the resort, buy this house, throw down a million and a half on a sports car only twenty-nine other people in the world would own?

I'd learned from my father and some of the cheating scandals in the sports world that the cream did not always rise to the top without some help along the way.

How did all of this belong to Dane Bax?

As I pondered the mystery of him—and shoved aside the notion of any potential scratching and clawing his way to the top—I prowled the kitchen and then raided the fancy Sub-Zero fridge, which was fully stocked. I found fresh salmon and used the stovetop grill to cook the fish. I made up a spinach salad that I drizzled with an olive oil, lemon, and dill dressing and added thick slices of warm French bread on a separate plate. I was just setting everything on the table when Dane joined me, a bottle of white wine in hand.

"Perfect timing," I said. It was just a few minutes after eight.

"I smelled the salmon down the hall. Delicious."

"You haven't tried it yet. I'm no gourmet cook—or five-star chef."

He kissed my cheek and murmured, "I bet it's fantastic."

Uncorking the wine, he poured two glasses. We settled at the table.

"Good business meeting?" I asked, dying to find out all I could about him.

"Excellent. There's a fund-raiser planned for mid-October that I have to attend in Scottsdale. I'd like you to go with me."

I smiled as my stomach flipped, the churning instantly dissipating. "Sure. Thanks for the invitation."

He gave me a sort of *as if I wouldn't invite you* look. Then asked, "How'd your work go?"

A diversionary tactic. Quickly off the subject of him and on to Ari.

That just wouldn't do. So I briefly said, "Since the grand opening is a week after Christmas, all of the holiday decorations will still be up—I presume." I crooked a brow at him. We hadn't yet discussed this.

With a nod, he told me, "They'll complement the launch perfectly. And we'll want them up for the pre-launch activities, anyway. The holiday season is a great time of year to show off the Lux."

"I agree." *Phew.* "So, that's my current focus. Every last detail, light strung, ornament hung, has to be *just right.*"

His grin was a grateful one that made his beautiful eyes sparkle. "I knew I could trust you with this. Really, Ari. How did you ever doubt yourself?"

I dragged in a slow breath, let it out on a long sigh. "Dane. I haven't done anything yet. I'm in reconnaissance mode at the moment. Needing to move on to the implementation phase ASAP, by the way. Chances are good it'll take most of December to get all the decorations up in time for the initial events."

"I have absolute faith you'll pull this off. Preferred planners don't miss deadlines or details, is my guess."

"Not so far. . . ." I picked at my salmon. Yes, I felt the pressure. I felt the significance of my role in the opening of the hotel. More than that, I felt the incredible need to bring it all together, flawlessly executed, not for my personal success but for Dane and the Lux.

Despite the weight on my shoulders and the constant *please, God, keep me from fucking this up* thoughts, I knew Dane needed me to be spot-on—so that he could contend with all the problems he continually encountered on-property.

"I won't let you down," I assured him. And hoped to hell I was right.

"I already know that, baby." He gave me the sexy grin. Literally turning me inside out.

I tried to focus on the food, because I really was famished, but his gaze remained on my lips, teasing a smile from me as the tingles ran rampant. I just wanted to climb all over him, have my way with him.

But I was missing the prime opportunity to quiz him more. I opened my mouth to speak—and his cell went off.

The angry ring.

He swore under his breath. "I have to take this."

I eyed him curiously and asked, "Is it Ethan?"

"Yes." He pulled the phone from his pocket. "I'll try not to be long." He kissed my cheek and stepped out onto the patio.

He'd finished his meal, at least. I polished off mine and then rinsed the dishes and put them in the washer. I went back to the great room, a little frustrated that I hadn't learned anything new about Dane. And why was he cool about missing calls when he was with me but never skipped Ethan's?

That was another piece to the puzzle I wanted to figure out. Ethan had been Dane's mentor—still was? And they were business partners on some level. I didn't know the extent. It had sounded last night as though Dane's investors weren't involved on such a grand scale that he'd had trouble supplementing funds for the Lux when he'd cut out the five corrupt associates.

Clearly, I was on hold for answers, so I gathered up my catalogs from the coffee table in the great room and retired to Dane's bedroom, flipping through pages and just trying to absorb thoughts as much as possible while blocking the questions from my mind.

It was nearing midnight when I heard him walk in. I'd been drifting in and out of sleep and was on the drifting verge again, a bit groggy.

He climbed in behind me and reached around to pry a magazine from my hand.

"Baby, you're going to OD on Christmas decorations and it's not even Halloween yet." He placed the book on the nightstand and switched off the light.

His arms were around me in the next instant and he surrounded me again with his heat and strong presence.

"So much to do," I mumbled.

"Hire someone already," he insisted. "Patricia said you had strong candidates."

"Haven't had time to follow up."

"Then . . . fuck. Get Kyle to help you."

My sleepy grunt filled the quiet room. "You'll take that back in the morning, when I'm refreshed."

"Probably."

His lips skimmed over my temple. "Don't overdo it, Ari."

"This is a dream come true, Dane. When it comes to planning, don't ask—or *insist*—I slow down. I'm really, really excited about this."

"Fine. But let's get you some help."

"I'll decide on staff this weekend and have HR make calls on Monday. Happy?"

"Not totally. I'm still pissed about today."

"Dane—"

"I'm going to be tied up most of tomorrow, here with the investment group. We're through with the bullshit. It's time for action."

An eerie feeling caused goose bumps to pop up on my skin. "Dane. What does that mean?"

"That's not for you to worry about. Just work from here tomorrow, okay? Where I can keep an eye on you."

"Whatever you want," I whispered.

My yawn gave him the chance to say, "What's happening at the Lux will be over soon. I'll make sure of it."

I didn't like the ominous undertone. But I was too exhausted to dwell on it. With Dane's body practically enveloping me, I was in heaven—and out like a light seconds later.

I woke up alone and immediately discovered I didn't like it, after just two nights of having Dane wrapped around me.

I spared a glance at the small crystal clock. Half past eight. And I had so much to do.

I threw off the covers and went into the bathroom to shower and put on some makeup and add a few curls to my hair. Then I crossed the hall to the dressing room and selected a navy-colored yoga suit with a white tank top under the jacket. I slipped on the lightweight sneaks I'd brought with me and went straight to the great room.

Dane, Ethan, and two others were on the patio, at one of the smaller tables, huddled over paperwork and talking animatedly. I grabbed some catalogs and my laptop and headed into the kitchen. Dane had left a plate of scrambled eggs with green chiles and chorizo wrapped in cellophane on the counter. Small flour tortillas and fresh *pico de gallo* accompanied the heavenly smelling breakfast.

I bellied up to the island and nibbled as I assessed whether the printer by the iPad on the far counter, beneath the flat-screen TV, would sync via Bluetooth to my laptop. When it did, I printed out the photos of the Lux that I'd taken. Then I used some of the printer paper to handwrite notes for each photo, determining what would go where when it came to accessorizing the lobby.

While I contemplated wreath placement, it occurred to me that I had more than the lobby to focus on. The tall columns between the wrought-iron and gold-leaf fencing needed wreaths. The lanterns atop them called for some sort of sophisticated decoration as well.

I resisted the urge to bang my head on the marble counter. Instead, I buckled down and drafted a plan.

Around noon, Dane and his group were still hard at it, so I trolled the freezer and found Kobe beef patties. There were brioche buns and cherry tomatoes, so I sliced and lightly sautéed the tomatoes, added mozzarella to the patties to melt, and then assembled the burgers and spooned a little balsamic vinegar reduction on them before topping them off with the bun. I added lettuce and thick slices of red onion on the side. Found a bag of sea salt and vinegar kettle chips in the vast pantry and loaded up my arms with four plates.

Dane caught sight of me heading his way, since they'd moved to the larger table just outside the breakfast nook. He jumped up and opened one of the doors, helping me with the food. I then delivered beers and refreshed their pitcher of iced tea.

"Thank you," Dane said with a kiss on the cheek. He made the introductions. "Ari, this is Nikolai Vasil and Sultan Qadir Hakim."

*Sultan?*

More questions instantly sprang to mind.

"Gentlemen, Ari DeMille."

We shook hands. This time it didn't bother me at all. Dane had helped to ease that phobia of mine.

He added, "And, of course, you know Ethan."

"Yes, it's nice to see you again. And to meet you all." I gave a smile. "I'll leave you to your business."

"Thank you for lunch," the sultan politely said.

"It's my pleasure."

I returned to the kitchen island, where I had paperwork and images spread across the countertop.

Dane and his associates disbanded in the early evening. I couldn't begin to fathom what they'd spent an entire day discussing. Ethan stayed for dinner, which was Cornish game hens and steamed vegetables that Dane cooked.

I used the opportunity to grill Ethan.

"I understand you're an economics professor."

He nodded. "Recently retired from my tenure at Harvard."

"Where you and Dane met?"

I heard Dane snicker behind me, from his station at the stove. Ethan and I sat on upholstered barstools at the island, which I'd cleared of my work. Dane knew what I was up to, obviously.

Ethan said, "Yes, Dane was a student of mine. A brilliant one, at that."

"Were you involved in the hotel he built in Tahoe?"

"No, he went solo on that one. I invested in the Vegas casino, though."

"I imagine that was a substantial undertaking."

"Dane has a gift. Excellent taste, an eye for luxury, and a good sense of what's appealing architecturally."

"Agreed," I said. "And do the two of you share other interests, besides business and golf?"

With a grin—because Ethan apparently also discerned my tactic for trying to find out more about Dane—he told me, "We were each on rowing teams when we were students. Both rowed in the annual Harvard-Yale Regatta."

"And won," Dane murmured in my ear as he leaned in close. Then he crossed to the table to set out the dishes.

So there had to be some pictures floating around of the crew, right? Unless he'd conveniently excluded himself from photo opportunities. But, why?

I frowned.

Ethan nabbed my attention again. "He's also an amateur pugilist—could have gone pro. Boxing's not something I ever picked up."

"Probably had your nose in a book instead," Dane joked.

"More than likely."

It was nice to hear them banter, to not see Dane quite so tense.

I asked more questions over dinner. Dane begrudgingly answered some of them; Ethan filled in most of the blanks. All surface stuff, really. Dane told me he'd selected Tahoe for his first hotel because he'd liked the lakeside location. Vegas had been more about making money on a flip, since it had been prime real estate on the Strip. The ultimate goal had always been the Lux. For him and his associates.

Not wanting to spoil the more relaxed evening, I didn't dare ask about the problems they currently encountered. After dessert and brandy that I served, Ethan bid us farewell. As the door closed behind him, Dane took me into his arms.

"You're a very gracious hostess." His warm lips skimmed over mine before he took my mouth in a searing kiss.

I melted against him, in his tight embrace, forgetting all about the trouble at the Lux. And everything else.

Everything except Dane. As his tongue tangled with mine, I slipped the small disks on his shirt through their holes and peeled the material away, smoothing my hands over his sculpted chest. I could make a hobby out of touching him.

Breaking the kiss, he said in his seductive tone, "Let's take this into the bedroom."

# chapter 19

"Which one?" I asked.

With a mischievous grin, he swept me into his arms. "You like being naughty."

"I do. With you."

"Only me."

"*Only,*" I assured him.

We bypassed the first room and continued down the hall toward the back of the house. I teased, "No playroom tonight?"

"I prefer you in my bed."

"Mm, I like your bed, too."

I nuzzled against the side of his neck and dropped kisses along his skin, up to his earlobe, which I flicked with my tongue before suckling it. "And I love everything you do to me."

"I suspected you were feeling a bit more adventurous after the other night."

"Which was incredible. As was the morning after. Yesterday in the—"

"I don't want to talk about yesterday," he said, his tone a bit gruff. "I have half a mind to not let you back on-property until I've resolved this situation."

"Dane!"

"It'd be for your own good. And for my sanity."

"I swear I won't go anywhere without Amano from here on out. But I can't do my job remotely."

We entered Dane's bedroom and he set me on my feet. "Then I have to work quickly."

I stared at him, seeing the consternation in his eyes, wondering what the hell he planned to do—and why it sent an ominous sensation down my spine.

Taking my hand, he gave it a gentle tug, and we crossed to his California king. He reached for the zipper on my fitted yoga jacket and slid it down the track. He peeled off the garment and then lifted the hem of the tank top over my head. My shoes, socks, and pants followed as he piled my clothes on the bench that ran the width of the bed.

"Better," he said, his tone returning to the seductive timbre that made my insides simmer.

His shirt hung open and I splayed my palms over his ridged abs. The delicious tickle along my clit caused the corners of my mouth to quiver into a small smile. The man was too gorgeous by far. I had the insane urge to lick and kiss every inch of him.

I moved my hands upward, to his shoulders, and pushed his shirt over them, then down his arms. He caught the material with one hand and tossed it onto the mounting heap.

Leaning in close, I inhaled the scent of him. So masculine and sexy, I would have been thrilled just to bask in his nearness—but, of course, he had other thoughts on his mind.

My smile widened when he guided me down onto the bed. His fingers trailed along my throat and then between my breasts. He whisked aside a lacy cup and his head dipped. His tongue swirled tantalizingly around my areola before paying my taut nipple the same attention.

I threaded a hand through his hair as he suckled deep. My spine arched, pressing my body against his. A moan escaped my parted lips.

Heat rushed through me and my eyelids fluttered closed, blocking out the dim lighting from a floor lamp in the far corner. The room was quiet, save for the snap of the fire and our shallow breaths.

Dane took my free hand in his, twining our fingers. He kissed mine, then left sensual touches with his lips along the inside of my wrist and forearm, to my biceps.

"I love how sweet you taste," he whispered, his breath wispy against my skin. "And you're so soft." His mouth grazed my collarbone. "Yet strong. Even if you don't realize how much."

He kissed my throat, his tongue pressing against sensitive spots that made me writhe beneath him. His chest melded to mine. Our fingers were still entwined and my other hand was buried in his thick hair.

"Your nipples are so tight. And you're wet for me, aren't you, baby?"

"God, yes." It was all I could do not to move slightly so he could settle between my legs and feel my dewy folds against his stomach. But I was too enthralled at the moment to move.

His mouth swept slowly down my neck, to my breasts. He kissed the inner swells, then drew my puckered nipple against his tongue.

He was going to torture me with his leisurely seduction.

He kissed the undersides of my breasts and then his lips skimmed down to my stomach, making my flesh ripple. His tongue grazed the dip of my waist and he whispered, "You want me inside you."

"More than you know."

His mouth slid lower and his teeth latched onto the strand of my thong, dragging the material to the top of my thigh. I instinctively shifted so he could do the same with the other side. He pulled the panties down just enough to uncover my sex, then blew a gentle breath over the moist skin.

My pussy clenched. And he hadn't even touched me.

"Dane. God, you turn me on."

My eyes were still shut, and I focused solely on the excitement he elicited, the anticipation that mounted. I felt the nearness of his lips, the taunting sensation of what was to come. He lingered so close, it was all I could do not to raise my hips to initiate the contact.

It was a wicked game. One he was a master at; I was the slave. A slave to the burning, the craving, the unwavering need.

I'd give up my soul just to feel his mouth on me.

I fought temptation, because he thrilled me with his sensual teasing.

With his tongue, he swirled lazy circles on my inner thigh. Pinched gingerly with his teeth.

"Dane," I breathed. My fingers tightened around strands of his hair.

"Yeah, baby?" His voice was a mere rush of air against my sensitive skin.

I wanted to beg him to take me in this way that had been so unfamiliar and too intimate before I'd met him but that now was as critical to binding us together as him being inside me. Because I'd accepted the intimacy. The connection. The ecstasy that came with him pushing my boundaries.

"Don't stop," was all I said.

He let out a sexy sound and then went back to his beautiful torment. His lips inched closer and closer to where I wanted him the most. I felt the natural compulsion to rush it—the urgency raced through me. Conversely, the fire inside only raged brighter with anticipation. With the tender strokes and the gentle nipping. I couldn't lie still, but I forced myself not to arch toward him, not to demand too much, when it was so erotic to let him do his slow-seduction thing. Which drove me crazy in the most exciting way.

Likely I didn't beg him to go for his ultimate goal because I loved how his toying with me made his breath come in heavier pulls and made me beyond desperate for him.

It was intoxicating. Addictive. Another escalating high from which I didn't want to come down.

When he finally, *finally* reached the apex of my legs, his mouth hovered. He inhaled deeply. I sucked in a breath.

"Fuck," I said as I let the air out on a long sigh.

"Jesus, Ari. You're going to come, aren't you?"

"Yes." I squeezed his hand that still held mine. "You know what I like."

"Everything I do to you."

"Exactly."

I felt the heat intensify as he lowered his head that tiny bit and his tongue swept over my slick folds. A small cry tore from my lips. The tip of his tongue fluttered over my clit. Once again I fought the urge to thrash on the bed, though my hips bucked and my pulse shot through the roof.

"Oh, Christ. Dane. I—oh, God . . . I—" Fire raged through my veins.

I came hard, the deepest, darkest moan wrenching from low in my throat.

I was suspended in a weightless, motionless state for endless seconds. So mind-blowing. Absolutely breathtaking.

Thoughts didn't exist in my head. Sensation reigned. Emotions swelled. I couldn't remember what had happened the day before. I didn't care what would happen tomorrow.

All that mattered was Dane—and the way he made me feel in those few glorious moments. The way I wanted to make *him* feel.

I had no idea how long it was before I returned to myself. But when I did, I still had a voracious need for him.

"Take everything off," I said of his clothes and my lingerie. My chest rose and fell quickly and I was limp from a fantastic orgasm.

But the intense desire to crawl all over him and bring him the sort of pleasure he brought me was unrelenting.

He whisked off my bra and panties. He undressed himself swiftly as I, his captive audience, watched with lust thrumming through me.

Dane was hard. Before he'd even settled on the bed again I rolled onto him and straddled his lap. He let out a sexy laugh.

"I like you so aggressive," he said.

"It's more of a desperate need than aggression." As I eyed his hunky body and desire flashed through me, I added, "Actually, I have a better idea."

I climbed off him and the bed. Dane's brow dipped.

I backed toward the door and crooked a finger. He sat up and stood.

"Come with me," I said.

His look turned lascivious, exciting me more.

"What are you up to?" he asked in his low, arousing tone.

When he closed in on me, I grabbed his hand. "Let's get nasty."

I continued out of the room and down the wide hall, walking backward as his gaze remained on me and he followed.

We reached the spare bedroom and I stepped inside, relinquishing his hand. The candles were still scattered about and I found the igniter to light some of them. Then I asked, "Where's the satin sheet?"

He pulled the folded rich navy material from the nightstand drawer and snapped it open, covering the bed. "Freshly laundered."

I scanned the ledge of the headboard and found the bottle of frankincense oil still there.

His gaze followed mine, and he said, "I told Rosa to leave this room be. I had the sheet dry-cleaned but left everything else as is. Well, except for the rose petals. I had to toss them."

"I was mostly interested in the oil," I told him with a coy smile.

Crossing the room to where he stood, I gave a gentle push

against his pectoral ledge. He fell onto the mattress, taking me with him. I sat astride his midsection and reached for the bottle.

"My turn," I said as I drizzled the lovely scented oil over his chest. I returned it to the table and ran my hands over his hard muscles and ripped abs. Across his shoulders and down to his bulging biceps, my fingers and palms sliding along his elbows to his forearms.

Clasping his wrists and raising them above his head, I rocked slightly against his ridged stomach.

"You know that makes me crazy," he said in a tight voice.

I inhaled deeply and told him, "Every scent I ever want to breathe in again is right here in this room." Exotic spice, orange, candles, and Dane.

I leaned into him, my breasts gliding against his slick chest, puckering my nipples. I nipped at his clenched jaw and whispered, "What if I just slid all over you?"

His eyes blazed. "You think you're going to make me harder than I already am?"

"Ah, a challenge." I winked. The satin sash was still attached to the floor post. I snatched it as it curled in the corner of the bed and tied Dane's wrists. Then I leaned back, still straddling his torso.

My hands were slightly coated with the oil and I palmed my breasts, massaging them and pinching my nipples with my fingers and thumbs.

"Goddamn, Ari." His gaze was fixed on me.

"Let's see how you do when *you're* the one who's restrained."

"You don't really think I'll just lie here and not touch you?"

"What choice do you have?"

He smirked. Tugged on the silk binding. It loosened. *Shit*. I should have known he was too strong for any knot I'd tie.

"Fine," I said. "You'll do it because I want you to."

He didn't dispute my logic.

Quite pleased with myself, I stroked his chest and leaned toward him, giving him my own searing kiss, thrusting my tongue into his mouth to take the lead and kiss him deeply, empowered by how strongly he reacted to me.

The sudden flash of dominance created a heady sensation and I tugged at the corners of his mouth with my lips.

Sitting back, I spared a glance at the sash he'd loosened even more, as though he really couldn't resist touching me but held himself in check because I'd asked it of him.

I grinned triumphantly. "You really will give me whatever I want, won't you?"

His look was a steady, intense one. "I've been saying that all along, haven't I?"

My heart fluttered. My hands skated over his pecs, down to his abs. I peered at him under my lashes. "And if I want to drive you completely crazy, so that you *have* to have me instantly . . . ?"

"Note that I've already freed myself from your ties. But I'm still playing your game."

A wicked thrill chased through me.

With one hand, I continued to caress my breast. The other hand skimmed over the satin to wipe off the oil. Then I lifted off him, coming up on my knees. I rubbed my clit with two fingers in a slow, circular motion, the way I had that night in my office when he'd demanded it of me. When he'd watched me. When he'd gotten so hard, his cock had strained the fly of his pants.

I already felt his erection nudging against me from behind. I wanted to make him half out of his mind.

My gaze locked with his as I stroked in a measured pace that heightened my own arousal because of the way Dane stared so intently. The way he absorbed the full effect of what I did—and the impact it had on him.

"You know I want to do that for you," he said in an edgy voice.

"That's the point you made when you were on the phone with Ethan. If you can't, you still want to watch."

"I'm not on the phone."

"But it makes you hot, right?"

His biceps tightened, as though he were just about ready to give up the pretense of me restraining him.

"It makes me want to flip you onto your back and fuck you hard," he said. "The way you like it."

The intensity of his expression, and his words, jolted me.

"Stop talking," I said as I worked myself a little faster. "You're not the one who's supposed to be getting me off."

"But you want me to get you off," he challenged.

"Of course. But what I really want is for you to watch and get absolutely wild over the fact that it's *not* you . . . at the moment."

His gaze smoldered. "How long do you think you can last before you beg me, baby?"

I already knew the answer to that devious question. But I played the game. "How long do you think *you* can last before you rip through that sash and finish the job yourself?"

His hips jerked. His stomach rippled.

I snickered. Then I placed a hand on his shoulder, pinning him down. Leaning over him, I stared into his eyes and slipped two fingers inside my wet pussy. I pumped vigorously. He watched every expression that crossed my face. I alternated between rubbing my clit and stroking my inner walls. I could see he resisted the urge to take one of my nipples in his mouth, because he followed my rules.

I lifted my leg and planted my foot flat on the mattress next to his hip, not only spreading myself wider but also giving him a clear view of me pleasuring myself. I pushed my fingers deep inside and massaged quickly. My breath hitched. My eyes likely danced with excitement.

"You think you're going to win?" he said in a husky voice.

"Yes."

"Think again."

He tore free of the sash, gripped my shoulders, and flipped me onto my back—as he'd said he wanted to do. His hard body was slippery against mine, the most tantalizing sensation. My hands roved his front and he felt magnificent under my fingertips as he let me explore his chest again.

Then he had a foil packet ripped open and a condom on before I could even process all the sparks shooting through me. Seconds later, he was thrusting deep and I came with a lustful cry and the sheer realization that I would never beat him at any challenge.

And that was okay.

I woke in the middle of the night. Alone.

It was an odd, empty feeling. Leaving me a bit cold when I'd so quickly become accustomed to Dane's heat and presence. The way he wrapped himself around me and held on tight.

The oddity, I realized, came from the fact that I missed him lying next to me, missed him filling the space with his muscular body. I tossed off the covers and climbed out of bed. His bed, because he'd said that was where he liked me. *I* didn't like that he'd slipped out on me.

Dressed in the pants he'd worn earlier, though he'd left the top button undone, Dane stood at the windows, staring out into the darkness. There were glowing embers in the hearth yet nothing for him to see outside but inky night.

I slipped on his shirt, capturing the smell of him again, and stole behind him. I circled my arms around his waist. "What are you doing?"

"Thinking."

My hand moved up to his chest, the temptation too great. His hands covered mine, warm and strong.

"About what?"

"How I'm going to get my revenge."

A chill ran down my spine. "Dane—"

"It's nothing for you to worry about."

I considered this. On the one hand, I didn't like how menacing his words were—or the implication behind them. Once more,

I was faced with the concern of how far Dane might go to protect what was his.

The other risky piece to the puzzle was that he deserved to fix this situation his way. The investors he'd cut out were trying to capitalize on his blood, sweat, and tears. I could fully understand how furious that would make him. And I honestly didn't know enough about what was going on to judge.

So what I worried most about was how he would react—and how accepting I'd be of his wrath. Because I walked the tightrope with him, wanting him to get his revenge but fearing what sort of person it made me if I approved of whatever he did to resolve the situation.

But that wasn't something I could reconcile just yet, so I said, "I support whatever you're doing. I know it doesn't really matter, but—"

"It does, Ari." His hands squeezed mine and our gazes locked in the glass pane as I looked around his broad shoulder. "You have no idea how much."

I kissed his upper arm. Then he turned and led me over to one of the oversize leather chairs in front of the fireplace. He sat and pulled me into his lap, my legs curling as I huddled close and flattened my palms against his pecs.

"What's really going on?" I asked in a soft voice.

"There's so much I don't want to tell you. To keep you safe."

"Seems like, after yesterday, it's better that I know everything. Knowledge is power, haven't you heard?"

He chuckled, without humor.

"How do you know a sultan? And is Nikolai Vasil Russian?"

"Yes, he is. I met them through Ethan."

This confused me. "Was he really a professor at Harvard, or is that some sort of cover?"

"You have an active imagination."

"Not so much. I just know there's more to this situation than meets the eye. You and your friends spent all day discussing the Lux—"

"It wasn't just about the Lux. And we're not friends. We're associates, partners. There's nothing social related to my acquaintances with them."

That sounded rather ominous. "Except with Ethan, right?"

"He's the one exception."

"Why?"

"Ari." His hand smoothed over my bare leg, caressing lightly.

"You're trying to distract me," I murmured against his neck.

"Why isn't it working?"

"Because I'm trying to learn your deepest, darkest secrets."

"Maybe I just need to put a little effort into this." He unbuttoned the shirt I wore and slipped a hand inside, cupping my breast.

"Clever. But I'm still asking questions." Despite how torn I was, thinking I ought to say to hell with knowing what he hid from me and let him take me to bed. "How do you know these men?"

His head fell back against the top of the chair. "Is this a 'must know'?"

I kissed his tight jaw and whispered, "I love you, remember?"

His head lifted and he pinned me with a serious look. "You never actually said the words."

"But you already knew I felt it. And I'm telling you now. It's only fair."

"You're a little bit devious."

"You made me that way."

"Hmm." He didn't seem to like that reality.

"It was the promise of hot sex from the get-go that corrupted me," I said. "Since we're in this boat together, tell me what's going on."

"Fine." Though he sighed miserably when it came to my logic. "Perhaps it might be best if you know what you've gotten yourself into."

What I'd been *seduced* into, was a bit more accurate. But I couldn't deny my own accountability. I'd been reticent along the way, but I had willingly given this devilishly handsome man my heart.

He posed his own query. "Have you heard of the Illuminati?"

My brows dipped. Strange direction for him to take. "Sure. In a Lara Croft movie."

He gave that hollow laugh again. "Okay, that's a start, I guess."

"Are you about to tell me it's real?"

"No . . . and yes."

"You can't make this easy for me, can you?"

"It's not something I can simplify. The origins of these groups began with the Bavarian Illuminati, though it was supposedly dissolved in 1785. There have since been offshoots—descendant factions—that continue to influence the political and financial environment, worldwide."

I didn't say a word. Just stared at him, knowing I was about to be blown away by the direction of this conversation. And not surprised there was so much more to him than words could describe.

He said, "When I was at Harvard, Ethan recruited me into a poli-econ secret society. The purpose of this particular Illuminati faction is to track, trend, analyze, and predict political and economic climates, with the goal of influencing leaders to effect positive change. *Positive* change," he emphasized in a tight voice.

I was speechless for a few seconds, eventually asking, "How did Ethan get involved with these people?"

"You were actually close to the mark when you suggested his tenure at Harvard was a cover. It was—of sorts. Ethan is a brilliant forecaster of economic trends. He studies world markets, trades, industries, and basically has a sixth sense about fiscal impacts and expectations. His great-great-grandfather formed the poli-econ group. With the exception of myself, all the nine members are descendants of the original secret society. It's generational—or, rather, it's supposed to be."

"They made an exception for you? Because you're so brilliant?"

Graduating from an Ivy League school with the highest honors and summa cum laude spoke volumes. So, too, did his success.

"I showed potential," he corrected. "I was recruited during my second year at Harvard. The youngest member to ever join."

"How, exactly, does this society work?"

"We're the heart of a network of global billionaires and scholars we call upon to influence the political and business realms to guide changing times. It's very complex. Cloak-and-dagger. No one speaks outside the network of what's to be done, what has been done. And within the inner sanctum . . . I took an oath to never reveal my involvement. To *anyone*."

"Oh." I did not miss the significance there. He'd broken his promise to the society—for me. "Dane—"

"Things have gone wrong, Ari." His expression turned grim. "It's a majority-rules bloc. Five of the nine members plotted a different course during a fragile economic time. We predicted another downturn, similar to that of '08. We've managed to keep it from happening—that *is* the premise of the secret society. But the five used the intellectual property of our think tank for personal gain. *Substantial* personal gain."

"Criminal corruption." A chill ran through me. This was growing darker by the moment.

With a nod, he said, "Fortunes have been lost, legacies obliterated—to their benefit. And there's some other stuff—" A sharp grunt fell from his lips. "I can't say for sure. I have no concrete evidence, but some political changes of late and a few 'fortuitous' deaths make me suspicious as to how far they'll go to increase their own empires."

"My God." My stomach roiled. "Dane. That's a huge assumption."

"That's why it's currently just speculation on my part. Like I said, I can't confirm anything. But what I do know—from the resources I've provided for the society—gives me a strong enough indication of the direction the five have taken so that I am carefully trying to extract myself before their course becomes more destructive."

"And part of the extrication is cutting these people out as investors in the Lux."

"Yes. But it hasn't gone over well."

"How did you manage it?"

"I had a legitimate loophole. Thanks to my legal team."

"Okay, maybe I didn't need to know all of this." Christ, the implications were enormous—and dangerous. "Dane, their retaliation is already wreaking havoc—and is dangerous to the people who work for you. They could come after you, or anyone else, with something much stronger if you refuse to bring them back into the Lux fold. They could—"

"Ari, stop." He caught my chin gently between his thumb and forefinger and stared into my eyes. "Don't start worrying like that. Don't worry about anything. We're taking care of it."

"How?" I demanded.

"We have our ways."

"Are they legal ways?"

"Don't ask me that. The less you know about our plan, the better."

I gaped. How could it be that behind all the luster and beauty of 10,000 Lux lay something sinister and foreboding?

Worse . . . could it be deadly?

I slipped from Dane's grip and his lap. I stood in front of the fire, trying to warm the frigid blood in my veins. Dane joined me, his large hands clasping my biceps.

"Ari, don't let this upset you. We'll get it under control."

"By whatever means necessary?"

"I have the right to protect *my* empire. To protect everything that's mine—I told you that before."

"But within the limitations of the law. Right, Dane?"

"Of course, Ethan, Qadir, Nik, and I want to rectify this as simply and efficiently as possible. Understand, though, that when people of this magnitude strike, you have to strike back. It's the only way they'll respect *our* power."

I didn't want to hear any more. I didn't want to agonize over what lengths they might go to save 10,000 Lux from shady poachers.

So much of me believed that Dane was correct—he'd had good intentions with the secret society. He'd had good intentions with the Lux. It was perfectly within his realm to want to defend and safeguard what he'd worked so hard to build. I didn't doubt that for a second.

The terrifying part was that I truly did support him, because he deserved to be able to fight for his own legacy. It was the darkness around the fringes that tore at me. What was he willing to do? How far were he and the others willing to go—on both sides?

And why did I feel I was somehow caught in the middle?

That incident in the stairwell . . . Had it been all coincidence and really bad timing on my behalf? Or had that snake been lying in wait for me? The one person who used that emergency exit more than anyone else—maybe the *only* one to use it.

What about the fire? I'd been the only one around the media room at the time.

I shivered. Dane wound his strong arms around me.

"I will take care of this, baby. You just have to trust me. Do as I ask."

"Stay out of stairwells and the media room?"

"For now."

"Damn it, Dane."

"I know. I'm sorry." He held me a bit tighter. "Believe me, I'm not happy about any of this. But when you're dealing with the sort of capital wrapped up in the Lux, investors getting greedy isn't uncommon. When it's within their reach, these men are like junkies, Ari. Money is their drug. It's never enough. They want more and more. It's a natural rush, a high they don't want to come down from, so they need bigger and bigger deals. No matter what they have to do to acquire them."

"That's what scares me. If they're so bent on owning the Lux, won't they do *anything* to get their hands on it?"

"Something tells me we're about to find out."

I wiggled out of his embrace and faced him. "Dane. This is serious."

"Yes."

Okay, he already knew that, but still.

His hands cupped my face. "You'll be safe. Here with me."

"I'm not quitting my job to be some caged animal, no matter how beautiful the house."

"I didn't suggest that. I agreed to let you return to the hotel. You just have to allow Amano to stay close."

I nodded.

Dane said, "It'll be okay, baby. I promise."

I wasn't wholly convinced. But I believed in him. So I said, "All right. Whatever you want me to do. Please don't worry about me."

"Impossible. I love you, remember?" He mimicked my words.

"Now's not exactly the time to joke."

"No joke," he said in a fierce tone. "I love you, Ari. And no one's going to hurt you or take you away from me. *Ever.*"

That riveting sentiment elicited a thrill as much as it alarmed me as to the lengths he'd go to keep me from becoming a victim of the Lux's troubles. But the former turned out to be a much stronger sensation and I told him, "I trust you. Thank you for telling me everything—and for standing your ground. It scares me, but you've worked too hard to let anyone steal your glory. I love 10,000 Lux, too, Dane. I don't want you to lose it."

"I won't."

His confidence was reassuring. Yet there was one more tidbit that burned in the back of my brain.

Given that Dane was currently being forthcoming with information, I took the opportunity to ask, "What about Mikaela? How does she factor into your life?"

"I've known her since we were kids. She was my closest neighbor in Philadelphia. Her father is gone a lot—estranged from the family, actually. He served as a U.S. ambassador in France for some time and now he's in England. The latter assignment started not too long after 9/11, when there were numerous threats against the embassy in London. The perimeter was barricaded with a security post and armed guards were placed at all four sides. The building was difficult to get into, even if you were an American. There were even concerns about snipers on the rooftops of adjacent buildings, dignitaries and their families being their target. Mikaela wasn't allowed to visit."

"I'm sure that was difficult."

"Yes, it was very hard on her. Maybe that was why we bonded, initially. I didn't have a father, either."

I absorbed that a moment, recognizing the significance. Then I asked, "And now?"

"Now when she needs help with something, I'm there for her."

I had to wonder how often she "needed help." But then, I couldn't bristle too much over her presence in Dane's life. He didn't seem to think of her as more than a friend. Maybe even a sister. I didn't doubt for a second that Mikaela's take on their relationship was more skewed, that their connection was more romantic than sibling-related in her mind. She was a little too touchy-feeling with him, a little too flirtatious. And for that matter . . .

"Why is she in Scottsdale, rather than Philadelphia?" I asked.

"She came out to look at the Lux when we broke ground and decided Old Town would be a great place for her new shop. She just needs to work through the politics a bit better. Mikaela's used to getting whatever she wants. The City Council isn't quite so accommodating."

And if she got her tenant issues worked out, she'd be around for the long haul. I wondered how much of her we'd be seeing.

Dane didn't seem to dwell on thoughts of his childhood friend. He kissed my forehead and said, "Let's go back to bed."

We snuggled under the covers, me finding my happy place despite it all, now that Dane's body surrounded me and he held me to him.

# chapter 20

On Sunday, we played a round with my dad at his golf club. The disapproval over my and Dane's obvious relationship radiated off him, but he kept his comments to himself. I think it disturbed him greatly that he couldn't help but like Dane. They were constantly engaged in conversation, though I noted that my father didn't miss the way Dane kept one eye on me. I felt their protective presence with every move I made.

After lunch at the nineteenth hole, Dane and I parted ways with my dad and returned to the house so I could continue my research. Kyle sent me an e-mail to say he'd been offered the Marketing Specialist job.

Like just about everyone else, Patricia apparently worked the weekends, too. There was just so much to do. And about five seconds later, she sent me a list of those candidates we'd narrowed down for my department, indicating she'd make offers in the morning. I was about to officially have a full staff. That helped to take some of the pressure off.

I shot a note back to Kyle.

> Congrats! I suspected all along you'd slay it!

No need to mention he was a shoo-in because it was what I wanted. I truly had been impressed with his online portfolio and didn't want him to think I had any sway over his hiring.

> The VP of Marketing told me in the interview
> that my main projects, if they selected me, would
> be the invitations to the grand opening and all
> the events leading up to it. Nervous much?

I laughed. Then sent another message.

> Please, I'm stressing out over which Christmas
> trees to buy for the lobby. Everything about this
> launch is crucial—and, yes, nerve-wracking!

A few moments passed; then another e-mail came in from him.

> I don't officially start until tomorrow, but I'm off
> to get a jump start with some images and design
> work. See you in the morning?

It would cost me succumbing to Dane's will again—not exactly torture—but I suggested to Kyle that we meet for lunch in the main dining room. Kyle agreed, and then we both went back to our work.

Dane spent most of the afternoon in his office. He'd offered me space in there, but I opted for the kitchen island again. I wouldn't get anything done with him in such close proximity. If I wasn't staring at him I'd be touching him, and that wouldn't be productive for either of us. And too much was at stake to lose my focus.

We did, however, knock off for dinner. Afterward, we got cozy on the sofa in front of the fireplace in the great room. Dane had just started Hawthorne's 1851 *The House of the Seven Gables*, and since I hadn't delved into it in the past, he went back to page one and read aloud.

I missed half of what he said, too caught up in the rich, intimate tone of his voice for all the words to register. Plus, nineteenth-century literature was sometimes lost on me. I enjoyed the evening nonetheless. Especially when he swept me into his arms again and carried me off to his bed.

The place I loved the most.


A week of uneventful happenings at the Lux was a huge relief. I felt the weight lift from my shoulders. I suspected Dane felt the same, tenfold. Whatever tactics he, Ethan, Qadir, and Nikolai agreed to employ against the others seemed to be working.

All of the security systems were green-lighted. More cameras had been installed and worked properly. The IT issues had all been resolved. No more deactivations of badges occurred. Everything was progressing nicely.

A multitude of samples arrived for me and my office dripped wreaths and garland, with decorations hanging from the walls for me to evaluate. Dane was probably right. I might be sick of Christmas before December even rolled around.

I had lunch with Kyle in the courtyard just about every day, since Dane had meetings and was sometimes off-property. On Friday, Kyle showed me a draft of the invitation to the private party Dane wanted to host prior to the opening of the Lux. He had used the same multitextured, gray-on-gray feel as on the hotel's business cards and incorporated a few of the professionally taken photos of the property.

"This is stunning. I love the font—very elegant." The silver-embossed script was gorgeous and stood out against the darker, layered background.

"The printer did a great job with my first few mock-ups. I liked this one the best."

"Good call," I said. "Dane will agree."

He eyed me curiously. "Because you do?"

I tried to bite back a smile, but it tickled the corners of my mouth. "Yes. But also because it's awesome. Sophisticated and glamorous, with that avant-garde look and feel he prefers. How do you plan to top this with the grand opening invites?"

With a half snort, he said, "I have no fucking clue."

I laughed. "You'll think of something."

I dug into a Mediterranean salad—my new favorite—and Kyle took a few healthy bites of his overly decadent foie gras burger.

He nodded his approval as his eyes nearly rolled into the back of his head. After wiping his mouth with the linen napkin, he said, "I didn't think this would work for me, but damn it's good. Melts in your mouth. I never thought I'd like foie gras."

"Are you planning to eat your way through the menu?"

"Yeah. And I'm in luck, since Chef D'Angelo keeps changing it up. I don't think I'll ever have to eat the same thing twice. Though . . . I could probably live off this burger. Want to try it? Or the garlic-Parmesan fries?"

"Thanks, no. I just about OD'd this morning on the petit fours our French pastry chef whipped up for the PR meeting. She wants them at the launch and I told her she'd better make a gazillion batches, because they're going to be devoured. I ate a half dozen myself."

"Pig."

I laughed again. "Totally. Every meeting I go to has food and wine. If I don't stick to these salads, I'm not going to fit in the elevator."

Since I'd been banned from using the stairwell . . .

Kyle said, "You have nothing to worry about." His gaze slid over me. "You're perfect."

"Hardly." I snickered.

He added, "Come on, Ari. You're beautiful." His blue irises deepened in color. "Maybe you'll have dinner with me tonight?"

"That's not going to happen. Now or ever."

My head snapped up, since I'd been spearing romaine lettuce and Kalamata olives with my fork.

Dane stood over Kyle's shoulder, shooting me a *really, this again?* look.

I tried a placating smile. "Mr. Bax."

He scowled.

Kyle's brow furrowed.

Dane rounded the table and said to me, "We have a meeting in my conference room with all of the department heads."

I consulted my watch. "In fifteen minutes."

"I thought we could discuss a few agenda items beforehand."

My heart skipped several beats. Could he be more alpha? And did he honestly think he had anything to worry about when it came to Kyle? I was in love—head-over-heels in love—and I'd told Dane that already.

But he did like to hold what was his close to the chest.

I said, "Take a peek at the private party invitations Kyle made up." I handed one over, hoping to diffuse some of the sudden tension. "Gorgeous, right?"

He actually grinned. "Am I allowed to form my own opinion on this?"

"I'm just sayin'," I casually told him with a wave of my hand.

Dane studied the cardstock and nodded. To Kyle, he said, "Excellent work. I really do like it."

I breathed a sigh of relief. Kyle's chest puffed out a bit, though I could still see how he bristled over Dane being so territorial with me.

"Thanks," he said. "I've got more tweaks, but I thought it'd make a good base."

"Agreed. I appreciate the time and effort you've obviously put into this." That was about as much of a truce as they'd reach, I suspected, because Dane's attention returned to me. "Now, let's have a quick chat before our meeting."

I left my salad, since one of the servers was closing in on the remnants anyway. The hotel wasn't fully staffed, but there were plenty of workers not only learning the ropes but also perfecting their positions. Dane wanted a smooth-running operation before the Lux even opened. That meant allowing everyone to run through the paces on a daily basis with other staff, as though they were actually catering to members and guests.

"I'll talk to you later," I said to Kyle, who appeared a bit perplexed over the entire exchange.

"Sure."

As Dane and I walked off, I felt his irritation. He said, "How many times has he asked you out?"

"That might have officially been the first." I didn't think it wise to mention our conversation at the Delfinos'. "And you can't get mad at him."

He crooked his dark brow at me. "Oh?"

"Dane. No one knows that we're together. So it's not his fault."

We'd miraculously kept our relationship a secret thus far. I was shocked, considering the way his eyes smoldered when he looked at me and the fact that every time he was near I felt as though I'd spontaneously combust. I wouldn't go so far as to say that my colleagues didn't appear to speculate, but I hadn't encountered any under-the-breath comments or outright insinuation.

Dane and I didn't spend enough time together at the hotel for anyone to put two and two together was my guess. With the exception of Kyle, because he'd already begun formulating that idea—and Dane had clearly just confirmed it.

"The only reason no one knows about us," he told me, "is because I don't want it somehow getting back to my former investors."

I drew up short. "Are you suggesting there might be a—what do you call it?" I searched my brain and said, "A mole on-property?"

"It wasn't beavers that destroyed my security wiring," he reminded me.

I continued down the pathway with him, saying, "You do background checks on employees. For God's sake, I've experienced the in-depth paperwork. How would someone slip by, when—"

"Don't forget who we're dealing with, Ari."

I sighed. "Right." Secret society. Wealthy, affluent, influential, powerful. "So anyone could be the bad guy."

"Yes." He gave me a solemn look. "Just . . . not me."

"Dane."

We entered an elevator and I turned to him. "I never thought that. Not once."

"I know you don't understand what this is all about."

"I understand that you've poured everything into the Lux. Of course you're going to want to see this through—and keep the wolves at bay. I told you I'm supportive. I mean it."

I spared a glance at the video camera in the corner and frowned. I wanted to kiss him. But every angle was recorded and monitored now that the security systems were fully functioning.

With a hint of frustration, I simply told him, "I get what you're doing."

"Thank you."

We stepped out on the fourth floor. I collected my notes from my office and we headed to the conference room in Dane's suite. It, too, was monitored, so I took a seat and shifted gears to business.

Saturday evening, we had dinner alone on the terrace of 10,000 Lux. More decadence that made my insides thrum. And Dane couldn't seem to take his eyes off me. I wore a new dress. A one-shouldered number in sapphire. I'd pinned my hair in a loose updo, with a few long, curly strands left free.

Over our arugula, strawberry, and feta cheese salads, he said, "PR wants to bring more media crews out in the next month to build up a bit of hype. What are your thoughts by way of hosting?"

"The property sells itself, but I can pull together a reception for them, showcase our food and desserts. Have a jazz ensemble offer background music while they take photos. It'd be good if you were casually mingling to answer questions and give some clever sound bites."

He grinned. "I never doubted for a second you were the woman for this job."

"I love it, honestly." I glanced toward the gardens and fountains and told him, "Seriously, this can't be beat. And I think it deserves to be shown off." Gazing back at him, I asked, "How many for that evening, do you think?"

"Around a hundred reporters. As many as we can get, exclusively, this side of the Mississippi."

I shrugged. "Why not go global? Make it a sneak peek for the international crème de la crème before you orchestrate the full-scale media blitz?"

Dane pushed aside his empty plate and said, "Maybe you should manage PR, too."

"Not a chance," I was quick to say. "I've got more than enough to do. And Traci is awesome, anyway."

Miyanaga appeared to clear our salads and deliver our entrees. Rib eye with crab béarnaise sauce.

"You didn't get to finish yours last time," Dane coyly said.

"That's because you were tempting me with a spectacular office."

"And I'm so glad you took the bait."

I sliced a thin piece of steak and sighed dreamily over the

tender medium-rare meat and the rich sauce. "I don't know where you found Chef D'Angelo, but he's a dream come true."

Dane said, "Don't make me jealous of him, too."

I laughed. "You aren't seriously jealous of anyone. You just like intimidating the hell out of everybody. And you know I am completely, totally yours. So lighten—"

Something dropped from the terrace above us and landed on my plate, cutting me off. Three nasty little black somethings, actually. And they practically lunged for me.

I screamed as I shoved my chair back and leapt to my feet as two scorpions raced over the edge of the table and fell to the ground. The third remained on my plate, blessedly trapped in the thick béarnaise.

Dane was beside me in a heartbeat, pulling me farther away. My stomach launched into my throat.

"Go inside," he demanded before stepping on the creepy little suckers that were on the move.

"If they're female, they release the babies from their back," I warned.

He stomped around the area. I screamed again as the third one broke free of the sauce.

"Inside, Ari!" Dane barked.

Before I could move, one more dropped onto my shoulder. I instinctively flicked it with my hand—and felt the searing pain as its tail curled and stung me.

I let out a bloodcurdling scream and dropped to the marbled floor. I clutched my injured hand, which felt as though a Mack truck had just run it over, crushing the bones.

"Ari!" Dane was next to me in an instant, helping me to my feet.

"Mr. Bax! Is something wrong?" Miyanaga asked, panic in his voice, likely because of my Freddie Krueger freak-out.

"Scorpions on the terrace," Dane said between clenched teeth.

"*Scorpions?*" This took the other man aback. "Not in this area. I've never seen them. And we have pest control."

"Get the company on the phone," Dane hissed out. "I want them checking every square inch."

He wrapped an arm around my waist and tucked me against his hard body, leading me to the bank of elevators as I cried from the excruciating agony. The doors slid smoothly, silently open and we stepped into the car. My entire body shook. The venom spread quickly through my veins, racing toward all my extremities.

"I hate them," I ground out as the doors closed. I could barely speak but said, "I was stung when I was a kid and had a severe neurological reaction to the venom that took tons of meds to correct. And then for years, I'd wake up in the middle of the night and swear they were crawling all over me."

I'd gotten over my aversion to spiders pretty damn quick. They didn't compare to quick-moving scorpions with pinchers and lightning-fast tails that coiled upward for the strike. The babies were the worst, because they didn't know when the threat was over, didn't know when to stop stinging. They just kept pumping in venom. I knew from experience.

My heart thundered and I couldn't catch my breath.

Dane said, "I should take you to the hospital."

"No. Let me ride it out. He only got me once." Though the pain was nearly unbearable. And my heart raced.

Amano met us on the fourth floor. He'd been waiting outside my office and followed us in. Dane explained what happened.

Amano went for ice at the wet bar, saying over his shoulder, "We don't have a scorpion problem on-property."

"Yeah, my thoughts exactly," Dane ground out. "Check her office."

"You don't think—" I started to say, when a terrifying thought occurred to me. "Oh, my God. Dane."

"What?" he demanded.

"We were standing *right here*. Remember?" I urged through my tears and the throbbing in my hand. I thought of the night he'd come in while we were working late. He'd done all manner of wicked things to me—then fabricated the beavers chewing-through-wire story after Ethan had called. "The security lines had just been cut and I said at least it wasn't an infestation of—"

Dane raised a finger to his lips and whispered, "Shhh." Turning to Amano, he said in a low tone, "Sweep for a different kind of bug."

Amano's expression darkened. He clearly caught Dane's meaning.

Dane said, "My office next, then the entire floor."

Dane pressed the ice pack to my hand, then collected my things again. He left me with Amano for a few minutes while he gathered his bag as well. Then we headed downstairs.

Brandon brought around the SUV and Dane dismissed him for the evening with a hearty tip for the extra hours he'd put in.

I still burned with pain as we drove to the creek house. It was even an effort to speak. "So they know about me."

"Obviously." Dane was about to take angst to all-new levels. He was incredibly tense, massively on the edge, distressing me greatly.

"That means they've been watching us for a while."

"Possibly."

"Possibly?" I shot back, turning in the seat to face him. "I announced my two biggest scare factors—rattlesnakes and scorpions. And guess what? That's *exactly* what I got scared by!"

"Ari—"

"No! Do *not* try to calm me down!"

I started crying again.

"Fine." His tone was strained. I couldn't help but think of the conversation we'd had after the snake in the stairwell. I already felt the wrath building. He would find out who was behind this—and I had no doubt they'd pay dearly for what they'd done to me.

I couldn't reconcile how I felt about that. Instead, I asked, "What does Amano know about bugs?"

"He has equipment. Knows to check for phone taps, too. He did it frequently at my parents' estate."

"And who were they that there was a concern over someone listening in on them?" I asked. It helped to keep my mind focused on something, rather than the sting rushing through my veins and the pain in my hand.

"My father was a political strategist. He died before there was an Internet, and since most news articles hadn't begun to be posted until around 1985, including a lot of those archived, it was easy to keep just about everything related to him off the Web. My mother, too."

"Why do I feel as though I'm part of one big conspiracy theory?"

"You sort of are," he deadpanned.

"Jesus." My eyes squeezed shut. More tears streamed down my face. I concentrated on the questions. "What happened to your parents? How did they die?"

His tone radiated his frustration as he said, "Plane crash. Their private jet went down outside of New York City after a night at the Met. They saw the operatic version of *Sweeney Todd*. Ironic." He gave a disgusted laugh. "He was a murderer."

My pulse jumped. "You don't think your parents were—"

"No," he was quick to say. "I was just pointing out that it's about tragic deaths."

I hated hearing the pain in his voice. "Dane, I'm so sorry." I would have reached over and covered his hand with mine, but I still clutched my throbbing hand to my chest. "How old were you?"

"Not quite a month. My aunt and Amano were looking after me that night."

"A month," I said on a heavy breath. "You never even knew them."

"Aunt Lara was good at making sure I did—with photos and stories. They were very well respected in Philadelphia society, though apparently quite private. They kept personal matters to themselves. Not easy to get to know beyond their philanthropic efforts."

"Must be where you got your secretive ways."

"Amano always thought it was a smart tactic, due to my father's political affiliations. In D.C., you never know your true enemies."

"Zoe Barnes can attest to that," I mumbled.

"Sorry . . . not following you."

"From *House of Cards*. She got thrown in front of a train by a congressman because she knew too much."

"Dangerous game to play," he concurred.

"Yeah. So's this."

We both fell silent until we reached the house. As we entered, Dane said, "You'll work from here the rest of the week."

"Dane," I instantly protested.

"Don't say a fucking word against it, Ari." He took my nearly melted ice and left me. I sank into a chair in the entryway. He returned minutes later with a fresh ice pack that he gently placed on my hand. Kneeling in front of me, he said, "Baby, I'm so sorry about this."

As he brushed tears from my cheeks, I said, "It's not your fault."

"You keep saying that." He stood. "But it *is* my fault. And I'm going to do something about it, once and for all."

I didn't like his ominous tone.

"Dane—"

"This all ends, Ari. All of it."

He helped me up and to his bedroom.

"Dane, I can't hide out here. I have staff. Meetings. Measurements to take around the lobby. I have to get Facilities involved as well, since their people will be hanging the decorations."

His jaw set and a hooded look clouded his eyes. "I'm not comfortable with you at the Lux right now. Not until I'm done."

I blinked. "Done?"

Was I even sure I wanted to know what that meant?

"I've got some calls to make. Final straw. I'm about to shove hard. I don't want you caught in the cross fire."

"What about others at the Lux?"

"Have you not noticed you're the target?" I could see he fought to keep the razor edge from his tone. He wasn't all that successful. "I'm willing to bet ours will be the only two offices bugged. Your badge was deactivated when you needed it most. Even you said it—rattlesnakes and scorpions terrify you. And you've gotten a healthy dose of both. *Only you*."

My nerves were shot to hell and I still felt the disturbing tingle of venom. I sank onto the mattress before my legs gave out. A tremor started in my toes and worked its way through my body.

"I don't want to be here alone, Dane. You and Amano will be at the hotel. That's where you *need* to be."

"You're safe here. That's a fifteen-foot-tall fence surrounding the property and it's fully monitored. I have access to the security cameras on my iPhone, my iPad, my computer. And I can give Amano access as well."

With a shake of my head, I said, "You'd rather have me close by and you know it."

He raked a hand through his hair and muttered under his breath. He paced before me.

"I'll give you my schedule for the week," I offered. "You'll know where I am at *all* times. They tried to scare me and they did. Okay? I am officially freaked out. And in a serious amount of pain. But I still have work to do and I will be *extremely* careful, Dane. I swear."

He pinned me with a tortured look that made my heart twist.

"I can't just sit here and worry," I said. "Even if you send Amano over, I will go completely stir-crazy. And we'll be behind the eight ball with the grand opening. I don't want you to have to postpone again."

"Neither do I," he said with conviction. He walked away, balled his fist, and put it through the drywall next to the door.

I jumped. "Dane!"

He didn't turn back. As though he couldn't look at me. He put another hole in the wall.

I sucked in a breath.

Then he stalked into the bathroom. When he returned, he handed over a pill. "Ibuprofen, eight hundred milligrams." He offered me a glass of water to wash it down, then took a pill of his own. I noticed his bloodied knuckles.

"Trying to feel my pain?" I asked.

"I can't feel your pain," he said in a tight tone. "You won't let me."

He set the glass on the nightstand.

My eyes squeezed shut for a moment. Then I said, "Doesn't that put us at an impasse?"

"No impasse. You're in danger. I'm going to end it."

"Dane—"

"You know how I feel about you, Ari. You mean everything to me."

"So does the Lux," I said. "It means *so* much to you. And it means something to me, too—because it's *yours*."

I got to my feet, just to prove to him that I could. That I could reach past the scorpion sting to prove a point. "I will do whatever you and Amano ask. I won't go anywhere without him, or you. You have my word. You know I would never do anything to make you worry about me or put myself in further jeopardy."

I tormented him. I saw it in his agonized gaze.

"Dane," I pleaded. "Trust me. *Please*."

"I do." He swept his good hand through my hair. "This is killing me, baby. Thinking you might be harmed because of my involvement in something that was supposed to be legit. Goddamn it."

I felt his anger. His regret. "You had no idea this would all happen. You've been so careful about us at work and even in public. But someone has obviously been paying very close attention. Is it possible it's not even the axed investors at all?"

"I'm convinced it is. But you're right. It's almost as though they knew about you from the beginning."

He took me in his arms. I knew he contemplated who might know about us and how or why they'd use that knowledge to their advantage.

"You can go with me to the hotel in the morning," he eventually conceded. "But you're with Amano or myself at all times. At the very least—" His tension mounted as he nearly squeezed the air out of me. "Kyle."

*Whoa.* Now we were getting serious. To resort to *approving* of Kyle sticking close to me?

I had to do something to break the strain between us. "That'll make stops in the ladies' restroom awkward."

"Damn it, Ari."

"Dane. You're just scaring me more. You realize that, right?"

Releasing me, he stared into my eyes. "I love you."

I smiled, despite it all. "Lucky me."

With a sharp shake of his head, he said, "Maybe not."

"Dane." I gripped his shoulder with my good hand, my fingertips curling into his hard muscles and heat. "Don't say that. Don't *ever* say that. My whole life has changed since the moment I met you. Even the not-so-pleasant stuff has made me open my eyes and see that I was just going through the motions until you came along."

His brow furrowed.

I rushed on. "I lived vicariously through happy couples, convinced I'd turn out like my parents and grandparents if I dared to try to have a relationship. Beyond that, I never experienced any sort of impossible to resist attraction the way I did the instant I saw you. It was like—I suddenly woke up."

Sleeping Beauty coming to life even before that first kiss. The fucked-up part was that she, too, had to contend with an evil force.

I had to believe Dane could defeat his nemesis. Whomever it might be.

Exhausted from the turmoil of the evening, I sat back down on the bed. Dane slipped off my shoes and helped me out of my dress.

"Do you want something to wear?" he asked.

"Your shirt."

He gave me a shadow of a grin. At least he tried not to be so sinister looking. "I'll go get you one."

"I want the one you're wearing. Smells like you."

Loosening his tie, he whipped it off, then worked the cuff links as best as he could with what had to be a throbbing hand. He set them on the table next to the water, slipped out of the shirt, and assisted me with getting it on and buttoned.

I crawled under the covers. Dane joined me.

"How do you feel?" he asked.

"Like I stuck my hand on a hot stovetop burner. At least my brain's not scrambled the way it'd been the last time."

"Jesus, Ari." His muscles tensed all around me.

"I'll be all right."

He possessively kept me pressed to his body until I fell asleep. When I woke in the middle of the night, it was because I knew he'd slipped out of bed. I'd sensed it even in slumber.

I scanned the room, finding him on the sofa in front of the large fireplace, working on his laptop, his fingers softly skating over the keys. He was also speaking in a quiet tone into the phone wedged between his ear and the crook of his neck.

"That's not enough," he said insistently. "Dig deeper. We're close but we need more. Yes, I know they're already panicking. I've been watching their market shares and portfolios. I'm seeing the results of our efforts. It's not enough. If they think they can fuck with us—with *me*—they've got to be seeing right now that it's *not* a good idea."

Dread slithered through me. Dane was poking the snake. This alarmed me. But what else was he to do? Roll over and play dead? Give in to them? Let them steal the Lux from underneath his nose?

I would concede that it was property and money. Difficult to part with—painful, even. But, all in all, potentially replaceable.

Yet that just seemed too simple a solution and too easy. I had to respect the fact that he fought for all that he'd built, all that mattered to him. He'd had a dream, he'd worked hard to achieve it. Now it was up to him to save it.

I really was torn between right and wrong with this scenario but definitely leaning toward the full understanding that if I had wrapped my entire future around such an enormous endeavor I'd want to protect it as well.

What would I do to safeguard the things that meant the most to me? I didn't know. I'd never been in that position before. When it came to my parents' fallout, I'd had no clout to help one side over the other. Obviously, I'd sided with my father. But I couldn't bargain with my mother to leave Dad the hell alone, because she didn't care enough about me to worry what she might lose if he threw his hands in the air and walked away, instead of fighting for me. In other words, giving her everything she wanted so he could have me.

I'd been a stand-on-the-fringes kind of person for the majority of my life. Now that I had a better understanding of what could be gained, built, *fought* for, I could appreciate the fact that Dane would do anything and everything in his power to protect what was his.

That did not mean it all sat right with me. I was a bit scared of what that all entailed. But he'd done his best to keep the poli-econ society on course—on the up-and-up. He and Ethan both. They'd failed. So now Dane was taking another stand. And I had to give him credit for it, even if I wasn't wholly sure what that meant in the long run.

I pulled on the robe Dane had bought for me in Paris and curled up next to him on the leather couch. I didn't bother stealing a peek at his work—I didn't want to know his new course of action. Perhaps it was wiser to not pry for information I couldn't quite decipher anyway.

He draped the throw over me and I closed my eyes, my head on his shoulder. I was content just being near him.

"I love you," I whispered. And drifted off.

# chapter 21

Two days passed without incident. I did exactly as Dane and Amano instructed. When something mysterious cropped up that they both had to contend with they waited until lunchtime, when I could meet with Kyle in the courtyard. It didn't take him long to catch on that all was not right in my world.

"Why is he not scowling at me this week?" Kyle asked over his prime rib sliders.

I shrugged nonchalantly. "He knows we've become friends. He's okay with it."

Kyle nearly spewed food. "Yeah, I totally believe that."

"Look," I said, conspiratorially, because I trusted him. He didn't seem to have any ulterior motives or inclinations, other than to steal me away from Dane, because he still asked me on dates. "We've tried to keep this private, but we're very seriously involved."

I gave Kyle a moment to digest that and his slider.

Then I added, "The thing is . . . well . . . we're in love."

He blanched. It was actually a bit comical, given his athletic build and all-around macho-jock attitude.

"Are you fucking kidding me?" he all but hissed. "I mean, yeah, I can see you're close to drooling when he's around. And he's all *hands off, dude* when he sees us together, but still . . . Shit. Ari. *Really?*"

"Yes," I confirmed. "Really. I am literally the *hopelessly devoted to you Sandra Dee.*" Since I wasn't sure he'd ever seen *Grease,* I amended, "Or Princess Buttercup. Take your pick."

He set aside his slider and glared at me. "Buttercup was always in jeopardy."

"Not because of Westley," I reminded him.

"Need I reference the snake and scorpions?"

"Kyle!" *Bit of a low blow.*

Dane and the PR people had thought it best to share the news with all the employees, wanting them to be aware of the unfortunate events for their own safety. And because he didn't want to hide anything. "The grounds crew are sweeping this property all day long to make sure there aren't any more problems like that. They've found absolutely nothing."

Crossing his arms over his massive chest, he said, "You're making my point for me."

"I'm not in danger because of Dane." Wee little lie. But I had confidence in Dane and I knew he'd solve this problem once and for all.

"I'd be a hypocrite to criticize him when he gave me a job," Kyle begrudgingly admitted. "I really like the people I work with and the projects. But damn it, Ari." His arms dropped and he leaned toward me. "Cut the bullshit and talk to me about what's going on. I see Amano following you around. Shouldn't he be holed up in a security booth somewhere, monitoring the cameras? No, he's like a . . . a—"

"Bodyguard," I said. "Yes. Dane trusts him. But, Kyle, he also trusts you. When they can't be around, he's okay that I'm with you. Doesn't that say something?"

"That he has *no choice* but to be okay with it?" Kyle scowled. "Whatever. Semantics, right?"

I picked at my salad.

Kyle glowered. "So he thinks I can lasso a rattlesnake with my bare hands?"

"Well, I suspect you could," I lightly teased, hoping to keep this conversation from getting too intense. "The point I'm trying to make is that he has some faith in you."

"Because or in spite of the fact that I want to date you?" he asked with a jerked brow and a perplexed look.

I smiled softly. "You know that's not possible, right? I mean, I've deflected all along. I've never led you on. We're friends."

My smile faded as a new thought occurred to me.

"What?" Kyle promptly asked.

"I'm really not thinking clearly. Christ, I'm so sorry."

"Hey, it's okay that you just want to be friends at the moment. We're getting to know each other. Won't be long before you realize I'm a much easier-going, less-intense guy to hang out with than the one who stews over everything."

Kyle's grin was a dazzling one, all straight pearly whites, with a hint of a dimple in his left cheek. His blue eyes sparkled, and I really did like how he calmed me on so many levels.

Yet there was still a critical issue at hand. I said, "I hadn't quite considered that my hanging out with you might be bad for *your* health."

He seemed to instantly catch on, because he winked. "No worries. I really can lasso a rattlesnake with my bare hands," he joked. "Don't tell anyone, though. I don't want to become some sideshow freak, ya know?"

He went back to his lunch.

I watched him a few minutes, all confident in himself that he truly was bodyguard material. I couldn't dispute it, though in the back of my mind I wondered how dangerous that might be for Kyle. And whether I should have Dane fire him for his own protection.

When we were finished, we walked back to the lobby. He asked, "Why so quiet?"

I sighed. How had this all gotten so complicated?

"I like that we're friends," I told him. "I like that we get to hang out at work and that everyone's raving about what a great job you're doing. Dane really likes the invitations you're producing—and that has nothing to do with me. I'm not even commenting on them, just letting him choose the ones he wants. And I can tell it's been a difficult decision for him, because they're all good."

"But . . . ?"

"But," I said with a grimace. "There are some sketchy things going on around here. Between you and me, they might have to do with some of Dane's former investors. I don't want you finding yourself in trouble because of me, any more than Dane wants me caught in the cross fire because of him."

We reached the elevators and Kyle leaned against the wall and grinned again. "Because you like me."

I smirked. "Your arrogance knows no bounds."

"Come on, toss me a bone. You like me a little, don't you?"

Leaning in, I said, "As friends."

"That's a start, remember?"

He'd told me that at the Delfinos' house. God, that seemed a million years ago. So much had happened since then. And along the way, I'd fallen madly, addictively in love. With Dane.

In answer to Kyle's comment, I told him, "On your way to being a BFF."

"Ah, the best friend curse. Though," he added optimistically, "the more you're exposed to my rapier wit and these muscles"—he flexed his biceps—"the better chance you'll have of ditching the brooding, intimidating guy for someone much more fun."

"You do have a way about you. Just . . . don't forget what I said earlier, okay? *All* of it."

The elevator arrived. Though I missed my daily stair-stepper routine, I moved inside with Kyle.

"Is it his money?" he asked.

I shot him a look. "Oh, please."

"So . . . what? Is it that whole *I'm as tall as the Empire State Building* thing he's got going on?"

"I can't tell you exactly what it is," I said. "Because it's everything—but mostly the way he makes me feel. And do you really want to hear about this?"

He frowned. "No, I guess not."

With an empathetic smile, I said, "I'm sorry. It is what it is, whether I can explain it or not. I can't do anything about it. I can't help how I feel."

"Yeah, well, *I* feel very strongly that you'll get over him soon and come knocking on my door." He gave me a smug look that I could see was feigned.

"You're probably right," I played along. "I mean who wants to be in love with the Empire State Building?"

The elevator chimed and the doors slid open on the third floor to let Kyle off.

"If you change your mind," he said, "you know where to find me."

"Duly noted—and thanks. For everything."

He stepped out and I returned to my office.

I'd pulled together an entire theme for the launch and was in the process of creating a collage I could show Dane, to give him the full impact of my concept. It was hugely helpful to have something so massive to concentrate on. I didn't even notice the time whizzing by until Molly announced over the speakerphone, "Kathryn DeMille on line two for you."

I froze. Christ, I'd put her out of my mind—but that clearly didn't mean she went away completely. And why the hell was she calling me at work after hours, rather than on my cell? What game was she playing?

I reached for the receiver as distress rippled through me. "This is Ari."

"Of course it is, darling. I'm sure you knew it was me calling. How lovely that you have an assistant."

"What do you want?" I had no desire to engage in small talk with her. I knew what prompted the beast to rear its ugly head— money. Plain and simple.

"Wouldn't you like to hear how I'm doing?" she asked in her delicate tone. The one I had little patience for because I was onto her. "The Olstead Benefit is this Friday at the Biltmore, so I'm busy with salon appointments and still on the lookout for the perfect gown. I really don't want to buy off the rack, in the event someone else has selected the same Louis Vuitton or Oscar de la Renta. You know, everyone has been copying Amal Clooney's wedding gown and I just don't want to match anyone or wear some sort of knockoff—"

"Mother, you're living the life of a socialite when you are, in fact, *not* one. Use the Dillard's certificate I gave you—along with the others you've likely stockpiled because they're 'not Nordstrom'—and buy a damn dress the way normal people do. At the fucking mall." Okay, so I'd just snapped. But I knew it was only a matter of time before she showed her true colors. Why beat around the bush about it?

"Aria Lynne DeMille," she scolded in her haughty voice.

"Mother, I'm at work. Working. A concept that goes well beyond your comprehension, obviously. But it's how I pay my rent and expenses. I'm under a lot of pressure here and I don't have time for you to suddenly drop into my life pretending to be my parent. I've been perfectly fine with our disassociation. I accepted a long time ago that all you care about is *you*—not Dad, not me. So stop with the bullshit and tell me why you're calling."

"Well, I just . . ." She huffed, as though I'd hurt her feelings. One would actually have to have feelings in order for them to be hurt. So I didn't take the bait. "When did you become so cruel?"

I closed my eyes as tears burned. Me, the cruel one? I'd spent the first eighteen years of my life trying to get this woman to love me. At the very least, to *notice* me. The next eight years had been wrapped around self-therapy, trying to survive my messed-up childhood.

I thought back to the time before I'd met Dane, when I kept everyone at arm's length, not letting anyone close, not letting anyone touch me except on those rare occasions when I'd craved it a bit too much to deny a quick interaction.

That had all changed. I had friends now. I was surrounded by people all day and I liked them. Finally, I was normal. Well, relatively speaking, since I was addicted to one very dark and broody man, but still . . .

I could honestly say that, despite the drama in my life, I was happy. I was in love and loved in return.

The woman on the other end of the line who professed to be my mother was, in all honesty, simply someone I used to know. And while I wasn't a proponent of severing parental ties, in this case I had to admit that it was time.

I pulled in a long breath, then said, "Look, I understand that you feel some false sense of entitlement. Maybe it's because of all the money Dad made before his injuries. Maybe it's all the trendy, prestigious places we were invited to, the circle you were all a part of in the professional world of golf. I don't know. Frankly, I don't care. You willingly chose to screw up your marriage, and for the life of me, I still can't fathom why Dad was the one who had to suffer because you were the one to do something wrong. But I am smart enough to know why you're suddenly dropping into my world, and I'm telling you it's pointless. So stop calling me."

Her tone turned downright vicious—the voice I remembered from my childhood. "You're not the one in control here, Aria Lynne. You hurt me, I'll hurt your father."

I slammed the phone into its cradle. My heart pounded. Anger flashed through me. So, too, did anxiety.

How could I have forgotten who she truly was? Why hadn't I recalled from the onset that it was Maleficent I dealt with?

I dropped my head in my hands. I could rattle off some stone-cold words to her but they meant nothing in the grand scheme of things. They tore at me more than they ever would at her, because it was my own mother I lashed out at. Even if she was the furthest thing from being my mother, it wasn't easy to rise to her level. The fact that I had worried me a little. But above that, I had the very distinct and sinking feeling that I couldn't walk the walk.

How was I going to protect my dad and still make my car payments?

"Ari?"

*Oh, shit.*

Dane.

I sniffled and swiped at my tears before lifting my head.

"What is it?" He was instantly alarmed and stalking across my office.

Damn my mother for calling me at work. This was a private matter and yet here I was, painted into a corner with one more person with whom I couldn't go toe-to-toe.

"*Mommie Dearest* has taken to phoning me at work. I'm trying to get her to stop."

His gaze narrowed. "I thought the two of you didn't speak."

"We didn't. And I'd gotten over it. Then she started seeing my name and photos in papers and magazines. Suddenly she wants to be besties."

That was a total lie—she didn't want friendship or anything beyond more checks. And Dane saw right through me.

Taking one of the chairs in front of my desk, he rested his forearms on the glass top and steepled his fingers. Fingers that distracted me. I'd much rather have his hands on me than have this conversation with him.

"What's really going on?"

"Nothing for you to worry about," I told him. "I can handle it."

Wow, I was doling out a few whoppers today.

He regarded me closely for several seconds, then nodded his head. "If you say so."

It was my turn to eye him curiously. "And that's that?"

"If you needed my help, you'd ask for it, right?"

I smiled, despite knowing I wasn't on par with my mother's wily ways. She was much more cunning—which meant I had to either resort to Dane rescuing me yet again or step up my game. Because I didn't want him involved any more than I wanted my dad tormented further.

"She wants money," I confessed. "But it's my problem and I'll figure it out."

He hedged. I saw the wheels churning in his brain, caught the hint of alpha in his eyes.

"Dane," I warned. "This is a family thing I need to deal with—not something for you to fix."

"But you know I can."

"And you hear me asking you not to," I challenged.

His jaw worked rigorously for a moment. Then he said, "If you insist."

"I do." And I meant it.

Luckily, a knock on my opened door saved me from continuing this discussion.

"Hey," Kyle said. "We have a meeting in the conf—" He frowned. "Why are you crying?"

"I'm not crying." I swept my hands over my face to erase any evidence to the contrary.

Dane stood and faced my friend. "Everything's fine, according to Ari."

"According to Ari." Kyle stepped into the room. "But not you?"

I got to my feet as well and rounded the desk, standing between the two men.

"It's just a little family drama," I said. "Let's go to our meeting."

Behind me, Dane scoffed.

Kyle simmered. "You just can't stay out of trouble, can you? Ever since that day in the bar when the guy with the tattoo grabbed you, you've been living on the edge."

"That's not fair," I bit back. "I didn't ask for him to—"

"Wait a second," Dane interjected. "Kyle has a point."

I whirled around and glared at Dane. "You're siding with *him*? What sort of alternate universe did I just wake up in?"

With a grim look that conveyed displeasure with my glib comment as much as it revealed a new level of consternation, Dane said in a gruff voice, "That guy in the bar had a diamondback tattoo. There are no snakes on this property. I have people who make sure of it. There isn't an infestation of scorpions, either. And yes, your office was bugged."

"Holy shit," Kyle said. "Okay, am I the only one who thinks this is all jacked to hell?"

Ignoring him, Dane told me, "A snake sitting on the fourth-floor landing would have been planted. Security cameras weren't operating at the time, so it would have been easy for anyone who had access to release it there, knowing you always took the stairs."

"Someone who had a thing for snakes?" I ventured as my blood ran cold. "Someone who might even have pet rattlers?"

"And if he doesn't have a problem handling snakes, he wouldn't mind collecting a few scorpions, either."

My stomach churned. "I just might be sick."

"The guy was pissed that I stepped in at the bar," Dane said. "Pretty easy to exact his own revenge when all he had to do was open a newspaper and see your face—just like your mom. Not difficult to put two and two together when it's a well-known fact I own the hotel where you work."

I sank into the chair he'd vacated. "Oh, boy. Now I know why you've been so adamant about keeping your exposure on the Internet and elsewhere to a minimum. With the exception of the very obvious and simple-to-discover detail that the Lux is yours."

"This is fucking unbelievable," Kyle muttered. "Are you

saying . . . ?" He shook his head as his fists clenched at his sides.
"Great. This is just great. So it's not Ari who's the trouble magnet." He glowered at Dane. "You're the reason she's constantly in
danger."

"Kyle," I pleaded, not quite having the wherewithal for a confrontation between the two of them.

"Way to go, Buttercup," he lobbed back at me. I smirked.

Dane dragged a hand down his face. "What?"

"Inside joke," I explained. Instantly realizing my mistake as his
head slowly turned and he shot me a *you did not just say that* look.

I'd made the entire scene worse.

"So she really is the target here," Kyle said, agitated. "Because
of you."

Dane's attention returned to Kyle. "I think you've made your
point."

Kyle took several steps forward. "Have I?"

I jumped up and moved between them again. "Knock it off," I
demanded, my pulse racing. To Kyle, I said, "He's a boxer. You're
a quarterback. I don't doubt it'd be an interesting showdown, but
fighting amongst ourselves isn't going to solve the problem."

"*I'm* going to solve the problem," Dane said as he stormed
around us and headed to the door. "All of them, now that I know
all the sources."

"Dane—" I called out, not liking the sharp edge to his voice or
the tension in his shoulders.

"Stay here, Ari. Kyle . . . Goddamn it. Make sure nothing happens to her."

"Definitely not on my watch."

Dane let out a low, primal growl before stalking off.

"You just have to provoke him, don't you?"

He glanced over at me. "And you can't resist all this risky business."

"It's not as though I'm enjoying this. Have you ever been stung
by a scorpion?"

"No." His jaw clenched again. "I'm a little more careful."

"Stop kicking me when I'm down."

His entire visage softened instantly. "Ari . . ."

I waved a hand at him. "Don't worry about it. I'll survive. Let's go to our meeting."

"Right. Like you can concentrate on work when you have no idea what Dark Knight there just set out to do."

It'd be hell to focus on business, but what choice did I have? "We have a ton of things to tackle. I'm not letting anything fall through the cracks because of me."

I collected my files and notebook and preceded Kyle out the door and down the corridor to the main conference room, where I did everything in my power to get through the rest of my day, keeping my shaky hands in my lap and forcing a bit of calm into my voice.

On the inside, however, I was nothing short of a nervous wreck.

# chapter 22

My mother called my cell the next morning. My tension hadn't eased the slightest bit from the day before. Especially when Dane had told me he'd learned the identity of snake-tat guy and that he'd apparently skipped town after paying off a few debts. Dane suspected he hadn't acted solely on his own—that someone had likely offered him substantial cash to torture me. The very cryptic, "Don't worry, I'll find him," from Dane only made me more apprehensive.

"I don't have anything new to say to you," I told my mother.

"It was all a bluff," she unexpectedly blurted, her voice cracking. "There is no synopsis, chapters, proposal. I made it all up."

I sank onto the armrest of a sofa in the great room and asked, "You what?"

"I had no choice but to blackmail you, Aria Lynne. I needed the money."

"Needed?" As in past tense.

"Everything's fine now," she rushed on, as though she wanted off the phone ASAP. "I won't bother you again. Ever. I understand you don't want me in your life and that's fine. Consider me gone."

My stomach knotted. "Just like that?"

"I don't know what sort of people you associate with—I'm not even really sure who you are. But you won't hear from me again." The line went dead.

I sat for a few minutes, trying to process what had just happened. Then I slowly got to my feet and sought out Dane in his office.

"You couldn't be in two places at once yesterday," I said without preamble. "So while Amano tracked down tat guy, you were . . . what? Buying off my mother?"

"She won't cause trouble for you in the future. I made sure of it." He didn't even look up from his laptop, just kept typing.

I stared at him, momentarily at a loss for words as anger roiled through me. I tried to tamp it down, but there were some seriously conflicting feelings clawing at me and I couldn't get a grip on them. My mother thought I'd become some sort of monster. Had I?

Because I was perfectly happy that I wouldn't have to deal with her ever again. That she wouldn't hurt my dad any more than she already had. It was a monumental relief, really. A huge weight off my shoulders.

Conversely . . .

"You had no right to take care of this. I was handling it."

Finally, he glanced up. "Were you? Or were you just feeding into her scheme? Because she kept calling you, didn't she? And five grand here or five grand there would have only snowballed into more and more—until all you were doing was signing over your paycheck to her. And, baby, you work too damn hard to make that sort of sacrifice."

I wanted to cry. He was right, of course. At the same time, I honestly feared how he'd reconciled the issue. My mother had not sounded normal on the phone. In fact, she'd sounded terrified.

"You threatened her?"

"I got her name from Molly, since she's called twice at the office. I had someone who works for me locate her. She happened to be at home, which made it easy to write her a check and tell her to stay the hell out of your life."

"You just said money wouldn't solve the problem."

"I said five grand here or there wouldn't solve the problem. Trust me, she understands that my offer was a one-shot deal."

"Because you threatened her," I repeated.

"I did what I had to in order to get my point across."

That flash of danger in his eyes—the darkness that rimmed his emerald irises—told me very specifically why my mother had been so nervous on the phone.

And the dark side of me that I'd not known existed until now made me pleased that she'd finally gotten a taste of her own medicine. She'd tormented my dad. She'd broken both of our hearts. And she hadn't cared that she'd done it.

"Ari," Dane said as he stood and came around to take me in his arms. "None of this is new to me. My entire life has centered around protecting what's mine. Sometimes there are simple solutions, sometimes not. I'm willing to do whatever I have to do. *Anything.*"

I gnawed my lower lip. Then asked, "You know when to draw the line, though, right?"

"I currently don't have any lines. Too much is at stake. You. 10,000 Lux. Hell, even your dad's reputation. You really think I'd let her publicly rip a hole in him again? He's your father. You love him. And I respect him. So I stood up for him—and you."

I realized that all of the shadowy parts of our life together were not strictly Dane's doing or a result of his personal and professional dealings. I'd brought baggage along to darken our doorstep, too. I wanted an end to it all as much as Dane did.

What kind of a person did that make me?

Regardless of good intentions or the need to protect the people and things we loved, the bottom line seemed to be that we'd both do whatever we had to do.

The question was, could I live with that?

———

In the afternoon, Kyle joined me on the terrace outside my office.

"You okay?" he asked as he rested an arm against the railing.

"Sure. You?"

He gave a sardonic laugh. "I've lost a little sleep over you."

"Don't," I was quick to say. "It's not worth it, Kyle."

He stared at me for several suspended seconds, then said, "I happen to think it is."

With a sigh, I told him, "I care about you, too."

"Which is why you didn't want to see my devastatingly handsome face rearranged? Though, for the record, I'd put money on the quarterback."

"I'd prefer it if we didn't find out whether you could last a few rounds with Dane." I still had no doubt who the victor would be. Kyle could hold his own for a while but I knew Dane would channel all that territorial intensity into a standoff. And it wouldn't be pretty.

A tremor ran down my spine. I didn't even want to think of the two of them taking swings at each other. I'd had enough drama, enough danger, to last a lifetime.

"So where is Surly, anyway?" he asked.

"Off doing whatever it is that he and Amano do when they're not here."

"Then I'm on bodyguard alert, eh? Cool."

"Try not to enjoy it so much. You could get hurt as easily as I could. In fact, it would be best if—"

"Huh-uh," he cut me off. "You don't bother dipping your toe in hot water; you dive right in. So I'm hanging out with you this afternoon. I'll go get my laptop and set up shop at your conference table."

As he headed back inside, I said, "Kyle, you really should think twice about this."

He turned to me and smiled. The pearly white, vibrant one.

"And miss out on the chance to twist the knife because your boyfriend knows I'm spending all this time with you? Not a fucking chance."

While he was gone to retrieve his computer, Molly popped in with a beautiful floral arrangement in her hands.

"These just arrived," she said as she set the red and white roses in a square crystal vase on the corner of my desk.

I causally asked, "Has Mr. Bax returned yet?"

"No. I'll phone when he's back, if you'd like."

"Thank you."

She left and I quickly snatched the small card from the florist's stationery. The flowers were from Dane, and he'd obviously ordered them online, because he couldn't write out the card himself. Instead, it was a computer-printed one that read:

> Ari,
> Again, I'm so sorry about what's happened. I'm fixing
> it, I promise. Meet me out front at five. Dane

I was more than happy to slip off with him at the end of the day. And I hoped he was in a better frame of mind, with whatever current plan of attack he had underway. Which I wanted to know about, yet . . . I didn't.

I went back to my collage of decoration images, prepping it so I could display it for Dane this evening. Kyle joined me and we both immersed ourselves in our respective projects. Close to five, I packed everything up. Kyle went downstairs with me, since he was done for the day as well.

The tall doors were opened by the valet taking over Brandon's shift. I hadn't met him yet.

"Ari DeMille, Events Director," I said. "This is Kyle Jenns."

"Wayne Horton," he introduced himself as we all shook. "I'll bring your cars around."

"Actually, I've got a meeting with Mr. Bax." Dane's Venom F5 sat in the circular drive. I turned to Kyle. "Thanks for babysitting me."

"Not a problem. Be careful."

"Of course."

Wayne escorted me over to the flashy sports car.

Staring up at him, I asked, "Are you new?"

"No, I've been working with various departments the past few months—IT, Facilities, Distribution Services, Grounds crew—whatever they need me to do. I'm sort of a jack-of-all-trades."

"That sounds handy for the hotel."

"Seems to be working out." His smile held a hint of mischief that perplexed me. He pulled open the door and I slipped inside, setting my bag on the floorboard between my legs. I glanced back at him, trying to read his expression. He added, "Have a nice evening, Miss DeMille."

"Ari is fine."

"Very good." He closed the door and engaged Kyle in conversation. I reached for the seat belt, an uneasy feeling seeping through me. The car peeled away, rounded the center fountain, and raced down the winding road.

I turned toward the driver's seat while saying, "No need to show off for—oh, my God!"

My heart leapt into my throat. It took several seconds for my brain to overcome shock and catch up.

"You're not Dane!"

# chapter 23

The dark-haired man flashed me a sinister grin and said, "No, I am not."

He had an accent with which I wasn't familiar and he wore sunglasses. With just a quick glimpse he could have passed for Dane.

"Who are you?" I demanded as I reached for the latch on my belt and unhooked it.

"Vale Hilliard. And don't think you're going anywhere, Miss DeMille."

"I'm not going anywhere with *you*!" I searched the door panel, mumbling in a panicked voice, "Where the hell is the lock?" Prepared to throw myself out of the speeding vehicle and onto the stone drive, I was that desperate to escape.

"Sit still and buckle up—it is the law, after all."

I shot him what I'd hoped was a menacing glare, though I knew it turned into one of terror when I saw he had a gun in his lap. And it was pointed at me.

"Shit." My pulse beat erratically. My eyes flashed to the dash-board, noting a different stereo and other options. "This isn't even Dane's car."

"It's a loaner. I told the owner in Las Vegas who has it up for sale that I was interested in a test drive."

"To Arizona?"

"I told him I'd need it overnight—and paid him handsomely."

*Fuck!* He'd found a car that, on the outside, looked identical to Dane's. The guards at the entrance of the property wouldn't have batted an eye as it came barreling toward the gates—as we did now on our way out. I wanted to scream at the injustice. This man drove a vehicle that was so rare, only twenty-nine people other than Dane had one.

We blew right through the opening without slowing down. Then he punched it, driving so fast that even if I could have found the lock on the door and had the nerve to attempt to get out just hitting the pavement might have killed me.

As though he sensed I contemplated an escape, Vale Hilliard said, "If you cooperate, you won't get hurt."

"What are you planning to do?"

"Kidnapping you is a start."

With an aggravated shake of my head, I said, "You sent the flow-ers, didn't you?" *Damn it!* I'd fallen right into his trap.

He grinned again. "Dane will panic when he realizes you're missing. I'll call him and tell him he can have you back, unharmed—for a price."

I swallowed hard. "You want part of the Lux."

"No. My father does."

My gaze narrowed. "Your father?"

"Well, I get something out of it as well." He slowed—barely—and I screamed as we took a hairpin turn onto a red-dirt road, the tires squealing as we left the asphalt behind. The car splashed through a puddle, coating the car crimson. The rugged terrain jarred me and we slipped a bit in the mud.

My heart now pounded fiercely.

"Where are we going?"

"We'll stay in the canyon, since there's no cell reception here. No reason for you to try to call Dane yourself. Or 9-1-1. I'll have to leave you in order to phone him. But don't worry, I'll tie you up nice and tight. And since there's no one within miles, you can scream as loud as you'd like—not a soul will hear you."

It took a bit for me to recover. Eventually, I said, "You're not seriously going to leave me in the middle of nowhere?"

"One of us will come back for you." His tone turned dark as he added, "For your sake, hope it's Dane."

"Oh, my God," I whispered. My stomach roiled. This couldn't be happening. And there was no way out of it. The man had a gun. I couldn't outrun *bullets*. Or him. Even if I had two seconds to reach for my phone and hit Dane's speed dial number, it would do no good. I knew there was no service this deep in a box canyon. I even had trouble sometimes at the Lux.

*Son of a bitch!* What was I going to do?

What about Dane? He'd spit nails when he found out I was missing. Not to mention, he'd be hellaciously worried about me. Would blame himself for my precarious predicament.

My mind reeled. What had he done to piss off the senior Hilliard enough for his son to resort to taking me hostage and extorting some of the shares in Lux from Dane?

We came to a jerky halt alongside a two-story house with scaffolding lining the font. Brush and sycamores surrounded it, creating a secluded alcove.

Vale said, "I noticed construction had stopped because of the rain."

How long had he been scouting a place to hide me?

He continued. "Roof's on. At least you'll be dry."

*At least?*

"You can't just leave me here." My panic reached all-new levels.

"But I must. I can't take any chances. Now sit tight for a moment."

He got out of the car. I wanted to make a break for it, but I'd get my feet in high heels and thick mud.

I unbuckled and went for the phone in my laptop as Vale rounded the back of the F5. With trembling fingers, I held up the cell—no signal whatsoever. Not a single fucking bar.

The door flung open and he yanked me out, my bag falling to the wet ground, the contents scattering. My phone dropped from my shaking hands. He gripped my arm firmly and forced me toward the house. I stumbled along the way. His fingertips dug deeper into my flesh, despite the suit jacket I wore.

We took the steps to the porch and crossed to the door. The inside wasn't finished. There were still exposed two-by-fours and tresses. Weaving our way through the mess of sawdust and plastic sheets, we reached the staircase with a metal railing on one side, clearly a safety measure while the banister was being built.

I let out a strained laugh. There was nothing *safe* about this scenario. Not for me.

The landing at the top of the stairs opened into an enormous room. In the middle sat a chair. At its legs were piles of rope coiled high.

I screamed and tried to wrest free of Vale's grip. He hauled me up against him and said, "Don't make this difficult. We want our money. My father's investments and assets are challenging to liquidate. Profits from 10,000 Lux are to be paid out quarterly. We need access to that capital. *I* need access to that capital."

"And you're willing to tie me up and hold me for ransom to get it?"

"I am willing—and have the authority—to do whatever's necessary." His intimidating stare unnerved me further.

"Whose authority?" I managed to ask, the fear distinct in my voice.

"The others who were part of the investment group for the hotel."

"You're the one behind all the problems on the property? On their behalf?"

"They paid me to *persuade* Dane to bring them back into the fold. He's already figured all of this out and has been wreaking his own havoc. No one's happy about that. It also causes trouble for me. So now it's time to put an end to this, once and for all."

I did not like the sound of that. Did they intend a hostile take-over of the Lux? What if Dane flat-out refused? What if Ethan, Qadir, and Nikolai stood their ground as well? Would this man really shoot me? Or leave me here? It could be two weeks before the construction crew returned. There was still rain in the forecast, since we had experienced a record-breaking monsoon season.

None of this boded well for me. Or Dane.

So as Vale slipped his gun into its shoulder holster, I lifted my foot and brought my four-inch heel down hard, stabbing his toe.

He let out an agonized growl and released me. I ran straight to the staircase. Reaching it before he reacted. I kicked off my shoes and had almost made the first step when he grabbed a fistful of my hair and tugged heartily so that I cried out from the pain.

He jerked me to him and ground out, "Big mistake, Miss De-Mille." He turned me to him and the back of his hand struck my cheek so hard, I screamed and fell facedown to the wood-covered floor several feet from him.

I lay there, stunned, an excruciating throbbing spreading from my cheekbone to my eye and temple. The thumping in my head was deafening and I felt disoriented and hazy.

"You stupid girl," Vale spat. "The last thing you want is to make me angry." His threatening voice rang in my ears.

I tried to latch on to the sound. Tried to let it pull me from the fog and the sharp ache.

His heavy footsteps came closer. I couldn't imagine what he'd do now that I'd pissed him off. I didn't want to find out.

Spying a small piece of discarded board within inches of my

hand, I waited until he descended upon me and clutched my hair again to pull me up. As my body lifted, my arm shot out. I grabbed the wood and slammed it against his jaw with all the strength I possessed, fueled by rage.

"You fucking bitch!" he yelled as he reeled, letting go once more.

I didn't wait around. I was on my feet again, miraculously, because the throbbing intensified when I moved. I raced to the stairs, made it to the midway landing, and was on my way down when he shoved hard against my back. I screamed again as I tumbled to the first floor, my head smacking against the damn metal safety railing that mocked me.

I might have lost consciousness for a moment or two. Huddled in a heap of sheer agony, I could barely breathe. It hurt too much.

"I'll give you credit for fighting back," he said in a deadly tone. "But you picked the wrong man to go toe-to-toe with."

Ripping me from the floor with his hand wrapped around my arm, he pushed me through the shell of a living room. Dry lightning crackled and lit the clouds as we passed by a window. He shoved me against a two-by-four that helped to form an entryway into the dining room or den. I clutched it for support, because my knees were about to give out on me.

My body was wracked with pain, radiating unbearably from head to toe.

"You've fucked this whole thing up," he insisted in a low, ominous tone. "For everyone. Including yourself."

Swiftly he whipped off his suit jacket, followed by his tie. Before I could even react, he had my wrists bound with it and pulled my arms up and over my head as he secured the tie to the beam above us.

"No," I uttered on a harsh breath. My throat felt raw and tight, my mouth dry.

"I listened that night you were in your office with Dane," he said in my ear. "Before you talked about the rattlesnakes and scorpions."

He let out a gruff laugh. My insides chilled.

Continuing, he said, "I knew that day in the bar that you were going to be his downfall. He's never let a woman get to him, never gave one the power or opportunity to screw up everything for him. But that's exactly what you've done. He lost sight of his goal, dropped the ball—because of you."

"I'm not to blame for what's happened at the Lux. You already admitted it's all your doing."

It was a wonder I could speak, but anger and fear propelled me forward, even as blood ran down the side of my face from where I'd hit the railing and dripped into my eye so that I had to try to blink it away, along with my tears. My cheek burned and my breath was still scarce. I'd never fathomed such pain in my life. Had I not practically been hanging from the rafters, I would have crumpled to the ground.

"How'd you do it?" I asked. I might have been stalling. I wasn't wholly sure, because I really couldn't think straight. It just seemed that the more he talked, the less damage he'd do to me. That was likely wishful thinking but I encouraged him anyway. "All of it. How?"

"I was there that day in the bar." He still remained too close to me, whispering into my ear. "I followed Dane to see who he'd meet with off-property. It was Ethan Evans. I knew I had to find out what they were planning. Then you came barreling in and he lost all concentration. He couldn't take his eyes off you. *Fool.*"

A lump of emotion swelled in my throat.

*Dane.*

Maybe it was true; maybe his attraction to me, everything we felt for each other, had kept him from working out all of his issues at the hotel. I didn't know. I doubted I'd ever know. I wasn't exactly convinced I was getting out of this mess alive.

"Later on," Vale continued, "when the two of you spoke at the restaurant in Tlaquepaque, I knew he'd offer you a job at the Lux. I have someone on the inside. He was aware of the office Dane assigned you, because he took delivery of all the furniture and set it up. It was easy for him to wire the place."

I had no idea why, but Wayne Horton's voice cut through the hammering in my head.

*. . . I've been working with various departments the past few months—IT, Facilities, Distribution Services, Grounds crew— whatever they need me to do. I'm sort of a jack-of-all-trades.*

And that smile he'd given me. As it flashed in my head, it seemed less mischievous and more . . . *devious.*

*Fuck.* How convenient. Working with IT, Wayne could screw up the Web site and deactivate my access badge. With Facilities, he could have the furniture Dane ordered for the penthouse delivered to Monaco. He could have cut the security wires while part of the Grounds crew.

"How'd the snake get into the stairwell?" I asked.

"Brilliant, really," Vale murmured. "Dane helped with that. So, too, did you. By wanting to keep this—what did he call it? oh, yes— *sensational* body in shape for him, you offered an easy way for me to prove how serious I am with my plight."

His hands moved over my hips. I recoiled. "Don't touch me."

"I'm going to do more than that," he said, his tone pure evil. "But about the rattler. Do you remember the gentleman in the bar whom you bumped into? The one with the diamondback tattoo on his neck?"

My blood ran cold. "Yes."

"Seems he took offense to being shown up—and foiled—by Dane and was all too happy to help me out when I offered him the chance for retribution. I ascertained that a man with a snake tattoo likely had access to the creatures you loathe. As a matter of fact, he helped me with the scorpions as well. And if you ruin my negotiations with Dane, I'll not only leave you here alone, tied up, but I'll fill this house with everything that terrifies you."

So Dane had been right. I wanted to scream again. I didn't have the strength. My heart beat way too fast and more tears filled my eyes, cresting the rims and streaming down my cheeks, mixed with the blood still oozing from the cut on my forehead.

He said, "I was also listening when he got you off that night. All your moaning and begging him to fuck you . . ." His hands slid along my rib cage. "That made me hot." His lips grazed my throat. My eyes squeezed tight as a violent tremor ran through me. "I had my dick in my hand, pumping with every hitch of your breath and every cry of pleasure."

My stomach revolted. Bile burned my throat.

His hands moved upward and he ripped apart the buttons on my blouse.

"No!" I screamed through all the pain and fear.

"I told you this could have gone so much smoother for you. Now . . . I get payback." Cupping my breasts through my bra, he squeezed roughly. Too rough. I cried out again. "That's what I like to hear. And, Jesus Christ, these are nice tits. I'm going to rub my cock between them, pushing your head down, making you suck me hard."

I screamed again. It didn't matter that no one could hear me. I yelled out for Dane, Amano, anyone. I wailed loudly, even if not coherently.

His hands shifted, shoving under my skirt. He jerked down my panties to mid-thigh, then knelt behind me. I thrashed against my bindings, but he clasped my calves and held them as steady as he could, so I couldn't kick him.

"Let's see how hard I can make you come when I eat your pussy."

"No!" I hollered once more. "Stop touching me! Please, God, stop touching me!"

Vale had been at the bar. He'd known that, in addition to the reptiles, I didn't want anyone but Dane to touch me.

This was torture. I wasn't even sure he wanted to rape me. I didn't believe that had been his intent all along. He was doing this to torment me—Dane, too. And dear God, once Dane saw me—if he ever saw me again . . .

I sobbed a little harder, struggled more against my restraints. This would kill Dane. What would the retaliation for *this* be?

"Let me go now," I said. "Don't go any further. This is too much. Dane won't let up. This will only make it worse for your family and the others."

"We can handle Dane," Vale assured me. "And if knowing what I've done to you cripples him . . . that's even better."

"Stop touching me!" I yelled again.

His hands hadn't moved from the backs of my thighs, but I knew it was only a matter of seconds until—

A resounding *thwack* echoed all around me, followed by the jolting of my body as Vale's hands tore from my legs and he let out a furious and agonized roar.

My eyes flew open. I saw him sprawled on the floor inside the dining room. Dane stood over him, a board in his hand.

Amano's arm was around my waist in the next instant. With his free hand he retrieved a knife from his pocket, flicked it open, and slashed through the tie binding me. I collapsed against him.

A startled and clearly injured Vale attempted to roll onto his side and either stand or crawl away. Dane didn't give him the chance.

Through my crimson-tainted vision, I saw Dane kick my assailant in the gut, so that he flopped onto his back again with a low grunt. Then Dane was on him, his fists pounding and making contact no matter how desperately Vale tried to deflect the blows. I heard the cracking of bones. Blood splattered everywhere. For several moments, I was riveted, unable to think, process, accept what my gaze remained locked on. I didn't even think about the gun Vale had. Clearly, it didn't matter that he was armed—he couldn't get to it with Dane's vicious attack.

I barely even noticed Amano maneuvering me just so in order to yank up my panties while still holding on to me so I didn't drop like a ton of bricks at his feet.

Dane continued to punch, and the bones snapping became

gruesome to listen to. Finally, it registered in my mind the length he was willing to go.

He'd kill for me.

And I almost let him.

"Dane," I squeaked out. "Enough."

He kept at it. Vale's legs vibrated, then stilled. His entire body went limp.

"Dane!" I mustered the strength to shout. "Stop! You'll kill him!"

Dane could have been a professional boxer. And he unleashed a violent rage that horrified me. Mostly because, in that dark part of me, I knew he deserved this revenge. I wanted him to get it. I wanted Vale to pay for what he'd done to the hotel—and, especially, what he'd done to me.

So much so that I could have retracted my protest. Let Dane finish what he started.

But then my mother's words taunted me.

*I don't know what sort of people you associate with—I'm not even really sure who you are.*

I wasn't so sure, either.

"Dane," I called out again. "Just stop. It's over!"

Wrenching myself free of Amano's loose embrace, I hurled myself forward, tackling Dane, shoving him off Vale. I lay sprawled across Dane, breathing heavily.

"That's homicide." I pointed my finger toward Vale. I had no idea if he was dead or alive. He was certainly unconscious. "You're not a killer."

"I have the right," Dane shot back. "I have *every* right!"

"No," I insisted, staring into his wild, dark eyes. "You don't. This isn't who you are. *This isn't who I am!*"

"Ari," he said with conviction. "This *is* exactly who I am."

I tried to climb off him, tried to stand. Amano had to swoop in and lift me to my feet while holding me firmly to him. I quaked and a peculiar dreadfulness consumed me.

Dane stood, breathing heavy. He extended a bloody-knuckled hand to me. "Ari."

I shrank away.

"Ari," he said again, his gaze connecting with mine. "Christ . . . Your face." His jaw clenched. His irises burned with fury. "Goddamn it. Look what he did to you! And he would have raped you. *Goddamn it.*" The fury was like nothing I'd ever seen, heard, witnessed. Not even my parents' poisonous tantrums had been this treacherous.

"We can't do this," I told him, my voice cracking. "We can't be these people. This is too much, Dane. This is all just too much!"

"Ari, I've said from the beginning that I would do anything to keep you safe."

"But I'm not safe if I lose you to this rage. Can't you see that? It's because of me that you've refused to draw a line. It's because of *me* that you've gone this far."

"Just let me help you," he quietly offered as he took a step closer.

I moved backward, forcing Amano to as well. "I am as much a destructive force as you are—don't you see that?"

"Ari. Baby, I—"

"No," I said as tears flowed down my cheeks.

"I'm not the bad guy here," he insisted.

"I know that. But Vale might be *dead*, Dane. Dead!"

His head snapped back at my angst, my pain. As though I'd slapped him.

To Amano, I said, "Take me home, please." My gaze was still locked with Dane's. "To *my* house."

"Of course," Amano agreed. Though I was sure he gave a questioning look to Dane, whose eyes didn't leave mine.

"Don't do this," he said, his tone pleading, tearing at me.

"I have to," I told him as the sobs welled in my throat. "And you have to let me go. This is wrong. What's become of us is wrong. My fault as much as yours, but still . . . It's *wrong*, Dane."

The panic over those words made my chest hurt. Like someone had ripped out my heart.

"I love you," he said with steely conviction.

"I feel the same—and it's devastating us both. This is not healthy, Dane." I could barely breathe, as though I'd been gutted. Shredded from the inside out. It took all the willpower and resolve I possessed to finally steal my gaze from his.

"Get me out of here, Amano."

He had to do most of the work, because my legs were wobbly. When we reached the front door, he seemed to realize I wasn't wearing shoes and lifted me into his arms. He carried me to Dane's Escalade and carefully deposited me in the passenger's seat. Then he collected my muddied bag and phone and put them in the back.

I kept my eyes on the windshield, looking straight forward, not glancing out the side window to see if Dane would appear.

I didn't want to know what he'd do about Vale or how he'd clean up this mess. All the blood in someone's partially constructed house.

I couldn't allow myself to think of anything at the moment. The demons clawed at me, but I mentally fought them back so I didn't fall apart.

As was his normal practice, Amano uttered not a word as he drove me to my townhome. I was grateful for the silence. It helped me to concentrate on blocking everything from my mind. *Everything.*

When he delivered me to the front door, he dug out my keys and unlocked the dead bolt. I stepped inside and he followed so that he could set all of my belongings on the kitchen counter.

Finally, he said, "Ari . . . whatever I can do."

That started the waterworks again. I turned to him. "Can you get my stuff from Dane's? My suits are in the dressing room and there are some clothes in the two top drawers. A tote in the bathroom. Not the silver robe and nightgown. I don't want them." My voice was scary. Distant sounding, yet laced with a fragility that made me fear how strong my freak-out would be when he left me.

"I'd rather take you to the hospital," he told me.

"They'll ask questions. You know that." I stared unwaveringly at him. I knew this Secret Service–type lifestyle was something he'd embraced for decades, after all, whether he knew Dane's Illuminati association or not. "I can't exactly say I walked into a door, right?"

His jaw clenched. Then he said, "At least let me clean you up. See if you need stitches."

"I'll do it." I wanted to be alone. I felt the hysteria coming on and I needed for him to leave. "Will you please just get my things?"

"Yes."

I could see he didn't want to walk out on me, but I said, "Before Dane makes it home."

"Right."

Likely I tested his loyalty to Dane. But in the end, I suspected he knew that Dane would want him to do whatever I requested. Do whatever needed to be done.

"Lock all the doors and windows," he said, his worry making me shudder. "Don't open up for anyone but me."

"I promise."

He gave me another unfaltering look that conveyed remorse, an apology, condolences. Making me wonder exactly how fucked up my face was. The pain throbbed in wicked beats but a certain numbness flowed through me.

The misery of losing Dane eclipsed the physical agony.

# chapter 24

When I was alone, I went into the bathroom. A peculiar sickness moved through me. Seconds later I was curled over the toilet, heaving. It took some time to get past the sights and sounds in my head. Then I pressed a damp washcloth to my mouth and the nausea eased.

I brushed my teeth and stripped off my clothes, wanting to burn them. Destroy all evidence of the evening so I never had to think about it or confront it, ever again. But that was impossible. Because I couldn't burn away the memory.

Cranking on the hot water, I waited until it steamed my bathroom. I wanted it as scalding as I could stand. I needed it to overpower every other feeling, every emotion. I needed it to obliterate the hands that had squeezed my breasts and clasped my legs. To incinerate the words that had been whispered in my ear.

I was creeped out, disgusted, revolted. The list went on and on. Literally, worse than scorpions was another man, any man other than Dane, touching me the way Vale Hilliard had.

Standing under the spray that made me squirm with its intense heat, I let it wash away the blood and tears. I stood under the water as long as I could, but it couldn't dissolve the pain seizing me. I sank onto the edge of the tub and the sobs came hard and fast, making my body quake again.

I wept for everything I'd started to believe in with Dane—the love, the bond, the dream we'd been building together. I wept for all that I had just lost—him, the faith I'd finally embraced, the hope that I could be different from my parents and grandparents, the optimism surrounding something that had made me come alive and had brought so much pleasure.

I was thoroughly wrecked. And so disassociated from myself. Like appendages were missing.

It took a small eternity for me to finally shut off the water and grab a towel. I patted it against my face, the trickles of blood staining the white material. Still feeling numb inside, I swiped at the steam on the mirror and bit back a gasp at the reflection staring at me. The cut on my forehead didn't look as though I needed stitches, though I'd definitely have to keep an eye on it—and it promised to leave a scar. I squirted Neosporin on a Band-Aid and applied it to the laceration.

Inspecting the bruises made me cringe. My entire right cheek was black-and-blue. My jaw was bright red. My lip was split, though thankfully not bleeding now. Regardless, I was a fright. My dad couldn't see me like this. He'd wig on a level I couldn't even begin to process. And it'd be a good week or so before I could cover the remains of the damage with makeup.

I also worried whether my cheekbone might be fractured, but I'd monitor it as well.

Somehow, the physical wounds didn't compare to the emotional ones. I'd left Dane at that house and, with him, I'd left a huge part of me. Making it difficult to breathe. But what was I to do? Just thinking of the ferocity of his wrath on Vale was petrifying.

Yet the devastated expression on Dane's face when I'd told

him to stay away. *My God.* That recollection sent razor blades through me.

I wiped away more of the fat drops that wouldn't stop flowing. My doorbell rang and I jumped. Then I realized it was Amano. I wrapped the towel around me, adding my thick terry-cloth robe. I pulled the sash tight at my waist. I was still crying when I glanced through the peephole and opened up for him.

He arranged my clothes and bags neatly on the kitchen table. Then he turned to me. "You don't look any better."

"I'll never be better," I said. More tears fell.

"Ari. Vale Hilliard isn't dead. He'll recover in a private facility. He won't come near you again."

"Dane has seen to that?" I asked a bit acridly. I didn't understand how all of this worked.

"It's complicated. Hilliard has disgraced his family by failing the charge given to him."

Really, who were all of these people that they had such control over these background Machiavellian machinations? It was too surreal.

"So it's over?"

With a nod, he said, "I think so. Dane's with Ethan right now. They'll figure it all out. But, Ari, he's—"

"Don't," I softly pleaded. "I can't talk about him. I don't want to hear anything about him, Amano. What I want," I explained as the apprehension and agony ripped through me, "is for you to take my laptop back to 10,000 Lux and tell Dane I quit. He'll have to find someone else to fill the Events Director position."

From what I'd gleaned over the months, Amano was not an expressive man. But he was running the gamut this evening. He dragged a hand down his face and said, "Ari, he'll never accept that."

"He has no choice."

"You don't understand what you're saying . . . suggesting . . . doing." He shook his head in dismay.

"I can't be with him, around him. Not after what happened. What I saw." My eyes closed. I envisioned Dane whaling on Vale. My lids snapped open. "There was no stopping him. I had to tackle him, Amano. He could have killed that man. I can't be a part of that. Not now. Not *ever*."

"Sometimes the lines aren't black and white, Ari. There's a lot of gray area when you're dealing with billions of dollars and people who want things from you that they can't let go of—and they won't let you out of their crosshairs."

"I'm going to naively stick with the adage that two wrongs don't make a right."

"Understood." He headed to the door but spared a glance over his shoulder. "I'm going to stay in the SUV tonight, outside. If you need me."

"Amano. You don't have to make all these sacrifices for me. I'm not with Dane anymore."

The tears flooded my eyes again.

"I can see that." He watched the fat drops crest the rims and roll down my cheeks. "I'll be here anyway."

"Wait." I reached for his arm. "Wayne Horton. I think he's your inside guy. Vale had him work on-property to send everything awry."

"You're sure?"

"Best guess."

"Okay. Thank you. Call me if you need *anything*."

I nodded. He left me to the crying jag that started anew.

How, exactly, would I exist post–Dane Bax?

I shoved a chair from the kitchen table under the doorknob because I was that terrified someone from Vale's faction might break in. Despite the bodyguard holding vigil in the parking lot. Then I made sure all the windows were locked and I searched for things sturdy enough to set in the metal tracks to keep anyone from being able to slide open a window in the event they could bypass the locks. If there was a fire, no way in hell would the firemen get to me unless they crashed through my patio doors. Over those I pulled the drapes closed.

I settled on the sofa, my pulse still rapid. My heart aching like nothing I'd ever known before.

Deep in my soul, all I wanted was to be wrapped in Dane's arms, engulfed in his heat and essence. I wanted all the beautiful and sensual sensations he evoked to chase away the terror and the shattered feelings.

Burrowing under the throw, I tried to clear my mind and calm my churning insides. I was highly alert to all the sounds around me, fearful even though I believed the threat had faded for now, with Vale in a hospital and Amano practically at my doorstep.

It wasn't so much the shadows and the unknown that taunted me. I was devastated, missing Dane already and needing him so much. Especially now, after everything I'd been through.

But I refused to turn on my phone. I couldn't renege on my convictions.

We were done. Through. End of the tragic love story.

That's when the really awful, body-wracking sobs came.

And didn't subside . . .

I didn't check the next day to see if Amano kept his watch on me. Or the next.

I didn't have to, because he rapped on my door a couple of times to let me know he had Dane's physician with him. No doubt someone from the *private* facility where Vale recovered. Someone who stuck to patient confidentiality and didn't call the police over this sort of thing.

For a price.

Both times, I went to the door and told them to go away.

For the most part, I remained curled on the sofa, huddled under the blanket. Sometimes crying. Sometimes staring at the drapes covering the patio doors. Occasionally, my mind wandered and I imagined someone jimmying the lock, throwing one of the doors open, and shooting me.

Trying to convince myself I was being melodramatic was futile. An hour or so would pass and I'd stare at the curtains again, pondering what might lie in wait for me beyond them.

Was it really such an easy conclusion to this entire clusterfuck of a situation that Vale had lost the game and that was that? Had Dane really won the war . . . or just one horrifying battle?

I didn't want to think about him, but that was near impossible. I couldn't get him off my mind and wanted desperately for him to be here with me, holding me. That's when the tears came again.

My combat tactic was to head to the bathroom or rummage through the fridge. But food didn't appeal to me. I forced myself to drink some water at first but eventually couldn't see the point in it.

I'd never understood hopelessness before. When my father had been wrecked by my mother, I'd poked and prodded him.

*Hey, Dad, let's golf.*

*Hey, Dad, we need groceries.*

*Hey, Dad, watch a movie with me.*

He'd gone through the motions to appease his daughter. I didn't bother. I had no one to appease.

Or so I thought. . . .

The pounding on my door on day three roused me from the sleep I drifted in and out of when I cried so hard, it exhausted me.

At first, I thought the horrendous hammering was thunder.

Then I heard the very distinct, "Ari, open up! It's Kyle."

I started. Holy shit, I hadn't thought about Kyle. He had to wonder where I'd been the past couple of days, when I hadn't shown up for work.

Crawling out of my cave, I didn't think about the way I looked. That was a big mistake. I moved the chair away and opened the door. The first words tumbling from his lips were, "Jesus Christ!"

I winced. "Sorry." My throat was raw and I went to the sink for a glass of water.

"What. The. *Hell?*" he demanded as he entered the townhome and slammed the door shut behind him.

"Lock it," I said between sips. "Put the chair back under the knob."

"Fucking A, Ari," he said as he did as I'd asked. Then he gently clasped my biceps and demanded in a low tone, "What the hell happened to you?"

His gaze roved my face. I saw the shock and pain in his blue eyes. Mixed with instant anguish.

Shifting away from him, I set the tumbler on the counter and said, "I walked into a door."

"You fucking—Goddamn it!" His outburst filled the room. "You can't just say shit like that! Tell me, *seriously*."

I turned back to him. "Why are you here?"

"What?" His brow furrowed. "You haven't been at the hotel in two days and Dane looks like . . . Christ." He shook his head. "I don't know what the hell Dane looks like, but the best way to describe it is the walking dead. He's so . . . not there. Even when he is." Another shake of his head. Then he said, "I had to get up in his grill, you know? Demand to know where you've been and why he looks all zombie-ish . . . I mean, still intimidating as hell. What is it with that guy?" he added under his breath.

I knew that expression he was talking about—the one where Dane was clearly someplace dark and scary in his mind. "So, what . . . he *told* you?"

"Sort of." Kyle whirled around and slammed his hand on the counter. "Fuck, Ari. Your face."

"Stop looking at it if it bothers you," I hissed. "I didn't invite you here."

His head whipped in my direction, his jaw tight, his eyes flashing with anger and concern. "Hell, yes, it bothers me. One side is black and purple. You've got a bandage peeling off a cut that might actually need stitches. Your skin's sallow and you have the most vacant expression of anyone other than your goddamn zombie boyfriend."

"He's not my boyfriend." I returned to the sofa. "Not anymore."

"Ah, fuck."

Kyle sank into the chair adjacent to me. "What's going on, Ari? I mean, I got all Rambo on the dude and he let me. In what world would that happen?"

Ignoring that sentiment, I asked, "What'd he say?"

"That he'd appreciate it if I checked on you. That I was probably the only one you'd see, the only one you'd talk to."

I gave a small, humorless laugh. "He knows me too well."

Between clenched teeth, Kyle said, "It was these people fucking with the Lux that came after you, right? Or . . ." He glanced away, then flicked a look back at me that was pure challenge wrapped in agony. "Or did he do this to you?"

My eyes bulged.

*Oh. My. God.*

I pressed a hand to my mouth as my heart wrenched. Acutely painful as the days before. Would this torture *never* end?

Dragging my hand away, I insisted, "You can't think that. Don't ever, *ever* think it. He wouldn't do this to me. He *never* would, Kyle." My tone became more assertive. "All he wanted to do was protect me—and the Lux. All he cared about was making sure no one hurt me. *No one.* He's been twenty-four-seven tormented with anything bad happening to me for reasons beyond his control. My God!" I jumped to my feet, even though that made the throbbing in my face and head return. "He's not the bad guy!"

I stared at Kyle as something shifted inside me. Tears burned my eyes. I sank onto the sofa. "Oh, my God."

"What?" he demanded.

The drops rolled down my cheeks once again. My insides were raw, as if I'd been sliced open by my *own* machinations.

"He didn't do this to me," I whispered. "He did everything he could to keep me safe. Same with Amano—for Dane's sake as much as mine. It's just that someone was a step ahead of him, from almost the beginning. It's not his fault. None of this is *his* fault."

The tears came faster.

"Hey, Ari." Kyle moved to the sofa, sitting next to me and draping an arm around my shoulders. "Come on. This is crazy."

"Yes. It is. And so beyond fucked up. But Kyle, it's not Dane's fault," I insisted. "I thought he was the villain when I watched him beat the hell out of the guy who'd kidnapped me and almost ra—" I shook that thought out of my head, not wanting to share it. "I couldn't reconcile any of it in my mind, because I was so terrified. But everything Dane has done, *did* that night, all comes down to saving what's his. The hotel. *Me*."

Kyle grunted.

I gripped his hands and said, "I'm sorry. I know you came here as a friend. But I also know you harbor thoughts we might someday be more. You have to understand, *accept*, that I loved—" I shook my head. This was all so insane. But I had to be honest. With Kyle and with myself. "I *love* Dane. I will always love him, no matter what. It's unconditional. It's . . . forever."

Between clenched teeth, Kyle said, "He is much too dangerous for someone like you, Ari. Why can't you see that?"

"That part doesn't matter. I told you, I'm not with him anymore. But that doesn't mean everything I feel for him will go away. It won't."

Kyle lifted his hand, but it lingered in the air, as though he wanted to cup the side of my face in a consoling way. But it was the wrong side, the damaged side. His hand dropped.

"This is all such bullshit, Ari."

I nodded. "These people defy comprehension. You have to believe me, though, when I tell you that Dane did absolutely nothing to hurt me. He never would. It's the situation, Kyle. Not him." I gave this more thought, then added, "I pushed him down this path. Inadvertently, I guess. The way he feels about me—that makes him willing to do whatever he has to in order to keep me safe. And it makes him want to pummel anyone who touches me."

A shiver ran down my spine, but I didn't mention the horrifying state Vale had been in or my fear when he'd gone still that Dane had killed him. Or that he was privately being tended to, likely laid up much longer than me, what with all the breaking of bones I'd heard. Some of them might have been Dane's. I didn't ask if he wore a cast on one or both of his hands.

I certainly didn't feel right as rain, but speaking about all of this to Kyle and having him here with me helped to ease some of the tension in my chest that had led to my seemingly endless sobfest.

I let him make dinner—canned soup—and ate a little to satisfy him, since I still didn't have much of an appetite. I didn't want him any more frazzled with worry over me. His consternation was pretty intense as it was.

I drank about a gallon of water, maybe to replace all of the tears. Sadly, there were still so many of them unshed. I held them in check for Kyle's sake.

We returned to the sofa, me curled in the corner with my blanket again.

"How did all of this happen, Ari?" he asked in a quiet voice. "To your face, I mean."

I wasn't inclined to relive that evening, but he deserved a bit by way of explanation.

I said, "You remember the valet, Wayne?"

"Sure. New guy."

"No, not new. He said he'd been around awhile. Working in all the functional areas that invariably fell victim to sabotage. He was chatting me up when I got into what I presumed was Dane's car. He distracted me so that I didn't look at the driver's seat."

"What do you mean by *presumed*?"

With a shake of my head, I told him, "It wasn't Dane's car. Looked exactly like it from the outside, with one minor detail. Well . . . not so minor. I think it's what saved my life."

His gaze narrowed. "What are you talking about?"

"Wayne kept my attention and yours, too. So that neither of us noticed that the F5 didn't have an Arizona license plate. It had a Nevada one. The car was from Las Vegas."

"Shit. I never even looked."

"I didn't, either. But my guess is that even though we blew through the security gates because the guard recognized Dane's car, and never stops the boss, he spotted the plate. Called Amano, who happened to be with Dane."

"Goddamn." He exhaled heavily. "Is this Mafia shit we're talking about?"

"No. Not exactly." I debated telling him everything but then decided against it. "The less you know, the better. Suffice it to say, Dane has tried very hard to make sure his investors are on the up-and-up, and to keep out the greedy bastards who don't subscribe to that ethic."

"And those greedy bastards are the ones who came after you?"

"Because Dane cut them out of the Lux."

"Wow. You really know how to step into the quicksand with both feet."

"Yeah."

"You had a visitor today, too," he added.

My thoughts instantly shifted to my mother. Making my spirits plummet further. I didn't think that was possible. "Who?" I tentatively asked. Not really sure I wanted to know.

"Another skyscraper. A chick this time. Mikaela something. Legs as long as the pillars in the lobby."

I groaned. "Please don't remind me." She was outrageously gorgeous. And clearly quite clever, knowing how to keep Dane at her beck and call while she played damsel in distress.

Would she be delighted I was no longer in the picture?

*A no-brainer, Ari.*

"Do you know what she wanted?"

"Dropped off a gift bag for you while I was in Dane's reception area, delivering mock-ups."

That seemed odd. "How'd she get onto the fourth floor?"

"Apparently, she has her own security badge."

"What?" I stared, incredulous. Dane was a massive stickler for security and yet he'd issued Heidi Klum an electronic card? That made no sense at all. Nor did her bringing me a gift.

Except for that wise old adage—*keep your friends close and your enemies closer.*

Was that what Mikaela was up to?

Well, fool on her. She didn't have anything to worry about where I was concerned. Dane and I were over. That gave her the wide berth she needed, if her intention was to pursue him or to otherwise be the only woman in his life.

I tried not to seethe over that prospect. I had no right. I had no claim on him anymore.

We were over.

As more tears burned my eyes, Kyle turned his attention to the TV to keep from wallowing in my agony, I surmised. Switching it on, he surfed while I nodded off again, fatigued from my injuries, crying, and explaining everything.

When I woke in the morning, Kyle was crashed out in the chair, the sound off on the TV, though he'd clearly been watching it while I slept.

I forced myself up and made pancakes and coffee. The scent roused him and he joined me at the table.

"So, what happens now?" he asked between bites.

"I'm not going back to the Lux." I sighed. That was a painful thought unto itself. Thankfully, I'd earned enough income while I'd worked there to feel comfortable with my nest egg. I had plenty to live off of until I got my wedding business back on track. Especially now that Dane had put an end to my mother's attempt to extort money from me.

"What about Dane?" Kyle ventured.

"I'm not going back to him, either. I told you that."

Sitting back in his chair, he eyed me curiously. "You can't stay holed up here forever, Ari."

"I don't intend to, believe me. I'll get my bridal consulting going again. I just have to wait for my face to heal so I don't terrify any-one, looking like Frankenstein," I tried to joke. He didn't see the humor. Nor did I.

"What can I do to help?" he asked.

"This is perfect," I assured him. "You came at just the right time. It probably wouldn't have been a good idea for me to be alone much longer. I haven't even showered."

"That's what that smell is."

"Asshole."

Finally, we laughed. And it felt damn good.

# chapter 25

I eventually had to turn on my phone, so my dad wouldn't worry. As I scrolled through missed calls, the vast majority were from Dane. I deleted the log and all the voice-mail messages. Didn't bother reading the texts. Then I checked in with my father, telling him I'd lost my cell at the hotel and just found it. Big apologies.

"You'll come out to the driving range and have lunch on Sunday, right?" he asked.

That was still a few days away. I spared a glance at myself in the mirror hanging over the kitchen table. The bruises remained but had faded decently. The cut on my lip had healed. The one on my forehead had an angry look to it, so I kept antibiotic cream and a bandage over it. I could find some way to camouflage all of the wounds with makeup, sunglasses, and a visor, so I said, "Sure. Usual time?"

"Yes. And . . . bring Dane." He said this hesitantly. I recognized the olive branch for what it was. And cringed. My dad was trying to reconcile and accept my choice in boyfriends. Not knowing I no longer had one.

I said, "How about I bring a friend, instead? I work with him at the hotel." I wasn't ready to spring the news of my departure, nor did I want anything to appear too suspicious while I was still so wrecked . . . and physically wounded.

"Him?" That one word in my statement seemed to perk up my father.

"His name is Kyle Jenns. I don't know if he golfs, so this could be fun for him to get lessons from you." I knew my dad liked doling out his professional opinion.

"Sounds great. Everything else okay?"

"Sure." I swallowed hard, hoping I sounded normal. Because I sure as hell didn't feel normal. And wondered if I ever would.

"All right then. See you on Sunday."

"Yeah." I was about to disconnect but hastily added, "Hey, Dad?"

"Hmm?"

"I love you."

He was quiet for a moment, then said, "I love you, too, Sweets."

Tears pooled in my eyes. I hung up. And started crying all over again.

Sunday came and went, and Kyle played it cool so that my father didn't suspect any trouble in my world. As it turned out, Kyle never had golfed before, so it was an eventful morning, followed by a comfortable lunch, with him carrying the majority of the conversation, for which I was grateful.

The final week of October was spent on intensive last-minute preparations for my Halloween wedding. I'd had my doubts on how we'd pull off the theme, but it was gorgeous as a formal black-and-white affair, with fiery blood-orange and gold accents. The orange lilies used for the decorations and centerpieces were the deepest, most vibrant I'd ever seen, thanks to the extensive research I'd done with the florist I typically subcontracted. We'd looked high and low for a grower who would give us exactly what we wanted, and everyone had delivered all the way around.

On my recommendation, Grace tended bar in the private clubhouse. I enjoyed seeing her again.

I stayed for the dancing because it was healthier to my psyche than spending another night alone at my townhome. I chatted it up with some guests but didn't hit the dance floor, despite a few requests. It felt as though it'd be a betrayal to Dane so fresh in our split. And the fact that I refused to take or return any of his calls.

Unfortunately, the evening had to end at some point. My euphoria over the striking wedding and the deliriously happy couple dissipated as I drove home. I was exhausted from the hard work and running around but my mind wasn't quite ready to shut down. So I made out my check for the vendor booth at a huge bridal fair at the Civic Center in downtown Phoenix in January and updated my Web site with both the Delfino-Aldridge festivities and tonight's Halloween wedding.

I wasn't one to boast about things of this nature yet I decided it best to add the cover of *Southwest Weddings* magazine with my photo on it. I needed to leverage what I could in order to get back in the game. My only other event on the books was Shelby Hughes's wedding next summer.

As I considered that, I thought it a good idea to compose some snippets about event planning so that I could branch out in that arena as well. If I couldn't manage parties at the Lux, I could do it independently. Just not on the same scale. At the same magnitude. With the same grandeur. For Dane.

I definitely needed more work. Something to focus on other than him. And the rug that had been ripped from underneath me, as I'd predicted would happen all along.

Powering down my computer, I left that room and went into

mine. I slipped into my Gretzky jersey, but that reminded me of the night on the phone when Dane had talked dirty to me and I'd had my first of many stellar orgasms because of him. I yanked off the jersey and returned it to its drawer, opting for a pair of yoga pants and a tank top instead.

The weather was mild and much more normal than the lengthy and violent monsoons we'd experienced this year. Yet I felt chilled to the bone as I crawled into bed.

My theory of not being touched so that I didn't miss it when instances of it were too few and far between turned out to be a valid one. I'd gotten used to Dane's touch, his heat, his essence surrounding me. I'd even relied on it in some respect, because it had become a part of me. *He* had become a part of me. Now there was nothing but loneliness. Emptiness. A bleak feeling.

Would I ever recover?

Did I even want to?

I pulled the comforter over my head. The very disturbing reality of the situation was that as long as I was devastated I'd keep the living, breathing reminder of what I'd once had. I'd be able to hold on to the beauty of Dane and the way he'd loved me. Fiercely, possessively. Sweetly, tenderly.

But there was so much crimson that seeped around the edges of that beauty. So much darkness.

The night Vale Hilliard had kidnapped me could have ended fatally for me, for Vale. For Dane and Amano. Anything could have happened. That continued to scare the shit out of me.

But I also continued to miss Dane. To crave his touch, burn for the intimacy we'd shared.

Throwing back the covers with a frustrated sigh, I climbed out of bed and went into the kitchen. If I were the type to believe in a soothing glass of warm milk, I might have gone that route. Instead, I dug my phone out of my tote and placed a call.

It was picked up on the first ring.

"I need a favor," I said. "A ride, actually."

———

"Are you all right?" It was the first thing Amano asked as I pulled open my front door.

"Not even close." Why lie? He'd lived the nightmare with me.

Dressed in jeans, sneakers, and a white oxford with a tank top underneath it and wearing lip gloss and mascara, I knew that—other than the scar on my forehead—I didn't look as torn to pieces as I was. But I still felt it inside.

"Where do you want to go?" he asked.

We'd had a sparse conversation when I'd called. I'd asked the favor; he'd said he was on his way. That was all.

"I never got the gate code."

"Right." With a sharp nod, he turned. I followed him out, locking up behind me.

On the drive to Oak Creek Canyon, I asked, "How did you find me that night?"

"The guard at the gates called me to say the plate on Dane's car was from the wrong state—and that he'd flown out of there quicker than normal."

So I'd been right about that. "I hope you gave him a raise."

It wasn't Amano's style to crack a smile, so I didn't expect one. "Naturally," was all he'd said.

I dug around a little deeper in my head. "How did you know where to find me?"

"We didn't. Except that on the drive back to the hotel Dane noticed tire marks veering onto a dirt road. Neither of us had seen them before. Someone took that turn ridiculously fast."

"Indeed," I muttered, recalling my scream as the car had shimmied and I'd feared it would roll. "What did you do about the car, by the way?"

"Had one of my guys locate the owner based on his plate number and return it in excellent condition, with a bit of extra cash for the delay in getting it back to him. He didn't seem to mind."

Considering that *bit* of extra cash had likely been in the six-figure range, I didn't think he would mind.

"So Vale's brilliant plan to keep me hidden in that box canyon so close to the Lux, where I had no way of reaching you or Dane by cell, actually foiled his kidnapping attempt."

Amano's jaw clenched. "I wouldn't say it was totally foiled." He spared a glance my way. I winced.

"Point taken."

I was tempted to ask how Dane had fared through all of this, but I'd already gotten the irritated zombie report from Kyle. And, really, it'd be too painful to hear it from Amano. I'd come to see the bond between them, which stemmed from three decades of camaraderie and Amano's devotion to Dane and his family. I wouldn't be surprised if there was an indirect father-son connection, given how close they'd always been. And Dane had no other paternal presence in his life, since he'd once told me his aunt Lara had never married.

I was suddenly compelled to ask, "How are *you* doing with all of this?"

He scoffed.

"No, really," I said. "I want to know."

For all his mammoth stature and stoic, borderline scary disposition, I'd long ago learned he was as loyal as a Labrador and as protective and territorial as Dane.

"I understand what upset you that night."

My brow jerked up. That was putting it mildly but I supposed it helped him to do his job when he kept his own emotions on an even keel.

"Okay," I ventured.

"You don't seem to realize that a man like Dane . . ." He pinned me with a look and said, "He'd die for you, Ari."

My jaw fell slack. His gaze returned to the road.

The words rooted in my head. There were songs like that. By Prince, Bon Jovi, Bruno Mars, however many others. Romantic connotations, for sure. But not something *I* would ever expect to hear in real life.

I stared out the windshield, trying to process the full extent of what Amano said. It didn't change the fact that I'd been terrified that night with Vale. It didn't exonerate Dane from nearly killing him. It didn't make me any less fearful of what I'd become embroiled in.

The problem lay in the all-too-real inevitability that I would have preferred Dane never see me in the shape I'd been in. Bloody, near hysterical, in pain, horrified, weak. Beyond that, he'd heard me screaming—and he'd known what Vale had planned to do to me. Dane had heard me begging Vale to stop touching me. He'd seen me with my blouse ripped open and my panties mid-thigh.

And even though nothing beyond that had happened—I had not been raped or otherwise molested—he still had to live with the very striking reality of how far it had gone and how much worse it could have been.

The truth was, I figured it would have been a hell of a lot easier on him if I'd just disappeared. If he and Amano hadn't been able to find me. Instead, Dane had gotten the sucker punch of a lifetime, seeing me tied up and at another man's mercy.

Unable to stop myself, I looked over at Amano and asked, "How bad off is he?"

His grip on the steering wheel tightened. "Bad."

Again, I suspected that was not at all the word he wanted to use.

I sat back in the seat. "Is he expecting us?"

"Yes."

*Loyal as a Labrador.*

I wrung my hands in my lap as we drove the winding dirt path through the trees and arrived at the massive wrought-iron gate. My nerves were a jumbled mess. I wasn't sure what I was doing here. It'd been an impulsive decision because I hadn't been able to stand the solitude of my bed without Dane next to me.

I didn't know what I wanted the outcome of a confrontation to be. I wasn't even certain a confrontation was the sane way to go. I had some recognition of his current mind-set, given Kyle's and Amano's comments. But I had no idea how Dane felt about me at this moment.

"Perhaps you ought to stick around," I said, anxiety closing in on me.

"He wouldn't appreciate that." As Amano spoke, Dane pulled open one of the double doors and stepped onto the patio.

The night was silvery, with a hint of fog and slivers of moonlight through the dense forest surrounding the house. He wore inky jeans and boots. A black shirt that hung open. The soft illumination revealed the hard angles of his face and his bunched muscles. He took edgy and brooding to all-new levels.

*Maybe this is a mistake. . . .*

I didn't reach for the handle. Amano alighted from the SUV and came around to my side. I hadn't even unlatched my seat belt. My gaze locked with Dane's. I wondered what I was doing here. What I *was supposed* to do.

Amano opened my door. Still, I couldn't move.

I hadn't seen Dane in over three weeks. Aside from in my head, in my dreams. None did him justice. He was mesmerizing. So masculine and sexy. Perfect.

Everything I'd never known I wanted.

My eyes drifted closed. He'd said those words to me, with astonishment in his voice. He'd known long ago, from the onset, some sort of destiny was at play between us. I just wasn't sure what that fate might be. My fairy tale hadn't exactly turned out sweet and innocent. And hadn't he also told me that?

"Ari?" Amano's low voice broke into my thoughts. I opened my eyes and turned my head to eye him curiously. "I wouldn't leave you here if I didn't think it was safe. Not for a heartbeat."

The corner of my mouth lifted. So, I'd won over the stoic. And he probably felt as much guilt as Dane that he hadn't protected me from Vale's devious plot.

"I know I'm safe with him." Dane could be hurt, angry, destroyed . . . he wouldn't take it out on me. I knew that to the depths of my soul.

I unbuckled and slid from the seat. Took a few long breaths. Then I said, "Thanks, Amano."

"Dane's not all right with this, either," he finally admitted.

I nodded. "I'm not sure we ever will be." I moved past him and walked the stone path.

Dane had propped his shoulder against the doorframe while I'd debated my course of action. He watched me approach, an unreadable expression on his devilishly handsome face.

My heart wrenched. Everything about him created that magnet-and-steel effect that had drawn me to him from the very beginning. I drank in his tall, sculpted form, hypnotized by every inch of him.

Yet a hint of caution trickled down my spine, a reminder that this wasn't a casual meeting. That he wasn't your everyday, ordinary man. He lived in a different, mysterious, dangerous world. He was someone who went after what he wanted and fought to keep it.

I couldn't dispute that he deserved to be able to fight for what he'd built. What he'd earned. After all, I'd been appalled for him when I'd learned the extricated investors now wanted to capitalize on all of Dane's hard work. His dream.

But there were some extremes I couldn't accept, couldn't live with.

Perhaps that was why I was here. To find out if I held enough power over him to draw a line in the sand and demand he not cross it. Ever.

Risky business, definitely.

My pulse raced at the sight of him, but my stomach churned at the prospect of what I wanted. And the very real possibility that this might be the last time I saw him.

I could barely breathe by the time I reached the front doors. I heard Amano leaving in the Escalade. Things snapped and sizzled inside me, a combination of apprehension and sheer excitement over the man standing just two feet away.

I felt his presence, was compelled to lean forward and inhale his scent.

But I still walked a tightrope, having no clear idea how this might play out. I might be calling Amano in ten minutes to come pick me up again. I should have told him to stay close.

Dane pushed away from the door frame and took a step toward me. My heart launched into my throat.

His gaze unwavering, he said, "This is a surprise."

"Yes, I know." I gulped down a knot of nerves. "Sorry it's so late in the evening."

"I was up."

I'd figured he would be.

"I couldn't sleep, either," I admitted.

A scowl darkened his features, as I was accustomed to. "You want more answers?"

"No." I shoved my hands into the front pockets of my jeans. "I think I have them all."

"Not all of them." He stepped aside and gestured for me to enter his house.

I hedged, anxiety mounting. Was this wise? Did I know what I was doing?

"Ari."

*Right.* I'd come to him. The ball was in my court this time.

Moving inside, I set my phone and house keys on the entryway table. He closed the door behind us.

I resisted the overwhelming urge to just walk into his embrace and let him swallow me up with his body and heat. Not say a word, just let him consume me.

Finding some inner strength, I said, "You sent Kyle to check on me."

"Yes."

"But you didn't tell him exactly what had happened."

"He needed to hear it from you."

"Why?"

He gave me a *come on, Ari,* sort of look. "He'd believe me? If I'd warned him what he'd find—about your injuries—do you think for one second he'd trust that I didn't physically do that to you? He'd latch onto *any* possibility to make me a demon when it comes to you."

"It did take some convincing that you weren't responsible."

"Jesus." He shoved a hand through his hair and started to pace, looking painfully tormented. "This has eaten at me, Ari. Sent me into a fit of rage I never knew could exist. I admit I'm at fault and—"

"Wait," I interjected. Everything inside me seized up, but I propelled myself forward. "I don't blame you for what happened. Vale plotted it out perfectly. I've never blamed you for how I got trapped in it all. Even I played a part, Dane. I'd just accepted that you were out front in your car, waiting for me. Because I wanted you to be waiting there for me."

Really, it'd all been such a fucked-up situation.

I said, "What I can't deal with, accept, is you *killing* someone. Even for me. For the Lux. It can't happen. It just can't."

"He's not dead."

"I know." Throwing my hands in the air, I demanded, "Don't miss my point!"

Tears stung my eyes. The sickness I'd felt that night threatened to return full force. I could still smell the scent of blood, because it had been everywhere. And it'd traumatized me enough to linger in my memory.

Dane gently gripped my biceps and stared deep into my eyes. "I'm not looking to be absolved, Ari. I lost control. Not because of the Lux. I can work that out, pay them all off, if I have to. Not easily, but . . . It's different. The hotel used to mean everything to me. Then I met you. I fell in love. And whatever I might have to rebuild, I never wanted it to be a relationship with you. I can figure out other funding sources. There is no other you. Not for me. Not *ever.*"

I saw the agony, the misery, the desperation in his beautiful emerald eyes, and his pain tore at me.

"Dane."

"I should have just brought them all back in. No one would have hurt you."

"No," I insisted. "You can't just bring them back in, Dane. They wanted to exploit your efforts, extort profits from you. And in the long run, you'd still be connected to the members you disagree with and want to be disassociated from. How could you ever live with yourself if you just . . . caved?"

I suddenly remembered that moment at the bar when he'd slammed snake-tat guy's shoulder to the table and Ethan had grumbled at him with both admiration and shock.

Looking beyond everything I found confusing and scary, I realized I felt as Ethan had.

"It can't happen again," I said with conviction. "What you did to Vale. But you can't hand over the Lux, either. And . . . even though you terrified me, I respected that you saved me, that you fought for what you've dedicated yourself to, for defending what belongs to you and what you love."

His hard features softened.

I repeated, "It can't happen again. You have to find another way to fight them, if they're still a threat to the Lux."

Dane released me. As he walked away, he quietly said, "I already have."

"What?" I followed him into the great room. He poured two brandies and handed one over.

"Vale won't be a problem going forward. You don't screw something up that badly and get a second chance to rectify the situation. Not with these people." His shoulders still bunched, so I knew we weren't out of the woods yet.

"Then, what? How will you save the Lux?"

"Legally." His gaze captured mine. "I'll bring them down legally, Ari. I'll find a way. I just . . . I need you to trust me. Give me some time."

"Dane." Emotion welled fast and furious. I set my drink aside and crossed to where he stood in front of the fireplace. I hadn't experienced many defining moments in my life but the ones I had seemed to all be centered around this man. And this particular moment was no less significant than all the others. "You'll make a promise you won't ever, *ever* break? No matter what?"

He stared down at me, clearly not wanting to give up his inherent need to do whatever necessary when it came to safeguarding his assets.

"Dane," I urged. "It has to be this way. Otherwise . . ." God, these words were going to gut me again. But I had to say them. "I'm gone. Done. No more. Forget you ever knew me."

More tears spilled down my cheeks. Christ, I'd already faced the cold, hard reality of what it was like to be separated from him, to walk away. I'd suffered the excruciating loss, and for the life of me I never wanted to go through it again. Yet I had to draw that line I'd thought of earlier. I had to know that when he assured me he wasn't the bad guy it was true.

"Please," I said. "If Vale would have pulled his gun on you, that would have been different. He didn't and you couldn't stop . . ."

I shook my head. Here was the really twisted and confusing part about all of this. Dane was justified in attacking a man who'd attacked me. I was justified in being horrified over the violence and the lengths to which Dane would go to protect me.

This was what I'd mulled over since I'd relayed the situation to Kyle, a semi-impartial audience.

There had to be a compromise, a balance. Justice was just so damn tricky to achieve with this scenario.

I said, "You and Amano rescued me. No need to kill the guy who'd kidnapped me—I was safe at that point. You still have to worry about the Lux, but if you have a legal way to come at this problem, great. It puts us on the same page with each other, right?"

He scowled.

I simmered.

We stared.

Endless seconds ticked by until he finally lifted his arm, drained his brandy, and returned his glass to the wet bar.

I stood where I was, riveted, as he sauntered toward me.

"What is it that you really want, Ari?"

My breath suddenly came in slower, heavier pulls as heat burned through me. Closing the gap between us, I splayed my palms over his bare chest and nearly melted at the warmth and hardness beneath my fingers. I'd missed him more than anything I could imagine. And knew, very simply, that I couldn't live without him. Not a second more.

His head dipped and he whispered, "Answer me."

There was no way to escape this. I instantly knew why I was here. Why I couldn't stay away.

"I love you," I said. "I can't—" Tears flooded my eyes and emotion choked me up. "I can't live without you. I can't . . . *exist* . . . without you. I love you," I told him again. "You own my soul, Dane." I stared up at him, the fat drops spilling down my flushed cheeks.

He held my face in his hands. Tenderly. "Ari. Baby." He let out a strangled sound. "I'm so sorry, for everything. You have to forgive me and you have to believe that I will make this all right." His lips pressed to mine. Against them, he murmured, "Because I can't exist without *you*."

My arms circled his neck. His hands shifted to my back and he held me tight, crushing me to him.

My tears fell against the crook of his neck.

He stroked my hair and said, "Ari, don't cry. Baby, please. I don't ever want to make you cry again."

"I know. I can't help it. It's just been so awful, Dane. So horrible without you. I couldn't go another night without being with you, without you holding me."

"Stay with me, Ari," he said in his low, sensual voice. "Stay."

"I'll call Amano and tell him I don't need him to give me a ride home tonight."

"Or ever. Stay with me, Ari. For good."

I choked on a sob. Pulling away slightly, I stared up at him. "You want me to move in?"

With a nod, he said, "Live with me. You like it here, right?"

"You know I do."

"Then I'll make more room for your clothes."

A smile tugged at the corners of my mouth. "You're probably the only man who willingly gives away his drawer space."

He swiped at some of my tears. "I'd give up the whole damn room if you asked me to."

"That's not necessary. I don't have that much stuff. I will need a little office space. I have this boss who expects me to work some nights and weekends."

"Baby, I never once said you had to put in all those hours."

"It'll be worse since I have almost a month to make up for and—"

"Ari, sweetheart. You have staff. They've been receiving the orders you placed and they have your collage. They know your exact vision and have been moving forward."

"With everything?"

"Yes."

*Oh, thank God!* And how fantastic that they'd found the collage when Amano had returned my laptop and bag to the Lux. I'd packed the collection of photos in there to show Dane.

"So I'm not behind?"

"Not that I'm aware of, though no one in your department works as hard as you. And they've missed you."

"So, it's okay that I come back?"

"More than okay. I couldn't pull off this launch without you."

"It means a lot to me, Dane. Because it's your dream."

His fingers grazed my cheek, the one that had healed. He stared deep into my eyes and said, "I hadn't realized, until you started working there and embraced everything about the Lux the way I do, that a dream is infinitely more important—more personal—when you share it with someone."

"I fell in love with it. As much as I fell in love with you."

He crooked a brow.

I laughed. "Of course that's not possible. I am ridiculously, insanely, hopelessly in love with you."

He brushed more tears from my face and said, "Then no more crying. No more worrying. No more fear. Because I'm going to make sure everything is perfect for you."

"Dane, that's a promise you can't make. All I'm asking is that . . . we're safe."

His lips swept over mine and the electric current returned. "Amano is working with me. Ethan and the others, too. It'll be different this time, Ari."

"I know. That's why I'm here. Kyle said . . ." I shook my head, not wanting to get my friend in hot water. But needing to clear the air. "He said you weren't yourself. Without me. Amano said you were in bad shape, too."

He glowered. "So happy to hear everyone's been keeping tabs on my mood."

"You're sort of hard to miss, brooding or not. But when you're in a mood, yeah, people tend to no—"

"Your point is?" he asked, spearing me with a look.

"I'm just saying that . . . I wouldn't be here if I didn't believe you could accept how I feel. I wouldn't be here if I didn't believe in you."

His head dipped and he kissed me. A slow, sexy one that drew me in and nearly made me forget my own name. I gripped his biceps, having missed his rock-hard muscles beneath my fingertips.

When he turned the heated kiss into a teasing tangling of our lips, I whispered, "Dane. I need you."

"You don't know how much I've missed you every single night. It's been hell. Like nothing I've ever known. You didn't return my calls, my texts. Amano told me not to go to your townhome. He warned me. That, Ari—that was damn-near impossible. To stay away. But he said you didn't want me there, didn't want the help I sent, either."

"I had to get through it on my own. But, Dane, that's all over. Now . . . Please, I can't stand another second without you kissing me, without you inside me."

His next kiss was an intense, searing one. His tongue delved deep and his arms crushed me to him.

No doubt I left scratches as my hands slid to his back and I held on tight. But it wasn't enough.

Tearing my mouth from his, I said, "Right here, Dane. Right now."

My chest rose and fell harshly. Desire ran rampant. I wanted him more fiercely than ever before.

I shoved his shirt off his shoulders and down his arms, letting it drop to the floor. He discarded mine as well, then lifted the tank top over my head, tossing it aside. He deftly worked the button fly of my jeans and yanked the denim down my legs, pausing to slip off my shoes and socks.

His hands skimmed up to my thighs as he knelt in front of me. He stared up into my eyes for several erratic heartbeats. Then he palmed my ass cheeks and his head dipped to the apex of my legs. He inhaled deeply.

I moaned.

His mouth pressed to my sex, his tongue sliding over my lace-covered lips. Excitement shot through me.

But a dark, incessant need claimed me. In a quiet, demanding voice, I said, "You have to be inside me. Now."

He took my hand and pulled me down to the thick area rug with him. He unfastened my bra and then guided me down, reaching above my head toward a chair where he snagged a pillow. As I lay back, he whisked off my panties and his clothes. I got lost in the beauty of him. His edgy perfection. His magnificence.

My hands roved his body, over his smooth skin. My pulse raced as his muscles tensed beneath my touch and his eyes blazed.

"I can't live without this," I said.

He swallowed hard. "You don't have to. I swear it."

My hand swept up to his neck and I tugged him forward. His lips grazed mine and fire ignited low in my belly.

"I want to feel you," I said, our gazes locked.

His emerald irises glowed seductively. "Are you saying—"

"I started the Pill after that first night here. It's hasn't been three months, but I think it's an okay time. If I count correctly."

"And if your math's not so hot?"

I didn't say anything. Safe Aria Lynne DeMille was not the Russian roulette type. But I had to have him this way. Just as he'd always wanted all of me, I wanted that in turn. Was desperate for it.

So I kissed him and let him decide.

His hand slid around to my back, pressing me against him as my spine arched. My breasts nestled under his pecs. Our legs tangled, as did our tongues. His kiss went on and on, a sizzling, revealing one. He would give me whatever I asked for, whatever I wanted. Of that I had no doubt. Especially when we'd both suffered so much from being apart.

My fingers threaded in his hair and I felt his erection against my hip. I drowned in ecstasy, and that was how I knew I'd made the right choice by coming here tonight. Because nothing else registered in my mind. Nothing else mattered to me. Except the moments when the world melted away and all that existed was the two of us.

Dragging my mouth from his, I murmured, "I want to feel you come inside me."

He let out a low sigh. So intimate and sexy, it sent a tremor through me and a flicker of heat against my clit.

His gaze captured mine again and he stared deep as he sank into me. My breath caught. Every delicious inch of him filled me. My hips rose to meet his unhurried, provocative thrusts, our eyes still searching, agreeing, accepting.

He made love to me slowly, intensely. Passion sparked in my core and spread out, flowing languidly, enticingly, through my veins.

Dane held me to him. I held him to me. We never broke the eye contact.

I felt the first wave of heat and then the subtle trembling. I wasn't sure if it was me who shook slightly or him. Maybe both of us. Our breaths were steady but labored, a bit harsh—coming in time with each other so that they became one. The way our bodies did. Our hearts. Our souls.

Everything that I would have ever wished for myself, had I been the type, crystallized the deeper he moved inside me, the more seductive his gaze became.

"Dane," I whispered as the sensations mounted.

"Yes, Ari. Yes."

I felt the shattering of every inch of me, the evidence that I belonged to him, only him. No one else. Ever.

"Ari," he said. "You are *everything* to me."

And then the hot rush of him filled me and he shuddered against me with one of those arousing, primal groans that told me how powerful my sway was over him.

That told me he was mine.

# epilogue

## KYLE

Ari returned to 10,000 Lux the first week of November. I'd been shocked to see her coming through the double doors of the lobby. Shocked to see Dane walking beside her. Not so shocked to see Amano close behind them, eyes alert.

Everyone was happy she'd come back. They'd been concerned about her absence, which they conveniently explained had been due to a car accident. That lie covered the scar on her forehead and the fact that Dane drove her to work, since she'd apparently "totaled" her SUV. I wondered what they'd done with it.

Dane cut me some slack with the intense, intimidating looks and even thanked me for helping her when she'd needed it most. That sentiment had been a reluctant one but I'd told him I'd always be there for her. Warned him, actually.

It was a bitch of a situation to be in. I didn't like her choices, plain and simple. I didn't like that she'd been in danger—could still be—or that she'd gone back on that vehement declaration she'd made in her living room, when her cheek had been bruised and swollen, causing me to want to put my fist through a wall . . . or Dane's face. She'd sworn they were over. I'd believed it.

So seeing them together now infuriated me, tore at me. I wanted to feel "happy" for her—for getting whatever it was that she wanted. Still . . . why'd it have to be *him*?

Now I was stuck with having to pretend I didn't know what she was involved in, pretend I didn't know she'd been kidnapped and attacked, that her face had been fucked up and she'd had a vacant, tormented look in her eyes that had damn-near killed me.

But he'd shown his true colors once, and I was convinced it would happen again. And when it did, I'd be there to pick up the pieces for her.

Just as I'd warned Dane . . .